DOWNTOWN

Anne Rivers Siddons

HarperPaperbacks
*A Division of HarperCollins**Publishers**

This is a work of fiction. The characters, incidents, and dialogues are products of the author's imagination and are not to be construed as real. Any resemblance to actual events or persons, living or dead, is entirely coincidental.

HarperPaperbacks *A Division of* HarperCollins*Publishers*
10 East 53rd Street, New York, N.Y. 10022

A hardcover edition of this book was published in 1994 by HarperCollins*Publishers*

Cover illustration by Jeff Cornell

First HarperPaperbacks printing: July 1995

Printed in the United States of America

HarperPaperbacks and colophon are trademarks of HarperCollins*Publishers*

❖ 10 9 8 7 6 5 4 3 2 1

By Anne Rivers Siddons

*Hill Towns**
*Colony**
*Outer Banks**
*King's Oak**
Peachtree Road
Homeplace
Fox's Earth
The House Next Door
*Heartbreak Hotel**
*John Chancellor Makes Me Cry**
*Downtown**

*Available from HarperPaperbacks

For JIM TOWNSEND and BOB DANIELS,
without whom,
one way or another,
this book would not have happened;
and for BILL SHINKER,
without whom many wouldn't have.

———

Dear Reader:

Just a moment of your time could earn you $1,000! We're working hard to bring you the best books, and to continue to do that we need your help. Simply turn to the back of this book, and let us know what you think by answering seven important questions.

Return the completed survey with your name and address filled in, and you will automatically be entered in a drawing to win $1,000, subject to the official rules.

Good luck!

Geoff Hannell
Publisher

Author's Note

EVERYONE WHO WAS FORTUNATE ENOUGH TO FIND HIM-or herself in Jim Townsend's orbit during his time at *Atlanta* magazine, in the early and middle 1960s, will have a different notion of the man, the time, and the magazine. Jim was never the same to any two people—and neither, I suspect, were the sixties. Both remain elusive these thirty years later. Very early in the writing of *Downtown* I gave up trying to catch the precise essence of the early *Atlanta* magazine and its contentious, incandescent founder and editor; I realized that it couldn't be done—not, at least, by me. So I tried instead to capture a slice of a particular city in a very particular time in the world, and let the characters become no more and no less than themselves. I am a fiction writer, not a biographer.

So anyone who knew him will see immediately that Jim Townsend is not Matt Comfort—is, in fact, far from him, though perhaps they share some notable eccentricities. Nor is anyone else in these pages anyone I know, or you do, though many quirks will have overlapped.

But the city and the times are as close to my own time Downtown as I could come. No, I'm not Smoky—she's a better woman than I, by far, and very little that happened to her happened to me. But I know her and her time and her world. In essence, if not in incidence, they were mine.

Atlanta was a wonderful, terrible, particular, and special place in those cusp days of the sixties; it could have been no other place on earth, and it will not come again. That luminous particularity is what I strove to capture in these pages. It may not be precisely as you remember it, but to Smoky O'Donnell and to me, this is how it was, and this is the way we were.

Prologue

A<small>LL OVER</small> A<small>TLANTA</small> <small>THAT FALL</small>, <small>IN THE BLUE TWILIGHTS</small>, girls came clicking home from their jobs in their clunky heels and miniskirts and opened their apartment windows to the winesap air, and got out ice cubes, and put on Petula Clark singing "Downtown," and sat down to wait. Soon the young men would come, drifting out of their bachelor apartments in Bermuda shorts and Topsiders, carrying beers and gin and tonics, looking for a refill and a date and the keeping of promises that hung in the bronze air like fruit on the eve of ripeness.

Atlanta in the autumn of 1966 was a city being born, and the energy and promise of that lying-in sent out subterranean vibrations all over the just-stirring South, like underground shock waves—a call to those who could hear it best, the young. And they came; they came in droves; from small, sleeping towns and large, drowsing universities, from farms and industrial suburbs and backwaters so still that even the building firestorm of the Civil Rights movement had not yet rippled the surface.

It was a time for youth. A tall, new young president had sent out a call of his own, and the young rose up for him with joy and purpose and the unbroken surety of his invincibility, and theirs. That he had died what was considered a true martyr's death in another slow, smiling, murderous Southern city did nothing to stem the rush of their ascendancy. On the contrary, it gave them focus and outrage to leaven their callowness; lent them a touch of becoming darkness. It was, after all, a very heady thing to have a new-slain hero of one's own. Strengthened and salted with his blood, the young surged toward the sun, and nowhere did they preen and jostle and mass themselves so thickly for the coming of . . . what? . . . than in Atlanta.

The city was suddenly full of them: pretty girls in new Carnaby Street knockoffs, streaming into the heart of town to their secretarial jobs; young men in dark suits and narrow ties and polished Cordovans and self-conscious new sideburns, marching into banks and brokerage offices and law firms and the budding businesses that they would ride, like the tails of comets, up to meet the high young sun.

They met, of course they did; they met, and came together in pairs and groups and broke apart and reformed, like patterns in a kaleidoscope. It was a common saying in the first singles' apartments of the city that if a girl couldn't get a date in Atlanta, the nunnery was the next step. And it was said, too, that if a man couldn't get a girl there, he'd do better to go back to Birmingham. And it was largely true.

A girl, a man, a career, a romance, a life . . . it was all out there, just ahead. I remember those autumn days of hope and exuberance and pale lemon sunlight, of softly chilled nights with scarlet leaves lit to translucence by city lights, so full of portent and promise that I often felt my very heart would burst with it.

Oh, wait, just wait, ran the song in mine and many hearts.

Oh, soon. Soon.

1

THE FIRST THING I SAW WAS A HALF-NAKED WOMAN dancing in a cage above Peachtree Street.

It was a floodlit steel and Plexiglas affair hung from a second-story window, and the dancer closed her eyes and snapped her fingers as she danced in place, in a spangled miniskirt and white go-go boots, moving raptly to unheard music. It was twilight on the Saturday of Thanksgiving weekend, 1966, when we reached Five Points in downtown Atlanta, and the time-and-temperature sign on the bank opposite the dancer said "6:12 P.M. 43 degrees." The neon sign that chased itself around the bottom of the dancer's cage said "Peach-a-Go-Go."

"Holy Mother of God, look at that," my father said, and slammed on the brakes of the Oldsmobile Vista Cruiser that he loved only marginally less than my mother. Or rather, by that time, more.

I thought he meant the go-go dancer, and opened my mouth to make reassuring noises of shock and disapproval, but he was not looking up at her. He was looking at a straggling line of young Negro men and women walking up and down in front of what I thought must be a delicatessen.

There was an enormous pickle, glowing poison neon green, over its door. It was raining softly, blending neon and automobile and streetlights into a magical, underwater smear. The walkers seemed to swim in the heavy air; they carried cardboard placards, ink running in the mist, that read "Freedom Now," and "We Shall Overcome." My heart gave a small fish-flop of recognition. Pickets. Real Civil Rights pickets. Perhaps, inside, a sit-in was in process. Here it was at last, after all the endless, airless years in the Irish Channel back in Savannah, drowned in the twin shadows of the sleeping Creole South and the Mother Church.

Here was Life.

Caught in traffic—a significant, intractable traffic jam, what a wonder—my father averted his eyes from the picketers as if they were naked, and, lifting them toward the alien heavens above him, saw the dancer in her cage. He jerked his foot off the clutch, and the Vista Cruiser stalled.

"Jesus, Joseph, and Mary," he squalled. "I'm turning around this minute and taking you home! Sodom and Gomorrah, this place is. You got no business in this place, darlin'; look at that hussy, her bare bottom hangin' out for all the world to see. Look at those spooks, wantin' to eat in a place that don't want them. And have we passed a single church in all this time? We have not, and likely the ones that are here are all Protestant. I told your mother, didn't I? Didn't I tell her? You come on back with me now, and go back to work for the insurance people, them that want you so bad. Didn't they say they'd let you run the company newspaper, if you'd stay?"

Behind us a horn blared, and then another.

"Pa, please," I said. "It's nothing to do with me. I don't think my office is anywhere near here. Hank said it's across from a museum. I don't see any museum around here; I bet this part of town is just for tourists. And Pa? I'll go to Mass every Sunday and Friday, too, if I have time. And after all, I'm staying in the Church home for girls. What on earth could happen to me at Our Lady?"

"We don't know anything about these Atlanta Catholics," my father said darkly, but he started the Oldsmobile and inched it forward, into the next block.

"Catholics are Catholics. You've seen one, you've seen us all," I said in relief. We were past the go-go dancer and the marching Negroes now.

"I heard some of them take that pill thing—"

"Of course they don't!" I said, honestly scandalized. "You're just talking now. You heard no such thing."

"Well, I wouldn't be surprised if I did hear it," he said, but my shock had reassured him. He looked at me out of the corner of one faded blue eye and winked, and I squeezed his arm. My father was in his late sixties then; I was the last child of six, spawn of his middle age, born after he had thought the five squat red sons who were his images would be his allotted issue, and he was a bitter caricature of the bandy-legged, brawling little man upon whose wide shoulders I had ridden when I was small. But his wink could still make me smile, still summon a shaving of the old adoration that his corrosive age and his endless anger had all but smothered. Most of the time now I no longer loved my father, but here, closed in this warm car with the jeweled dark of my new city all around me, I could remember how I had.

"There's nothing for you to worry about," I said. "Aren't I Liam O'Donnell's daughter, then?"

The convent school where I had spent twelve millennial years back in Savannah, Saint Zita's—named after the patron saint of servants and those who must cross bridges; apt for my contentious lower-class neighborhood—was big on epiphanies. It was a favored mode of deliverance among the nuns in my day, perhaps because no one stuck in Corkie could conceive of any other means of escape. I had a speaking acquaintance with every significant epiphany suffered by every child of the Church from Adam on. But I had never been personally seized by one. It seemed somehow déclassé, bumbling and rural; my best friend Meg Conlon and I used to snicker whenever Sister Mary Gregory trotted out another for our edification.

"Zap! Another epiph has epiphed!" we would whisper to each other.

I had one then.

I sat in the warm darkness of my father's automobile, for the moment totally without contact with the world outside and newly without context of any sort, and saw that indeed I was Liam O'Donnell's daughter, wholly that, just that. Maureen Aisling O'Donnell, known as Smoky, partly for the sooty smudges of my eyelashes and brows and my ash-brown hair; smoke amid the pure red flame on the heads of my brothers. Twenty-six years on earth and all of them within the fourteen city blocks near the Savannah wharves that was Corkie, for County Cork, whence most of us who lived there had our provenance. Daughter of Maureen, sister of John, James, Patrick, Sean, and Terry. But unquestionably, particle and cell and blood and tenet, daughter of Liam O'Donnell.

It stopped my breath and paralyzed me with terror, and in the stillness my father laughed and pummeled my thigh, pleased and mollified, and said, "You are and no mistaking. See you remember it."

And we inched on up Peachtree Street toward midtown Atlanta, where the Our Lady's Home for Catholic Girls waited to receive me in its red Medusa's arms.

I know that he was handsome once. There are yellowed, sawtooth-edged snapshots stuck in old albums and curling in drawers at home to attest to that. Never tall, of course, but powerful through the chest and arms from his years of wrestling reams and bales of Monarch paper products on and off the freighters that wallowed at the Savannah municipal docks. He was dark, too, from the malignant kiss of that coastal sun, even though his hair was as thick and red as molten copper. Even in the old photographs it looked red, like lava. His eyes were bright blue, though in the photos they were always narrowed with laughter; he laughed constantly when he was young, it seems. Laughed and sang and cursed and flirted; I have heard the stories of his legendary charm ever since I was old enough to understand them, and some of it I remember. He was still a force to be reckoned with when I was a child.

I remember running down to meet him at the edge of the docks when his shift was over. I was not allowed to go any farther into that den of iniquitous cursing and brawling and innuendo than that, but I would stand with one or more of my brothers, waiting for him, and I heard the laughter and the admiring jeers about his sexual prowess from the small crowd of men that always surrounded him. The talk would stop when the men reached my brothers and me, and change to the mindless, crooning endearments that Irishmen always have for girl children, and the sly, freighted teasing that they keep for boys. But I knew the sense of it. All of us kids in Corkie knew, early on. You could not live in the warren of small row houses and tenements that bordered the docks, off Gallien Street, and not know about sex. You would have to have been deaf and blind. The great, smothering mantle of Saint John the Baptist may have effectively stifled our actions, but it could do nothing about our minds and our groins. I never knew of more people in one time and place who thought more about sex and did less about it than the children of Corkie, in Savannah, Georgia, in the last two decades before the pill.

So I always understood that my father was two people: Liam O'Donnell who was my father and the head of our cramped, noisome household, whose savage hand lay heavy on all of us and whose sentimental, conventional Irish tongue glibly celebrated the joys and values of Family; and Liam O'Donnell the laughing, quick-handed rogue male, who, not unlike Browning's last duchess, liked whate'er in skirts he looked on, and whose looks went everywhere. For a long time I loved the one and was awed by and proud of the other, even as I pretended to know nothing of him. Not knowing has been the way of the women of Corkie since time out of mind.

Of my mother I have always had less of a sense. She was when I first remember her as she was, to me, all of her life: gray of hair and face, deft and constant as a robot in her kitchen, silent and smileless, heavy-footed, and red-handed from daily washing of the family's clothes and dishes. She wept when my father bought her a washer and dryer, when I was about ten, and not from joy, either. She wept because she said that the Blessed Virgin never had such, and nowhere in the scriptures did it say that a virtuous woman should, and she might be only plain little Maureen Downy O'Donnell from Pritkin Street, but there was no woman in the parish that kept a better house or did more for her family. Even Father Terry said that. She kept the washer and dryer, but she made sure that we all knew she made an act of contrition.

That's what I remember most of her: her great, limitless, blind, joyless faith. For a very long time it maddened and embarrassed me. By the time that I saw that it was what she had in place of love or laughter or joy or even contentment, she was gone. Of all the things I never did, telling her that I understood that is the bitterest to me. I wish I could have seen it, or, failing that, I wish I had had the wit to lie and say I did. But in those days I had little of understanding and less of the sort of wit that breeds kindness. When James and John, my oldest brothers, used to speak of the slender, curly-haired young woman who laughed in the hot evenings on the stoop as the children of Corkie played around the marble doorsteps, or who sang in the mornings while breakfast cooked, I could only look at them. They might have been talking of someone they saw on the screen at the Bijou on Saturday afternoons.

I look like her though, or as she once looked. I have the old photos, and they do not lie. I am, as she was, pale of skin, with her soot-fringed, water-clear gray eyes and her coarse, unruly dark curls; deep-breasted and small-waisted, with round hips that I used to try, vainly, to subdue with fearsome junior girdles. I have not bothered with these in many years. One day, perhaps, like her, I will be as soft as a pudding, but so far I am not. I have her deceptively sweet face; I will always look younger than I am, a fact that I hated for many years and have come, now, to appreciate. Sometimes, I am told, I can look almost sanctimonious, with a cloying, missal-saint's rapt stare; this, usually, when I am lost in thought or tired to mindlessness. Those who tell me this do not mean it as a compliment, and I do not take it as such. I am very far from saintly. I have from my father, in addition to his smallness of stature, his pigheadedness and swift, hot temper and his sentimental penchant for lost causes, although the nuns and my mother taught me early and well to put a cap on all of them. From the time I was four or five I could hold my own in a fight with my brothers, and learned soon after that I could devastate them with my tongue. But from almost as early an age, I was wracked with guilt when I did either one. I think if I had not gotten out of Corkie I would eventually simply have exploded from the force of all those warring, tightly repressed factions roiling within me. Many Corkie women did explode, or, like my mother, simply and gratefully turn to stone.

During the last terrible, irreparable argument I had with my brother John he told me that she changed when I was born, but I know that he was only trying to hurt me with that. In his eyes I had brought scalding shame on the family, and he fought me with what weapons he had. I knew that what he said was not true. My mother changed very gradually, and if I had been older I could have seen it happening. She began to change, I think, when my father started with the women and drinking, and she changed for good and all when he did, when the laughing and the kissing and the spontaneous snatching-up and dancing around the kitchen stopped, and that was when he and many other Corkie men were fired from Monarch for trying to unionize.

Before that my father had been a fierce partisan of all things American, loudly scornful of those who clung to the ways of the old sod. It was, by his lights, a good life Monarch had given him and his family; to him, "made in America" was more than a public relations slogan. It was one of the tenets that he lived by.

But Ireland will not, finally, let her sons go, and the dark need to argue and shout and rage in the name of injustice, real or imagined, came crawling out of the core of Liam O'Donnell like a tapeworm. When the first black men—spades and spooks and niggers always to my father and the men of Corkie, even though they had long bossed black gangs on the docks and laughed and eaten with them—began to aspire to and get minor supervisory posts, better pay, brighter prospects at Monarch, Liam O'Donnell and the Monarch men of his age began to lobby for organization and unionization. Georgia was a right-to-work state, and companies like Monarch were not about to let that change. Anyone not blinded and maddened with prejudice could have seen that it was a lost cause. But despite that—or perhaps, being the man that he was, because of it—my father took his rage to the pubs and street corners, and gathered a sizable army of red-faced, furious, bellowing Irishmen around him before Monarch bothered to fire them. It was a terrible shock to him. I truly don't think he ever recovered from it.

I was around nine when it happened, in that last somnolent year of the decade, and I remember almost to the day when the man I had known came home from work for the last time and sat down in front of the large new Dumont television set he had bought and turned into someone I no longer knew. This man laughed no longer, made no more insulting, infectious jokes, took us no more for ice cream or to bingo, went only on high holy days to Mass, and carried me never again on his shoulders on a hot, still summer night. He stared silently at the flickering black and white screen in the living room while the life of the house stumbled awkwardly around him, waiting only for five o'clock, when he could escape to Perkins's Pub on the wharf, under the great shadow of the river bluff, where he and his mates had always stopped off after work three or four times a week. Now they met there and drank, steadily, watching the shifts change and the crowds, increasingly dotted with black faces, surge back and forth across the docks like the tide, while they muttered together in their spleen and sadness. And what they talked of in those twilights now was Ireland.

It was during those days, when he would come stumbling home, often on the arms of his cronies or one of my brothers, sent to fetch him, that I began to hear the old stories of Ireland. Stories of soldiers and poets and kings and virtuous maidens, stories of heroes and battles and glory and blood. Stories and songs that we had not known he knew. Perhaps he had not known, either. In those days, and the days that followed, my laughing, devilish, handsome father became one of those ludicrous and heartbreaking professional Irishmen who could be found drinking and weeping in pubs up and down the East Coast from Boston to Savannah; a straggling, frayed rosary of beads that had yearned to be gold but could not, in the end, transmute themselves. Ireland, they intoned endlessly, Ireland. If it was not Irish, it was not worth the gunpowder to blow it to hell.

It was then that he began to call me Smoky. Before that he had called me, as everyone else did, Reenie, after my mother, or, if he was angry with me, the more formal Maureen. I had almost forgotten that I had a Gaelic middle name; the old grandmother who had insisted on it, my father's nonna, had died when I was not yet two. It is spelled Aisling, and it means, literally, "beautiful dream." I remember being told that back during the Troubles, when their English oppressors had forbidden that poetry about Ireland be written, Irish poets used the word *aisling* in place of *Ireland.* My father remembered it suddenly one evening when John and James had brought him home much the worse for wear, and seized upon it as if it had been the pot of gold at the end of the rainbow.

"Beautiful dream," he crooned, over and over, his voice thick with Jameson and tears. "Beautiful dream. Ah, and 'tis Aisling you are from now on, darlin', and I'll not be hearing anything else under this roof."

He often sounded like Barry Fitzgerald after a session at Perkins's.

When pronounced, the name sounds like "ashling," and it was only a matter of time until one of my brothers, tormenting me, stumbled upon "ashy," and then Smoky. I hated it, and ran sniffling to my father, sure that he would reestablish by fiat the slightly less objectionable Aisling. But something in the cheeky, common little nickname pleased him, or else his perversity demon was sitting on his shoulder that day, because he laughed uproariously, and repeated it several times, and the boys all laughed, and even my mother smiled, and Smoky I have stayed until this day. As I grew older I tried, without success, to reintroduce Aisling or Maureen or Reenie among my schoolmates, but without success. Something in the combination of syllables, some essential foolishness, obviously had great charm. It is a nickname without dignity or substance; a man I once loved told me that it sounds like a stripper's name or a professional lady roller skater's—Smoky O'Donnell, queen of the steel wheels. It might as well be graven on my forehead. If I should ever win a Pulitzer Prize, it will be presented, not to Maureen Aisling, but to Smoky O'Donnell. It has outlived by far its perpetrator, and bids fair to outlive its owner. It is not the least of the reasons, that first night in Atlanta with my father, that "Liam O'Donnell's daughter" struck me to stone.

We crawled with the Saturday night traffic out Peachtree Street, past the great department stores, lit for Christmas, past the towering new hotels that were springing up like white mushrooms—one, I had heard, had a cocktail lounge on its roof that revolved, presenting a spangled panorama of the entire city—past office buildings and restaurants and movie theaters and shops. There were people everywhere, heads lowered against the mist, hurrying across the streets and down the sidewalks. Many carried Christmas packages and shopping bags from stores that were names out of legend to me: Rich's, Davison-Paxon, J.P. Allen, Muse's. There were many couples, heading into the movie theaters and restaurants, and who knew where else. Most walked quickly, some arm in arm, and it seemed to me that all of them were smiling. It was a world made of light; light was everywhere. Streetlights wore opalescent collars, neon signs streamed and flared, automobile lights blazed and flickered, tires left iridescent snail's tracks on the shining black streets. Even closed away in the Vista Cruiser's overheated interior, I could hear the music of the city: horns blaring, tires swishing wetly, brakes squealing, sirens, snatches of laughter and shouts at intersections, from somewhere the heavy beat, though not the melody, of rock music. Saturday night in downtown Atlanta.

I swiveled my head from side to side, heart beating high in my throat, trying to slow my breathing so that my father would not think me inflamed by this Sodom, this Gomorrah. I was close to weeping with an excitement that was the nearest thing I could imagine to the holy rapture Sister Dinitia once described to us. We had been force-fed Latin by Sister Mary Gregory, in whom the world had lost a great Classics scholar when she cast her lot with the cloister, and I said silently, with Cicero long before me, "The city, the city—residence elsewhere is mere eclipse."

We slid out of the canyon of tall buildings and fetched up abruptly in stalled traffic in a part of town that was light-years, eons away from the romantic, MGM cityscape we had just passed through. On either side of Peachtree Street now were modest, two- and three-story buildings housing anonymous, largely unlit businesses and services, overhung with a bleak litter of electric wires and signs and frayed awnings and the crossbars of utility poles. But it would not have mattered if it had been Park Avenue, Worth Avenue, the Rue de la Paix. The show was not the street, but the people on the street. Shoals of them, a great river of them, packed so tightly that they seemed to move all of a piece, like the tide, eddying slowly along the sidewalks on Peachtree Street, seemingly oblivious to the nearly stopped carfuls of people who were gawking out windows at them.

"Hippies!" My father spat. "Will you just look at them dirty hippies, now! Dear Jesus, there must be five thousand of them!"

He was right, or nearly; there were not, of course, five thousand of them, but there were a lot, and hippies they were, and more: I saw bikers and out-and-out addicts, so stoned on what they were smoking or had just swallowed or shot up that they were clearly not in the same universe with the rest of us; ragged and eerie children whose bizarre costumes owed more to economic circumstance than the current flower-child craze; supine bodies that might be stoned or ill or even dead; young girls who, even to my untutored eyes, could only be prostitutes; plumed and preening black youths who could only be pimps. Smoke lay in solid strata in the air above the sidewalks; even inside the car, its acrid bite advertised its backyard origins. Music keened and thumped from guitars and radios; ragged and belled cuffs and vests and beads and bare feet and a sea of thin, faded denim challenged the raw fog of the night. Everyone moved slowly and hypnotically, as if underwater; no one seemed at all bellicose or threatening—indeed, most merely looked wackily exalted—and virtually everyone was young. There was nothing at all in the entire lot to threaten, except the sheer numbers of them and perhaps their studied grotesquerie. But I saw many windows in the cars around us fly hastily up, and my father quickly locked the Vista Cruiser's doors.

"It's straight home we're going, and I want no sass from you," he said tightly.

"Pa—"

"No! I'll not leave you here by yourself where dirty hippies and God knows what else are shootin' dope in their veins on the street, and fornicatin' in the gutters! No decent Catholic girl should have to see that; no daughter of mine will have to go through that mess of whores and whoremongers to get to her work."

I was silent. We were at the heart of it now, the thing inside Liam O'Donnell that had killed my love for him; the thing that had driven me, ultimately, away from home. It was not the potheads and freaks and the affluent white teenagers playing at being hippies; it was the sex implicit among them. It was sheer bad luck that we should blunder into the fabled Tight Squeeze area of Atlanta that even we in hermetically sealed Corkie had heard of, but I was not surprised. If it had not been Tight Squeeze it would have been something else, anything. I turned my head away from him, feeling the old bile of anger and resentment rise up into my throat, wondering if I had the courage simply to snatch my suitcase out of the car and shut the door and walk away from it, and find my way to the Church's Home on foot.

Remembering . . .

From the time we reached puberty, even before, we were taught by our mothers and the nuns and the Church in general that chastity was the only normal, desirable, permissible, or possible state for an unmarried girl, and that even thinking about "doing it" would result in instant corruption, begin the long slide into ruin. To actually do it meant pregnancy, disgrace, death, everlasting hell. No ifs, ands, or buts. I don't know precisely what the boys were taught, but it must have been something similar, only with the added threats of defiling the temples that were their bodies and bringing shame and anguish to their mothers' hearts. The natural consequence was that we thought about it all the time—the Black Act, the Dirty Deed—and not a few of us did it. We wept, afterward; we burned inwardly with shame and fear; we suffered agonies of guilt, but we did it.

I never did, but I was a late bloomer, and had not yet begun to date in earnest by the time I was sixteen. But my best friend, Meg Conlon, had. She had gone steady with Frank Callahan since they were thirteen, and by the time she was sixteen, desperate with love and hormones, they did it in the back of Frank's father's car after a Demolay dance, and then they did it again, and yet again, and the February before she turned seventeen Meg got pregnant. I never did hear how she figured that happened; I knew that Frank was using the rubbers that his older brother got for him at Malone's Drugstore. Perhaps the nuns were right; birth control of any kind was a sin, and the sinner would inevitably pay.

I didn't know about Meg's pregnancy. I don't think anyone else did, either, perhaps not even Frank. Meg attempted to abort herself one night with a coat hanger, and ended up in Sisters of Mercy with a raging infection that brought her near to death for many days, and ended, we heard, any chance of her ever having children. I wanted to go to her but my father forbade me, and when she was well enough to come home she went, instead, to her mother's mother in Jacksonville, ostensibly to care for that terrible old harridan in her long last illness. She never came back. Frank left Corkie the day after his high school graduation, and we never saw him again, either. My father forbade me to talk about either of them.

"She was no better than a whore," he said when he found me in tears for Meg, soon after we heard. "And what happened to her is no more than should have happened."

I looked at him incredulously. If I had not been so shocked and outraged, I might have seen the living fear that looked out of his white-lashed blue eyes. But I did not. I saw only that his face was red with rage, tight and twisted and terrible.

"Why is she a whore when she does it," I screamed at him, "but when you do it with half of Corkie you're not—"

He slapped me. Before he did that, I still loved my father after a fashion, as best I could. After that, I did not.

His words and the slap had finished the work that the Church had begun, though. After that I became a classic good girl, a model of Catholic young womanhood, the flower of my family. I was a true child of Saint John the Baptist and Corkie. I dated, decorously, many good Catholic boys, but never more than one at a time and never seriously. When things began to get serious, I fled. I still do not know if it was fear or anger that kept me, as the Church puts it, pure.

I had little time at Armstrong College for serious relationships; I studied endlessly to keep my Demolay scholarship and worked in the college bookstore after classes to help pay expenses. There was one young man, a dark, silent, awesomely gifted young Pole from Pittsburgh named Joe Menkiewicz, the editor of the school paper, for which I wrote a column and served as feature editor, with whom I might have thrown caution and Corkie to the winds, but he transferred to Columbia journalism school before the relationship could catch fire, and no one like him happened to me again. I found and nurtured as best I could a talent for writing and editing, and graduated with honors and as editor of the *Armstrong Argonaut,* and went to work in the office of a large marine insurance company on Bay Street, on the bluff above the docks where my father had worked for so long. I lived at home, paying room and board to my mother and father, and advanced quickly at work, and dated steadily, all good young Catholics from the old neighborhood, trainees in insurance offices like mine, banks, real estate firms, or perhaps the sons of prosperous local Irish merchants. A few of them were truly interested in me and wanted for me just what my family wanted: marriage, children, a life of service in the Church, a neat house on a neat square in the old city a little—but not too much—more affluent than the ones we grew up in, a prosperous middle age, an old age full of years and respectful grandchildren, an honorable death, and a huge funeral at Saint John.

I wanted none of that, but I did not know what I did want. Like Scarlett O'Hara I would, I decided, figure all that out tomorrow. I bent myself to my work. Before I even raised my head I was twenty-six years old and a rising star in my company and more than half-seriously involved with a handsome young claims adjuster there who was on what would one day be known as the fast track and who was still a virgin.

And I still did not know what I really wanted.

And then one day I did. It was the night Hank Cantwell, my best friend from Armstrong days, the art director of the *Argonaut* and the college yearbook, called me from Atlanta and said, "You remember those photoessays we did on the *'Naut* about the old town? The cityscape things that I shot and you did the captions for? Well, I showed them to somebody, and he wants to talk to you."

And a voice like rich honey, like poured wine, deep and complex, came on the line and said, "Hello, dear heart. My name is Matt Comfort, and I'm the editor of

Downtown magazine, and I want you to come up here and work for me."

I said nothing for a moment, while the rest of my life roared in my ears. I knew in that instant that I would go. I knew before I knew who this man was, or even what manner of magazine his might be, that I would go, that I would go if I had to walk every step of the way to Atlanta, and that nothing forever after would be the same. All that was in the extraordinary voice, and more.

Before I could speak, Matt Comfort said, "Hank has told me about your daddy. Is he around? If he is, put him on."

I looked at the phone and then at my father, sitting as he always sat, in front of the television set, drinking John Jameson. The set that year was an RCA. He looked up at me when I did not speak, and I simply walked across the room and handed the phone to him, the cord stretched tight. And I sat down to wait.

It was not a very long conversation. Mostly my father said, "Uh-huh. Uh-huh. Yes. Uh-huh. I see."

Finally he said, "Well, she'll be calling you back, Mr. Comfort . . . Matt, then . . . in the morning. You, too. Good-bye, now." And he hung up the phone and studied me in silence. My mother had come in from the kitchen, and we stood looking back at my father.

"Fellow Comfort thinks highly of your work, Smoky," my father said, as if it had only just occurred to him that I might have any sort of proficiency. "Starting a new magazine up there for the chamber of commerce, he is, says it's going to be the best one of its kind in the world. Says it's already more than halfway there."

I nodded. My father looked at my mother.

"Wants Smoky to come up there and work for him. That Cantwell fellow that Smoky had here once, the one with the glasses and the fat behind, you remember, he showed this fellow Comfort some of the work our girl did while she was at college, and this Comfort told him to get her right on the phone. What do you think of that? Mama?"

My mother started to shake her head, and my father lifted a hand. She subsided.

"Fellow says he knows how we must feel about letting her go all the way up there by herself, but says he's a Catholic, too, and he's on the . . . the board or something of the Church's home for working girls or something like that, right near this magazine office, and he'll see she gets a nice room there, and makes friends with some other Catholic girls—he's got two working for him—and he'll look after her himself, and even take her to Mass with him until she's found her way. Goes to a big church called Saint Matthew's. Says he can't pay Smoky much, but he can see that she comes to no harm, and he says she's got that kind of talent ought to be given a chance—"

"Is he married? Does he have a family?" my mother said.

"Well, of course he does. I mean, he didn't say, but no chamber of commerce is going to be giving a grand new magazine to some young, unmarried upstart, now are they?"

My mother said nothing.

"Well, Smoky girl?"

"Oh, Daddy, oh my God—" I breathed.

"Don't blaspheme," my mother said automatically.

And so I was on my way at last.

It was the first of the many miracles I personally witnessed Matt Comfort perform, that toppling of my father's towers without a shot being fired. It gave me a great and giddy sense of possibilities, the sense that, in that city to my north, on fire and on the make, assorted minor miracles might truly be within beck and call, at least that of Matt Comfort.

Then send me one right now, I thought desperately from the passenger seat of the Vista Cruiser stalled in Tight Squeeze, watching from the corner of my eye my father's face harden into the resolve to take me home to Corkie. God or Our Lady or Matt Comfort or somebody, send me a miracle or this whole thing is surely going to end right here in this car.

And it being the night for them, miracles as well as epiphanies, my deliverance presented itself at that instant, standing on a street corner under a streetlight on the corner of Tenth and Peachtree Streets.

"Look, Daddy," I said, incredulous laughter bubbling up like ginger ale in my chest, tickling giddily behind my eyes. "Look over there."

He followed my pointing finger and saw them, too. Three young nuns in full habit and a young priest in jeans and a crewneck sweater over his dog collar, standing in the middle of a throng of the tatterdemalion, half-naked young, strumming guitars and singing and laughing as if the whole scene were a Sunday School picnic. Over my father's silence I could hear, faintly, the sound of the chords, and their singing: "The answer, my friend, is blowin' in the wind. . . ."

My father did not speak again until we had cleared the lights of Tight Squeeze and were at the corner of Fourteenth Street, where we were to turn left for the Church's Home.

"I'm leaving you here against my better judgment, Maureen Aisling," he said. "And I'll be in touch with this Matt Comfort at least once a week, and if he notices the slightest thing amiss with you, the slightest wee thing, I'll be up here for you before he hangs up the phone. Don't you forget that."

"I won't, Daddy," I said meekly.

When we had reached the forbidding dark-brick pile of Our Lady, my father decided that he would not come in with me. His innate sense of otherness from all but Corkie had gotten hold of him, I knew; I had seen it happen before. His plan had been to deposit me safely in the arms of the Church, to find himself a cheap motel room nearby, and drive back early the next morning, but I knew that he would get back into the Vista Cruiser and start for home when he left me off, fleeing for safety in the cradling arms of the huge car. He would play the radio all the way, the sentimental stations he favored fading out as he left the city behind and the raw all-night gospel stations of the wiregrass and the coast coming in, singing along with them, emerging whole and vigorous once more as he neared Savannah and Corkie, like a photograph in developing solution.

He carried my bags to the sagging front porch and set them down and rang the bell, and when he heard a ponderous tread coming toward us, he hugged me stiffly, ruffling my careful new Sassoon cut, and kissed me on the cheek.

From the bottom step he called after me, "Whose daughter are you now?"

"I'm Liam O'Donnell's daughter!" I called back obediently.

"And don't you be forgettin' it!"

"I won't."

But I began to forget in that instant.

"Look out, Atlanta," I whispered as the lock on the forbidding front door to Our Lady began to turn. "Look out, *Downtown* magazine. Look out, Matt Comfort. Here comes Maureen Aisling O'Donnell. And don't you be forgetting it."

2

I HAD NEVER BEEN TO NEW YORK, BUT CAROLYN RENFROW in my class at Saint Zita's had, to visit her older sister Deirdre. Deirdre married a Corkie boy who simply never came home after he disembarked from his Korean-war troopship, but stayed and went to work for a taxi company. By the time he sent for Deirdre he had his own cab, and they married and lived in Levittown, and Deirdre worked for the city in the Tax Records Division until her children began to come. But before she married Jerry Sullivan she lived briefly in the Barbizon Hotel for Women, and it was there that Carolyn visited her. I thought Carolyn's account of Deirdre's life there was the most magical thing I had ever heard.

I thought Our Lady would be like that. I can't remember why, but I did.

In my mind I knew every inch, facet, and nuance of it before my father and I even set out for Atlanta. There would be laughing, wisecracking young women streaming out to their jobs downtown in the mornings and back in the evenings. They would be sleek and modish, dressed in Mary Quant, their shining blunt-cut Sassoons swinging, their long legs flashing in patterned tights of white fishnet. They would be self-assured and up-to-the-minute on where to shop, dine, be seen in Atlanta, but of course they would be out-of-towners like me, too, so there would be just a touch of endearing unsureness about them; I would not stand out in their ranks in my Corkie greenness. They would welcome me as a sister; we would sit on our beds in our shortie pajamas and curlers at night, smoking and drinking Coca-Colas and trading the secrets of our hearts; we would do each other's hair and lend each other clothes, maybe we would experiment with body paint. We would introduce each other to our boyfriends' urbane friends, and we would go in crowds of youth and laughter and kickiness to movies and discos and restaurants and concerts. There would be a housemother, of course, a wise, eccentric older woman who saw in us her own youthful dreams and foibles, and she would shake her head, smiling, when we came in late or violated some minor house rule, and comfort us when we fetched up—briefly—between boyfriends. We would call her Muggsy or Gertie or something, and she would call us all "kid." At Christmas we would pool our resources and buy her a satin negligee, and she would crack bad jokes about it, and her eyes would shine with tears.

One evening, across the warm, disorderly, Miss Dior–smelling parlor, our eyes would meet those of a handsome stranger come to call on someone, and would lock. . . .

In truth, my vision probably owed more to a recent rerun of *Stage Door* at the Bijou in Corkie than to Deirdre Renfrow's tenure at the Barbizon Hotel for Women at Madison and Sixty-fourth in Manhattan. Neither one had anything at all to do with Our Lady's

Home for Catholic Girls on Fourteenth Street in Atlanta. Our Lady was inexorably moored in the early, Vatican-blessed fifties, and though I could not have seen it, so was I. It is incredible to me, looking back, that the woman whose fantasies that night included *Stage Door* and body paint was twenty-six years old. But such was the power of Corkie and the Church. The distance from Atlanta and the dock neighborhoods of Savannah was measured in far more than miles.

Even though it was just past nine when my father dropped me off, Our Lady was largely dark. Standing on the porch waiting for the door to open to my ring I saw a dim, grayish light from a foyer lamp through the grimy stained glass panels on either side of the door, and one or two slits of light on the second floor that looked as if they might be escaping from beneath lowered shades. Otherwise the ungainly old house and those around it were steeped in darkness like thick tea. I had little sense of the neighborhood, except that it gave off a stink of semicommercialism. I knew without even thinking about it that all of the darkened houses around me had once been single family residences, and substantial ones at that, but that now they were rooming houses or businesses of some sort: AAA Personnel Service; Peach City Temporaries; Dr. A. E. Moorvakian, Chiropractor; Madame Rhonda, Psychic; T. Plasters, DDS. Except for the sharp, cold night mist on my face and the distant river-roar of traffic over on Peachtree Street, I might have been back home in Corkie. There was the same slight, sour effluvia of defeat, slackness, decay. I would have known it on the other side of the universe.

The door opened. I could not see the face of the woman who stood there, but I could see the white of her wimple and the dark skirts to the floor, and my heart sank. Why had I not expected a nun? Who better, after all, to guard the daughters of the Church in a strange city? But I had not. My vision of Muggsy in sentimental tears over her satin negligee vanished.

"Maureen O'Donnell?" the sister said in a voice that seemed a piece of the night, harsh and affectless, overlaid with the singsong of the brogue I had thought I had left behind me.

"Yes. Ah . . . at least, it's Maureen Aisling, but everybody calls me Smoky," I said into the darkness. I wished she would step back into the light. I felt as if I were talking to a statue.

"I will call you Maureen. That's what Mr. Comfort's letter said, and that's how you're registered with us. I am Sister Mary James," she said, and turned and went back into the house. I picked up my bags and followed her. Inside the light was the color of pale urine, and scarcely brighter than it had been outside. I could see only that she was heavy, wore flesh-colored plastic-rimmed glasses, had tight-stretched shiny skin, and might have been any age at all over thirty. All the doors off the foyer were dark fumed oak and closed, and the walls were painted the self-same green of those at Saint Zita's. I thought perhaps there was a company somewhere that made green paint specifically for Catholic institutions.

Sister Mary James moved ponderously and silently up a dark oak staircase. A runner of sour taupe carpet muffled my footsteps as I followed behind her. At the top of the stairs a crucifix hung over a scarred oak table holding twelve or so Thom McAn shoeboxes, each with a slit in its lid and a name crayoned under the slit.

"For your mail," Sister Mary James said, not pausing. "We sort it and put it out once a day in the midafternoons." She turned left and padded on down the hall. On either side, doors were shut. Squares of cardboard taped on them had names, but I could not read any of them in the murk. The only light here came from a night-light attached to the baseboard about halfway down the hall and from a pink and green neon sign that flashed through the high window over the mail table: "Life of Georgia," it winked. "Life of Georgia."

The thought came, unbidden and suddenly threatening to swamp me with choking laughter, that the night-light, when I passed it, would prove to be a plastic one of Jesus. But it was, after all, only a tiny bulb in a seashell. That, though, was plastic.

At the end of the hall Sister Mary James opened a door using a key that hung from a chain around her neck and entered. She motioned me to follow her. As I passed I could see that the sign on the oak door read "Callahan, A." and "O'Donnell, M." I stopped still, suddenly shy. My daydreams had all had a roommate in them, but now that I was here, I felt bumbling and insensitive, and annoyed at Sister Mary James, simply unlocking the door and crashing in upon the sleeping Callahan, A.

But the room was empty. A bare overhead light fixture showed two single beds, each tightly covered by a military-cornered chenille spread and a folded gray blanket. I knew those blankets: the few rooms at Saint Zita's kept for boarders had them, and the infirmary. Perhaps as well as paint, there was a central emporium for blankets. Or, more likely, an enormous central Catholic commissary.

One of the beds had a stuffed monkey and a ruffled pink pillow on it. The other was bare except for one thin pillow, hardly making a rise in the chenille. Between the beds was a metal desk with a green goosenecked lamp on it, and over each bed was a plain metal cross. Two enormous oak-stained wardrobes stood on either side of the door, and a round hooked rug, faded and obviously homemade but somehow warm and softening, lay in the middle of the linoleum floor. In the corner a radiator hissed and rattled.

It was so Spartan a room as to seem a nun's cell, and my heart, already poised to dive into the pit of my stomach, would have made the final great leap with no further delay except for the window. It was much larger than the other few I had seen in Our Lady, and it lay over the desk uncurtained and shining like the door into heaven.

I drew a soft little breath. By some twist of geography I could not yet figure, the window in my room looked straight out over the treetops of Fourteenth Street and those on the streets beyond it, into the river of light that was Tight Squeeze. I could see the shoals of drifting, wildly dressed hippies that had so outraged my father, and the flowing-lava lights of the traffic crawling along Peachtree Street, and the towers of downtown rising beyond it all, gleaming in the mist.

"Oh," I said softly. I did not realize that I had spoken it aloud until Sister Mary James nodded in quick annoyance and strode to the window and pulled the shade down firmly.

"I know," she said. "It's a terrible annoyance. Shameless young heathens. But it's the only vacancy we had, and Mr. Comfort didn't give us much time. I'm afraid you'll just have to ignore it. We've petitioned and petitioned for someone from the diocese to come and do something about it—shutters on the outside, or something—but of course no one has. Ansonia keeps the shade down all the time, but there's still the glow, and in the summer the infernal noise—"

"It will be just fine," I said, itching for her to leave so that I could raise the tattered shade. Ansonia, whoever she was, would just have to make other sleeping arrangements. Perhaps I could get her one of those chic black satin sleep masks you saw in movies. Audrey Hepburn had worn one in *Breakfast at Tiffany's*.

"Well, then, here you are," Sister Mary James said. "I hope Mr. Comfort will be pleased with your room. I must say we don't usually take girls on such short notice and without written references from their parish priest, but he said your Father Terrence Moore would be writing us in a day or two, and it was Mr. Comfort who got us our bus, so of course we did what we could. I'm sure you'll be comfortable here and will try to do him proud. We don't have many rules; you're all young working women and too old to be treated like children, but the rules we do have are quite firm. You'll find them in the little pamphlet in your mailbox. Any other questions you can ask me or Sister Clementia in the morning. Breakfast is at eight, so you can have it after early Mass or before the nine o'clock. Saint Joseph's is one street over and two down. Almost everyone has gone home for Thanksgiving, but they'll be coming in tomorrow. I believe Ansonia said she would be back about four. She's visiting her parents in South Carolina. Rachel Vaughn down the hall is here and will no doubt be happy to take you to Mass with her. She goes to the eleven o'clock when she goes. And you may have company in the parlor tomorrow from one P.M. until nine in the evening, if you have friends here."

She paused and looked at me. The eyes behind the flesh-colored plastic glasses clearly did not believe that I had any friends in Atlanta.

"No, I thought I would just . . . walk around and get to know the city a little bit," I said lamely.

"You'll find it very quiet on a holiday Sunday," she said and made as if to leave, and then turned back. "We had thought to meet your father," she said. "Sister Clementia made a cake, and has waited up, I believe. But I see that he has gone on—"

"He had to get back," I said, the lie sliding out smoothly on a little rush of annoyance. "My mother isn't well."

"I am sorry. I will remember her in my prayers," Sister Mary James said, nodded at me, and closed the door. I could not hear her footsteps going away, and somehow had the fancy that she was standing just outside the door, listening. But for what? It was an absurd notion.

All the same, I did not move from the edge of my bed for a long time, and it was even longer until I reached over the desk and raised the shade and let the blaze of city lights stream back into the room. They set me free, and I moved about the room in my stocking feet putting away my clothes in the unlocked armoire, my eyes drawn over and over again to the blaze of light and life outside.

I got into my nightgown and robe and slippers and tiptoed down the hall peering at doors until I found the one labeled bathroom, went in and washed my face and brushed my teeth among the bulbous old white fixtures, examined my face in the wavering, underwater mirror. The dim, sterile light and the speckled, greenish glass made me look like something at the bottom of the sea, blanched and sodden, long drowned. I bit my lips and rubbed my cheeks hard, but the drowned girl still looked back at me, and I shook my head hard and went back, silently, to my new room. I will never sleep, I thought. I will simply never sleep.

But despite the strange, bare room and the clattering radiator and the prowling of the night wind in the branches outside, and despite the cold radiance of the lighted streets pouring down over my narrow bed, I did sleep. I knelt and said the mechanical small prayer that I had said almost every night of my life, slipped into bed, turned my face to the streaming window, whispered, "I'm here. Wait for me," and closed my eyes. And when I opened them, it was morning.

That afternoon I went out in search of Atlanta and couldn't find it anywhere. By the time I lay again in bed under the window into the soul of the city I was almost ready to call my father and tell him to come and get me. And to call the insurance company and say that I would, after all, be coming back to edit the employee newspaper. I have always wondered what would have become of me if it had not been forbidden to use the communal upstairs telephone after ten P.M.

I got up late on that first morning. The previous night's mist had slumped into a ceaseless, defeated rain, so that it was not possible to tell what precise time it was, and my watch had stopped just after midnight. But it felt late. The bare room around me had the slightly hangdog air of a place where no one should be, but was. I started downstairs, where I thought I might find breakfast, in my robe and scuffs, met Sister Mary James on the stairs and was told "We dress for breakfast." I went back and put on my blue suit and high heels so as to be ready for Mass if the late-rising Rachel Vaughn seemed, as Sister had said, amenable to company, then went back down. When I found the breakfast room, a large room at the back of the house off the kitchen with a great round oak table and chairs and a sideboard and a battered upright piano, there was no one there but a thin redhead in a ponytail so tight that it gave a Chinese slant to her eyes. She was slumped on a chair with her stockinged feet propped on another, drinking coffee and reading the Sunday comics. She wore, oddly, a khaki London Fog raincoat, the twin of my navy one, buttoned up under the chin, and there was a great deal of makeup on her sharp little fox's face. Her eyes were heavily shadowed and feathered with jet lashes that I knew were not her own because the end of one set had pulled away from her lid and arched into the air like a caterpillar. Her mouth was small and round and thick with pale pink frost. The shoes that lay on their sides under the table were Cuban-heeled, square-toed affairs constructed almost totally of cobwebby straps. Perhaps, I thought, she is going on to a party somewhere after Mass, though I couldn't think what sort of party might be held, even in Atlanta, on a Sunday afternoon that occasioned bare sandals and false eyelashes. She was smoking a cigarette from a pack of Salems that lay on the table beside her plate, which held only a half-empty bowl of cereal. There were ashtrays all around the room—the Church forbids a great deal, but is fairly pragmatic about what it will allow; it has never pushed its luck. When I came into the room she smiled and put her cigarette out in the cereal bowl.

"Good morning and welcome," she said over the sizzle. "You have to be Maureen O'Donnell. Who else would you be? Isn't it a horrible morning? I'm Rachel Vaughn. Sister told me you might like to go to eleven o'clock Mass, so I waited for you."

She rolled her eyes toward the door into what I supposed was the kitchen, and mouthed, "Say yes. We don't really have to."

I grinned.

"Thanks," I said loudly. "That was nice of you. It's nice to meet you."

She put her hands together over her head and shook them in a victorious prize-fighter's gesture. She chattered aimlessly while I had coffee and cereal: about the others who lived there; her job in a beauty salon ("I'm almost finished with my course at Brower College of Beauty and I'm going to work full-time at Antoine's when I do"); my job at *Downtown* ("Are you a secretary? No? An editor? Really? Like on a newspaper? Fabulous!"); her boyfriend, Carl, who worked for Triple A right around the corner; her boyfriend's friend Lee who would simply flip over me, no kidding; the Beatles, who were rumored to be making an American tour and might even come to Atlanta; current movies around town; my age ("No kidding? Twenty-six? You don't look it. I thought you were maybe eighteen"); my romantic status ("Well, don't worry about it. There're so many single men in this town you have to step over them on the street. You won't have a bit of trouble, cute as you are. Whyn't you let me fix you up a little?"); and, in response to my query about how many nuns there were at Our Lady, a terse, "Two. At a time, that is. Different ones, but always two."

This was accompanied by a parody of suicide, her white-lacquered nail being drawn across her throat, her red head flopping to one side, her pink tongue sticking out the corner of her mouth, and the caterpillared blue eyes crossing. I could not suppress an explosive giggle, but turned it into a sneeze.

"Let's go on before the rain gets worse," she said, projecting her voice toward the kitchen. "I have an umbrella. You ready? Bye, Sisters! See you at dinner!"

An indistinct mumble from behind the doors followed us out of the kitchen and onto a small back stoop, and she put up her umbrella and we clattered under it down the three rain-slicked steps, through a dismal alleyway where rusted old garbage cans leaned, and out onto Fourteenth Street, our shoulders touching, our heads bumping together as if we were old friends.

"You didn't really want to go to Mass, did you?" she said, pausing on Our Lady's front walkway.

"Well . . . I guess not," I said, thinking I could go later that afternoon, or to evening Mass, if I had to. Surely the

Church would want me to make friends among its flock. "But where else would we go?"

"To the IHOP and get a decent cup of coffee and a stack of potato pancakes with sour cream," she said. "My treat, since you're new. I got a humongous tip yesterday. And after that . . . who knows? We'll scare up something. That is, if you want to. And I hope you do. You're the first inmate of that joint I've ever seen that didn't look like a junior Sister Mary James. Just please don't tell me you've given all your worldly goods to the poor and have come up here to do missions among the heads and freaks. It's a big thing with the Church."

"Not me," I said. "I don't have any worldly goods. What's the IHOP?"

"The International House of Pancakes. The first reason you'll be glad you left—wherever you left."

"Savannah."

We picked our way through the skin-prickling rain down to the corner of Fourteenth Street and turned south onto Peachtree Street.

I'm walking down Peachtree Street, I said to myself. I'm walking where Scarlett O'Hara walked, where Margaret Mitchell walked. Where, as a matter of fact, she was fatally injured. But I did not know that yet.

I waited for the frisson of exaltation to begin in my stomach, where all my raptures had their genesis, but nothing happened. The rain-slicked street was largely bare of pedestrian traffic and even the cars that swished by looked dull and furtive, seeming to sneak through the heavy air. As they had been the night before, the tops of the buildings downtown were lost in cloud and mist, and I could not see clearly more than a block ahead of me. There were few lights in the buildings along this section of Peachtree; structures that crouched stolidly, none more than five or six stories high, largely mustardy yellow stone or dark red brick weeping black soot. A movie theater's marquee advertised, dimly, Ingmar Bergman's *Persona,* but there was no line waiting to see it, and in the lighted drugstore across from it I saw no customers among the Hallmark Santas and folding bells and scanty displays of tinsel. At the far corner, nearly lost in mist, a red, black, and white Texaco sign flashed on and off. Far beyond that, an anonymous building glowed yellow and faint. Everything was dingy, indistinct, as if someone had dropped dirty stage scrim down over the whole of midtown Atlanta. There was an astonishing amount of litter in the gutters.

"Uggh," Rachel said, skipping over a rich mound of dog excrement at the curb. "Watch your step. Come on, let's run. This is gross."

I huddled closer to her under the umbrella and put my head down and we trotted off down the sidewalk. Under the bumping umbrella I could see very little but our feet. The air that crept under my raincoat collar and around my legs was cold, raw; I seldom felt air of this temperature in Savannah.

Savannah—for a moment the sense of it enveloped me so totally that I was lost in it, drowned; I perceived it, in that instant, more sharply and wholly than I ever had in all the years I had spent there. I saw, through the wet black dome of Rachel Vaughn's umbrella, the lush canopies of live oaks in its small, beautiful squares; the surging banks of ruffled azaleas and camellias in the long, warm springs; the spectral gray curtains of hanging moss; the lovely woman-curves of wrought iron balconies and stair railings; the grimy, tight-packed, once-beautiful row houses that lined the noisy cobbled streets of Corkie. I heard the hooting of the great ships that wallowed at the docks under the bluff and the liquid spill of mockingbirds in the crape myrtle trees; I smelled the ineffable perfume of the night-blooming Cape Jessamine along the slow river, and the thick, dank, shrimpy smell of the river itself; smelled sweat and linseed oil and iron fittings heating in the sun and exotic spices from who knew where in the world, that was the breath of the docks. I tasted on my lips the salt of the sea and the sweet, fetid aftertaste of the sulphurous water and the nectar of sun-ripened peaches from roadside stands out toward Tybee Island. I felt the dark, amniotic water of the August shallows of the ocean in my own blood; felt the soft, blood-warm rain of summer under the icy needles of the rain I ran through; felt as well as saw the strange, silken spring light that seemed to rise from the greening marshes.

Savannah . . .

"Look out!" Rachel cried, giving a little hop, and I looked down and saw a used condom lying on the sidewalk almost directly beneath my blue pumps, and sprang over it like a startled rabbit. When I came down I landed in a puddle, and felt the filthy water spatter my pale new stockings.

"Somebody must have had an awfully good time last night," Rachel laughed. I could not answer her. My cheeks flamed and my voice seemed to have died in my throat. I had never seen a condom before, used or otherwise. My brothers and father had conspired to keep me mindlessly chaste all my life. I could not have said how I know that that was what I had seen, but I did know.

We fetched up in front of a little Permastone chalet blazing light and full of people, its windows frosted over with their breath and the warmth inside.

"Here's the IHOP," Rachel said. "Is this okay, or is there any place else you'd rather go?"

"I'd sort of like to go down to Tight Squeeze," I said. "We drove through it last night, and I could see it from my window till all hours. It looked . . . I loved the way it looked. I'd love to really see it—"

"You just did," she said. "That was Tight Squeeze right about where the guy left his calling card on the sidewalk. We were the only living souls in it. Take it from me, you'd rather see Tight Squeeze on a nice sunny day, or a warm spring night. It's the pits on Sundays and in bad weather."

I felt like a small child who had just been told about Santa Claus. In silence I followed Rachel into the International House of Pancakes. I still go to IHOPs sometime, when I happen upon one. It was the first place I ever went in Atlanta beside the Church's Home for Girls, my first journey out, and it still makes the best potato pancakes with sour cream I have ever eaten. And I have eaten them everywhere, from the Russian Tea Room to neighborhood delis in half a dozen countries.

The crowd was mostly young, half-obscured by clouds of cigarette and other smoke and steam from many cups of coffee, and dressed in plastic, beads, boots, fishnet, sunglasses, flips and bobs, and a great deal of skin. The men's hair was, in many cases, longer than that of the women and often more lovingly coifed, and there was a thick frosting of Max Factor on every female mouth in the place. The room was full of eyes drooping under the weight of caterpillars like Rachel's, and there were enough clunky, square-toed boots to stomp an invading army to death. Rachel shed her coat and threw it over the back of our booth, revealing an A-line dress in what appeared to be shiny white vinyl, with cutouts that showed a coy sliver of her belly button and more than a slice of the top of her freckled breasts. When she sat down it climbed so far up her white, cross-hatched thighs that I instinctively averted my eyes. I blushed, hating the treacherous tide of heat in my face. It was another legacy from my mother, that involuntary pink suffusion from chest to hairline, and I still do it today, even though there is little now that startles me and almost nothing that embarrasses me.

"Well, aren't you going to compliment me on my new dress?" Rachel grinned, lighting a Salem and looking around the room to see who was watching her. Everybody was.

"It's stunning," I said truthfully. "Courreges? I'm going to try some of his, but I thought I'd wait till I got up here. There's bound to be a better selection than we get at home."

"God, no, but it is a good knockoff, isn't it?" she said, drawing in smoke and letting it drift from her nostrils in twin plumes. "If you're serious, I'll show you where to get some neat stuff really cheap, but somehow I don't think you are. You're blushing, you know."

I gave up trying to pretend that I was merely waiting for a wider selection of Courreges and Quant to pick up a few things. She had a shrewd eye and probably a sharp, banal little mind behind the shutter-lashed eyes. I was maybe six years her senior, but she was decades, a lifetime older than me. I felt younger and rawer by years, provincial and diminished. And I was angry that I cared. She and this group of outrageously winged young butterflies jostling and preening in the IHOP might be far more outwardly sophisticated than I, but I was the new senior editor of *Downtown* magazine, and I was willing to bet that there was not a college degree or the aspiration toward one in this entire group. I would hold on to that.

"Actually, I'm not," I said. I was not going to play games with Rachel Vaughn. "I don't own a miniskirt; at my old school the nuns make you kneel, and if your skirt doesn't brush the floor they send you home to change. And miniskirts aren't even allowed in Vatican City. We don't see them in Corkie, except on TV. It's no great loss. You need to be long and skinny, like Twiggy. My brothers are always telling me I'd look like a beachball in one."

"Your brothers are jerks," she said. "You have a knockout little figure, even if it isn't right for this stuff. Of course, that suit doesn't do anything for you. Jesus, I know that suit. There's one in the back of mine and every other good Catholic girl's closet in the country. They ought to just go on and issue them at Confirmation. I put mine in the poor box when I first came to Our Lady of the Eternal Virgins. I've got a closet full of these, but I lock it every morning when I leave, and I always wear my raincoat. London Fog is A-one, Pope-approved. Hang on to yours, and lock your closets. Sister Mary James and Sister Clementia both snoop."

"What are they going to do, throw us out because of our clothes?" I said. "It's not a school. There's nothing about clothes in that astonishing little rule pamphlet. We're all adult women."

"Not in their eyes. To them we're lambs who just can't wait to go out and get shorn, or worse. And no, they can't throw you out over what you wear, but if they disapprove they can poke and pry and wait until they find something they can use. They've done it to a couple of girls since I've been here. I can't wait to get my own apartment."

"Why do you stay?"

"Are you kidding? It's the cheapest place in town. That's the only reason anybody stays. The minute you have enough money you go to Colonial Homes."

"Where's that?"

"Out toward Buckhead. It's this apartment complex where all the swingers live. It's where you go to meet the Buckhead guys—the lawyers and stockbrokers and bankers. My friend Joyce moved out there and she says there's a sports car in every garage and a party every night. They've got a pool, and after work and on the weekends the guys go from door to door to get drinks and meet the new girls. And a lot of the girls grew up in Buckhead, so they've got a lot of money—"

"What is this Buckhead business?" I said.

"You really don't know anything, do you?" Rachel said, looking around the IHOP with bright, avian eyes. "It's where the rich people live. You ought to see some of those houses; they're humongous. And some of them are real old. There's one that they've made into this fancy country club that's almost a hundred years old. Joyce—she's a cocktail waitress and a dancer—she worked this party out there that was like a go-go club, you know, and she said all the faucets in the bathrooms are gold. When I'm living at Colonial Homes I'm not going out with anybody except guys who belong to that club. You ought to see Buckhead. We'll go out there next weekend, if you want to. The Twenty-three Oglethorpe bus goes through there."

Old? Almost a hundred years? I thought of the mellow stucco row houses off the squares in Savannah, gentled by the quiet centuries that had drifted over them, and the great white houses out by the river, older by decades than that. I was not beguiled by the spell of years as were many Savannians—no one in Corkie was—and indeed, I was in full flight from it. But just for a moment the dark resonance of the thick-piled years called after me, all these miles away. Back there, you might fall endlessly down through the centuries and not hit bottom; here, you sensed hard red clay just beneath the surface of time. I did not miss the endlessness, but I was sharply aware of the clay.

"I think Twenty-three Oglethorpe is the bus I take to work," I said. "I've got it written down somewhere. . . . I thought you said you already had a boyfriend, who worked for that automobile thing . . . Carl?"

"Carl is fine for the Church's Home," Rachel grinned. "You've gotta have some fun, after all. But when I hit Colonial Homes it's good-bye Carl, hello Buckhead. And let the good times roll."

"I hope you haven't told Carl that."

"I'm not a fool. Carl's going to think he's the greatest thing in shoe leather until he's on the way out the door. But listen, it's all a game. He knows. He'd bounce me out on the sidewalk so fast my head would spin if he got something better. It's just the way you do things up here. You gotta move fast and travel light."

I said nothing, thinking that if this was the way the game was played in Atlanta, I would never get the hang of it. Nothing here was like it had been back home. My clothes were wrong, my expectations unfounded, the experiences of my entire lifetime totally alien.

But then I thought, well, that's why I'm here, isn't it? To learn how to move fast and travel light? So I'll learn. I can learn anything this silly child can.

And when Rachel said, "Let's cruise around a little and see what we can scare up," I said, "Fine," and got up behind her, and took a deep breath and squared my shoulders under my all-wrong navy blue coat and followed her into the crowd.

I can remember few more uncomfortable journeys in my life. Rachel seemed to know many of the brightly plumed young in the IHOP, and reached out to lay a hand on this shoulder and that; tossed back the red hair, now unbound and kinking furiously on her shoulders; laughed and blew smoke and dodged away from grasping hands. But she never stopped, and behind her, I plowed on, a stiff smile pasted on my mouth, feeling with every step the four or five all-wrong extra inches of cloth around my knees, feeling flat, assessing eyes on me, hearing barely muffled laughter that I did not doubt was aimed at me. When Rachel finally stopped beside a booth where two pasty-faced, wolfish young men in lank, collar-brushing hair and scuffed ankle boots lolled amid overflowing ashtrays, I said lightly, "Ladies room," and found it and ducked gratefully inside. It was cramped and filthy, but blessedly empty, and I drew a deep breath and let it out, and then ran cold water into a basin and splashed my burning face repeatedly.

Some minutes later Rachel came in. Her face was flushed and her eyes were very bright. She opened her shoulder bag and fished in it for makeup, and began brushing brick-red blush on her cheeks and applying a thick icing of chalky lipstick to her mouth. She was excited; I could smell the musk of her body through the sharp-sweet perfume she wore.

"Bingo," she said. "We're invited to a party. Those two guys say there's a great one going on over on Lindbergh; there's some kicky apartments over there, and they want us to go with them. They've got a car, and they'll bring it around and pick us up. The dark one, Earl, thinks you're cute. He wants you to be his date."

"Rachel, I really don't think—"

"Come on. He's older than he looks; he has a good job at Lockheed. And there's nothing else to do but sit around Our Lady and wash out pantyhose. It's dead on Sunday. Here's your chance to meet some swingers and get to know the party scene. Here, let me poof some of this on you, and do up your eyes a little. . . ."

She dug deeper into the purse and it spilled its contents over the counter. A small cardboard wheel tumbled out. Tiny pills were embedded in it. About half were gone. I stared as if an asp had crawled out of her handbag. I knew as surely as I knew anything, as surely as I had known the condom, that they were birth control pills. I felt my chest and cheeks flame, and snapped my eyes to my own reflection in the mirror, busying myself with fluffing my hair. I wanted to say something hip and funny, but I could think of nothing. Embarrassment almost strangled me.

She said nothing for a long moment. Then she swept the pills back into her purse and clicked it shut. I expected her to make a wisecrack, but she said, sullenly, "I suppose you think I'm going straight to hell, don't you?"

"No, I—"

"Well, I don't give a shit what you or anybody else thinks. I'm up here to swing for a change, to have a little fun before I get old and ugly and stuck with a million screaming brats, and nobody, not you or the Church or anybody else, is going to tell me how to live my life. Come or don't come, I don't care. But don't stick up your nose at the way I do things."

I did not reply. She went to the door, opened it, and looked back.

"Coming?"

I shook my head.

"I really thought you were different," she said, and went out of the door and closed it. Through it, I heard: "You can make the last Mass at Saint Joseph's if you hurry."

I stayed there for a while, looking at myself in the mirror, my heart finally slowing its pounding. And then I put on my raincoat and walked through the crowd out onto Peachtree Street. Rachel and the two young men were nowhere in sight. The rain had stopped, but last night's heavy fog had come down again. I set off through it back the way we had come, stepping over the puddles and the litter, feeling more sharply than ever the rawness through my thin coat. I felt shamed, chastened, humiliated by my shock at the pills and her scorn at my prissy naiveté; disoriented, near to tears, and lonelier than I had ever been in my life. Loneliness was an emotion almost entirely alien to Corkie; we all lived, simply, too packed together for loneliness. I almost did not know what the emptiness was.

I had meant to find my way over to Saint Joseph's, but suddenly I wanted, instead of dimness and stale incense and the mustiness of a dingy winter church, lights and chatter and the warm, buttery smell of popcorn. When I passed back by the little theater, I went in. Two hours later I came back out into the lowering darkness as one pulling exhaustedly for the surface of dark water, nearly drowned in somberness and obliqueness and Bergman's enigmatic flickering, doom-charged images. I could not have made a worse choice, on this dark Sunday, to show me the Atlanta I had come in search of.

Walking the last empty block toward Fourteenth Street, watching the pale streetlights making shallow pools in the foggy emptiness, my shoulders felt weighted, literally burdened with the great freight of wrongness. Why had I thought it would be special, this upstart young city so far to the north of everything I knew? Why had I known so surely that I was coming to Camelot? I could not remember. I had only been to Atlanta twice before: once to a Beta Club Convention when I was in the eleventh grade at Saint Zita's, when I and another girl had slept in the same room with the chaperoning nun and never left the anonymous downtown hotel; and once to visit my father's younger brother Gerald in his little house in Kirkwood, when I was perhaps nine. We had only stayed two nights before my father and my uncle got into a fight over some fancied slight to Ireland and we left and drove back to Savannah. I had thought of Atlanta, before I came here this time, as a place much like Corkie, except that it had yards and did not smell of ships and shrimp and sulphur and the sea. Indeed, except for a trip to Ponce de Leon Park to see the Atlanta Crackers play and one to the great, dark brick Sears Roebuck on Ponce de Leon, I had done nothing here that we did not do at home in Corkie.

But it was different; somehow I had always known that it was. It was Camelot, the Camelot of the wonderful stage play, the movie. Splendor, glamour, it was all here. If I could only find the key.

In that dark twilight, I knew for the first time that perhaps I would not.

When I got back to Our Lady, I went straight to the dining room, for I felt a great, whistling hollowness inside, and thought that part of it, at least, might be hunger. But the room was bare and dark. Sister Mary James, putting her head out of her quarters, told me that there was no dinner served on Sunday nights.

"So many of our girls have a heavy Sunday meal with their families. I thought you would have seen that we do not serve, in the pamphlet. In any case, I supposed you would have a meal somewhere with Rachel. She is usually out on Sunday evenings."

"I'm not really hungry," I said.

"Did you enjoy Mass?" she said. "I believe Father Diehl takes the eleven o'clock."

"It was very interesting," I said. "Well, I think I'll go and write a few letters, and meet some of the others—"

"I believe most of them have retired for the night," Sister Mary James said. "I was up a few minutes ago and all of their doors were closed. You'll be without a roommate for one more night; Ansonia's mother called to say that Ansonia has another of her sinus infections, and will not be coming back until tomorrow or the next day. Poor child, she suffers terribly in weather like this.

Remember breakfast is at six, in case you want to go to
early Mass. You'll hear the bell."

"Thank you, sister. Goodnight," I said, and went up
the stairs and down the silent hall to my room. Sister
Mary James was right. None of the doors was open.

Much later, after I had set out my clothes for the next
day and written a brief, determinedly cheerful postcard
home, and taken a quick, uneasy bath in the chilly, too-big
bathroom, I turned out my light and crawled into bed.
This time I did not lift the shade that Sister Mary James
had let down over the window. I lay in the thick, airless
darkness and listened to the thumping, pinging radiator
and thought, Well, I can call them in the morning and tell
them it was a mistake and I want to come home. It's not a
disgrace. At least I would know my way, know how to live
there. It may be all I do know, but I know it well. I could
be somebody there, a big fish, a kind of queen. . . .

No, I can't, I thought then. Whatever happens to me
here, that is not an option. This may turn out to be the
worst mistake I ever made, but going back is not an
option.

For the first time I could remember I had not said my
prayers, and I started to get out of bed and kneel on the
floor beside it, but then I did not. The thought came,
ridiculous but powerful, that I would simply be too
exposed there. I closed my eyes and said, rapidly, "Holy
Mary, Mother of God . . . "

The words crashed into the ceiling and scattered
back down over me. I tried again: "Holy Mary, Mother
of God . . . "

It was no use. Apparently the Blessed Virgin had
turned her head as inexorably away from me as her
handmaiden downstairs. I did not try again.

Far down the hall I heard someone begin to cry. The
sound was muffled behind the thickness of old oak and

perhaps thin layers of old percale, but it was unmistakable. In my house in Corkie I had heard that and all the other sounds of living through the paper-thin walls. I knew tears when I heard them. I lay still listening to the crying, wondering if I should get up and make my way down the dark hall, listening at each door in turn, until I found it. But then I heard heavy footsteps ascending the stairs and moving down the hall, and stopping, and the sound of a door opening and closing, and soon the weeping stopped, and at last I slept.

3

I DREAMED OF HOME AND EARLY MORNING AND BREAKFAST, and when I smelled coffee and the hot steam of pancakes I tried at first, in the manner of dreamers waking, to work it into my dream.

Then I felt and saw light spilling over me, and heard a voice on the edge of laughter say, "Good morning, sleepy head. Don't you have a date downtown?"

I raised my head groggily and saw a young nun setting a covered tray down on the desk. In the dazzle of light from the window her face seemed to gleam with a kind of translucence. She sat down on the edge of my bed and held out a cup of coffee.

"Drink up," she said, and her voice was crisp and light, like the first bite from an apple. It was neither Southern nor Irish. "Sister Mary James told me you missed your dinner last night, and I know it's your first day at your new job, so I thought a little head start on it might come in handy. Don't go thinking breakfast in bed is part of the service, though."

"Thank you, Sister," I said automatically, blinking in the brightness of the diamond light through the window, and the music of her voice. The whole room, the whole world, seemed transmuted by light. After two days in murkiness I could scarcely take it in.

"Are you Sister Clementia?" I said, not believing it. She simply could not move in tandem with the dark Sister Mary James.

The young nun laughed. "Sister would not thank you for that," she said. "No, I'm Sister Joan. I'm one of the two weekday sisters. Sister Clementia and Sister Mary James take weekends. I saw them when we changed shifts, though, and they said that you'd spent your first day out with Rachel and come in too late for supper, and I knew then that neither of them would have offered you anything on the side. I'm afraid they're both convinced that Rachel is their cross to bear on this earth. And I knew you'd be in a hurry to get to your job. What a grand one, too. An editor, now. Do you know that *Downtown* just won some kind of fancy award for best city magazine, or something? Everyone is talking about it, and Mr. Comfort, too. I think it's fully as good as any national magazine I see."

"You read *Downtown*?" I could not help staring. She laughed again. Her eyes were warm and brown, and there was a scattering of freckles on her nose. I thought she could not be much older than I.

"I graduated from the Chicago Art Institute," she said. "I know good graphics when I see them. You must be very good. Mr. Comfort said you're coming in as senior editor."

"You know Mr. Comfort?" I knew that I must sound like a parrot.

"We all know him here. He's on the board. And I serve on a kind of unofficial commission he and some other city leaders have started, an ecumenical council on race. There are representatives from all the churches, black and white. Rabbi Jacob Rothschild is on it, and our Archbishop Hallinan. It's going to do great good, I think. Anyway, Mr. Comfort said to look out for you. And," her eyes crinkled, "not to let the weekend sisters get you down. They're some of the most devout we have, but they're having a hard time with the twentieth century, and Vatican Two was a great shock to them. This is not a good town for the old-liners."

Something clicked behind my eyes. "Sister Joan, were you . . . could you have been playing a guitar and singing in Tight Squeeze Saturday night? My father and I were passing through, and—"

"And saw two renegade nuns and a priest singing to the hippies and ran your poor father's blood pressure sky high? I confess. That was me, and Sister Catherine and Father Mark from Saint Stephen's. We call it a street ministry, but we all enjoy it as much as the kids. I hope your father wasn't too upset. I realize we do things here that some of our older church members have a hard time with. But we think—the archbishop thinks—that there's a great need for them. Atlanta is a town for the young."

"No, Daddy was all ready to take me home, and seeing you all did the trick," I said, feeling a rush of love for her, a surge of something near sisterly, in the filial sense, sitting on the edge of my bed with her freckled face screwed up in laughter. I had never felt anything like it for a nun before.

"Good. Well, I'll get on downstairs and let you get dressed. I just wanted to say hello, and welcome. Oh, and to see if you knew where Rachel might have gotten to? She wasn't at breakfast, and her bed hasn't been slept in. We're all a little worried."

Cold fingers brushed my spine. "She was going on to a party with some boys we met," I said. "It was at some apartments that she said were popular, but I don't remember their name. The boys seemed okay—"

"And were, no doubt," Sister Joan said. "Don't you go worrying about her. She's stayed out before. I just thought I'd ask. The other sisters are upset—"

"I hope she won't . . . you know, lose her room or anything," I said, wishing I had not informed on Rachel.

"We're not her keepers," Sister Joan said. "The only way she can lose her room is to not pay her rent, or do something much worse than the hours she keeps. I think about her a lot, though. Sometimes, God help me, I think she may simply be one of the lost ones."

I blinked at her in surprise. This was a woman-to-woman conversation, not nun to parishioner, or teacher to pupil. I thought of the little cardboard wheel of pills in Rachel's purse. I would have bet anything, in that moment, that Sister Joan knew about them.

"Thank you for breakfast and everything, Sister," I said.

"You're very welcome. I'll be waiting to hear about your first day. Do they call you Maureen, by the way?"

"Some people call me Aisling," I said, thinking to try again to circumvent Smoky.

"Ashley." She misunderstood me. "Ashley O'Donnell. How very pretty. It sounds like a byline, doesn't it? Very smart and now. Well. Happy landings, Ashley O'Donnell."

And she was gone in a swirl of skirts.

I stood looking after her. Ashley O'Donnell. Ashley O'Donnell . . . I liked it. It did not sound Irish, or Catholic, or anything except young and smart and rather glamorous. That was it, then. From here on out, I would be Ashley O'Donnell, senior editor of *Downtown* magazine, Atlanta, Georgia.

When I left Our Lady and ran out into the cold, dazzling morning, I had rolled the waistband of my blue skirt until the hem brushed the tops of my knees, and brushed and shaken my hair until it sprang from its accustomed careful flip and fell over my forehead and one eye in a tousle of curls. I rubbed my cheeks and bit my lips for good measure. Aisling O'Donnell of Corkie might not wear miniskirts and Sassoon hair, but Ashley O'Donnell of Atlanta most certainly would.

The city pulsed with light and morning; the sidewalks danced with them. The streets were crowded with people on their way downtown, and they looked wonderful to me, vibrant and smart and eager to be on their way. The 23 Oglethorpe bus rocked along between shops and office buildings glinting in the morning light, and everyone on it seemed to be young. The drivers of the bright cars caught in traffic beside the bus looked young, too, sleek and well-groomed. I felt ginger ale bubbles of glee rising in my chest, and bit my lips to keep from laughing aloud with joy and anticipation. Wherever they were going, these chic young men and women alongside me, only I was going into the heart of the city to begin being the new senior editor at Matthew Comfort's remarkable *Downtown* magazine. Only I. Ahead of us the city came wheeling up in the dazzling sun. Bronze and silver and blue towers rose up around me.

"Oh, yes," I whispered. "Now."

Looking back, I can see—though I could not then, caught in its midst as I was—what a strange, exhilarating, and contradictory time that was in the country. It was a cusp moment in our national life, the year before the love turned to anger, the peace to militancy. Everything that had gone before us hung shimmering in the air, along with the unseen bulk of everything yet to come. At a Human Be-In in California, heads and freaks had announced happily that the number of live people equaled, for the first time in history, the number of the dead. From that *outré* coast the sound of mantras and chanting from yogis and the wailing of Janis Joplin and Jimi Hendrix drifted East; the Beatles reigned supreme everywhere; the hippies and yippies met in their trajectories. Gidget and go-go dancers and Timothy Leary and Ken Kesey and the Merry Pranksters competed for the national consciousness, along with Hugh Hefner and the Bunny Hutch. Stokely Carmichael and Eldridge Cleaver were moving toward their time in the sun as Martin Luther King Jr. and his doctrine of nonviolent change moved out of it. The war in Vietnam was not yet called a war, and the great protests still lay ahead, as did the militancy of the Black Panthers, the body of the sexual revolution, and the sisterhood of the women's movement. In late 1966 the young said "fuck" as often as possible but the pill was still an innovation, and no one had yet bombed a chemistry building. In that year, women were still called "chicks," even in the most radical circles, and Bunnyhood was as desirable a thing as sisterhood. NOW was in its infancy and both Twiggy and Doris Day were at their apogee. The ferocious, militant love of Woodstock Nation—the Hippies' Last Hurrah—was more than two years away. The first terrible death, that of JFK in Dallas, was three years past.

In the year I came to Atlanta, it was still possible to regard that assassination as an aberration, a terrible accident. I rode a crowded bus along a literal fault line, one that would soon cleave America apart, and I had no thought of anything except that the sun was shining and I was careening toward the rest of my life.

When I got off the bus at the Five Points turnaround, I took a deep breath of cold, electric city air and looked up and saw the dancer's cage, empty now, and above it, on the fourth floor of the gray stone building, a small sign in a window that said "Museum of the Deep South.

Exhibits and Artifacts. Open by Appointment." Below that a smaller sign said "See Big Snake."

I began to laugh. My poor father. His Good Catholic Girl had been delivered into the very jaws of the enemy by the 23 Oglethorpe bus. When I got off the packed elevator on the eleventh story of the Commerce Building, in a crowd smelling of youngness and cold wool and Miss Dior and cigarette smoke, I was still smiling.

I stopped before a red-lacquered door that said DOWNTOWN in bold black capital letters, smoothed my hair, bit my lips, and took a deep breath. I could feel the smile still on my lips, stiff and frozen. I could not seem to make it go away. I closed my eyes, and then opened them and turned the knob and went in. Still smiling, I stood in the small lobby and looked around for the people who would soon shape my world, hearing my heart in my ears and feeling it in my throat.

There was no one there. I could hear, off behind one of a row of closed red-lacquer doors, people laughing, and someone who seemed to be singing, but there was no sign of anyone. The lobby was so crowded that it was hard to take it in at first glance. A blue sofa piled so high with coats and cartons of glossy magazines and books and records that they spilled over onto the tweed carpet sat against one wall, and red tub chairs similarly laden were grouped around it. A coat rack held more coats, and, in front of the sofa, there was a coffee table on which sat a real stuffed coyote or timber wolf—it was so scruffy it was impossible to tell precisely what it was. On the coyote's head was a Mexican sombrero. Three steel desks stretching toward the back of the lobby held signs that had women's names on them, and typewriters, and in-boxes overflowing with papers. Two tall windows gave onto the jumbled rooftops of the city, shimmering with light. After the windows the individual offices began. There were names on these doors, too, but I could not read them. From the ceiling hung a miniature outhouse with a sign on it that said "Southern Comfort." I simply stood there, not knowing what I should do next.

From behind one of the floor-length drapes at the first window an arm with its hand formed into a claw emerged slowly. I stared at it in silence. The fingers opened and closed like a spider flexing its legs, and the arm stretched farther from behind the drape, and then its owner followed. He was a tall, swarthy young man with thick black hair falling over hooded brown eyes, and he had a dark hawk's face and the most elegant body I had ever seen. His shoulders were wide and square and his long waist tapered in a narrow vee toward lean hips and long legs. He wore a soft, beautiful gray tweed coat and lighter gray flannel trousers and a white oxford cloth button-down shirt. His tie was askew.

"Speak," he commanded solemnly. His voice was soft and deep.

"Mr. Comfort, please," I said. I could hear it as plainly as he must: my faint Irish brogue, almost vanquished by now, had so thickened with nerves as to make my speech almost unintelligible.

A slow, very white grin broke his brown face.

"Well, darlin', and who might you be, then?" he said, in a perfect parody of Corkie. "Sure, and 'tis shamrocks you'll be sellin' us this fine mornin'."

The people I had heard but not seen came out of the last office in the row and stood looking at me. My chest caught fire.

"I'm Ashley O'Donnell," I said faintly, thinking as I said it how silly and contrived the name sounded, like something from a comic book for teenage girls. The fire spread to my cheeks and forehead.

"I work here," I whispered.

Hank Cantwell broke out of the small crowd and caught me up and swung me around, my feet bumping against his shins.

"Well, old Holy Smoke," he yelled exuberantly, and set me down, and they moved in then, crowding around me. Over their murmurs of greeting I heard for the second time the rich music of Matt Comfort's voice, demanding "Is it her? The once and future Smoky O'Donnell? Bring her in here and let me get a look at her, by God!"

"This is your new senior editor, Smoky O'Donnell," Hank said to the people around me, and they smiled and said, "Hi, Smoky," and "Welcome, Smoky O'Donnell," and "Glad to have you on board," and other things like that, and walked behind me as Hank ushered me into the last office in the row.

And so my time with Comfort's People began.

After I had known him for a while, I realized that Matt Comfort could have had no other office than the precise one he had; that given another he would have stamped his imprint on it swiftly and indelibly, and it would have come to look exactly like this one did. It was the corner office, twice as large as any of the others, and it was at once elegant and eccentric, refuge and crucible, more a home than an office to the man who sat behind the great black rosewood desk before the windows. It was carpeted in deep, velvet-gray plush, and had a gray tweed sofa and two of the legendary, consummately beautiful Eames armchairs and ottomans. A glass and chrome étagère stood between the windows, and glass and chrome end tables and a cocktail table made a conversational grouping around the sofa and chairs. An Oriental area rug glowed like a jewel against the gray plush. Twin speakers hidden somewhere on the wall of books blasted out "England Swings Like a Pendulum Do." There was not a vacant square inch of surface in the entire room.

People slumped in the Eames chairs and crowded onto the sofa, sat on the floor around the coffee table, sprawled on the Oriental. Some smoked and some drank coffee and some did both. The surfaces not occupied by people held things: books piled until they spilled onto the floor; magazines and record albums; sheets of photographic prints and contacts; large dummy sheets; mail both opened and unopened; cameras and agfaloupes and magnifying glasses; jars of rubber cement and mugs holding pencils and Pentels and others holding the dregs of coffee; overflowing ashtrays; a tarnished silver tray with a beautiful, dusky black bottle of something surrounded by small crystal glasses. On the walls were framed covers of *Downtown* magazine from its inception; awards and citations; photographic portraits of many people I did not know and some, incredibly, that I did—all signed; and a great white calendar sheet that read December 1966, most of its squares penciled in, crossed out, rewritten. I looked around giddily, unable at first to see the man who lived at the epicenter of all this.

Then he rose and came around the desk and gave me a swift hug and a kiss on the cheek, and said, "Welcome to hard times, dear heart. I'm Matt Comfort."

"Of course," I said, and began to laugh. Everybody else laughed, too.

Because who else could he be? He looked just like his office. He was elegant and eccentric and wonderfully appointed and charged with particularity, and there was not an inch of him that was not in disarray. Until the last day that I saw him, he looked, as someone said of *The New Yorker*'s legendary Harold Ross—whom Matt admired inordinately—like an unmade bed, even though that bed was of the very best quality and outfitted by Porthault.

He was very small. I had not thought of him like that, and even after I had known him intimately for years, I still never did. But he was scarcely five foot six or seven, and thin to wiriness; he looked, always, as if he had been fashioned out of fine copper tendrils. He was so far from handsome it was almost laughable: round-shouldered and a little stooped, with a large head and sharp, chis-eled, ruddy features that looked sometimes Lincolnesque and sometimes vulpine; he appeared to be always in motion, even when sitting down. The air around him seemed to ring, as if with silent percussion. It was his hair that first drew the eye and somehow saved him from simple ludicrousness: it was a great, shining shock of pure chestnut that fell over his forehead and into one nar-row green eye, and it was glorious. In that time of strag-gling beards and lank sideburns on the one hand and residual John Wayne brush cuts on the other, he had the glinting, sun-anointed head of the young Kennedy. This was never lost on anyone, and certainly not on Matt Comfort. He wore round, wire-rimmed glasses mended with adhesive tape, and dressed beautifully, in custom-tailored tweed and flannel and oxford cloth, though his clothes were invariably rumpled and semi-buttonless and his face and forearms smudged with ink. But even the few times I saw him in old clothes or a bathing suit, he still had more pure style than anyone I have ever known. In the panache-starved South of his day, he was Merlin and Huck Finn and Casanova rolled into one small body, and I don't think there was anyone who ever met him who did not come away from the meeting convinced that he was tall.

Holding me by the arm, he scowled at the sofa and said, "Goddammit, get up, Gordon, and let this lady sit down. You too Stubbs. Alicia, dear heart, run get us all some fresh coffee, will you, darling? The rest of you guys go on back to work, unless Patterson just fired the lot of you. I ain't your mother."

The tall, hawk-faced young man grinned and unfolded himself from the sofa, followed by a stocky, bearded man in sunglasses. A stunning young woman in a muted plaid wool mini and red tights on her endless legs stood up from one of the Eames chairs and gave Matt Comfort and me both an unreadable look and glided out of the office, trailing clouds of silky ash-blond hair and Joy perfume. I would have bet her duties, whatever they were, did not ordinarily include fetching coffee for the new girl. Except for Hank and a compact, snub-nosed girl in a navy A-line skirt and white turtleneck, the rest of the people in the office— young men, all of them—got up and straggled out, grumbling good-naturedly. Hank patted the sofa and I sat down on the edge of it. It was low, and I could find no place to put my knees that did not hike my rolled-up skirt indecently up my thighs. I put my purse in my lap and dropped my knees as far as they would go, and Matt Comfort laughed and tossed me an afghan from the arm of the sofa.

"God bless miniskirts," he said. "I had the sofa legs shortened when it was obvious they were more than a passing fad. Well, let's see. The lazy sonofabitch on your left is Tom Gordon, our art director. That there behind those Foster Grants is Charlie Stubbs, our other senior editor. He's just back today from his honeymoon; we won't know till he takes his glasses off if he had a good time or not. Hank you know. This precious muffin here is Teddy Fairchild, who handles production. Look upon her with abject terror."

The chunky girl smiled and murmured hello. She wore little makeup and had her brown hair pulled back with a hair band, and she had a nice smile that crinkled her brown eyes and her nose. I smiled back. The blonde came back with a tray of coffee and put it down on the coffee table and sank down onto the floor beside Matt Comfort's chair all in one sinuous motion. She brushed the long, shining curtain of hair out of her eyes with the back of one slender hand and waggled the fingers of the other toward Tom Gordon, who was fishing a Viceroy out of a pack. He handed her one, and she put it between her pink lips and waited while he produced a lighter.

"This is Alicia Crowley, otherwise known as Tondelayo," Matt Comfort said. "She's a terrible secretary, but everybody upstairs at the Chamber wants to get in her pants, so we keep her around for insurance."

"Don't you wish," Alicia Crowley said. Her voice was tiny and breathy, like Jackie Kennedy's. I knew two things about her in that instant, absolutely and without question, though I did not know how I knew: that she would never be an ally of mine and that Matt Comfort was sleeping with her.

"This is the whole staff, except for our receptionist and editorial secretary and the ad salesmen and our comptroller, who's off somewhere comptrolling," Matt Comfort said. "Most of the editorial and graphic stuff we freelance out. That gang that just left are some of them; from the *Constitution*. They're good reporters and some of them are good writers in general, and they hang around here all the time because Gene Patterson won't let them sit around over there and drink coffee and smoke cigarettes, and because they want to get into Alicia's pants, too. So far it's no dice—I don't think— but they keep hoping."

I felt the hated blush surge up my neck again. I had never heard a man talk so around women before.

"It sounds like you're the most valuable member of the staff," I said, smiling at Alicia, acutely conscious that

I sounded prissy and was dressed like a five-year-old ad for Villager dresses and circle pins. She smiled back at me, a small, cool smile, but did not answer.

Hank showed me my office, a smaller one than the others in the line along the window wall, but private, and with a window of its own that commanded a sweep of the city to the south. It wasn't the breath-stopping vista that you would get looking north, where John Portman's revolutionary white urban complex was rising, but I stood transfixed, my heart singing. The dome of the State Capitol flashed in the sun, gilded with gold from Georgia's low blue mountains, and nearby were the white sugar cubes of the new state government buildings, and the scrollwork of the just-completed freeway system, and the blue bowl of the new major league stadium. Back in Corkie the talk of the Atlanta Braves' first season had been fierce.

I thought, looking out my window into the cold sun, that that one glass square commanded the essence of Atlanta in the middle of the decade. The stadium and the freeway had both been conceived and executed in a scant six years, and just out of sight to the southeast, along the ribbon of the interstate, the new Hartsfield International Airport hummed like the active beehive that it was. It was said that at certain times of the day it was the second busiest airport in the country, first being Chicago's O'Hare. I, who had never flown, was enormously proud of that. I may have drifted tranquilly in the backwater that was Corkie for all of my life, but even there we knew what was happening in Atlanta in the supercharged sixties, that a handful of men—scions of the old families, sons of the big Buckhead houses, merchant princes—were literally reinventing it. One of them, the exuberant Mills B. Lane of the Citizens and Southern Bank, was one of our own. C&S had had its genesis on the bluff above the docks in

Savannah, and in its sleeping cotton and cane fields. Mr. Lane had always been sort of a patron saint to me, the one who left Savannah and wrote his name across the face of Atlanta. It could be done. I would do it, too.

"It's kind of small, but it's all yours," Hank said. "So what do you think, Smokes? Does it beat the 'Naut office or not?"

I turned and gave him a brief, hard hug.

"By a country mile," I said. "Oh, Hank, I can hardly believe I'm here!"

"Me, either, but here you are, in the very considerable flesh," he said, giving my behind a proprietary pat, and I thought affectionately of the years of teasing, semisexual banter we had shared at Armstrong, working together in the *Argonaut* office. It had been the first completely easy friendship I had ever had with a male, and remained almost the only one. With Hank I found the work for which I was born; to Hank I said the things in my heart that I had said only to Meg Conlon, and not all of them to her. It was Hank who showed me the larger world that danced and crackled outside the bell jar that was Savannah and the Creole South; gave me my first sense of the changes that were sweeping it, and the change-makers. It was with Hank that I had sat, late into the night, in a coffee shop at the edge of the campus, crying in anguish and disbelief, when John Kennedy had been shot. Hank had driven all the way from Atlanta to be with me. And in all of Corkie, weeping maudlin tears for its fallen son, it was only Hank I wanted to be with. Corkie wept for the broken red head of a prince of Ireland; Hank and I for the beauty and symmetry of the dream that had been shattered with it. I loved Hank Cantwell with a whole, comfortable, and selfish love that took everything and questioned nothing. I could not remember wondering why he never asked me out, or thought of me in any way except as I did of him. As I said, I was not, then, in the habit of questioning.

By then the rest of the staff had come in, and I met Sueanne Hudspeth, the office manager and receptionist, a comfortable middle-aged woman with a sprayed beehive and a flat, wiregrass voice, who gave me a little peck on the cheek and told me it was about time they got another woman in there to even things up a little. The editorial secretary, Sister Clinkscales, was honey-blond and blue-eyed and wore her hair caught up in a huge powder blue ribbon bow that matched her angora sweater and mini. She looked to be about thirteen.

"Hey, Smoky," she said, in a sunny, little-girl voice. "I bet you know one of my sorority sisters from Savannah, Kitty DuBignon? I think she married somebody that works for the newspaper down there."

I did indeed know Kitty DuBignon, or rather, her family; the DuBignons owned controlling interest in Fournier Sugar, and I knew that one of the daughters had married Clay Gilchrist, whose forebears had established the *Savannah Morning Courier* in the late 1700s. All of Corkie had heard of Kitty DuBignon's escapades at the University of Georgia, which had culminated in her being dismissed for something so outrageous that not even her father's sweet money could mitigate it. She married young Clay Gilchrist weeks after that.

"Well, I certainly know who she is," I said, smiling back at Sister. I could not imagine her being a great deal of help to the staff of *Downtown.* She did not look as though she knew how to remove the cover from a typewriter. On the other hand, there was nothing in her sweet, snub little face of malice or privilege, and her smile was as infectious as a child's laughter.

"Ah, yes," Hank said, giving the end of her hair ribbon a tug. "Hot times at the ole Kappa house. Sister, you ninny; Smoky was out of school and working before you and Miss Kitty were out of training bras. Where is everybody, by the way?"

"Mr. Carnes called some kind of meeting upstairs," Sister said. "He wants all of us, too. I think we're going to get fussed at about the coffee cup holders again. You know he thinks we're the ones doing it. Mr. Comfort said for me to see if Smoky would answer the phones until we get back. She's too new to be one of the usual suspects, he says. It's just for a minute, Smoky. I'll show you how to work the switchboard."

"I can figure it out," I said, smiling at her chatter. She was a lovable child. She always was. Years later I heard that she went to Emory Law School after her second child was in day care, and made *Law Review* and Moot Court, and turned out to be a trial lawyer of fearsome ability. After my first shock of surprise on hearing it, I realized that I was not, after all, completely startled. There was always a bright, implacable intelligence just under what Matt Comfort called Sister's froufrou. I sensed it behind the wide blue eyes that first morning.

She and Sueanne and Hank went out of the office and I sat down at Sister's desk and studied the telephones until I figured them out. One rang, and I picked it up and paused, then said, with a small thrill of pride, "*Downtown* magazine. May I help you?"

"Yeah," an irritable masculine voice said. "This is Carithers from Dynatech. When the hell are you all getting the December issue out? My contract says the day before Thanksgiving, and it's six days past that already. You tell Comfort I expect a refund on this ad, too. Is he there?"

"He'll be back in a few minutes," I said. "He's in a meeting. May I tell him you called?"

"Sister?" he said.

"No, this is Ashley O'Donnell. I'm the new senior editor," I said.

"Christ," snapped Carithers from Dynatech. "He can't get an issue out on time, but he can hire senior editors all over the place. Tell him to call me." And he hung up before I could reply.

"Have a happy day, creep," I said, stung.

I had meant to glance at the new issue of *Downtown* that lay on Sister's desk, and perhaps to look over a few of the back ones, but the phone kept up a steady barrage. Most were for Matt or for the ad salesmen or our comptroller, Jack Greenburg, and most callers were not especially pleased. All of the calls had something to do with the lateness of the December issue. Well, I thought defensively, after all, it's not December yet.

There was a lull then, and I reached for the December issue and was admiring its cover, a wonderfully painted caricature of Coca-Cola's legendary, reclusive Robert Woodruff dressed as Santa, handing out stadiums and airplanes, when an astonishing aroma reached my nose. It was an indescribable confluence of smells: dank earth, woodsmoke, wet newsprint, sun-ripened garbage, raw old wine, some sort of machine oil, and a powerful underbase of long-unwashed body and clothing. It literally jerked my head up from the cover of *Downtown,* and when I looked up it was to see a man just wobbling carefully into the lobby on a bicycle, lips pursed in concentration. I simply stared.

He was tiny, gnarled and gnomelike, and quite old. There was white stubble on his slack, simian face, and his hair, under an old, filthy New York Yankees baseball cap, was lank and greasy and yellow-white, and brushed his shoulders. He wore grimy white flannel knickers and a vest of some sort over many layers of tattered sweaters, and old black high-top Converse basketball shoes over what looked to be three or four pairs of socks. On his hands were fingerless mitts that reminded me, crazily, of the lace mitts we had worn to dances at Saint Zita's, and in his bicycle basket was a pile of magazines and newspapers so old that they were brittle and yellow, shedding flakes onto the carpet. Around his neck, on a filthy string, was a large round globe of the world.

He propped the bicycle lovingly against the sofa and began pulling magazines from its basket, talking busily to himself under his breath. I took a deep breath, regretted it, and said, in a silly, strangled voice, "May I help you?"

Only then did he seem to notice me. He cocked his head this way and that, like a bewildered old bird, and said, in a gruff mumble, "You ain't her. That flibberty little one, you ain't her."

"No, I'm . . . I'm new. I'm Ashley O'Donnell," I said, wondering if I should phone for help. But to whom? Or perhaps dash past him and into the offices down the hall? Were there any? I didn't remember. . . .

He smiled, a sudden, sweet smile, and held out his hand, and I took it numbly.

"Francis Brewton," he said grandly, and swept me a low bow. "I'm in the travel and newspaper business. Everybody here are my clients. I have something for Matt, something he's been looking for for a long time. There's probably not another one in the country. It's going to cost him plenty, you bet."

"Well, ah . . . he's upstairs in a meeting," I said. "Maybe I could give it to him for you?"

"Naw. I want to see his face when he sees it," Francis Brewton said. "I'll go up and give it to him myself. But maybe you'd like to buy a few magazines? I have some *Ladies' Home Journals* nobody's seen before. In perfect condition, they are."

He pulled out four *Ladies' Home Journals* that I had to agree no one had seen before, at least not in living memory. They were dated 1911, 1912, and 1914. But they were, indeed, in good condition. I looked at them helplessly, and then at Francis Brewton. He beamed, revealing brown gaps where several teeth had been.

"Umm—how much were you asking?" I said.

"Ten dollars," he said firmly. "Ordinarily I'd get fifteen, but I always give Comfort's People a discount. Some of my best customers, they are."

He stood there smiling happily at me, and I reached for my purse and pulled out a ten-dollar bill and gave it to him. Somehow I could not bear to argue with him. It was not fear, but a sort of hypnosis that his extraordinary self-confidence generated. It crossed my mind that he possibly lived rather well.

"Thank you," he said, and pocketed the money, and retrieved his bicycle. "I'll catch Matt upstairs."

He got on the bicycle and pushed away out of the office, and then stopped and put one foot down, and looked back over his shoulder.

"Oh, and by the way," he said, "If I should miss him, tell Matt I think we've got the Lutherans sewed up."

"I certainly will," I said, and he rode away. It was several minutes before the aroma faded from the lobby.

I was still sitting there, looking at the yellowing *Ladies' Home Journals* and trying not to remember that the ten dollars was busfare for two weeks, when I heard the elevator bell pinging around the corner, and the staff came trooping back in. At the rear was Matt Comfort with a tall, paunchy, bald man in a blue three-piece suit. He had a tight red face and a small round mouth, pursed like a woman's. When he saw me it broadened into a smile.

"Smoky, this is Culver Carnes, director of the chamber and my boss of bosses," Matt Comfort said. "Be nicer to him than you ever thought possible."

"Well, Smoky, glad to have you. I've been hearing about you," Culver Carnes said. He had a voice like an old-time radio announcer, someone I could barely remember from my childhood. Harry Von Sell?

"Thank you, Mr. Carnes," I said. "I'm glad to be here."

"She's just as pretty as you said she was, Matt," Culver Carnes said, clapping me on the shoulder. "Nothing wrong with your editorial eye, is there, boy?"

He winked at me and Matt Comfort, and behind him, Tom Gordon crossed his eyes and stuck his tongue out. I bit my lips.

"Fastest eye in the South, Culver," Matt said solemnly.

"You had a number of calls, Mr. Comfort," I said in as businesslike a voice as I could muster, given the fact that behind Culver Carnes's back Hank Cantwell and Charlie Stubbs were now making elaborate, silent punting motions at his blue-clad behind. "I've put them on your desk. Oh, and a Mr. Francis Brewton came by. He said he had something for you, and that he'd catch you upstairs. He just left."

"Jesus Christ," Matt Comfort laughed. "You really have had your baptism by fire, haven't you? I thought I smelled Francis when we got off the elevator. What did he sell you, the 1929 *Farmer's Almanac*?"

"Copies of 1911, 1912, and 1914 *Ladies' Home Journals*," I said meekly.

Matt Comfort sighed. "How much?"

"Ten dollars—"

"Shit, we're going to have to do something about Francis's price-gouging," Matt muttered. "Get Sister to give you five dollars from petty cash, and remember, we never give Francis more than two bucks. He knows that. It bothers me that he'd take advantage of your being new—"

"If that's the only thing about that lunatic that bothers you, you need your head examined," Culver Carnes said sourly. "I've told you and told you, Matt, not to encourage him. We can't have him hanging around here. Where did he say he was going?"

He turned to me.

"I think he said upstairs," I said in a small voice.

"Christ," Culver Carnes roared, and started for the door. "Do you know who I've got in my office, waiting for me? Only Todd Ingram, who's got more money at his fingertips than you'll see in your lifetime, Comfort, just trying to decide if he wants to invest it in an office complex here or a new stadium in Birmingham! That's all! And what I need most in the world right now is that goddamned fucking Francis Brewton rolling by on his bicycle looking for you—"

"Sorry, Culver," Matt said, his mouth twitching. "Send him on back down here if he shows. He knows he's not supposed to go up there, but he forgets—"

"How the hell did he get in here, anyway? I thought I told you to tell the guard not to let him in the building."

"Well, I told him to let him in when the temperature dropped below fifty. Jesus, Culver, he's been sleeping under the Spring Street Viaduct since Saint John's closed its doors. I'm not in the habit of freezing octogenarian loonies to death. What does it hurt? He doesn't go up to your place much anymore."

"It hurts when I've got the chairman of All-South sitting in my goddamned office trying to decide where to drop twenty mil and Francis Brewton rolls up on his bicycle looking for the editor of *Downtown*! What do you suggest I say to Todd Ingram?" Culver Carnes had moved up until he was shouting into Matt Comfort's face. His own face and neck were suffused with red.

"You could ask him if he can ride a bike," Matt said.

His voice was mild but his eyes had gone flat and dead. Behind Culver Carnes Tom Gordon and Charlie Stubbs stifled explosive laughter and retreated into their offices.

"One of these days you're going to push me too far, Matt," Culver Carnes said furiously. "You're just as good as the last issue of this two-bit local flak sheet. I hope you remember that."

"They know us in New York, Culver," Matt Comfort said, his voice casual. "I hope you remember that." I did not think he felt casually about what his boss had said, though. His face was white. He shoved his hands into the pockets of his wrinkled tweed jacket and strolled back into his office.

"The day that stops, Comfort, is the day your ass is back on a train to Humble, Texas," Culver Carnes shouted after him, and turned and strode out of the office. He slammed the door behind him. Tom and Charlie came back out of their offices and stood looking after him. I did, too. The shouting had disturbed me profoundly. I was suddenly terrified that Matt Comfort would be fired before my tenure with *Downtown* had even begun.

Into the silence I said, "He said tell Mr. Comfort he thought they had the Lutherans sewed up," and Tom and Charlie exploded into laughter. Matt Comfort came out to hear what was so funny and began to laugh, too. He gave me a brief hug around my shoulders and I joined in the laughter, lightly, pretending that I had known all along it was funny. I sensed that it pleased them that I should be ironic and quick. I would remember that.

I spent the rest of the morning upstairs meeting the chamber staff—with a few exceptions a sunless lot who acknowledged me coolly—and then Hank took me to lunch. It was a small, dim French restaurant called

Emile's a couple of blocks away from the Commerce Building, and it seemed to be full of men drinking cocktails and laughing, all of whom seemed to know Hank. At one corner table on the upper level a bushy-browed bulldog of a man with thick spectacles nodded and smiled, and I whispered breathlessly, when we had passed, "Was that—?"

Hank grinned. "Ralph McGill. Yeah, Pappy comes here a good bit, especially on chicken-liver day. That's kind of the unofficial *Constitution* table."

"You really know him?"

"Well, Matt knows him, and he knows who we all are. You're not going to ask him for his autograph, are you? He's awfully shy."

"Don't be an ass. But I wish I could. He's a real hero, Hank. Lord, though, my father would have a conniption if he knew I was even under the same roof with Rastus McGill. I wish he could see me now."

"You better be glad he can't," Hank said, and we sat down to lunch in the first French restaurant I had ever been in, to order, for the first time in my life, sautéed chicken livers on toast with sherry and mushrooms. I thought they were probably an acquired taste.

Hank asked me if I wanted wine, and I simply looked at him, and he laughed.

"I forgot," he said. "They don't call you Holy Smoke for nothing. I'm so used to eating lunch with Matt and the rest of the gang that I forget everybody doesn't have two martinis and wine with lunch. It's kind of nice to give it a rest."

"Do you all drink a lot?" I asked. I had heard of two-martini lunches, of course, but until now had assumed they were the stuff of bad novels about Madison Avenue.

He looked surprised, and then said, "I guess maybe we do. I don't think about it all that much. We're usually all together, talking and laughing, or there's some visiting muckety-muck from out of town that we're entertaining, and it just seems the natural thing to do. Almost everybody does it, at least when Matt's buying, and he usually is. He can drink more than anybody I ever saw and not show it. He'll go back after one of these lunches and put together an issue that will win another award, or get on the phone and set up an interview with somebody virtually nobody else could get, or sell twelve full-page four-color ads right under Jack Greenburg's nose. It's incredible. If the rest of us drank that much we'd be passed out under our desks."

"He must be rich," I said, thinking what five days a week of lunches like that for the whole staff must cost.

"God, no. It's kind of a local legend that when he got here he had exactly fourteen dollars in his pocket. He lived at the Y for six months. Tom Gordon still does; he's going through a messy divorce and he barely has the clothes on his back left. Nobody on the staff has any money except Teddy, whose daddy owns the biggest real estate company in town, and Sister, whose daddy owns South Georgia. Alicia has a dynamite apartment, but I'm fairly sure she doesn't pay for it. Matt lives in two rooms at the Howell House that the chamber pays for, along with paying for his car. The rest of us have roommates or live in one room. Matt likes to say that he's going to pay us half the salary we had wherever we worked before, and work us twice as long. Didn't he tell you that? I think he charges the lunches and everything else to the chamber."

Matt Comfort had indeed told me that about the pay and the hours, and it had charmed me, made me want to work twice as hard for him.

"Boy, he really must rate with the chamber," I said. "I mean, to charge stuff like that, and talk to Mr. Carnes the way he did this morning. That almost scared me, Hank. I thought Mr. Carnes was his boss."

"Well, he is, but it's a funny relationship," Hank said, frowning. "It's kind of a game with them, the insults and the yelling. Culver really resents Matt's smart-ass, seat-of-the-pants way of doing things and the fact that all of us on the magazine get away with bloody murder, are kind of local heroes. The whole chamber staff hates and envies us, for that matter. Don't think you're going to find any friends up there. But Carnes knows Matt is an authentic genius, and whenever we win another award, he takes the credit—he's the one that hired Matt out of the whole pack. And in a funny way he really loves Matt. He's not a dummy; he knows quality. He used to have his own public relations firm. What he said this morning is true; we're all of us okay as long as they know us in New York. And they do. Matt wasn't boasting there.

"And as for Matt," he went on, "well, he gets off on pushing Culver to the edge. He knows just how to do it. He's got this one-man war going against all that pomposity and blandness upstairs. He's always one step ahead of the pack and one step shy of overstepping. He knows that most of the chamber would just love to see him brought down. He simply flies too high for them. We all do. But the rest of the town absolutely eats him up. And then, I really think he's fond of Culver, too. It's complicated."

"So I don't have to worry about old Culver baby," I said. "Lord, Hank, he looks just like an emperor penguin, doesn't he?"

Hank put his fork down and looked at me seriously. "Listen, Smoky," he said. "Don't ever underestimate him. Don't underestimate any of them upstairs. *Downtown* depends on them; they subsidize us almost totally. We'd be drowning in red ink without them, the way Matt spends editorial money. They pay our salaries.

We can laugh at Culver Carnes, but he can fire us. He could fire Matt, too, come to that. We do the stories the chamber says to do in exchange for doing the stuff we want to do, and they have final say on everything. So far, thank God, Culver knows the good stuff, but he could nix any story he wanted to and we couldn't do a thing about it. Be as nice to him as you can and do the shit as well as you do the good stuff, and stay out of their way. We're okay as long as Matt is."

I thought about what he said. It gave me a heady feeling, the sense of dancing on the edge of an abyss. I realized that I liked it. The Irish always have.

"Is he married?" I said. "Matt, I mean?"

"He was, I think," Hank said. "He's not now. I heard there was a wife back in Texas—he really is from Humble, Texas; it's near Houston, population about three thousand. But so far as any of us know, they divorced before he came here. No kids that I know of. Nobody else knows anymore than that, except maybe Alicia, and she ain't talking."

"He's sleeping with her, isn't he?"

"Jesus, how'd you know that? We none of us ever admit by word or deed that we know about it."

"I don't know how I knew, I just did," I said. "You can just tell by the way he talks about her and to her, and the way she is with him."

"Yeah, well, it's really not such a big deal," Hank said. "There's a lot of sleeping around in this town. I don't know why that is, it just is. Maybe it's all the energy floating around, or the fact that everybody's young, or something. Everybody I know, practically, has somebody."

"What about you?" I said teasingly.

"God, I wouldn't have time even if I had the money," he grimaced. "I work six and seven days a week, sometimes eighteen hours a day. Sometimes I sleep on the sofa in Matt's office, when we're getting an issue to bed. We all do. Besides, now I got you, babe."

I ignored that. "You mean everybody works seven days a week, eighteen hours a day?" I said. "I don't think I can do that, Hank. When on earth would I meet anybody, or get to know Atlanta?"

"You'll do it and you'll love it, Smokes, just wait and see," he said. "*Downtown*—I don't know. It gets to be your whole life. The people there become your family. You'll spend all the time you're not working with them, as well as office hours; you'll come to really love them. Well, most of them, anyway. It's really funny, how it happens, but I've seen it over and over again. Gradually everything else drops away and there's just the magazine and all of us. And it's enough. There's more sheer excitement and . . . and . . . exuberance, more laughter, more intensity, in that one office than I ever thought there was in the world. In a way, Matt asks it of you. He doesn't come right out and say it, and I don't think he does it consciously, but pretty soon you'll know that he means for you to put it and him and all of us first, before everything, and by then you'll want to do it."

"What happens if I don't?" I said, knowing that, of course, I would. I did already. I had, from the night of Hank's phone call.

"I know you. You will. But if you don't, or can't, well . . . you just wouldn't stay. He wouldn't fire you, but you'd leave. I've seen that happen, too. Not so much with the ad people; they kind of go their own way, and Sueanne is an exception because she's married and has a family. But there've been a few editorial people who didn't want to be one of Comfort's People full-time, and sooner or later, they just left."

"Charlie's married," I said.

"And Charlie's on his way out," Hank said. "You can see it happening already. Whenever he goes home to Caroline instead of going out for a drink with us after work, or spends weekends with her instead of down here, Matt gets kind of quiet. Charlie used to be the closest one of us to Matt; the nearest thing he had to a close man friend. They spent a lot of time together. Now they don't. And I'll bet you a week's salary that in a few months Charlie will find something else that pays better and has better hours, and we'll give him a huge party at the Top of Peachtree and a going-away present that cost more than he makes in a year, and Charlie will be history."

I could think of little to say to that. On the face of it, it seemed unreasonable in the extreme to expect the staff, young and attractive as they all were, to forsake all others and cast their lot exclusively with Matt Comfort and his magazine. On the other hand, I could not imagine wanting anything else.

"Oh, Hank," I said, "what if I can't cut it, or I don't fit in?"

"You will," he said. "He wouldn't have hired you if he hadn't known you would. If all else fails, he'll simply make it happen."

On our way out I saw that Mr. McGill was still at the corner table. With him now were a square-jawed, blunt-faced blond man and a tall, thin dark one. They were deep in conversation.

"That was Gene Patterson, the editor of the *Constitution,* and Reese Cleghorne from the Southern Regional Council with Pappy," Hank said. "You don't often see them together. I wonder what's going on?"

"I feel like I just saw history being made," I said.

"You probably did," Hank said. "That's the thing about Atlanta that knocks me out, Smoky. Almost anywhere you look, on any given day, it is."

* * *

I worked the rest of the afternoon in Tom Gordon's office, learning to write photographic captions to fit a specific character count. It was frustrating, exacting work, and Tom was a stickler for captions that fit their spaces exactly. He wanted no gaps and no one-word lines. They were, he said, called widows, and no decent art director would allow them. By the end of the afternoon I had produced several galleys full of perfect, widowless captions, and was mussed and ink-smeared and aching of eye and head, but glowing from Tom's grave praise. He was gentle and sweet-tempered, and, in a sly, quiet way, extremely funny. I felt as close to him at the end of that day as I might a companion with whom I had been through some natural calamity.

"You're a quick study, Smoky," he said. "Charlie is a disaster with captions."

I stretched and looked around. Outside the day was ending; a glowing, grape-flushed twilight was falling down on the city, and lights were blooming in windows all around us. I looked at my watch. It was six-thirty, long past the usual five P.M. quitting time. Hank was right about *Downtown*'s hours, I thought. I wondered if I had missed supper at Our Lady, and what time the last 23 Oglethorpe bus ran, and if anyone would think it amiss if I simply got my raincoat and left. The thought made me feel oddly desolate. Our Lady seemed on the other side of the moon.

A great blatting blare broke the silence of the office, and Matt Comfort's rich bellow followed it.

"Quittin' time! Top in five minutes!" he bawled.

"What on earth was that noise?" I asked Tom Gordon. He grimaced.

"Somebody gave him a Bahamian taxi horn," he said.

"We've been trying to steal it, but it keeps turning up. Jack Greenburg is threatening to bring him a ram's horn, just to vary things a little. Come on, get your coat. We go to the Top of Peachtree around the corner most afternoons for a drink. It's got a sensational view of the city, and Matt pays."

"I don't know . . . " I had started when Matt put his head into Tom's office. He had on his coat and tie, but he still looked as if he had been wrestling alligators. The shining sheaf of hair completely obscured one eye.

"Champagne in honor of you tonight, Smoky," he said. "I think this is the start of a beautiful friendship."

"Well, the thing is," I said, feeling stupidly young and prissy, "I already missed supper once, and I'm not sure when the last bus runs, and I think there's a pretty early curfew on weeknights—"

Matt stared at me, and then said, "Oh, Christ, the goddamned Church's Home. I forgot. I'll call Sister Joan and clear you for being late tonight, and Hank or Tom will feed you and take you home, but we've got to get you out of there. I've got to have you available when I need you. That curfew shit is ridiculous, anyway."

"You're the one who put her in there, Matt," Hank said, coming up behind him. He was grinning widely. "You're the one that sits on the board."

"You know damned well I'm on that board because I owed the archbishop a big one and he called me on it," Matt grumbled. "And I put her in there, smart ass, because you told me her daddy wouldn't let her come up here unless I did. That doesn't mean she's got to stay there. Teddy, dear heart," and he raised his voice to a roar, "when is it your roommate is getting married?"

"Christmas," came floating out of the office where Teddy Fairchild had been cloistered away all afternoon with the door closed.

"Well, come on out here and meet your new room-mate," Matt yelled back, and I flinched.

"Oh, please, Matt, don't make her do that; she doesn't even know me. She'll have somebody she wants to live with her."

But Teddy Fairchild came into Tom's office and put her small, grubby hand on my arm and smiled her warm smile and said, "No, I'd love to have you. It'll be wonderful, having somebody who realizes what working here means. Polly stays mad at me all the time because I'm never there to cook when it's my week, or do my part of the housework. You might want to think about it, though. Colonial Homes is pretty far out for people who work downtown. There are lots of places closer."

I began to laugh.

"Colonial Homes will be just fine," I said. "And if you're sure, I accept with pleasure. I already don't fit in at Our Lady, and I've only been there two days."

"Polly's leaving the first of December to stay with her folks until she gets married," Teddy said. "There's no reason you couldn't move the end of this week, if you'd like to."

"Oh, boy, would I."

Matt came back into the room. "I've called Sister Joan and sprung you until midnight," he said. "A fine broth of a gal, that. Now, let's do it. I have a towering thirst."

We walked in a loose formation down the street and around the corner to the National Bank of Georgia building, which soared above any of the others down-town. The air was cold and clear, and swirls of people passed us, talking and laughing among themselves. Several of them nodded and spoke as they passed: "Hi, Matt." "Hello, Matt."

Matt Comfort spoke to all of them by name. Warm in the envelope of light that seemed to wrap us all, I smiled at them. I noticed for the first time that the sidewalks had small specks of glitter in them, like diamond dust.

We rode up in the elevator with other pilgrims seeking to wait out the motionless glacier of light that was stalled downtown traffic, and emerged into a vast cage of glass and soft gray velvet and plush, hung in the night sky. A great central bar of black leather had stools and drinkers two and three deep, and small tables lined the ceiling-to-floor windows. Outside, in the blue evening, the city pulsed and glowed like a single perfect jewel. I gasped, a small, soft, involuntary sound, and Matt Comfort grinned.

"City at your feet tonight, dear heart," he said.

Across the room a small combo played popular music, softly. When the piano player looked up and saw us he grinned and segued into Petula Clark's "Downtown."

When you're alone and life is making you lonely,
you can always go . . .
        downtown.
When you've got worries, all the noise and the hurry
seem to help, I know . . .
        downtown . . .

I thought, in that moment, that my heart would burst with joy.

We sat at a corner table next to the window and Matt ordered champagne, and when it came and the waitress had poured it all around, he lifted his glass to me and said, "To the new kid. Cheers, Smoky O'Donnell."

I tried, one last time.

"Ashley. I'm going to use Ashley as a byline, I think," I said.

"Not a chance," Matt Comfort said. "It's got to be Smoky. It's why I hired you, dear heart. Smoky

O'Donnell—it's the best byline I ever heard. With a name like that you'll be editing *Holiday* in five years. Ashley is a goddamned debutante's name. No offense, Teddy."

He reached into his briefcase and brought out a flat, oblong package wrapped in silver paper and tied with blue ribbons, and handed it to me. I opened it. Inside was a slim bronze plate that said, in *Downtown*'s distinctive Roman script, SMOKY O'DONNELL, SENIOR EDITOR.

I felt tears sting into my eyes, and took a deep swallow of the first champagne I had ever tasted, remembering that I had read somewhere that the monk who invented it said, on first tasting it, "It is like drinking stars."

And when the last stars had faded in my mouth, Maureen Aisling O'Donnell had gone with them, gone, I knew, for good.

Only Smoky remained.

4

THE CITY TO WHICH I CAME THAT AUTUMN WAS A metaphor for the times. It was changing at the speed of light, and it was young. No matter what it was before or what it became after, Atlanta in the midst of its great decade-long trajectory was a splendid town to be young in. It seemed to me that everyone around me was young, and everywhere I looked the sheen and gloss and leaping blood of youth glimmered and dazzled. Youth bloomed in the soft city nights; youth burned from the downtown skies; youth sat warm on faces and forearms like October sun. It was as if Atlanta had wakened from a hundred-year sleep and found itself, not old like Rip Van Winkle, but fiercely and joyously and ass-over-teakettle young.

It was, to us young newcomers, the best of times, period. There wasn't any worst. Oh, there might have been a shadowy underside, perhaps; a deep-running current of black water at the roots. Bound to be. This was the South in the middle of the twentieth century, after all; this was a Deep South city just struggling up out of stasis. How could there not be shadows on the grass in Eden?

But I think I speak for most of us when I say that we simply did not, for a long time, see them. I think we were, in the fullness of that time, about as canny and sophisticated and politically aware as the terrible, time-frozen and utterly charming denizens of Brigadoon. And the town had a sliver of Brigadoon through its heart. For all its big-city roar and bustle, it was a naive and insular town in many ways, eager to show the big mules and money from outside that it could compete. In 1966 it was still small enough to be perceived all at once, seen and tasted and swallowed whole. For the hordes of us who poured in on every freeway and Greyhound bus, it was a kind of enchanted village of the future.

Those of us who worked downtown belonged to a common fraternity. Most of us knew or had heard of one another, or we soon would, and we pursued our lives and our loves and our fortunes together, downtown. Petula Clark's poignant and galvanic ballad of the previous year was our anthem. It was, we knew, all true: the lights were much brighter there; we could forget all our troubles, forget all our cares . . . downtown. Everyone in a ten-block radius of Five Points, it seemed to me in that dying year, was young and talented and in a hurry, and the bellwether for us all was Matt Comfort. Our field manual was his smart, erratic, adolescent magazine that spoke to and for the city: *Downtown.*

To be on its masthead was to own a piece of the city. I learned that the first week I was there. We might, and did, work prodigiously, enormously, for twelve- and eighteen-hour spans, but when we went out into the city it was in a flying wedge, with Matt at our head, and there was literally no one I met in those first days who did not say, on learning that I worked for *Downtown,* "Oh, yes. That's got to be a dream job. I'll look for your byline."

Or words to that effect.

And, "Yes, it really is. I'm awfully lucky to be there," I said over and over, and meant every syllable of it. I could not, in those days, still quite believe where I had landed when I left Corkie in my father's Vista Cruiser.

The glamour of my first urban Christmas lay over everything that season. Downtown was awash in secular splendor. Rich's Great Tree, on the top floor of the bridge that linked its two edifices together, shone in the cold blue nights, and by day the Pink Pig Flyer on its roof ran round and round its track, bearing loads of enchanted children. I was enchanted, too; I spent a great deal of time at my window, elbows on the cold marble sill, drinking coffee and staring at the Pink Pig by day and the incandescent tree after dark. On my lunch hour I sometimes went with Teddy or Sister into the store proper, to wander the tinseled aisles and sniff the perfume of money and privilege and Joy and stare at the counters and racks piled and hung with things so beautiful and bountiful that I could not even take them in. I lost my head and a large part of my first paycheck in one evening there, getting a new haircut in the beauty salon and a new red wool dinner suit with black braid piping in the Wood Valley Shop and presents for everybody back in Corkie that I had wrapped in extravagant Rich's giftwrap. What change I had left over I gave to the Salvation Army girl outside in an exaltation of silver bells and city magic. I had to borrow lunch money for a week from Teddy, and did not do it again, but I still remember that no-holds-barred shopping spree with nostalgic delight. Nothing else I have ever bought, in New York or London or Rome, has ever come close to it.

It was the high social season for Atlanta, as I suppose it still is, those gold-bitten weeks preceding Christmas, and it seemed to me that everyone in town was having a party or going to one. Restaurants and clubs and theaters opened like parasols in a rainstorm. We went in our gilded ensemble to complimentary lunches and dinners at new restaurants, drinks after work and after hours at new clubs and discos, had front-row tickets to first nights and first-run movies, danced until one or two at discos and go-go clubs. Everywhere, people nodded and smiled at Matt and, by extension, at us and everywhere people told us how much they enjoyed *Downtown* and how lucky they felt the city was to have us. Within a fortnight, having learned to sip wine or champagne without getting sick or silly or feeling compelled to rush to confession, and to work like a tireless little engine on four or five hours' sleep, I had come to agree with them, totally and with little attendant modesty. Separately we were, I think, rather ordinarily nice young people; together, we were Comfort's People, and often near to being insufferable. What was said of Atlanta in cities like Charlotte and Birmingham—"if she could suck as hard as she could blow, she'd be a seaport"—might well have been said of us. I believe that if *Downtown* under Matt Comfort hadn't been as good as it was, at least for its time and place, nobody would have been able to abide us. Fortunately for us and *Downtown,* Matt's capacity for work and insistence that we share it saved us from drowning in our own egos. It was always the best of his gifts, that uncanny ability to sense what it took to get the best from each of us, and for almost as long as I knew him nothing, not the hours or the liquor or the adulation, ever dimmed it. Part of the headiness of those days for all of us was the sense that we were working over our heads and beyond our capacities. I still remember the magical feeling of sheer creativity bubbling inside me, spilling over like a champagne fountain, like a geyser. We all made leaps of mind, connections, that we never made again. After that, whatever heights we reached, we got there more by craft and persistence than by those first flowing parabolas of intuition. And even though I came to know them for the fickle foxfire that they were, they are what I miss most about my time as one of Comfort's People.

It was a time for heroes, and it was not long until I had a full pantheon of them. Some, like Dr. Martin Luther King Jr. and the *Gemini* astronauts and the remaining Kennedys belonged to the nation, but most of mine belonged uniquely to Atlanta. I have had no others like them since. They came to be called the Club, and together they remade the city.

They were Old Atlanta, or what passed for it, men with names like Ivan Allen Jr., Robert Woodruff, Ben Cameron, Richard Rich, who had lived all their lives in Buckhead within a four-mile radius of each other, grown up together, gone to the University of Georgia or Georgia Tech together, flirted and danced and married each other's sisters and cousins, godparented each other's children, laughed and wept and partied with each other, loved and sometimes hated each other, and often buried and mourned each other. A good many of them were rich, or what the world then called rich; men who had made millions from Coca-Cola, either directly or indirectly. Men who had built family businesses into international concerns; men who had dramatically altered the face of the South, and in some cases the nation, with their monolithic urban and suburban developments. Men who had, almost singlehandedly or in concert with a dozen or so of their peers, in the firestorm decade of their ascendancy, brought the city a major league sports arena, five professional sports teams, a great arts center, and a world-famous conductor to head its symphony, a world-class international airport, a state-of-the-art rapid transit system, a freeway system to boggle the mind, unparalleled convention facilities and the guests to fill them, and the harmoniously integrated school system—all of which lured the industry needed to fuel it all.

They were men altogether of their time and place, and in another age would not, perhaps, have been thought heroes, because their motives were never altruistic. They did it all in the name of business and to keep the good life in Buckhead good, and that it spilled over into the arena of humanitarianism was an agreeable but secondary benefit. They did it with money, largely their own. There was enough money at home to do what had to be done, to accomplish what they had in mind: the ignition of the rocket that sent Atlanta soaring to the edge of the known universe. After that, the money would have to come from somewhere else, and they knew that. They knew, even as they started out, even as they mapped its course, that theirs would be a self-limiting journey, that they themselves, as a political entity, would be doomed by their own success.

I remember the first time Matt took me, with the rest of the staff, upstairs to the lounge of the Commerce Club after work for a drink. Around us were several of the Club, though I did not know yet that they were. They sat bantering, as almost everyone who entered did, with Matt, and I sat listening. I was struck silent with awe at actually being in this all-male Holy of Holies and in the company of so much raw vitality and power. It is, in my head, Ben Cameron who said it, but it might well have been someone else. Ben Cameron shone over those days like the sun, and was the spokesman for a decade and a generation, and so it is his face in my mind, and his voice, but at any rate someone said, "We can do it at home. We have enough money here. We have just enough. After that, it'll have to come from outside, and

God knows who and what will bring it in. But for now, we have enough and we can do it."

In that moment I fell in love with the power structure of the city, and it was a love affair that did not end for a long time. It was my first glimpse of the pure force of personality, and though I have learned now that that is as susceptible to corruption and decay as anything else mortal, power still attracts me. Without it, I would have had no career. I have built a life chronicling it.

They were an impressive group, the Club, sitting together at one of their board meetings or luncheons. Attractive, easygoing, affable, with their own ritualized jargon, the argot of the well-born Atlanta male among his peers. "Hey, how you doin'?" one seersuckered man would say to another, smiling a slow smile and laying an arm easily over a shoulder. "Hey, good to see you, suh." This to a man with whom they had, perhaps, just come off a golf course or from a family dinner. That drawled "suh" was the group's familiar, as *tu* is to the French. It was not used outside the ranks.

But the ease and indolence were by way of protective coloration. To sit and lunch in the Capital City Club or the Commerce Club was to see pure power in repose, drinking its prelunch bourbon and branch water and eating its London broil. It was almost palpable; you could get dizzy from it.

"Let me write about them," I begged Matt over and over. "Let me do a piece on Ben Cameron. We haven't had a piece on him in two years. Let me interview Governor Wylie. Or Mills Lane. It could be a good piece, you know, a young newcomer from Savannah talking to its most famous expatriate here about the city? I know it could. . . ."

And it could have been a good piece, but Matt would not hear of it. All of my pleas to do pieces on the men who powered the city fell on deaf ears.

"The next three issues are all assigned," he would say, or "I really need you most on captions and the entertainment guide."

For the first three weeks of my time there, I wrote endless photo captions for the layouts that Tom did, and spent endless hours on the telephone getting time and place listings from galleries and theaters and clubs and restaurants and musical groups, and typing them on my secondhand IBM Selectric. Sometimes, by seven or eight in the evening, my eyes would sting and my throat would be closed from talking on the phone, my fingers stiff from typing columns of numbers and listings. I never stinted and I did well at what he gave me. But none of it merited the use of my new byline. And the more I asked for additional work, real stories to do, the more terse and annoyed Matt got. I did not understand; he had hired me, I thought, on the basis of the photo-essays I had done with Hank, but the ones that came in went to Charlie or to a freelancer.

"You need to hold it down with Matt," Hank said to me once, after a story meeting in which I had lobbied once more, unsuccessfully, to do a real piece. "If you get him pissed with you he'll never give you anything. Pay your dues first."

"I thought I had by now," I said sulkily.

"He needs to know you're tough first, before he gives you anything."

"How's he going to find that out if all I ever do is Guide listings and captions and subheads?" I said.

"Well, he just doesn't like it when people push him, especially women," Hank said. I could tell he was uncomfortable. "I know you've had to learn to hold your own with all those brothers, but it comes across as pushing to him."

And so I stopped agitating for byline pieces for a while, because I was still a child of Corkie and of Liam

O'Donnell, and pushing was not a thing that daughters of either did. But I was restless and puzzled. Tom Gordon, with whom I had a comfortable, sweetly flowering friendship from the hours spent toiling over layouts and character counts, interceded for me once in a meeting, saying he had a series of photos of the city in the spring from a new photographer that was the best thing he'd seen in a long while, and he thought I was just the person to do the text for a photo-essay using them.

Matt looked at him levelly from behind the wireframed glasses and said, "I want the next photo-essay to go to Bill Towery at the *Constitution*. I promised it to him when we killed the legislature thing for January."

"Well, let's give Smoky a photo-essay soon," Tom said stubbornly. "She's better at it than anybody we've got."

The green eyes behind the glasses narrowed. Alicia smiled creamily and lit a cigarette.

"When we find the right photographer," Matt said, and that was that. Tom did not persist, and I did not ask again. But there was, now, a slight edge to my joy in the city and the magazine. What was I doing that displeased Matt Comfort?

Teddy told me, finally and plainly, as we sat drinking milk and eating cookies on one of the rare nights we were not out with the staff. I had said, not really expecting an answer by then, "I wonder why he hired me if he's not going to let me write?"

She took off the granny glasses she wore to read and watch television and looked at me seriously.

"Matt really doesn't like women," she said. "Somebody should have told you before now. I thought Hank might have. You hear all about his legendary fucking, and how women find him irresistible and vice versa, but he simply won't hire a woman to do significant editorial stuff. It's not a policy, it's just something we all know by now."

"He hired you," I said. "He hired Alicia."

She grinned. "Well, Alicia. And as for me, I came on board to be managing editor. I was doing some good stuff at the *Constitution*. The deal was that I'd take over the ME's spot and Hank would go on to do traveling and the glamour stuff. Production is as far as I got, or will. I doubt that I'd have gotten this far if it weren't, you know, for Daddy. I'd leave and go back to the paper except that I'm hooked now. I can't leave all that *Downtown* stuff; who could? We all give up something for the magic."

I looked at her, solid and plain in her flannel granny gown, her round face innocent of makeup. She had rolled her brown hair on fat rollers so that it would fall into its smooth brown bob in the morning, but that was her one concession to preening. Teddy's looks were as they were, and her clothes, though expensive, were tailored and conservative, and she did not have a lot of them. It was possible to forget for long periods of time that she was the daughter of the house of Fairchild, whose octagonal residential and commercial real estate signs were as familiar in Atlanta as dogwood and Coca-Cola signs. I had not known until I read a piece we had run on him in a back issue that Oliver Fairchild's fortune ran, even in those days, into the high multimillions. Teddy and her brother, young Ollie, had grown up in one of the largest houses in Buckhead, and summered in another at Sea Island, and gone to Princeton and Wellesley, and skied at Aspen and sailed out of Northeast Harbor and played tennis almost every weekend at the Piedmont Driving Club, but you seldom got an inkling of it around Teddy. She did not hide it, but neither did she flaunt it. Her money, or even the sense of it, seldom came up. Her reference to her father tonight was the first I had ever heard her make. It was a measure,

I knew, of the friendship that was growing between us, and I smiled at her around a mouthful of chocolate chips, thinking that even my mother and father, who scorned loudly the rich and anything to do with them, would have to approve of Teddy. It would not have been hard, even, to convince them she was decorously and inalterably Catholic, though I knew that her family had been pillars of the great yellow St. Philip's Cathedral on the hill that commanded Peachtree Road, entering Buckhead. There was about Teddy an invisible aura of knee-length uniform skirts and shined saddle shoes.

"Well, why don't we change all that, you and me?" I said. "Be the ones who win equality for women at *Downtown,* and blah-blah-blah? The dynamic duo."

"Ain't gonna happen, O'Donnell," she said. "I'd say the only way it might would be to seduce him, women being his Achilles' heel, but even that doesn't work. Alicia tried it, I know. She was hired to be just what she was, his secretary, but she decided she wanted her own byline so she put a move on him you could see a country mile. All it got her was the greatest apartment in Atlanta and probably more money than even Tom or Hank makes. No byline."

"Poor baby," I said sarcastically. "What a bum deal. Does he pay for her apartment? I never knew anybody who was actually kept."

"Not directly. I think he trades it off to the real estate company for ads. He does that a lot. God help us if Mr. Carnes ever gets wind of it. No, if he paid for it I doubt if he could afford more than Colonial Homes. He doesn't really make much. There're just a lot of fringe benefits that go with the job."

"I'm glad she's not in Colonial Homes," I said, looking around at the snug living room that I shared now, miraculously, with Teddy. It was small and even rather

Spartan, but compared to Our Lady it was nearly sump-
tuous. "Wouldn't it be awful always to be worrying
about running into Matt Comfort at dawn in the parking
lot, or something?"

"He doesn't stay over," Teddy said. "It's the one rule he
has. He never stays over." She stopped and flushed, deep
red, and looked away. "At least that's what I've heard."

I was silent, dumbfounded. Teddy and Matt Comfort?
Here, in this cheerful fishbowl of a singles complex? In
this very living room, perhaps, with its worn brown
tweed sofa and the butterfly chairs from Teddy's college
room, and the faded Oriental and good, if slightly battered, oval cherry dining table and chairs from her family? In the little upstairs bedroom with the single window overlooking the fairway of Bobby Jones golf course,
on the narrow four-poster bed she had brought, also,
from home? I could not imagine it. It seemed as unlikely
as the mating of different species. There had never been
anything in their manner with each other but casual
affection—that I had seen, anyway. I thought suddenly
that if there had been anything between them, Teddy
was bound to have suffered from it. I knew her well
enough by now to know that she would never give her
body or her heart lightly. I felt a swift surge of pure dislike for Matt Comfort, followed by the old, hot embarrassment.

"Well, I'm not giving up on the byline," I said. "But
it's nice to know I'm not going to have to sleep with him
to get it. It would be like screwing Secret Squirrel."

She burst into laughter and reached over and
hugged me.

"I'm glad you decided to move in here," she said.
"Polly is an old and dear friend, but she's got the sense of
humor of a bull moose. She never said screw in her life; I
hope by now she knows what it means, but I doubt it."

I smiled back at her, thinking that I had said it perhaps twice now in my life, and had no more idea than the hapless, moose-witted Polly what it meant.

"I'm glad I did, too," I said.

The week before Christmas, Teddy invited me to a party at her parents' home. It was, she said, their annual open house, a long-held custom with the Fairchilds, and traditionally only their oldest and closest friends were invited.

"Which means about four hundred people," Teddy grimaced. "It will probably bore you to death; there won't be many people under fifty, and virtually nobody swings. But I always bring a special friend, and I hope you'll come. Otherwise I'm going to be stuck listening to some Buckhead matron tell me about her problems with her servants now that Dr. King has gotten everybody stirred up."

I knew Teddy was, like everyone on *Downtown*'s staff, a social and political liberal, and wondered for the first time how that must be for her in her own world. I did not think that many of the people of the big Buckhead houses would be liberal thinkers. It was a given, in Corkie, that none of Savannah's wealthy were.

"Are you sure?" I said. "Somehow I don't feel that your folks would have exactly chosen a blue-collar Irish Catholic for one of your special friends. And, if they're like mine, they'd much rather you brought a man. Aren't they always on your back to get married?"

She rolled her brown eyes. "Only about every second of their lives. You'd think I'd disgraced my entire caste or something by being single. But I think they've given up for the time being. I'd far rather take you than one of the guys I grew up with. Most of them have already lost some of their hair and voted for Barry Goldwater."

"Do you have somebody special?" I said tentatively. She had not dated since I had moved in, but that had only been three weeks. It did not mean that there was no one in her life.

"Not really," Teddy said. "I've had fairly serious boyfriends, but . . . I don't know. There's so little time after work. Right now, the magazine just seems enough—"

"I know," I said. "I feel that, too."

She smiled again. "You won't go boyfriendless long, I don't think," she said. "I'll bet you lunch at Emile's that you've got somebody by . . . Easter."

"Why do you think that?" I said, flattered.

"There's just something about you. A kind of vulnerability, I think. I know Atlanta guys. There are going to be a lot of them who want to take care of you."

"I don't intend to be taken care of," I said firmly, meaning it. "I just left home to get away from all that."

"Oh, I know," she said. "But it doesn't mean a whole slew of them aren't going to try."

And so, on a Saturday night pearled with the cold white mist that seemed to be endemic to Atlanta in early winter, I went in my new red suit and Rich's haircut and sweating palms with Teddy, in her smart little green Mustang convertible, to an enormous stone and stucco house on West Andrews Drive, in Buckhead, to attend the Fairchilds' annual party.

I had never seen a house as big as the one Teddy's parents lived in. Or been in one, at any rate. I had been driven past many of the old river plantation houses outside Savannah, of course, since I could remember, and some of them seemed to me enormous. But the homes in Savannah proper, even those of the very wealthy, tended to be tall, narrow, elegantly proportioned town houses. This house sat far back on the crest of a wooded hill, overhung with enormous old oaks and hickories. It was reached by a long, curving drive that swept between stone gateposts and described a circle in front of the portico. In the middle of the circle a huge evergreen glowed with outdoor lights, and each of the seemingly countless windows on both floors spilled out more light. Even from the street, I could see that they all had candlelit wreaths hung in them.

A steady stream of cars wound ahead of us up the shrub-lined driveway, where a uniformed Atlanta policeman, huddled into a leather jacket, was directing them. I could see that three or four young men in white jackets were helping people from their automobiles at the portico, and then driving the cars somewhere out of sight. Already intimidated by the drive among the old dowager houses of Buckhead, where I had not been before tonight, and by the blur of spangled Christmas lights and spotlit green wreaths on white doors, I felt my throat close up when we turned in between Teddy's gateposts. I had no business in a house like this; I did not know how to talk to people like these; I would say something irretrievably gauche and tasteless; I would trip on some fabulous Oriental carpet, spill something on priceless tapestry, break some treasured ancestral bibelot. . . .

The officer touched his cap to Teddy and she waved and mouthed, "Hi, Wayne," through the frosted glass, and pulled the car smartly up in front of the steps, where one of the young men opened the door for her. Another dashed around to my side.

"Merry Christmas, Miss Fairchild," Teddy's young man said. "You staying the night? I'll put it in the garage, if you want me to."

"Merry Christmas, Leon," she said, skinning out of the Mustang, her sedate navy satin climbing up her thigh. The boy tried to look as if he had not noticed. "No, I'm going on back to my place. But could you maybe just tuck it somewhere so we can make a fast getaway if we need to? I don't think I can take much of our esteemed lieutenant governor tonight."

The boy tittered. "Yeah, he's primed for bear. You could smell the Christmas cheer ten feet away when he got here. I'll put your car behind the poolhouse, headed out the back way."

"Is he talking about Boy Slattery?" I said, too intrigued to remember that I was nervous. Thomas John Slattery, Georgia's lieutenant governor, was known far outside the borders of his state for his boozy, good-ol'-boy—hence the nickname—antics, his drawling courtliness that masked a snake's venom, and his baroque racism. He was despised and feared by the liberal and moderate forces in the South, adored and venerated by the hardcore reactionaries in the state—my father and all of Corkie among them—and laughed at by almost everyone else. He was the son of one of these houses, I knew, but had made his political fortunes by courting the state's white rural poor, and got endless local and national press coverage for his boisterous high jinks in the state legislature before the present liberal young governor, Linton Wylie, made the worst mistake of his life and picked him for his lieutenant governor in the past election. Lint Wylie had thought to cash in on Boy Slattery's enormous grass-roots popularity and then put a firm lid on him, but it had not worked out like that. So far, he had managed to keep Boy from declaring open warfare on Dr. King and his young lieutenants, but only just, and there were no thoughtful Southerners who looked forward to Georgia's next gubernatorial election. Boy was twice as popular as Lint Wylie, and totally without the shackles of conscience and moderation. He kept a little Negro jockey hitching post at the curb of his Buckhead mansion, and flew the Confederate flag daily on his lawn. People who thought he was merely a colorful Southern clown were making a very bad error of judgment.

"Boy Slattery in the extremely unattractive flesh," Teddy said in disgust. "He was my dad's roommate at Virginia, and Mother and Daddy always feel like they have to ask him and Mrs. Slattery, even though they both hate the way he carries on. They've both known him and her, too, since they were all in dancing school, or something. I guess he wasn't always like he is. Every year my father says, 'By God, it's just too much, Lucy; I can't take him again. Half the people here will see him and have one drink and leave. I'm tired of that damned fool ruining this party every year,' and every year Mother says, 'We can't just cut him off, Oliver. I know he's an ass, but you have to feel sorry for Becky. This is about Christmas, not politics.' And so every year he comes and pinches Mother and me on the fanny and drinks all Daddy's liquor and insults half of their guests, and after he's gone Mother and Daddy both agree he'll never come again, and then of course next year he does—"

"Boy Slattery," I said half to myself, hardly hearing her. "What a profile he'd make."

She looked at me sharply. "Put it right out of your mind. Matt would run a profile on Satan before he'd do one on Boy."

"Yeah, but it could be, you know, a subtle indictment. We ought to be doing tough pieces too, not just things on people everybody loves—"

"Have you forgotten we're the official organ of the chamber of commerce, among other things? Half the chamber might secretly love old Boy, but the rest of the country doesn't. Run a profile of him and you can kiss most of the Fortune 500 companies good-bye."

"I can see that this chamber of commerce stuff is going to wear pretty thin before long," I said, following Teddy up the shallow steps of the portico.

"Well, tell Culver Carnes," she said. "He's always here. He went to North Fulton with Daddy."

A black man in a white coat opened the door, and I goggled at him. My lord, a real butler, or houseman, or whatever you called them in Buckhead. He said, "Good evening, Miss Teddy," and smiled, and she smiled back and said, "Hi, Frost. Merry Christmas. This is my new roommate, Smoky O'Donnell."

Frost smiled and nodded and held out his hand, and I took it. He looked at it as if it were a ticking package, and then at Teddy, and I realized that he was holding out his hand for our coats, and dropped his hand, my face and neck flaming. Teddy gave him her smart black, silver-buttoned coat and I handed over my London Fog, and we started into the party. As we did, she whispered, "Don't worry about it, for God's sake."

When I whispered back, "I'm not," my voice was thickly felted with the finest brogue Ireland had to offer. Dear God, I prayed silently, please take this miserable accent and let me sound, just for this one night, like one of these people.

But God was not doing accents that night, apparently. When Smoky introduced me to her mother and father, standing before a roaring fire in what looked to be the Great Hall of a small medieval castle, I still sounded like Deirdre of the Sorrows. Teddy grinned and her father, a tall, stooped, silver-haired man of astounding good looks, smiled and took my hand, and her mother, a plump duplicate of Teddy in floor-length red velvet, kissed me lightly on the cheek and said, vaguely and sweetly, "Hello, dear. Teddy said you were called Smoky, but she didn't say you were Irish. Isn't that interesting? The Irish part, I mean. Well, the Smoky, too—"

"Teddy's mother speaks in tongues," Oliver Fairchild said, patting my hand before releasing it. "Welcome, Smoky. Teddy tells us you're the new gal at that magazine of hers, and a very talented one, too. It's doing a great job for the city; we're proud of you young people. Comfort is something of a miracle worker. It's a treat to hear that pretty brogue; I spent some time at Oxford after Virginia, and I used to go up to Ireland for houseparties every now and then. You take me right back, you surely do."

I muttered something that I adjudged to be proper and followed Teddy into the dining room, where a table covered with white damask and shimmering with candles held more silver and more crystal and more food than I had thought there was in the world. A great mahogany bar at the far end of the room, set before a wall of French doors, was four and five deep with tuxedo-clad men and women in silks and satins and velvet. My cherished Wood Valley red wool felt too plain by half and too short by four inches, and my chest and face still flamed. If Oliver Fairchild had heard accents like mine at county houseparties in Ireland, he had been hanging around a lot of kitchens. I wondered if it was possible to get through an hour, or possibly two, with only smiles and nods.

I remember the following two hours as unquestionably the longest in my life. I moved among the handsome, sedate crowd of Teddy's parents' friends like a small dinghy being towed by Teddy, nodding and smiling brilliantly when I was introduced to someone, nodding and smiling brilliantly as I listened to this conversation and that, striving to look as though I were fascinated by the banal, alien talk of children and servants and other parties and absent friends, as if I moved each evening of my life among ease and privilege like this, as if I could wish for nothing more than to stand with the rich of Buckhead a week before Christmas and beam my good will upon them. I did not say another word. I did not dare. I felt as ungainly and inept as a village idiot who had strayed into a Romanov ball, and was profoundly surprised, shocked, even, when Teddy told me afterward that her parents and their friends all thought I was "such a nice, pretty girl, and so interesting, too." And, "How lucky Teddy is to find someone as nice as Smoky for a roommate."

"Nice," apparently, was an operative word in Old Atlanta.

Teddy was meticulous about staying at my side, never letting me stand tongue-tied in a strange group, seeing that my champagne glass was kept filled and my canapé plate laden. I think, without her, I would simply have opened my hands and dropped my glass and plate and dashed out the great front door into the night, leaving Old Atlanta goggling after me. As it was, her presence and the silky, fizzing champagne kept me nodding and smiling in a modicum of comfort, and by the time she whispered, "Let's blow this joint," I was able to say, with only just a lingering trace of Corkie, "Let's." Of course, it was only one word. . . .

"Let's just run downstairs first and say hello and good-bye to Ollie," she said. "I haven't seen him in over a month. He's been in Richmond opening an office for Daddy."

I nodded and she led me down a great, curving staircase to a huge paneled cave of a room, carpeted in muted tartan and hung with great brass lamps. Another mahogany bar was crowded around with people, mainly men down here. More clustered around the largest, grandest pool table I have ever seen. It shone in its polished mahogany grandeur like an island in the middle of the carpet. In the crowd of men I recognized many faces from the pages of *Downtown*. Half the Club must be in this room tonight, I thought.

A short, thick, red-faced man and a tall, thin, younger one leaned over the table, watched by the others. It was their match, apparently. The soft light from the hanging brass lamp fell on the heads of both; the younger one did not lift his, but kept his eyes levelly on the table, looking once or twice into the face of the older man. His hair was very curly, cut short around his narrow head like a rough cap, and it was almost silver in the light. His skin was the dull, matte gold that some blonds tan after long hours in the sun, and his eyes were so blue that they seemed almost to spark. He wore a plaid cummerbund and tie with his tuxedo, and was so handsome that I almost laughed aloud. He looked as if he were designed to go with this room, and others like it.

The older man lifted his bald head and looked at Teddy and me when we entered. It was Boy Slattery.

"Teddy, sweetie pie," he said in his loud, nasal drawl, and I realized he was quite drunk. "Come over here and give Uncle Boy a kiss." He put down his stick and came around the table, staggering just slightly. The tall blond man watched him expressionlessly. Several of the other men smiled in indulgent anticipation.

"Merry Christmas, Mr. Slattery," Teddy said, sidestepping neatly. "Hello, Brad. Long time no see. This is my roommate and *Downtown*'s new senior editor, Smoky O'Donnell. Smoky, this is Brad Hunt and Lieutenant Governor Slattery. We're just leaving, but I wanted to see Ollie a minute. Is he around?"

"He's in the kitchen," Brad Hunt said. "Hello, Smoky O'Donnell. You have eyes the color of rain."

I smiled at him, tentatively. Boy Slattery moved in on me and Teddy, both hands reaching.

"How about a little Christmas kiss, girls?" he said, leering showily at the watching men. "Christmas kiss for Teddy, hello kiss for the little new girl here. What did you say your name was, peaches?"

"I didn't," I said, wincing as the brogue reasserted itself. I would, I swore silently, find myself a voice coach the very next week.

Teddy melted away into the kitchen, leaving me standing there. She closed the door smoothly behind her before I could follow. Damn you, Teddy, I thought.

Boy Slattery bridled at my accent.

"Faith and begorra!" he bawled. "'Tis a little Irish lass, now. You know what they say about the Irish in my neck of the woods, sweet thing?"

I said nothing.

"Tell us, Boy," someone yelled, and Boy Slattery grinned and draped his hammy arm around my neck and prepared himself for his audience. I felt his fingers like slugs inside the collar of my suit.

"Come on, Boy," Brad Hunt said. "Play pool. You're just stalling. You know I've got your ass in a sling."

His voice was pleasant, but there was something solid and cool under it.

Boy Slattery was diverted. He let his arm drop from my shoulders and moved back to the side of the pool table. His stagger now was more pronounced.

"Okay, Brad," he roared. "Come on back over here. I'm fixin' to whup your ass."

He peered down at the tabletop, and then said, accusingly, "You moved your ball."

"The hell I did," Brad Hunt said mildly. The coolness was stronger, though.

"The hell you didn't. That eight was way over across the table a minute ago. I had a clear shot at mine before—"

"I know you're not accusing me of cheating, Boy," Brad Hunt said, his voice growing softer and more affable. "So maybe you just made a little mistake. As it were. Go on and take your shot and I'll buy you a drink. We've got folks waiting to play."

Boy Slattery scowled at Brad Hunt and then down at the table. He rocked on his small, fat feet and hunched

his shoulders so that his neck nearly disappeared in stub-
bled rolls between them. I knew that he was about to do
or say something offensive and irrevocable. Dislike and
contempt welled up in my throat.

I went over to the table and studied it for a moment.
Boy Slattery's red seven lay six or eight inches from the
pocket. The eight was directly behind it. The cue ball
was directly behind that. There was almost no way to hit
the seven without striking the eight.

Almost.

"May I?" I said, and took the cue from Boy Slattery's
fingers without waiting for him to answer. He simply
stared at me. I chalked the cue deliberately, walked
around the table, studied the balls for a moment, leaned
far over and, feeling my skirt climb far up the backs of
my thighs and not caring a whit, slid the cue smartly into
the cue ball, giving it just a touch of English. The cue
ball bowled smoothly into the far side, banked sharply,
and clicked gently against the seven. The seven slid,
neatly and softly, into the pocket.

There was total silence in the room, and then the men
broke into laughter and applause. I straightened up and
handed the cue to Brad Hunt. There was pure delight on
his face.

"How on earth?" he said simply.

"I have five brothers who hung around Perkins's Pub
in Corkie every day of their lives," I said, exaggerating
the brogue until it was a caricature of every stage
Irishman I had ever heard. "That's what they say about
the Irish in my neck of the woods, Mr. Slattery. They
play better pool than anybody in the world."

I turned around and walked out of Teddy Fairchild's
family rumpus room without looking back. I would wait
for her on the portico; she could damn well find me. It
would serve her right for running off and leaving me.

Behind me I heard Brad Hunt call after me, "Is it really Smoky?"

"It is," I called back, not turning. "Old Gaelic name. Been in the family for generations."

The next Monday Matt called our last editorial meeting before we scattered for the Christmas holidays. Almost everyone was going home for Christmas; or somewhere at any rate. Matt was going back to Texas, to Galveston, where his mother was in a nursing home now; Tom Gordon to the tiny town outside Macon where his large family farmed; Hank to Athens where his brother's family lived; Alicia skiing in Aspen with someone she refused, with a small smile, to name; Sister to South Georgia, to be, as Tom grinned, Christmas Queen of the Wiregrass. Charlie would go, grimly, to Charlotte to his new wife's family, and Sueanne and Teddy would stay in Atlanta. I was to leave for Savannah on the six P.M. Greyhound in three days, and felt a suck of dull dread whenever I thought about it.

The office was full of scraps of bright wrapping paper and curls of ribbon; fallen needles from the lopsided, drying tabletop tree in the lobby; piled gift boxes from Rich's and Davison's and Muse's and J.P. Allen's awaiting the talented ministrations of Sueanne, who was cajoled into wrapping everyone's gifts; cloying bleats from Alvin and the Chipmunks, from the Muzak; and still-unopened gifts advertisers had brought Matt. There would be a staff Christmas party upstairs at the chamber the next evening, but we were going on to have our own afterward, at the Top of Peachtree.

No one's mind was on the March issue, which we had met to try to finalize. Matt had to drag our flagging attention back to it so many times that he grew waspish and abrupt, the chestnut hair only partly veiling the annoyance in his slitted green eyes. He looked, in the watery gray afternoon light filtering in through the windows, like he had slept the last three nights at the Union Mission. Even though we knew we were pushing him, we grew sillier and sillier.

"All right," he said finally. "None of you are worth shit, and won't be until after New Year's. But by God we're going to finish this issue before you leave here, if it's midnight. What's next, Teddy?"

Teddy looked at her page layout boards.

"YMOG," she sighed.

Everybody groaned.

"Is it in?" Matt said, glaring at us.

"No. I don't think it's even started. Frank Finley over at the paper was doing it; I thought he'd have it in by now. But he called this afternoon from Dobbins and said he was on his way to Vietnam and somebody else would have to take it. There are some notes in his office if we need them. He said somebody would hunt them up for us."

"Christ, I hope somebody shoots the sonofabitch in the ass," Matt snarled. "Is it too much to hope he was drafted?"

"'Fraid so," Teddy said, and I thought her mouth quirked just a fraction. "Patterson finally sent him and a photographer over there to cover the First Cav."

"Some people will do anything to get out of YMOG," Tom said, grinning.

"Yeah, well, I'd give it to you, you bastard, if you could read or write," Matt said. "Okay, Charlie, I want you to get on it. You're going to have to move fast. You'll need to interview him tonight or tomorrow if you're going to get the piece in by the twenty-sixth."

"Shit, Matt, I did the last one!" Charlie Stubbs howled. "Be fair, dammit! You know we're leaving Wednesday morning; I'd have to write all through Christmas—"

Matt grinned ferally. "Poor baby," he said.

"What's Eemog?" I said. I could not imagine what it might be, to engender such animosity.

"Young Man on the Go," Tom Gordon said, safe in the certainty that art directors did not get assigned editorial pieces. "We do one a month. It's the chamber's pride and joy. A profile on some young up-and-comer from the local business and professional community, as they are fond of saying. A kind of gallery of local young Turks. Nary an unflattering or discouraging word is ever, ever said about an YMOG. All their daddies are chamber honchos. The pieces are long as hell and dull as chickenshit. Charlie and Hank usually take turns, but sometimes Matt gives up and farms them out. YMOG has driven more than one reporter to drink—or Vietnam, as the case may be."

"Well, Charlie's off the hook," Hank said slyly. "Because this YMOG just called me and named his writer. Said if he couldn't have . . . this person . . . the deal was off."

"Just what we need," Matt said between clenched teeth. "A fucking prima-donna YMOG. So who's the writer?"

"Smoky," Hank said, breaking into a grin. "Smoky or nobody."

I stared at him. Everyone else looked at me. Teddy began to laugh. I turned my eyes to her.

"It's Brad Hunt, Smoky," she said. "Bradley Hunt III, scion and heir apparent of Hunt Construction. Oh, Lord, y'all, wait till I tell you what Smoky did. . . . "

They listened as she told them about my encounter with Boy Slattery in her father's billiard room. By the time she finished almost everyone was weak with laughter, and one or two of them got up to hug me. Only Alicia did not respond with glee, and Matt. Alicia sat smoking silently, studying her nails and then me. Matt stared at me so long that I grew uncomfortable. Then he broke into the long-toothed grin that so totally transformed his ruddy fox's face. He reached over and squeezed the bulb of the Bahamian taxi horn, and said, "Way to go, Smoky. By God, I'd love to have seen you whip Boy Slattery's fat ass. You got talents I never dreamed of."

"Apparently," Alicia breathed.

"Okay," he said, sobering. "Brad Hunt's yours. Go call him now and do the interview today or tomorrow. I want the piece on my desk the morning of the twenty-sixth, no excuses. If you have to write it on the bus going home, do it. And Smoky, we don't sluff off the YMOGs just because they're crap. We treat them like the most important piece we've ever done."

"It's the only piece I've ever done, so far," I said.

"Smartmouth is a privilege we earn around here," he said shortly, and I flushed. Alicia's laugh tinkled. I got up from his sofa and went back to my office to call Brad Hunt.

"Well, if it's not Savannah Fats," he said. "My wild Irish hustler. I've been waiting to hear from you."

He took me to dinner the following night at the Piedmont Driving Club for our interview. He picked me up after work in an incredible little automobile that looked like a bird in flight; only later did Hank and Matt, who were standing at the curb with me, tell me that it was a gull-wing Mercedes.

"Holy shit," I heard Matt Comfort breathe, as Brad Hunt reached over and somehow raised the door up so that it did, indeed, look like the wing on an airborne gull.

"Long way from Corkie, Smokes," Hank said, handing me into the little car. It smelled of leather and cigarette smoke and a wonderful, bronzy aftershave. The car was so opulently ostentatious that I could only laugh helplessly, completely forgetting that a minute before I had been nearly mute with nerves.

"I hope this thing turns into a pumpkin one second past midnight, and you a rat," I said to Brad Hunt as he gunned the car away from the curb.

"It turns into my brother Chris's garage, from whence it came," he smiled. "He races it around the South, and this is only the second time in my life I've been allowed to drive it. If I get so much as a scratch on it, I do indeed turn into a rat, a dead one. I borrowed it because the gal who beat Boy Slattery at eight ball deserves something fancier than my four-year-old Pontiac. Hi, Smoky O'Donnell. You look mighty pretty tonight."

"Thanks," I said. "I needed that. I've been shaking in my boots all day. This is my first piece for *Downtown*. I've never interviewed an YMOG before."

"Thank God," he said. "I've never been one, either. Well, don't think of it as an interview. Think of it as a first date. I'm going to take you to the Driving Club for dinner and show you off, and then maybe we'll go somewhere and dance. Can you dance as well as you play pool?"

"No," I said. "And dinner would be fine, but I'm going to have to go home and start writing after that. You're due on Matt's desk the morning of the day after Christmas. I'll be writing all through the holidays. What's the Driving Club?"

He looked at me for a moment, and then laughed again.

"By God, I think we'll skip dinner and go to North Georgia and get married," he said. "It's this old club where we—where a lot of quote, Old Atlanta, unquote belongs. Supposed to be harder than heaven to get into; somebody has to die before there's a vacancy. Dull as dishwater. Terrible food. If you hate it, I will marry you."

I didn't hate the Piedmont Driving Club, but I was not comfortable there. I never was, in all the times I went there, with Brad or anyone else. It was simply too static, too assuredly placid, too steeped in its stone-and-oak exclusivity to get a deep breath in. It sat on its low, wooded hill north of the city like the fortress that it was, walled away by stone and mortar and money, and all of the well-dressed, middle-aged people who came in and out of it that night seemed to me the same person. There were many small Christmas parties in its private rooms that evening, and diners in the low, beamed tavernlike room where we ate before a huge fire were all decked in sedate glitter, and all spoke warmly to Brad, and asked after his mother and father, and smiled at me when he introduced me, and all might have been the same stocky, graying man in a dark blue suit, the same small, silver-rinsed woman in dark wool just touched with pearls or a lone diamond.

"What a cute nickname," the women all twinkled at me, assessing my suit and accent like Jack Russell terriers. "I bet it's your daddy's, too. Savannah, did you say? We have lots of friends in Savannah—"

"*Downtown*?" said the men. "Good boy, Matt Comfort. Heard him speak at Rotary. Real go-getter. Gon' do well in ol' Atlanta. You going to write stories for him?"

"She's the one who put Boy Slattery away at the Fairchilds' the other night," Brad said over and over, and all the men laughed. They had heard.

"They won't forget that," Brad said when we had been seated, and ordered drinks. "They may never read a word you write, but they'll remember that. Boy is not universally loved in this town. My father may be one of the few who really like him."

"Are they old friends?" I said, thinking of Teddy's father.

"Sort of," he said. "What they really are is soulmates. My dad thinks Boy's politics are right on. He thinks he'll be the next governor, and not a minute too soon. My dad's construction company builds, among other things, dangerously substandard low-cost housing for the Negroes in the southeast part of town. Saves the owners a bundle in niceties."

I looked at him curiously in the candlelight. He wore a beautifully cut sage green suit with a blue oxford cloth shirt and a striped tie, and looked like a fashion sketch in *Esquire* with his narrow head and good features and the cap of rough, silver-blond hair. He looked, it struck me suddenly, like a portrait of one of the young Medicis, which in effect was what he was, or this city's equivalent, at any rate. And yet he sat talking easily, even humorously, of what could only be called his father's racism, and something that was not at all complacent, something on the edge of anger, looked out of his blue eyes.

"Don't forget you're talking to a reporter," I said.

He laughed. "I know Culver Carnes and his precious YMOGs," he said. "You could write that my father is a Nazi war criminal and he'd just take it out. I'm safe, whether or not you like it, and whether or not I do."

"But you don't approve of the way your father does things. And I gather you don't approve of Boy Slattery, for governor or anything else."

"Right to both. That's no secret to people who know me, especially the younger ones of us. Boy Slattery would be the biggest disaster this state ever had, and Atlanta couldn't survive if the old-time hard-liners like Dad should prevail. Race is the single most important problem we'll ever have. A lot of us know that. We've got to do better than we have so far, by a long shot."

"I would like to quote you on that," I said. "Matt will like that. He thinks the same thing. He's on this committee, or council, or something, a kind of task force the mayor set up to help sort out the racial thing—"

"I know," Brad said, smiling. "Focus. I'm on it, too. Dad almost had apoplexy."

"I know somebody else on it," I said. "Sister Joan, from Our Lady. Matt got me a room there for a week or so when I first came here, until I moved in with Teddy."

"Sister Joan, yeah. Nice lady. Plays a mean guitar. Well, well. So you're one of Our Lady's girls. I can't wait for you to meet my father. He thinks the Catholics are the ones stirring up the Negroes."

"I can hardly wait," I said dryly. "Hadn't you better tell me something good about your dad, drop just a little filial loyalty, as befits a scion and future president of Hunt Construction? Mr. Carnes will make me invent it if you don't."

"My dad's probably the best businessman in Atlanta, and that's saying something," Brad said. "It's no secret I don't always get along with him. Chris doesn't, either, or Sally. It's why Chris races sports cars and Sally married a Jew and moved to Upper Montclair. In your face, Daddy-o. That doesn't mean I don't think we've got the solidest family business in the state, or that I don't plan to run it as well as I can one day. I'll tell you interview stuff after dinner. Let's don't ruin this . . . whatever this extraordinary meat is. . . with that. Tell me, why is it that you had an Irish accent last Saturday night, but you don't tonight?"

"I only do that when I'm very nervous," I smiled. "I'm not nervous now."

"No? I hope not. I sincerely hope not. All the same, I liked the accent. Don't lose it entirely."

We ate a middling bad dinner and drank a lot of wine, and had rich, wonderful Black Russians before the fire afterward, and laughed a lot, and he did, indeed, give me, tersely and as if he were reciting, more than enough to make an interview. I knew that I would do it well. I did not know if I could manage to capture the duality about him that intrigued me; the almost exotic— at least to me—mantle of the well-born Southern liberal that he wore; the wing-brush of darkness that I sensed about him. I had met no one like him. He made me laugh and he made me think, and by the time we stood in the chill air of the portico waiting for the Mercedes to be brought around, I realized that I had not felt in the least ill at ease with him since I climbed into his brother's ridiculous car at the beginning of the evening.

When we drew up in front of my apartment he did not get out immediately. He lit a cigarette and sat looking out over the dark golf course, at the lights of the houses along Northside Drive on its other side winking through the bare branches of the trees, then he turned and took my chin in his hand and raised my face to his and kissed me, softly. He kissed me again, not so softly, and then dropped his hand and studied me. In the green light from the dashboard his narrow, uplit face looked Oriental, eerie, a Chinese statue's face.

"Will you be back for New Year's Eve?" he said. "If you are, I'd like to take you to a party. One of my fraternity brothers from the university is giving it. We'll drop by my parents' open house beforehand. I want them to meet you. That is, if you're not tied up with family doings in Savannah."

"Brad," I said, "what happens at my house in Corkie on New Year's Eve is that my mother goes to midnight Mass and my brothers go to Perkins's Pub and my father gets drunk in front of the TV and waits for the ball to drop in Times Square. I want to be clear about all that from the very start. We're light-years away from . . . your parents' open house and the Driving Club. We're probably downright poor, truth be known, only I don't guess I ever realized that. Poor and Irish Catholic. I'd love to go to your party, and meet your parents, but I'm still going to be poor and Irish and Catholic after I do. That's not going to change. I'm not sure, from what you've told me, that your parents are going to think a whole lot of that."

He did not speak, only smiled.

"Or is that the point?" I said.

"Partly," Bradley Hunt III said. "Partly it is the point. But only partly."

And he kissed me again.

5

I DID THE YMOG PIECE WELL. I SAT UP ALL NIGHT AFTER
Brad left and wrote it. I could not have slept. There
was too much roiling around in my head. My first story
for *Downtown*; my first real foray into the insular, complex world of Old Atlanta; my first kiss since I came
here. I thought back, and laughed softly to myself: my
first non-Catholic kiss ever. Not bad, I told myself, for a
Corkie girl who's been in town less than a month.

I was pleased with myself. I knew I had written well.
The piece had seemed to organize itself swiftly and
surely, as they did when I was writing at the top of my
form. From the first sentence it found its voice; it was
particular and cogent and informative and laced with
small glimmers of irony. I thought Brad would like it,
and Matt. I write badly often enough to know when I
do it well, and allowed myself the small surge of self-
satisfaction because I knew that all too often in the days
ahead I would flounder in self-doubt. I had already seen
that Matt could do that to me with the lift of an eyebrow
or a drawled word.

I was just gathering up my papers when Teddy appeared downstairs, dragging her robe and knuckling her eyes.

"Lord, how long have you been up?" she said.

"I haven't been down yet," I said. "I thought I'd just go on and do this so Matt could have it today, instead of after Christmas. It'll give me more time if he wants a rewrite."

She put on coffee and flopped down heavily on the other end of the sofa. Morning is not Teddy's best time.

"So. What did you think of the Driving Club?" she said.

"It's big and pretty, and the food is awful."

She laughed. "And Brad?"

"Big and pretty."

"But not awful." It was not a question.

"Not awful. Not a bit awful. Strange, though. There are so many contradictory things about him. I wanted to dislike him on principle, but I don't."

"Nobody does," Teddy said. "What's to dislike? He's rich, handsome, nice, funny, and his heart is in the right place. He believes in all the right things—"

"So why isn't he married or at least taken? I'm assuming he's not."

"Not that I know of. He's always been the despair of my crowd, and our mothers. He dates all the time, of course, but when it gets right down to it he just . . . withdraws. Nicely; Brad doesn't do anything mean or vulgar, ever. He must have been through every girl in Buckhead between the ages of twenty and thirty, and none of them have taken. I think it's his mother."

"What about his mother?"

"Oh, God, she's awful. She's strident and touchy; you know, one of those women who finds something to be offended by in everything. And she's the worst racist I think I ever knew. That's not to say there aren't a lot of them in Buckhead, but mostly they're very seemly about it, doncha know. Marylou Hunt is horrible to her help, and talks about the niggers this and the niggers that in front of them. No wonder Brad and Sally and Chris went the opposite way. She's tried to run off everybody any of her children got serious about, and who knows, maybe she's succeeded with Brad. Or maybe he just doesn't want to get serious for fear his marriage will be like his parents'. Big Brad drinks all the time, and spends most of his time either on the golf course or off hunting down at their plantation in Thomasville. No ladies allowed down there."

"I wonder why he puts up with her?" I said.

"She's very beautiful," Teddy said. "When she was young she just took your breath. Brad looks like her. And the money's hers, most of it. Everybody knows her daddy just flat bought Big Brad for her."

"I simply can't wait to meet her," I said. "Brad's asked me to go by there for the open house on New Year's Eve, before another party. Maybe I should rent an Old Buckhead suit."

Teddy laughed and padded into the kitchen and came back with two mugs of coffee.

"You're getting open housed to death, aren't you? Well, it'll be interesting. Whoever of Ol' Buckhaid you didn't meet at my parents' you'll meet there. You'll know more of them in the short month you've been here than some of us who're supposed to be of them. We'll make a Buckhead matron of you yet; get you a tennis dress, maybe, and sneak you into the Junior League. Want me to help you figure out some protective coloration? Virtually nobody else would care about you coming from Corkie, but I assure you that Marylou Hunt will."

"Nope. I'm going in full Irish regalia, with a mouthful of the Old Country. I want her to know right up front what she's dealing with. I made sure Brad knew."

"He wouldn't care," Teddy said.

"No. He didn't. I think he wants to flaunt me under his mama's nose."

"Do you care?"

"Nope."

"Did he kiss you?"

I looked at her. She was sipping coffee and regarding me with interest over the rim of her mug.

"He did."

"Oh, shit. You're a goner," she groaned.

"How do you know? Have you ever kissed him?"

"I told you," Teddy grinned. "He's dated everybody female in Buckhead who isn't downright deformed or demented."

"I'm glad to know he has his standards," I said peevishly. "Were you in love with him or something?"

"No. I think we just knew each other too well. I used to go to dancing school with Brad, and he taught me to smoke, out behind the gym at North Fulton. We both threw up. That may be why he doesn't stick with any of us. Familiarity and contempt."

"You are a virtual walking encyclopedia of Atlanta folkways and mores," I said, heading upstairs to the shower.

"Think of me as your guide through all the levels of hell," Teddy said.

I left the profile of Brad Hunt on Matt's desk. Shortly before noon he came in and sat down on the edge of my desk and looked at me through the wire spectacles. His rich oxblood loafers were coated with dust and grime, and the Pentel in the monogrammed pocket of his oxford cloth shirt had leaked, leaving an ineradicable ink blossom there. Some of it had transferred itself to his hand, and from there to his chin.

"It's a good piece," he said crisply. "I'd probably want you to do some rewriting, but I'm not going to ask, since we're right on deadline. Maybe I'll put you on YMOG full-time. Think you could handle it?"

"Oh, yes! Oh, Matt, thanks—"

"Don't mention it," he said, and went out of the office as quickly as he had come. I waited until I heard his footfalls fade from the office and the elevator bell ding, and then I got up and ran into Hank's office and threw my arms around him and swept him into a stumbling dance. Tom Gordon, lounging in Hank's visitor's chair with his long legs stretched out before him, hummed a snatch of "The Rain in Spain."

"You won the lottery," Hank said.

"Matt liked my YMOG! He's maybe going to let me do them full-time," I caroled.

"Well, that son of a bitch," Tom said, grinning. "Don't you let him stick you with YMOG, Smoky. You'll never get out from under it."

"Yeah, but it's the first step, and I had to take it," I said. "It's only a short hop from YMOG to the good stuff. And it's a byline."

Hank gave me a swift kiss on the cheek and hugged me briefly, and sat back down.

"Way to go, Smokes," he said. "That's taking the YMOG by the old . . . well, I hope you didn't do that. How'd you like Hunt?"

"I liked him," I said. "I'm going out with him New Year's Eve. How 'bout them apples?"

"Uh oh," Tom said.

"If I'd known you were going to be back in town, I'd have asked you out myself," Hank said, scowling. "You want to watch out for the rich kids from Buckhead. Pretty soon you'll be running by Cloudt's on the way home and planning your fall around Fashionata."

Hank's eye and ear for social nuance never failed to astonish me.

"Come on," Tom Gordon said. "I've got a freebie for lunch at that new Chinese place on Luckie. I'll muscle you both in, to celebrate Smoky's first YMOG."

I danced along the cold, windy street arm and arm with both of them, dodging through crowds of gift-laden people, whirling by windows glittering with the bounty of Christmas, thinking that life in Atlanta could hold no more for anyone than had been given me.

But Savannah, now, held little. When I got in, at dawn on Christmas Eve, having sat up in my Greyhound bus seat the entire way, holding the armful of roses Brad had sent to the office, it was to be met by my father in the Vista Cruiser, and we had a swift, immediate quarrel. The rest of the holiday went rapidly downhill.

My father was still a little drunk, and much annoyed that he had had to get up early to come and fetch me. He glared at the roses in my arms and his color rose when he noticed the new haircut and the red suit and the length of opaque white tights that showed beneath its hem.

"And are you afraid the neighbors won't have seen your behind, is that it, that you have to come home showin' it?" he said sullenly.

I felt a great wash of fatigue, the first I could remember feeling since the day I left Corkie.

"Merry Christmas to you, too, Pa," I said.

He snorted, and picked up my Rich's shopping bag full of exquisitely wrapped packages.

"I won't be askin' how you earned the money to pay for these," he said.

My temper flared. This was past his annoyance with my haircut and skirt length. This was unfair.

"Yeah, maybe you'd better not," I said. "What's the matter with you, Pa? What are you so mad at?"

"I'm wonderin' why you had to move out of the Church's Home the minute my back is turned, is what," he said. "And not to tell us about it, but to let us call there and find out you've been gone for two weeks. Who is this Teddy Fairchild person that you're living with, pray tell? Is it a he or a she?"

"It's a she," I said, cursing myself for not telling them immediately. But I had been so happy, and I knew what they would have said.

"She's a very nice girl; she works for the magazine and is a good friend of Matt's . . . Mr. Comfort's, and she's from a very old Atlanta family, just the kind of friend you'd want me to have. I've already met her mother and father. And I'm only paying a few dollars more than I did at Our Lady, and it's a nice, safe apartment where a lot of other young people live—"

"And is she a good Catholic girl, like at Our Lady?" My father smiled at me slyly. I was suddenly so tired of it all, all the anger and the crazy, ritualized games and innuendo and insularity, and the eternal niggling Catholicism, that I could have simply gone back into the bus terminal and sat there, staring blindly at the wall, until the next bus left for Atlanta.

"No. As a matter of fact she's a mediocre Episcopalian girl, not at all like at Our Lady, and you'd better be glad of that," I snapped. "Some of the girls at Our Lady would have curled your hair. The first one I met, as a matter of fact, was on the pill."

"Don't you be lyin' to me!" my father roared.

"I'm not lying to you!" I cried. "Don't you be yelling at me."

"You have turned into someone I don't know," my father said bitterly, and that set the tone for the rest of the day, and the next one. My mother said little to me, and my brothers stared and retreated to Perkins's Pub and did not come home until early Christmas morning. When first Brad and then Hank and Tom called to say

Merry Christmas, my mother wept silently in the kitchen until it was time to go to Mass and my father roared something indistinct—for by then he was very drunk—about the kind of people I was running around with up there, and passed out in the rump-sprung recliner in front of the TV, where Lawrence Welk was exhorting him to have himself a merry little Christmas. I laid out my Rich's gifts in a row on the kitchen table and retreated to the little cubicle where I had spent twenty-six years' worth of nights under this roof, and sat in bristling misery in my red suit, thinking that my father was right. I had, indeed, turned into someone they did not know. It had not taken much.

When I left that barren, bitter house on the morning after Christmas I knew on some level that I would not come back again. I had already moved an irrevocably long way from Corkie.

Brad's parents' open house was the twin of the one Teddy's parents had given, except that more people were drunker earlier and Mrs. Hunt declared open war on me with practically her first sentence. She stood in her flamboyant, patently "done" drawing room wearing ice blue satin cut very low, her silver-blond hair drawn straight back from her beautifully modeled face—Brad's face—and assessed me with cold, level eyes, and did not smile, as Brad's father had done, when Brad introduced me. She simply stared. In spite of myself, I felt the flush beginning.

"Your house is lovely, Mrs. Hunt," I said, not caring, this time, that Corkie oozed out of every word.

"It does do, doesn't it?" she said languidly. Her voice was a peculiar deep growl, and her Southern accent was very thick and slow. I thought that it was probably the epitome of taste and class in her set, but to my ears, accustomed to the lilt of Corkie, it was flat and unpleasant.

"What an amazin' dress, darlin'," she added, and looked me up and down, with a smile. It was a lazy smile, and fully as unpleasant as her voice.

I looked down at myself involuntarily. Teddy had gone shopping with me the day before at J.P. Allen and had talked me into the dress, a black sheath cut low and straight across, with spaghetti straps and a short, rhinestone-buttoned jacket. I had thought the dress was both too short and too tight, not to mention too low cut, but she had pointed out that I had the small, curved figure to wear it (*petite* was the word she used) and that she knew for a fact that Brad loved women in black. And the sale price was good, so I bought it, and thought, when I left that evening, shoulders and bosom gleaming white, single pearl earrings borrowed from Teddy my only jewelry, that I looked as sophisticated as it was possible for me to look.

Marylou Hunt made me feel, with one sentence, that I should have been working a street corner in Tight Squeeze.

"Bradley, darlin'," she said to the square, red-faced man standing beside her, "this is Brad's new little friend. Bridget, isn't it?"

"No," I said. "It's even better than that. Smoky. Smoky O'Donnell. I'm from Savannah. There are a lot of us down there, you know, or perhaps you didn't. They call our neighborhood Corkie because so many of us came straight from County Cork."

"Oh, yes," she said. "The docks. I did know. Well, Brad, sweetie, you all come on in and have some eggnog. I'm sure everybody is going to want to meet . . . Smoky."

Her voice was still low and languid, but somehow it rang in the crowded room, and people turned to look at Brad and me.

"As a matter of fact, Mother, I think not," Brad said, smiling at her with a smile made of glittering ice. I thought suddenly that he looked exactly like her when his eyes were cold with anger.

"I think we'll get on over to T.J.'s," Brad said. "It's a little cold in here, besides being a little stuffy. Odd combination, don't you think? Not very attractive. Dad, see you in the morning. Maybe we can get in some golf."

And before his father could speak, Brad had turned me by my shoulder and walked me back out onto the veranda of his parents' great white brick house. Behind us, Mrs. Hunt was saying something in a light, amused tone, but I had seen her face as her son spoke to her. It was frozen in ice-sheathed rage.

I looked up at Brad, thinking to see something of the same on his face, but he was laughing, silently.

"That's one for me," he said. "She won't forgive me for saying that in front of her friends. It'll be a week before she speaks to me again."

"Is it a game with you?" I said. "Because if it is, I don't think much of it. You must have known she'd react to me that way. It embarrassed me, Brad."

"I'm sorry if it did," he said, and he did look contrite. "I didn't think it would, somehow; she's just so awful, and so transparent with it. Everybody in that room was on your side. But I'll try to think before I let her near you again. In fact, I'll see that she's not. I don't want to hurt you, Smoky."

And he bent and kissed me on the top of my head, very softly.

"You didn't," I said.

Brad's friend T.J. lived with two other young men in a rented carriage house behind a vast gray stone Tudor pile somewhere in Buckhead. I had little sense, yet, of where I was in its maze of wandering northside streets. The New Year's Eve party was in full swing when we arrived.

After the bone-chilling two or three minutes in Brad's mother's drawing room, the low-beamed living room with its blazing fire and Christmas decorations still glittering looked ineffably warm and welcoming, and I plunged in behind Brad as you would into a tub of hot water after breaking through the skin of a frozen lake.

I still remember it as one of the best parties I have ever been to. The room was full of young people, none much older than I and certainly no older than Brad and his former roommate T.J., who were in their early thirties. All of them were laughing and drinking and eating hors d'oeuvres and dancing to Frank Sinatra and the Beach Boys and Petula Clark, and all of them seemed somehow of a piece. The men wore dark suits and short, carefully brushed hair and polished shoes and the women wore smart, short sheaths like mine, or perhaps velvet pants and tunics, and had shining, swinging bobs and large, dangling earrings, and everyone seemed to know everyone else. At first that felt off-putting to me, but in the space of half an hour I had been enveloped in the surf of carefree uniformity that prevailed, totally submerged in the tide of the party.

It turned out that few of the people in the room had met before that evening. It was the first sense I had of the vast subculture that was emerging in the city: the newly arrived, ambitious, attractive out-of-towners. Except for Brad and T.J. and one or two others, no one I met that evening was an Atlantan. They came from towns and cities all over the South, and all were thrumming with the excitement of living in Atlanta, and all had come because "This is where it's happening. This is where it's at."

Everybody knew Matt. Everybody knew *Downtown*. Everyone said, with genuine feeling, "You're an editor for *Downtown*? Wow. You must be good."

Within an hour I felt just that—good. At the end of the evening, when we had eaten and drunk and danced a bit too much, I felt as if I were the newly crowned queen of the city.

"I loved it, I loved it," I sang to Brad, more than a little high on unaccustomed scotch, as we walked to his car in the deep, velvet black just before the winter dawn. I had my shoes in my hand, oblivious to the icy dew on my stocking feet, and I twirled round and round on the cobbled drive that led to the carriage house.

"I loved it, too," he said, and took me into his arms, and we stood in the driveway of T.J.'s carriage house kissing, deep, slow, lost kisses that left me loose-jointed and rubber-limbed. When he lifted his head to look down at me I made a noise deep in my throat and pulled his head back down to mine. We kissed some more, and then he pulled abruptly away and shook his head and said, "We're either going to have to stop this right now, or go somewhere and finish it. Your call."

I looked at him in confusion. I had not thought beyond the feeling of his mouth on mine, or his arms and hands on my body. But now I did, and realized that I truly did not know what I wanted. Every inch of my skin and flesh called out to be enfolded in his, but my mind withdrew and looked down at the two of us, and could see no further than where we were.

He shook his head again, briskly, and said, "It's not fair to ask you to decide. It's too soon. We've had too much to drink. I'm never going to push you, Smoky. But I want you to know that I would have liked to . . . go much further with this tonight. And that's not going to change. So be warned that down the road apiece I'm going to ask you to call it again."

"Well . . . all right," I said, my voice hoarse in my throat.

"Just so you know. Okay. Want to go get some breakfast?"

"Sure," I said, not wanting, yet, to lose the night, the feeling, the closeness of him.

We drove down Peachtree Street toward downtown looking for someplace open and found ourselves outside the very same International House of Pancakes I had gone to on my first day at Our Lady, with Rachel Vaughn. Inside, much the same mix of disheveled heads and hippies and freaks prevailed, with the addition of a few obviously drunk street people and one or two well-dressed, coffee-seeking couples like Brad and me. Everybody looked rumpled and used up, bleached and haggard in the white fluorescent lights. I caught sight of myself in the dark window wall, and flinched. My hair was a wild tangle, and my mouth was chafed and swollen and ringed with smeared lipstick and beard burn. Somehow, Brad managed to look, except for a smear of my makeup on his collar, like he was on his way to a Jaycee breakfast.

"I'm going to fix my face," I said. "Order me some potato pancakes with sour cream and coffee, will you? Did I tell you that I came here with a girl from Our Lady my first day in town, and she took off with some guys and left me by myself?"

"No. It must have made quite an impression on you, to be abandoned at the IHOP," Brad smiled.

"What made the real impression on me was that she had birth control pills in her purse. I saw them in the ladies' room, before she got mad at me and left," I said.

He looked at me pleasantly, obviously waiting for me to go on and tell him the startling thing that had so impressed me. I made a small, helpless gesture with my hands.

"I just . . . in Corkie, nobody takes them," I said. "I'd never even really heard of anybody who did. The Pope . . . I'd just never seen any."

I let my hands fall.

"Lots of girls in Atlanta have them, I guess," he said mildly. "Not that they . . . sleep around all that much, but you know, in case. It's better to take care of yourself than to trust some stupid guy to do it, you know."

I had not thought of it that way before.

"I guess so," I said, and got up and went into the ladies' room. It was as dim and grubby as I remembered, and for a moment Rachel's brave, slatternly presence was overwhelmingly vivid to me, so much so that I whirled around from the spotted mirror. But there was no one there but me, and my underwater-looking image. I wondered where Rachel was, what she was doing on this first morning of the New Year. No one at Our Lady had seen her again by the time I moved out.

When I sat back down in our booth, newly powdered and lipsticked and combed, our food was steaming in front of us, and Brad was pouring cream into his coffee. He smiled at me and raised his cup, and I raised mine to him.

"Happy New Year, Smoky O'Donnell," he said. "I hope it will be everything you ever dreamed it would, and more."

And it almost was. At least in the beginning weeks of 1967, I could not have imagined wanting to live in any other time and place, any other way. *Downtown* became, for me, a perfect biosphere, providing everything I needed to survive and flourish. In all that time, nothing outside its venue was ever completely real to me. It gave me shelter, warmth, laughter, companionship, friendship beyond any I had ever imagined, exhilaration, a deep sense of moving smoothly in the precise groove I was born for, and the patina of heady specialness that is, of course, what the young most avidly seek. It was why we poured in droves into Atlanta in those cusp years; Atlanta was a town that dealt in specialness. It was still new enough and small enough to celebrate the modest gifts brought to it, and large enough to need them.

There was an electronic sign in front of a large apartment complex that Teddy and I passed going to and from downtown every day; on it flashed, on and off, day and night, the precise number of souls living in the Atlanta metropolitan area. When we drove by it on the day in early 1967 that it passed one million, I began, abruptly and without warning, to cry. A million. A million people, eccentric and particular and kicking, living in this city that was now my city, too. And it was a city; nobody could argue with all those numbers. Take that, New York and Chicago and Los Angeles. Take that, Birmingham and Charlotte and Jacksonville. Take that, Corkie.

After that, the sign in front of the Darlington Apartments became to me as the green light at the end of Daisy's dock to Gatsby: talisman and totem and pure panacea. When I think of the city now, from wherever I happen to be, I see in my mind two things first. I see that sign, and I see the dancer in the glass cage over Peachtree Street. As afterimages, they have, I think, a singular enchantment.

Also in those weeks, there was Brad. Ours was by then a full-fledged relationship, an involvement that was, for me and I think for him, close to total, though for some reason I shied away from thinking of it as a love affair. But it was more than just dating; I knew that, too. We saw each other perhaps twice or three times a week: always once on weekends, to do something formal and planned and structured, such as dinner and a play or concert, or a movie with friends of his with a late supper afterward. At other times he might come with us for drinks after work with Matt and the staff at the Top of Peachtree and once or twice at the Commerce Club, or he would have lunch if he happened to be downtown. He often was. His office was at the firm's headquarters over in the industrial area near Georgia Tech, but he came in town several times a week to take customers and prospects to lunch, or attend meetings. Brad was the front man for the firm, the one whose persona was adjudged best by his father for dealing with the public. At the time I met him, he belonged to a dozen boards and committees and organizations. If he disliked it, he never spoke of it. He was totally a man of his time and place, and Atlanta was unquestionably his frog pond. Nobody doubted he would be one of its premier merchant princes one day. He was born, Matt teased me and Brad, to be an YMOG.

We did not go back to his parents' house. We did not even speak of it again. Since he lived in the guest house behind the family swimming pool, we did not go there, either; we spent what time we had alone together at Teddy's and my apartment in Colonial Homes. Because of that, and because of the hours I kept, our physical relationship did not progress any further in nature than it did in the beginning. It became more intense, I suppose, but in essence we were still at the stage of long good-night kisses. I don't know if that bothered Brad, but it never did me. Often, when I thought about Brad Hunt, I could not separate his image from the amorphous haze of joyous exhilaration that enveloped *Downtown*. In those early days Brad and the magazine were all a piece of the same thing.

The only cold wind in my Eden was Matt's refusal to let me do another byline piece for the magazine. My YMOG piece on Brad would not run until March, and in the gray hiatus between then and the holidays he kept me more than busy with captions and subheads and the interminable listings for the entertainment guide. He would give me no reason for it except that he needed me most there.

"But anybody could do that; it's just a matter of spending hours on the phone and typing," I argued. "Sister could do it. Alicia could do it."

"Sister is not a senior editor, and neither is Alicia," he said, not looking up from the proofs he was reading. "The people who list with us are prime ad prospects. They don't want a secretary calling them. Don't bug me about this, Smoky. Pay your dues and then we'll talk."

"How long will that be?" I could not seem to let it go.

"How fast can you pay?" he said.

And so the days passed, and I spent them on the telephone, and at the typewriter. And despite the dearth of real assignments, I fell more and more deeply in love with the people at *Downtown* who were now my family.

I remember an evening when Matt took us all to the Commerce Club for drinks after work. He did this perhaps once a month, when we had put another issue to bed and he was as pleased with us as he ever was. I suppose he might have done it more often, as he had carte blanche from the chamber, who paid his tab. It was one of the perks of his office that helped to make up for his paltry salary. But he kept it as a special treat because, as he said once, he saw no sense in putting weapons in Culver Carnes's hands. Especially since the booze and the view were better at the Top of Peachtree.

But on this night he was pleased with us, especially since the February issue looked as if it might actually come out within five or six days of its due date. We often, in those days, missed it by a couple of weeks, and on one legendary occasion before I came, the magazine was twenty-three days late coming out. The story is that when Culver Carnes came roaring into Matt's office threatening a mass firing Matt got on the phone in his presence and sold some overwhelmed soul a twelve-month, full-color ad campaign, inside front cover. That incident, apocryphal or not, gave birth to a favorite magazine epithet: "Great save!"

At any rate, there we were, in that mahogany-paneled, leather and lemon oil–fragrant, Oriental-carpeted holy of holies, sitting in the outer lounge because women were only allowed in the inner sanctum on Thursday evenings, drinking old-fashioneds and basking in Matt's foolishness and our own wonderfulness. Men whom I had seen in the pages of the newspapers and on local television came in and out and spoke to Matt and Tom and Hank—Charlie, by then, did not often join us—and gave me and Teddy and particularly Alicia courtly nods. We were on our second round of drinks and Matt on his third; he had taken off his watch and dumped it, with the change in his pockets, on the tabletop, and was fidgeting with them while he talked. His voice was rich with humor and ebullience. Something near to electricity rolled off him in waves.

"I'm going to go around the table and ask every one of you what's the most embarrassing thing you remember," he said. "The one who did the dumbest thing gets to jump Alicia's bones."

"Oh, wow, big deal," Teddy said.

Alicia tossed her fall of honey hair and made a small face at Matt.

"You start, Gordon," he said to Tom, and Tom thought and then said, "It was either the time I was holding a piece of my birthday cake and leaned over to get a drink out of the hose faucet and a chicken came up and grabbed the cake, or the time I was necking with my date out in front of her house way out in the country and her father came running out with his shotgun and I threw the car in reverse and stripped the gears and had to back home fourteen miles with my head hanging out the window. I couldn't move my neck for three days."

We collapsed in laughter. It was hard to picture gentle, elegant Tom, with his dark falcon's face and his worn, beautifully tailored suits, prey to chickens and Three-Stooges pratfalls. He might have owned a penthouse high above midtown Manhattan. But I knew that his family was not far from downright poor, and that in fact he was forever dodging his ex-wife's creditors and lawyer, and would not have eaten regularly if the magazine had not been accorded so many comp meals. I thought of his sweetness and humor, and felt an arrow of love for him pierce me.

"Teddy," Matt said.

"When my tights fell off in the middle of a cheer in front of the entire stadium," said Teddy, who had been a cheerleader at the prestigious Westminster schools.

"That's the Teddiest thing I ever heard," Matt said, and Teddy flushed and laughed.

"Hank?"

"When I told my entire seventh-grade class that they were conducting scientific experiments in the boiler room at school because I'd heard some of the guys say that Isobel Carsuncki was selling her body down there," Hank Cantwell said, and I reached over and hugged him. Hank was, in his heart, still the innocent who could have believed such a thing, and in that bourbon-warmed moment I loved him, too. I loved them all, all of us.

"Sister?"

"Oh, Mr. Comfort, it was awful! Once when I was in the Miss Junior Lowndes County contest I had these falsies, you know? Actually it was Mama who said I needed them; she said it would make my costume fit better, and my posture and all, and so I was doing my baton twirling in front of the judges, and they just popped right out of there and hit the stage and bounced. One of them ended up in a judge's lap."

It was a long moment before anyone could speak, we were howling so with merciless laughter.

"Did you win?" I said, ruffling Sister's hair, that had come loose from the headband she always wore. She was not that much younger than I, but somehow people often ruffled her fair hair.

"Oh, yeah, but it was still embarrassing," she said.

"Alicia." Matt looked over at Alicia, who was licking drops of maraschino cherry juice from her fingers. She always begged the cherries from our drinks. She looked back at him sleepily, and the air between them seemed to thicken and shimmer. How on earth could anybody miss what they are to each other? I thought.

"I can't remember ever being very embarrassed about anything," she murmured, and we all laughed again, and the men catcalled and whistled. She seemed in that moment as totally female, as exotically beautiful, as any woman I had ever seen, on or off a movie screen. How on earth did that bleak, fallow-dirt little mountain town of hers produce such a creation? What sort of life could she have had, to become what she was? It was as if she had invented herself a moment before, out of the air.

"What about you, Matt?" Hank said, and Matt grinned. "It was just two or three years ago, at the National Chamber convention in New York," he said. "I was sitting in that garden restaurant thing at the Museum of Modern Art waiting for Culver, and I was drinking a Coke and eating potato chips. This Negro guy sits down across from me, a dignified cat in a three-piece suit, looked like he might be a UN delegate or dictator of an emerging nation. And he's eating chips and drinking a Coke, too. So we nod, and I go back to my newspaper and he pulls out his, and then I reach for a chip from my bag and he's got his hand in it, and I glared at him, and he ate the chip and I took one and went back behind my paper, and when I put my hand back in my bag, his was back in there, too. So I thought, Well, hell, I love Dr. King better'n my own papa, but there ain't no way you're gonna steal my chips, bubba, and I glared at him and said, 'Excuse me,' and jerked the chip bag over to my side. So he looks back at me a minute, and then gets up and walks off. He never did say a word. And when I got up, I saw my full chip bag lying on the ground under my chair."

When we had stopped laughing, he looked at me.

"Smoky," he said.

"Every time an issue comes out and I don't have a byline," I said.

I thought I had pushed him too far, because he stopped jiggling and fiddling with his change and watch and stared at me, the cold green stare that I had come to dread. But then he smiled. It was a strange smile.

"Well, we can't have that, can we?" he said, and the moment broke and the evening flowed on. Presently we left the Commerce Club and everyone went home, or wherever it was that they went at night.

"I didn't like the looks of that smile," Teddy said as we waited for her car to come careening down from the multilevel parking lot.

"Well, at least it was a smile," I said. But I had not liked it, either.

Matt called me into his office the next afternoon, just as I arrived back from lunch with Hank and Teddy at Emile's. When I entered his office I could not see him for a moment. It was a mess of mind- and eye-boggling magnitude, its usual state at the end of one issue and the beginning of another. Matt was proud of his office, and picky about it as he never was about his clothing, but toward deadline, as time shortened and pressures grew, he forgot about it and allowed it to become the catchall for the staff's assorted junk, until it reached the stage it was in now. A living example of entropy, Hank called it. I knew that in a day or two Matt would sound the taxi horn and bellow for us to come get our goddamned junk out of his office now and it would go back to its original *Architectural Digest* stylishness. But for now it looked like the aftermath of an explosion in a shop run by an insane junkman.

"Come in here, dear heart," he said, and I followed his voice and found him sitting on the floor with Tom Gordon, looking at spread-out photographs. I picked my way over the piles of proofs and ribbons of galleys and assorted coats and parkas and an old blanket that someone had left on the floor and stood over him and Tom, looking down at the photographs.

"Oh, they're beautiful," I said. "Are you going to do something with them?"

They were beautiful. They were color shots of antique airplanes in all their aspects, close-ups and in midair, caught in the frozen grace of aerobatics, spidery open biplanes and monoplanes with fragile bones shining through the fabric of their bodies and wings, the wings themselves as attenuated and gossamer as dragonflies'. In some of them men in leather helmets and scarves held up circled thumbs and forefingers and grinned into the teeth of the wind; in others, they were one with the planes, caught in the wild rush of space and motion. From the light, I thought the photos must have been taken near dawn.

"We thought we might use them," Matt said. "There's a big chapter of the Antique Airplane Association of America here. These guys build and fly these things all over the country. There's a big fly-in in April. I'd like to do a photo-essay on it."

"Oh, yes," I said. "It would be wonderful. Who took them?"

Matt grinned and jerked a finger at the pile of coats I had just stepped over. I looked down. A head emerged from them, flaming red and exploding with wiry curls that spilled down a vastly freckled face and made a wild copper beard. The beard split in a cheerfully feral grin, and the narrow blue eyes above it slitted shut with the grin. A child's snub nose nestled in the drooping red mustache. It was like being ambushed by a jovial jack-o'-lantern. I gave a small shriek and stepped back, but not before the jack-o'-lantern produced a camera from somewhere and shot neatly up my miniskirt.

"Meet Lucas Geary," Matt said, and Lucas Geary unfolded himself out of the pile of coats and rose to his feet in sections. He was very tall and seemed put together entirely of wire. He put out the hand that did not hold the camera.

"I am pleased to make your acquaintance, whoever you are," he said. His voice was the musical treble that you heard on every street corner and in every pub in Corkie. Oh, God, I thought. Another Irishman.

"I am Smoky O'Donnell," I said, "and if you think it's funny, shooting that thing up my skirt, think again."

And I reached out and took the camera from him and unloaded it and spilled the film out onto the floor in a long, curling spiral. The camera was battered and dusty, but expensive, a new Leica. A fine instrument. I knew that much by now.

Matt and Tom and Lucas Geary all looked at me for a moment, and began to laugh.

"I like her," Lucas Geary said to Matt, slumping down into his nest of coats again. "I want her."

"You got her," Matt said.

"In a pig's eye," I said. It was the thing about them that I disliked most, the men of *Downtown* all together. In a group, they were capable of treating women, even women of nearly equal rank and ability, as what Matt called chicks. Singly, they almost never did. I was already angry at this boneless red Irishman. I was not going to be passed around like candy. I had seen Matt do it with Sister and Teddy and once or twice even Alicia: a visiting journalist or minor celebrity would come by the office, and Matt would summon one of the women and announce to the visitor that she would have dinner with him and show him the town, courtesy of the magazine, of course, and the woman would smile with clenched teeth and go. He had never done it with me so far, and I was not going to let him start now.

"Too bad," Matt said, turning back to the photographs. I saw that beside them lay one of Tom's page layouts, a double-page bleed spread with large photos and captions. The title read, "The Sunchasers."

"Matt's going to do the spread with new photos," Tom Gordon said. "We thought you might like to write it. Luke has final say, and he just said. I hope you'll reconsider. I'd like you to do it, too."

"You got me," I said, my heart rising up singing in my chest. I plopped down cross-legged on the floor beside them. "I'd do them with Josef Mengele. Ichabod Crane here is a bonus."

Luke smiled what we all, in time, came to call his shit-eating smile and rolled over onto his stomach and focused the Leica at my face. He shot and shot as I leaned over the photos, studying them and listening to Matt and Tom talk about the photo-essay. We talked for perhaps half an hour, and in all that time he did not speak again. I did not speak to him either. I did not even look at him. But I was acutely aware on every inch of my skin that he was there, tracking me with the third eye of his camera, pulling back, coming in so close that I could almost feel the cold kiss of the Leica on my cheek, on my neck. It seemed an extension of him; it

was like having him run his hands over my face just a
breath shy of touching it. I felt heat and color rise in my
chest and neck.

Matt rose finally, and so did Tom and I. Lucas Geary
still lay on his back, fiddling with his camera. I did not
look at him.

"Thank you, Matt," I said. "You won't be sorry you
gave it to me."

"Thank Luke," he said. "And you may be. Sorry, I
mean."

"No. Not in a million years. It's the kind of story I've
been dying to do."

He laughed. "You know not what you say. Here's the
deal, Smoky. You do the story and get a full byline. After
you go out and fly with these guys. I'm talking aerobatics. Immelmanns and barrel rolls and whatever the hell
they call those things. Up in the air, junior birdmen, up
in the air, upside down. Open cockpit. No chute. I got a
guy waiting to take you up at dawn in the morning in a
Stearman, if the weather holds. Hank'll meet you here
and take you out to the field; they fly out of Stone
Mountain. Luke'll meet you there. Take a change of
clothes. Luke tells me he threw up three times when he
went up."

The three of them smiled at me.

"I've never thrown up in my life," I said, and walked
out of Matt's unspeakable office. The trembling started
then, but I did not think they could see it.

I am terrified of heights. I always have been. I do not
know where it had its genesis, this humbling, debilitat-
ing terror. There is nothing in Corkie higher than three
stories. Until I came to Atlanta I had never been in a
building taller than five floors. I knew the fear was there,
but until I first stepped into the glass cage of an outside
elevator in John Portman's futuristic Regency Hotel, in

his fledgling Peachtree Center, I had not realized its extent. I made that trip soaked in cold sweat, eyes squeezed shut, holding on to Hank Cantwell so as not to simply sink to the elevator floor on my rubber legs and howl like an animal. I never rode it again. I took the freight elevator when I had occasion to go to the revolving restaurant on top. Nobody so far but Hank knew about the fear, I had thought, but it was possible that Matt sensed it somehow. I knew that he had an interior radar that was nearly uncanny.

He knows and he's punishing me for nagging him for a story, the thought came clear and cold and stony in my mind. He thinks I'll back out. And if I do I will have shown him that I can't cut it. This is his price for letting a woman do feature stuff for him. The bastard, I'll show him. Who the hell does he think he's messing with?

I cannot remember ever being quite that angry before. The anger went a long way in banishing the fine, silvery trembling that had taken control of my entire body. A long way, but not all the way. When I got to the door of my office I leaned against it for a second and wiped the sweat off my forehead with the heel of my hand.

"Hey, Smoky," a mellow voice behind me called, and when I jumped and turned, Lucas Geary clicked the shutter of the Leica.

I went into my office and slammed the door. Through it I could hear him laughing.

6

SOMETIME IN THE BLACK EARLY HOURS NEXT MORNING Teddy shook me awake. I had slept poorly and dreamed, just the dreams I might have expected, of darkness and aloneness and falling. I sat up, heart pounding sickly, when she wakened me.

"What?" I said thickly.

"Telephone."

"Who is it?" I could not imagine who would be calling me at this hour unless something was wrong at home.

"Some German," Teddy mumbled indistinctly, and stumbled away toward her bed.

I was still not fully awake when I picked up the telephone. It stood on a wrought iron table in the upstairs hall outside Teddy's door. My feet on the bare black linoleum were icy.

"Hello?"

"Goot morning, Fräulein," a rich voice said. "Ziss is von Richthofen. Ve fly at dawn."

Even with the execrable accent I knew who it was.

"Damn you, Lucas Geary," I said. "I had another hour to sleep."

"When von Richthofen awakens, everyone awakens," he said. "I vill meet you at the aerodrome at zero-six hundred hours."

He hung up and I went into the kitchen to heat water for coffee, but there was no coffee in the cupboard. Teddy and I cooked very seldom; it was a house joke that if we had not been invited along on so many freebies, we would have starved. At any given time there might be small swans of twisted silver foil in the refrigerator containing the leftovers from these elegant—to us, at any rate—repasts, but no staples. This morning I found half a desiccated surf and turf and three soggy, orange-glazed shrimp from a new Polynesian restaurant, but no juice and nothing you might fashion a breakfast from. The last of our bread was furry and gray. The single girl's pet, Teddy called it. I made green tea from a teabag left from a complimentary Chinese lunch and ate the accompanying fortune cookie.

"You will go far," the fortune said. I crumpled it up and flung it into the trash can. I sat on the sofa sipping the tea, my feet tucked under me, staring out at the opaque darkness until the tea cooled, and then I went upstairs and took a very long, very hot shower. Even after that, I was still cold, and my heart was beginning a slow, dragging pounding. I was very frightened.

Matt had said to dress warmly, so I put on two pairs of tights and a pair of socks under my new striped bell-bottoms, and pulled a ribbed turtleneck sweater over my head. Over that I put on a bulky knit cardigan of Teddy's and my London Fog. I was so bundled up that my arms stuck out like a child's in its snowsuit, and I trundled uncomfortably out to the curb to wait for Hank, who was picking me up at five-thirty. My heart lifted when I stepped out into wet, thick fog. I could not see my hand in front of my face. Surely, no one would expect a pilot to take up a small, frail biplane in fog. I felt almost gay as I waited for Hank, rakish and daring, a latter-day Amelia Earhart, now that I would not have to fly. We had been having a spell of the balmy April-like weather that Atlanta gets sometimes in late February, and the cool, wet kiss of the fog felt good on my hot face.

Presently Hank's sedate Chamber Chevrolet loomed up out of the fog, and I got in.

"You have any trouble sleeping?" he said, and I shook my head. He was not smiling. Hank was opposed to this whole affair. He knew my terrible fear of heights, and had, I knew, had words with Matt about my flying. Sister overheard the argument and told me about it.

"He said you could write it as well from photographs as going up," she reported, "and Mr. Comfort said he wasn't asking anything of you he wouldn't of any other reporter, and Hank said on the contrary, he thought there was a small element of punishment here, and Mr. Comfort said bullshit, he'd make any man go up, and if you were dead set on playing with the guys you'd have to play by the rules. And then Hank said the only thing wrong with that was that Mr. Comfort made up the rules as he went along, and Mr. Comfort said, 'Bite my ass,' you know, like he does when he's really getting mad, and Hank steamed out of there and slammed the door. I never heard him talk like that to Mr. Comfort. Why do you have to do this stupid story, anyway, Smoky? Now everybody's all uptight, and nobody's talking to anybody else—"

"I just do," I said.

And so Hank and I drove out to the field near the base of Stone Mountain through the swirling fog and said little to each other. When we reached the dark field, the sun had still not risen, and the fog was as thick as ever.

Lucas Geary was not there, after all, but almost everybody else on the editorial staff was. I saw Matt's car, and Tom's. Even Charlie Stubbs, who seldom spent time with us now except during strict office hours, was there. I recognized the new Camaro convertible his wife's father had given them for a wedding present. In the huddle of figures standing just inside the open, lighted hangar I heard Alicia's silvery laugh, and my face flushed with anger. So they had all gathered, then, to watch my ordeal. Matt did know about my fear. I supposed that they all did, by now. And they had come to watch the upstart get her just deserts, perhaps even disgrace herself. At that moment I was profoundly sorry for the fog. I would have showed them a thing or two. . . .

"Well," I said, walking into the light of the hangar. "My ground crew. What a surprise. How good of you all to get up so early."

"Hi, Smoky," Matt said amiably. He grinned at me. He was as rumpled as if he had slept in his clothes. They looked as if they were the same ones he had worn the previous day, and I thought maliciously that he had had to crawl out of Alicia's warm bed fully as early as I had had to get up. But then, he often looked precisely like this in the mornings. Alicia looked fresh and edible in a long cardigan coat of seafoam green mohair that turned her pale eyes a matching color. Her makeup was perfect. Maybe, I thought, she just varnishes it on and sleeps in it.

"You ready to fly, Tiger?" Tom Gordon said in his dark, sweet voice.

"But this fog—"

"Ground fog," Matt said, as if he flew dawn patrol every morning of his life. "It'll burn off by the time you're strapped in. Your pilot here says all systems are go."

He nodded at the man who came out of the shadows toward us, and I said, "Good."

My voice was a high, strangled bleat. The fog, I could see, was thinning rapidly, and a clear, pearled light grew in the East.

My pilot was a sunburned man with a dark, square face and a no-color burr cut through which brown scalp showed. His tan stopped at his neck and wrists; I could see pink flesh beyond the perimeters of his shirt. He looked like a laconic South Georgia farmer, but in fact turned out to be the president of a small aviation company nearby. He gave me a brief nod and shook hands with Matt, cocked an eye at the rapidly thinning fog, and said, in a flat drawl, "Ought to be clear enough by the time I get her suited up. You ready?"

He looked at me, and I nodded. I could not have spoken. I expected him to spit in the dirt.

He produced from somewhere in the hangar a large, heavy leather jacket and put it on me, and a leather cap with goggles that fastened under my chin with a strap. He got the strap too tight, but I did not care. Perhaps it would strangle me; at the very least it would preclude much talking. He added a long white silk scarf and told me to tuck it into the jacket, and found thick leather gloves that were too large.

"Ought to have boots," he said to Matt over my head, as if I were a monkey dressed for a moon shot, "but I couldn't find any that would fit her. Okay. If y'all are ready, let's get to it. I got a ten o'clock meeting in town."

He turned and walked around the hangar motioning me to follow, and Hank took me by the shoulder and walked me around behind him. The rest of the staff followed us. Like malicious ducklings, I thought in despair, waddling along behind the pilot, whose name I never got. But at least if he planned to be downtown in three hours, the possibility of imminent death was not on his mind. I repeated to myself, over and over, the little mantra with which I have gotten through many tight spots: in three and a half hours it will be over. I can stand anything for three and a half hours.

We rounded the hangar and I saw the Stearman, sitting alone in the brightening dawn on the empty runway. If Hank had not been firmly behind me with his hand on my shoulder, I believe I would have simply turned tail and fled in an ignominious fast waddle. The little biplane did not look large enough to lift two adults into the sky and bring them down again. It did not look large enough to sit down in. But there were two seats, one behind another, in a small aperture over and slightly behind the double wings, and they were open to the sky. The morning light streamed through the wings themselves, as if they were made of gauze. For all I knew, they were. The plane was a sparkling blue and yellow. I knew that the Stearman had been an early air corps trainer, but this one looked as if it were brand-new. Slightly comforted, I croaked as much to Hank.

"It is," the pilot said, not looking back from the propeller he was fiddling with. "Or as good as. I restored her myself, in my basement. She won the best-restored Stearman category in the fly-in in Ottumwa last year."

"Wow," Hank said reverently.

"Holy Mary, Mother of God, pray for us sinners now and at the hour of our death," I whispered under my breath, closing my eyes briefly.

"Well, let's do it," said the pilot, and simply lifted me beneath my armpits and swung me up into the second seat as if I were a child. I stared straight ahead as he buckled me in, and fitted a cold metal speaking tube in place. I would, I decided, concentrate on the texture of the metal struts, and the rivets, and the back of the seat ahead of me, and just not look out into the air until we were down again.

The pilot swung himself up on the wing and into his seat and buckled himself in. Over the speaking tube he said to me, tinnily, "I'm going to take her up and around

Stone Mountain, and maybe over it. We're going to do some simple aerobatics; I don't have time for much fancy stuff, and besides, your photographer got plenty of those last time. It ought to be a pretty smooth ride. There's no wind to speak of. If you think you're going to vomit, for God's sake lean away from the wind. Tell me first, if you can."

"I'm not going to vomit," I said in the tight little whinny that had become my voice. "But wait, isn't Lucas Geary supposed to be here? The photographer? I thought the whole point was so he could shoot some more."

"Naw," said the tinny voice. "So far as I can tell, the whole point is to scare the living shit out of you. I tell you, I don't much like ferrying around little girls, but I like less a man who'll try to scare one to death just for the fun of it. I'm going to fly us around the other side of the mountain and fiddle around some, and come back and tell your editor we did the whole nine yards. You'll have to put up with a couple of maneuvers so he can see 'em, but they won't be the big stuff. And I won't tell if you don't. Deal?"

"Deal," I said, thinking that if he asked me at that moment I would have married him. I could grit my teeth through a couple of gentle stunts, and then it would be over. I looked down at the staff, standing in the fresh morning, safe on the cool, damp earth and grinning up at me, and jerked my thumb back as I had seen Errol Flynn do in *Dawn Patrol*.

Matt's half-smirk gave way to a full smile, and he jerked his thumb in return. Alicia rolled her eyes and looked away. "Good girl, Smokes," I saw Hank's lips say, though I could not hear him.

Tom Gordon walked to the front of the plane and reached high and grabbed the top blade of the propeller. The pilot nodded, and Tom gave a mighty downward heave that pulled him up off the earth for a moment, and the plane's engine coughed into life. I pulled down my goggles. The pilot gave Tom a thumb-and-forefinger circle and the plane began to bounce, slowly, down the rough dirt runway. I burrowed deep into my seat and grabbed the bottom of it and closed my eyes. The goggles cut into my face.

"Thirty more minutes. Just thirty more minutes . . . "

We accelerated rapidly, and fled down the runway, bouncing high at intervals like a jackrabbit. For a long second there was only the roar of the engine and the interminable jouncing and what seemed to me great speed, and then, abruptly, we were up.

For a moment it was much better, and I opened my eyes, thinking, "Well, if this is all there is to it . . . ," and then the little plane flew straight up and sideways and dropped like a bird shot out of the sky. My stomach rose into my mouth.

"What was that?" I could not help crying.

"Little updraft," came the voice in my ear. "You get 'em in the early mornings this time of year; the sun's warming the cold ground. Relax. It's a smooth morning."

We did not hit any more updrafts, though the plane wobbled like a bicycle going too slow. The wind in my face was a solid force, and despite the goggles tears stung down my cheeks, drying almost instantly. My ears roared. I felt the cold, but somehow it did not register.

"You looking? This is something to see," the pilot said into the tube, and I opened my eyes, to see the great pewter granite bulk of Stone Mountain wheeling up beneath and above us. We were circling about two-thirds of the way up it, flying so close that I could see the scars and striations on its face, and the pockets of scrubby growth, and, just coming into view, Gutzon Borglum's monolithic equestrian carvings of President

Jefferson Davis, General Robert E. Lee, and General Stonewall Jackson. I watched, all fear forgotten, as General Lee's titanic gray profile streamed past me. I only realized my mouth was open when I felt the frigid air that was burning my throat and chest.

"Oh, Lord," I said.

"Right. Okay, brace up. Here we go," he said, and before I made the mental transition from awe to terror he took the Stearman up, steadily and inexorably, until we were nearly vertical. The engine drone built to a great scream and the little craft shook all over, and my own scream was totally lost in the roar of the wind. I closed my eyes.

Suddenly the awful sensation of falling upward into nothing stopped, and I opened my eyes again, and saw the horizon of the earth wheel over my head, slowly and majestically, and knew that I was hanging upside down from an open cockpit, and had no idea on earth what, except a webbing of straps, was keeping me in the plane. I saw the mountain, and the hangar, and small dots that I knew to be my treacherous compatriots, all upside down, and then we swept down again in a great, stomach-turning dive, and I screwed my eyes shut once more and kept them shut until I felt the plane, at last, level out in the air.

"Okay?" came the pilot's voice.

"Oh, yeah," I said, feeling my head swim as though I was going to faint.

"One more, then," he said.

We were much higher; the earth and hangar looked very small, and I could barely make out the staff. This time he nosed the Stearman into a deep dive that was worse by far than anything we had done; by the time he took it up, I was crying with terror. We did the inside loop again, but this time I knew to wait for the respite of the gravity-free moment at its apex, and that the downsweep that followed it would soon end. And it did. The pilot flew in low to where Matt and the staff stood, waggled his wings and pointed to the mountain, and roared off around it. Behind me I could hear, just for a moment, faint cheers. They were the sweetest sound I had ever heard.

He was as good as his word. We flew around to the other side of Stone Mountain and he did a few gentle curves and figure eights, and we killed perhaps twenty more minutes, and then he brought us home. It was Matt Comfort himself who stood beneath the wing to catch me when I crawled out of my seat, and I have always been glad that he was such a small man and my padded weight put him off balance so that he stumbled and nearly fell with me, because I could not, for that first moment back on earth, have stood. I could make myself smile brilliantly to their applause, and say the proper things, like "It was wonderful, like being a bird," but I could not make my legs hold me up. I think, of them all, only Hank knew that. He came running over and picked me up in his arms like a child and bore me back to the hangar, humming loudly the Triumphal March from *Aïda*.

"You did yourself more good today than you know," he whispered in my ear, and I said, "I hope so, because if I had to do that again I'd shoot myself."

Behind me I heard my pilot telling Matt Comfort that he had taken me behind the mountain and turned me "every which way but loose."

"One day," I said to Hank, still in a whisper, "I'm going to dedicate a book to that man."

Presently Hank set me down and I was able to make my legs work, and I walked with him and Tom Gordon into the hangar to divest myself of some of the layers of clothes. Matt had gone on to the office with Alicia, and Charlie had scratched off in the Camaro, top down in the warm, late-winter morning. When I reached the hangar, Lucas Geary was standing just inside it, drinking a Coca-Cola. With him was a tall black man I had never seen before, wearing, as Luke was, bleached, thin-worn blue jeans and a work shirt that had unquestionably seen many days of hard labor.

When Luke saw me he saluted me with the Coca-Cola bottle and smiled the lazy, feral smile I had noticed the day before.

"So you did it," he said.

"So I did," I said. "No thanks to you. I thought you were supposed to shoot it. Or did you just figure I'd back out, like everybody else?"

"Well, I thought you might," he said. "But just in case you didn't, we got here in time to snap a few of you coming down. Just for the record, in case Comfort should conveniently forget that you really did it."

I looked at him with interest; did he sense, then, what I knew: that Matt had been testing me with the flight and was not apt to be totally pleased with the result? His narrow blue eyes crinkled in their nests of freckled flesh, and I could read nothing in them but a sort of abstracted awareness. His eyes might have been cameras themselves.

As I thought it, he picked up the Leica that hung around his neck, shook what looked to be toast crumbs from it, and aimed it at my face. It is the shot that ran with the photo-essay: me still in the leather cap with the goggles pushed off my face, looking up at him with my lips slightly parted. It is an extreme close-up, and by some trick of light and shade in the hangar, in my pupils are mirrored the tiny thin reflections of another small plane that stood nearby in the hangar. It is a tricky shot, but it does have impact. I never minded the comparisons it drew, when it ran, to the young Amelia Earhart.

At the time, I merely said, "If you point that thing at me again I'm going to spit into it," and he laughed and dropped the camera. It bounced on its strap against his chest.

"This is John Howard," he said, and the black man stepped forward and held out his hand, saying nothing and studying me.

"Smoky O'Donnell," Luke said.

John Howard shook my hand briefly and nodded, but still did not speak. His hand was hard and dry and warm. I wondered who he was.

"I'm glad to meet you," I said.

"Thank you," John Howard said. He had an actor's voice, deep and musical, with the quality that I have always thought of as projection in it: I thought that he could make himself heard for a long distance without raising his voice. He had a long, narrow head with a close crop of only slightly napped hair, and a remarkable face. It was angular and seemed modeled of rough bronze planes, rather like one of Frederic Remington's statues, and the only noticeably Negroid trace in it was the slightly flared nostrils. His eyes were, instead of brown, a yellowish hazel that you could see into; a wolf's eyes. A long grayish scar ran through one eyebrow, bisecting it, and down across his left eye socket, just missing the eye. The scar raised one-half of his eyebrow so that he had a permanently quizzical look that saved him from mere handsomeness. But he was that, too. John Howard was always a man on whom it was a pleasure to look—up to a point. Little in his ledged face responded to other people. He was as still, in repose, as a bronze carving, much the color of one, and had the same surface warmth. At first I thought he was a workman of some sort, with whom Luke Geary had struck up a conversation, but when he spoke I knew that he was not.

Luke did not tell me what he was, though, and he did not speak again. After a moment or two of banter with Tom Gordon and Hank, Luke and John Howard turned and went out of the hangar. I watched them until they got into a small, square sports car of a type I had never seen, filthy beyond anyone's recognition with dried mud, and roared away. Hank told me later that it was Luke Geary's, a Morgan.

"Who is John Howard?" I said to Hank as we walked to the Chevrolet.

"A bona fide hero from the early days in the movement," Hank said. "One of Dr. King's closest lieutenants. Been with him since just after Montgomery. I'm surprised you didn't recognize him; Luke's picture of him on the Selma march was everywhere. *Life* picked it up. It's famous. That's where he got the scar."

"Somebody—hit him?" I said, flinching to think of that fine bronze face taking the brunt of a billy club.

"Cop on horseback got him in the face with his flashlight on the bridge," Hank said. "They thought for a while he was blind. I don't think he has much sight in that eye. Luke shot him just as it was happening, and the cop backed the horse up on Luke and just stomped hell out of him. The horse smashed his ankle. Didn't you notice yesterday that he's got a limp? He shot that too— the world's best shot of a horse's ass, he calls it. He walked out on that busted ankle with the film in his shoe. He and Howard have been friends ever since. They spend a lot of time together."

"I think maybe I remember the shot of John Howard," I said, thinking that I did. "But I didn't know that about Luke."

"He's one of the best young photographers in the country," Hank said. "He sells to *Life* and *Magnum* and *Black Star.* Any one of them would grab him full-time, but he doesn't want to leave the South. The Civil Rights movement is his thing; he's kind of obsessed with it. I'm really surprised he'd bother to shoot antique airplanes for Matt, but Matt's already worked the old magic on him. And I think he's given him carte blanche in the magazine. How he's going to square that with Culver is beyond me. I know he's the only photographer I've ever known who Matt lets pick his writers. We're lucky to have him."

"I guess I don't remember much about Selma," I said. "Not a lot about the Civil Rights movement was ever very real in Corkie. We were our own minority of choice, you know. Is he an actor? John Howard?"

"No," Hank said. "He's a minister. An ordained Baptist minister. Does that surprise you?"

"Yes," I said. "I don't know why it should, but it does."

When I told Brad about the flight in the Stearman, and about Lucas Geary and John Howard, he did not respond as I had thought he might.

"I don't like that flying business one bit," he said. "You could have been killed, you know. Comfort should have his butt kicked. I wouldn't have let you do it if I'd known."

"It's the best restored Stearman in the country, and the pilot is the best Stearman pilot. And Matt should indeed have his butt kicked, but not for the reason you think," I said, surprised and faintly hurt. I had thought he would be amused and proud of me.

"Well, I want you to tell me about your assignments ahead of time, from now on," he said curtly.

"Why, so you can forbid me to do the ones you don't like?" I snapped. "Listen, Brad, it's hard enough to get

Matt to give me assignments of any kind. You just don't know what I go through to get them. This is only the second byline piece I've done, after your YMOG. If I start refusing pieces because you think they're dangerous, or unseemly, or something, it'll be just the excuse he needs to stop giving them to me. I'll be doing the entertainment guide for the rest of my life."

"I don't think you'll be doing anything at *Downtown* for the rest of your life," he said, smiling his wonderful smile. "As for the entertainment guide, what's wrong with that? It's got a huge readership. You get to go to every new play and concert and restaurant and lounge in town. It's like a full-time, year-round party."

"That's why," I said sullenly, but I did not press it. I did not want to argue with Brad as well as Matt Comfort. I told him about Luke, then, and about meeting John Howard.

"Geary sounds like a madman," he said. "Just what you need, another Irish lunatic. Howard I know, or know of. He's a good man. Atlanta wouldn't be as far along in the race department as we are if it weren't for him and a few others."

"He intrigues me," I said. "He has a wonderful face. I'd love to do something on him, with Luke's photographs as a companion piece. There's this sense of tragedy about him, a kind of sadness underneath. I'd like to find out about him."

"Well, he's been beat up a lot, I think," Brad said. "And there's something I vaguely remember about a wife and kid who left him. Seems like he doesn't preach anymore; I think he does something over at the Atlanta University complex. And then he's something high up in SCLC. Most of the young ones are. I know Dr. King depends pretty heavily on him. Somewhere in all that there's bound to be some tragedy."

"I really want to do a piece on him," I said, the desire solidifying. "He stands for a lot of what this city is about, it sounds like. A symbol of the best and brightest of us."

"Yeah, well, good luck," Brad said dryly. "Matt might like to do a piece on him, but unless it's an YMOG Culver Carnes would as soon run a piece on Lee Harvey Oswald as do a big editorial darky piece."

I looked at him. Even though I knew he was right, I hated both the certainty in his voice and the ugly epithet.

He flushed.

"Bad choice of words. It's what Culver and some of his buddies call the Negroes, though. I've heard them do it. This piece is just not going to happen, Smoky. Don't get your heart set on it. Even if by some miracle Matt got to run one like it, he'd never let you do it. Not a woman. You know I'm right, don't you?"

"I'm going to do it," I said.

March came booming in on a high wind so full of light that the new green leaves seemed to shimmer and tinkle like crystal. The March issue came out with my YMOG featuring Brad and my byline in fat, solid black and white beneath it, and as far as an YMOG could do it garnered quite a lot of complimentary attention. Brad was popular with much of *Downtown*'s readership, and as Matt had said on my first night with the staff, my name proved to be an attention-getter. Sister announced, a few days after the issue came out, that she had had a number of calls wanting to know who the new guy was, and Matt said he was telling everybody I was a sportswriter from New York he'd lured away from the *Herald Tribune*. I did not care about the letters or Matt's teasing. I turned surreptitiously to the page with my byline so often that I had permanent ink ghosts on my fingers and forearms.

Tom Gordon, catching me at it, laughed and said he'd run a photo of me with the Sunchasers, in May, so everybody could see just who Smoky O'Donnell was. I packed up several issues and sent them home to Corkie, but no one there replied. Even that did not materially dim my pleasure. I knew that I would not be going home again.

I did not see John Howard again, but Lucas Geary soon became a permanent part of *Downtown*'s furniture. He spent a great deal of time lying on the floor of one office or another, and his piles of camera equipment and clothing took up continuing residence in Matt's office. At any given time that one of the staff went in, during an absence of Matt's, to stretch out for a while on the sofa, it was necessary to step over Lucas's equipment and often Lucas. Knowing that his shattered ankle often pained him, we smiled and chatted with him and stepped over him with equanimity, and soon got used to the ever-lurking Leica, whose cold eye followed us everywhere. I remember thinking, in that gilded spring, that possibly no group in contemporary history was so relentlessly chronicled as the staff of *Downtown* magazine was by Lucas Geary.

Lucas became, to most of us, rather like another of Comfort's more eccentric irregulars: like Francis Brewton, or tiny, wizened black Randolph, who came scuttling through each morning and made a small fortune shining shoes that did not need it, or like Mr. Tommy T. Bliss, an elderly gentleman who was such a rabid fan of the Atlanta Braves that he persisted in standing on his head on top of the home dugout whenever one of them hit a home run, despite the fact that the resigned constabulary removed him to the Fulton County Jail each time for disturbing the peace. It was usually Matt who bailed him out, and each time, Mr. Bliss would come up to our offices and stand on his head in the lobby, by way of thanks. We bought Francis's ancient newspapers and Randolph's shoeshines and applauded Mr. Tommy T. Bliss's headstands and stepped over Lucas Geary. They seemed all of a piece with Matt's world.

But Culver Carnes did not find him amusing or intriguing. Emissaries from the chamber of commerce upstairs, often escorting visiting dignitaries who wished to meet Matt, invariably had to step over Lucas, and the prim, tight-mouthed, beehived secretarial corps from the chamber hated him to a woman. There was not a skirt he had not shot up with the Leica, or a shocked face into which he had not grinned his shit-eating grin and drawled, "Thanks, toots." Soon there was a memo about him from Culver Carnes, which Matt read with glee and put, he said, into the growing file of memos concerning the Coffee Cup Wars.

"What the hell are the Coffee Cup Wars?" Lucas Geary said when Matt told him, and I stopped what I was doing and went to listen. I had heard references to them for a couple of months, but had somehow never investigated. Now, suddenly, I wanted to know.

"About a year ago Culver got the chamber offices all spruced up," Matt said. "He's always been bent out of shape because our offices are better looking. So he hired this little fag interior decorator, and spent a bunch of money, and got the whole shebang done over, everything matching, prettier than shit. Even had color-coordinated plastic holders for those paper coffee cups, you know. Theirs up there are yellow, to match the little fag's sunflower motif, doncha know. The ones we have down here are red. So somehow, I guess whenever one of us went up there for something, or when we all went up for the Wednesday morning meeting, our red holders would migrate up there and some of their yellow holders would end up down here. It wasn't on purpose; nobody down here cares what color their coffee cup holders are, but it just sent ol' Culver to the moon to see those sneaky red cup holders up there in his little yellow heaven. And he'd holler like a stuck pig if he came down here and found yellow ones. He sent a stern memo, and we did try, but somehow it just didn't seem a real big priority. So he fired off a whole series of memos that started off appealing to our pride and ended up threatening punishment for treason, and worse. And pretty soon those yellow cup holders started turning up in the damnedest places—in the window of Ham Stockton's store, or on the roof of the building that Culver's window overlooks, or in the goddamn Pink Pig flyer on Rich's roof at Christmas. Once the chick that does the disco in the cage across the street every night had a couple of 'em hanging from her watusi. It got very creative. Culver of course thinks we're doing it, but he can't catch anybody, and besides that, can you imagine grown men and women . . . ?"

And he grinned his doggy white grin at Lucas Geary. Lucas grinned back, a white crescent splitting the piratical red beard, framed Matt's face with his two hands, and said, "Shocking."

"How about we go get a drink?" Matt said. And the two of them shambled out into the spring noon, in search of Cutty Sark and chicken livers at Emile's.

It was, I think, the start of a beautiful friendship. After that, you seldom saw Lucas Geary that you did not see Matt. Lucas spent long hours lying on the floor in Matt's office, poring over his contact sheets and listening to Ramsey Lewis and the Modern Jazz Quartet on Matt's tape machine, and when he and Matt did not lunch or dine alone, he came along with us on our staff lunches and evening freebies, as if he were one of us. Hank told me that they went out together many nights, staying until all hours, and that often Matt slept over at Lucas's place in Ansley Park, an airy, secluded guest house behind the large, genteelly shabby home of the widow of the former conductor of the Atlanta Symphony Orchestra. It was, Hank said, surprisingly sophisticated and luxurious for one who seemingly lacked any visible means of support, and Matt thought that much of the furniture and many paintings and books and records had found their way there from the collection of the old lady. Lucas spent a good bit of time with her talking music, and she was frankly besotted with him. Hank thought a good bit of the musical chat was probably bullshit, but Lucas did seem to know a lot about all types of music, and did some chores and simple handyman work for her, and sometimes took her to the grocery store or the doctor in the Morgan, or walked her fusty old poodle. It was a good arrangement for both the old lady and Lucas Geary, and Matt enjoyed the aura of cultivation and the comforts of Lucas's guest house.

"I reckon Alicia is getting a lot of sleep these days," Hank said.

Alicia was not a happy woman in those first tender spring days. She said nothing, of course, but we did not see her getting into Matt's car with him after the trips to the Top of Peachtree often anymore; instead Matt and Lucas would go off together, leaving Alicia to wait tight-mouthed with the rest of us in the building parking lot for her little yellow VW bug to come hurtling down the ramp. Tom Gordon said that until that spring no one had even known what sort of car she drove.

For several weeks after Matt and Lucas became insep-arable Alicia appeared almost daily in a new outfit, with freshly done nails and, two or three times, a new haircut. But, though she still spent a great deal of time with Matt in his office, now Lucas was there, also, supine or prone as the spirit took him. He never, Hank said, seemed to take photographs of Alicia.

There had always been talk about Matt's women, and now gossip began to drift back about Lucas Geary's near-mystical appeal to anything under sixty and female. There were tales about women in other cities who pursued him feverishly on his out-of-town shoots, and women who slipped keys and pleading messages under his motel room doors all over the South, and beautiful women of all races who answered knocks at his door when he was at home, or soft voices that answered his telephone at all hours. He never stayed in a relationship more than a month or two, went the stories, and always had two or three going simultaneously, and there were even hints that there was an abandoned wife in this Northern city, or a small red-haired bastard in that one.

I could scarcely believe the talk. In the first place, what was there in this gangling, shambling, wild-haired, glib-tongued Irishman that could account for such massive, ongoing fatal attraction? Most of the time Lucas Geary seemed to me lazy, sarcastic, almost insulting, and good-naturedly indifferent to the women in our office. He was focused mainly on his photography and his conversations with Matt. In the second place, when did he accomplish his legendary womanizing? Unless he and Matt worked in tandem, I could not imagine when he could fit in dalliance. And somehow team seduction did not seem to me to be Matt Comfort's style. I wrote the stories off as the spillover luster of Lucas's very real aura as a precocious Civil Rights photographer, and to the enmity of Culver Carnes and his minions.

Lucas cultivated the latter assiduously. Besides shooting photographs of the underwear of all of the chamber secretaries, Culver's own personal helpmeet included, he took Francis Brewton and Mr. Tommy T. Bliss to lunch at the

Capital City Club and charged the meal to Culver Carnes's account. He went into the poorest, most blasted and simmering public housing projects and slum neighborhoods in the city, alone with only his camera, staying for days at a time, telling the justly suspicious inhabitants that he was shooting for Culver Carnes at the chamber of commerce.

"Matt says he's the only absolutely fearless human being he's ever seen," Hank told me one day. "It's not that he's macho or anything. Matt says that he just lacks the human capacity for fear. Everything goes into the photographs. Matt says it'll get him killed one day."

"I sort of figured he'd die in bed," I said. "Not, of course, his own."

"He been hitting on you?" Hank said, frowning at me.

"No, of course not. Don't be silly," I said. There was, I knew, an unspoken rule that women on the staff were off-limits to casual sorties from outsiders; I would have been truly surprised if Lucas Geary had made any sort of overture to me, or any other *Downtown* woman. But still, the stories that drifted around him like smoke were intriguing.

It was a beautiful spring, even for a city that bragged in national print about its springs. I still don't know a place with lovelier Aprils. The mornings and nights are fresh and cool, and the sun pours down like spilled honey, warm without the thick, wet weight of the coming summer. The damp earth is as red as flesh, or blood, and so fecund that you can almost hear the thrumming, rustling push of growth up through it. The new foliage is a thousand different shades of pink, red, gold, and green. I could not seem to stay indoors at night in that first spring; I was enraptured with the startling, ghostly white snowfalls of dogwood in dusk-green woods, and with streetlights shining through new leaves. Azaleas rolled like surf through the wooded hills of the north-west, where the great houses of Buckhead stood. Brad and I spent more than a few nights simply drifting up one street and down another in his brother's gull-wing Mercedes, drinking in the smells and sights of April. Teddy and I often walked on the dark sweep of Bobby Jones golf course, saying little, simply breathing in the sweet night wind. Even downtown, walking back to the garage after an evening out, the staff lingered, raising our heads to evening skies milky with stars, holding out bare arms as if warm rain fell upon them. I fell in love, that year, with spring.

On an evening in mid-April Brad picked me up after work and told me that he wanted to cook dinner for me in his guest-house apartment.

"I am a true artist with a small palette," he said. "I do terrific steaks, hamburgers, and spaghetti. We'll eat out on my terrace and sip champagne by the pool. We'd swim, but it hasn't been cleaned yet, and I don't fancy swimming in stuff that looks like lime Jell-O. Maybe we'll get drunk."

I looked sideways at him. He smiled at me, and winked. He looked relaxed and carefree and young in the soft twilight; he had thrown his seersucker suit coat in the backseat and loosened his tie, and rolled up his sleeves. The last sun glistened gold on the hairs of his forearms. They and his hands were tanned and corded with veins and thick with muscle. I forgot for long periods of time that Brad was a builder and had started out working with his father's construction crews.

"Your parents must be out," I said.

"Nope, but they're busy. They've got some people coming in. And besides, mother's so crazy about the YMOG you did that she ordered fifty copies of the magazine. You're way up in her book now."

"I'm so grateful," I said sourly, and he laughed.

"Relax. We won't even see them. We'll go straight on

back to my place. You can't see it from the big house when the leaves are out, only the lights. She'll never know you're there if you don't want her to."

"I'm not going to sneak past your mother to have supper with you," I said. "I'd rather get a hamburger at Harry's."

"I'll never ask you to sneak, Smoky," he said.

When we pulled in between the great, white painted-brick gate posts that guarded the Hunt house, I remembered something from a college English class and said, "Last night I dreamt I went to Manderley again, and for a time I could not enter, for the way was closed to me—"

"Yeah, I always thought Mother would make a great Rebecca," Brad said. "Or do I mean Mrs. Danvers?"

"You're a man of many parts, Mr. Hunt," I said. "When do you find time to read?"

"Saw the movie," he said. "I like that about the parts. Wanna see a few?"

"Shut up and drive," I said, and he gunned the car up the long driveway.

The drive curved around in front of the big white house and then looped on toward the back. I had thought we would follow it back into the thicket of tall hardwoods that made a backdrop for the house, but he braked abruptly and stopped. There were two or three other cars pulled up under the porte cochere, Cadillacs and Lincolns, dark and sedate.

"Are we going in?" I said, looking down at my hot pink–flowered Pucci bell-bottoms and skimpy pink T-shirt. "I'm not dressed for seeing people."

"Just for a minute. There's someone I want you to meet," he said. "You look fine. It's not a party, just some of Dad's buddies breaking a little ice and talking a little trash."

"What trash?"

"I think maybe your old buddy Boy Slattery has been a bad boy again, and some of the others are meeting to see what they can do to shut him up. He's been popping off to the press; *Newsweek* picked up a real cute thing he said about financing day care for little jungle bunnies the other day. He was talking about some federal funds Ben Cameron thought he had in the bag for a program of day care and early education down in the projects. He went to the feds because they love him after he fell off that car down in Vine City a few years ago, and he knew he wasn't going to get a dime out of the statehouse. Lint Wylie would have given it to him, but Boy and his yahoos, as Ben calls 'em, would have blocked even a penny for the Atlanta Negroes until hell freezes over. LBJ's folks were all set to dish out, I hear, and then Boy gets drunk at some legislature barbecue back in January and shoots off his mouth to the press pool, and now the White House is all uptight and publicly washing their hands of Georgia. You can't really blame them. Ben's going around to all Boy's old buddies and trying to get them to reason with him. I think he's wasting his breath with Dad, but I know Ben. He'll do whatever he has to do. Somebody ought to just take ol' Boy hunting and see that he has a little accident. Maybe that's what Ben's thinking. Boy and Dad hunt together a good bit down around Thomasville."

"I've got no business in a meeting like that," I said, meaning it, but I was intrigued, too. Ben Cameron. For several years I had been accustomed to seeing the tanned face and level gray eyes of the legendary Ben Cameron, mayor of Atlanta, in the pages of the state and national newspapers; I'd seen the thatch of iron-red hair and the wide grin beside the smiling faces of many of my heroes: John F. Kennedy, Robert Kennedy, Dr. Martin Luther King Jr. Cameron was a rich man, a patrician, and yet a tireless and pragmatic battler for the civil rights of all his constituency. He had done more than orchestrate legislation; he had put himself in harm's way more than once, as when he had stood in a mob of angry Negroes in one of the city's grimmest ghettos on a broiling hot summer day, atop a car, virtually the only white face visible, and shouted for order and communication until the crowd was diffused and he himself was knocked, as he said later, on his ass. I would give a lot to meet Ben Cameron. I would even face Marylou Hunt.

She was on the long screened porch that stretched across the back of the house, passing a tray of tall drinks to the three or four men who lounged about on the comfortable old wicker furniture. They were all in shirt-sleeves, and most had taken off their ties and rolled up their sleeves, as Brad had. Marylou Hunt wore a long flowered caftan that I recognized as a Lilly Pulitzer. Her silvery hair was pulled severely back from her wonderful face, as it had been the night of New Year's Eve, when I had last seen her, and there was a great flame-colored azalea pinned in her chignon. It matched the flame and salmon splashes on the caftan, and set off the velvety new tan that lightened her blue eyes to the color you sometimes see in the heart of flame. She smiled when she saw her son, and the smile widened into something else entirely when she saw me. Brad had her small, very white teeth. Both looked, at times, like beautiful animals snarling. That was how she looked now.

"Children," she said. "How nice. Come in and have a sundowner with us. These boys are almost done with their silly business. Bradley, I'm sure you remember Brad's little friend Sooty. Sooty, this is Evan Tarpley and George Carmichael, and of course you'll know our mayor and Bradley's and my dear friend, Ben Cameron. Gentlemen, Sooty . . . O'Leary, is it, dear?"

"It's Smoky," I said, feeling my chest ignite. Why had I let myself in for this? "Smoky O'Donnell. It's a pleasure to meet all of you."

They all smiled, and Marylou Hunt gave a small cry of patently false distress and said, "Of course, Smoky," and one of the men—Evan Tarpley, I think—said, "Well, well, Miss Smoky O'Donnell. I'm exceedingly glad to meet you. Didn't I see your name on a piece about this boy here a few days ago? And didn't I hear something about you whipping Boy Slattery's butt at pool awhile back?"

"I'm afraid so, to both questions," I said, smiling gratefully.

"It was a good piece of writing, Smoky," Ben Cameron said in the tenor voice that was familiar to me, and yet not. "And it was an even better piece of ass-whipping, if you'll excuse my French."

"Is this the little gal?" George Carmichael said, and Brad laughed and said it was. They all laughed, even Brad's father, although, I thought, unwillingly. He had had a flushed, mulish look on his heavy face when we entered.

Marylou Hunt laughed too, a high crystal tinkle.

"Boy's no match for the fighting Irish," she said.

"Doesn't seem to be," the mayor said. "Maybe Smoky's what we need on this team."

"As a matter of fact, that's why I brought her by," Brad said. "If you'll forgive the intrusion, Ben, I've got the germ of an idea that might end up making our side look pretty good and shutting Boy's mouth at the same time. I thought you might be willing to hear it."

Ben Cameron took a glass from Marylou Hunt's tray and settled back on his chaise and propped his long legs up. He smiled at Marylou and raised his glass at me and Brad.

"Always glad, Brad, you know that," he said.

"Well, it's this," Brad said, pulling up a chair beside Ben Cameron and sitting astride it, his arms crossed on its back, with the ease of one who has walked among powerful men all his life. His mother smiled fondly at him; his father gave him a guarded, unreadable look.

"You know Focus, that commission you set up a while back to pull in representatives from the business and professional and, ah—spiritual, I guess—communities, to sort of spotlight the places the private sector could help out the city? I'm on it, and Smoky's boss, Matt Comfort, you know Matt . . . well, you know everybody on it. Your office put it together."

Ben Cameron nodded, following Brad with his eyes.

"Well, I know it can't be official, or you'd have hell's own time with the city and the state people, but what if we gave it some real teeth? Put it to work on a continuing basis, like a really good ongoing PR campaign, only with more . . . dignity, more bite. Spotlight a different need, say, each month, along with a team from the private sector and a plan to address it? You've got a lot of talent on Focus, and you could beef it up some, with people who could tell us what the real problems are and the kinds of minds that could come up with real solutions. All you'd need is money. I think if the public was used to seeing problems set out with solutions suggested and ways to implement them, they might be willing to come up with some money. I feel like our business leaders would kick in, and I think if it was an ongoing media campaign, Washington might see that we mean business down here, and know how to get it done, and mean to do it no matter how much rednecks like Boy Slattery flap their gums. They might feel like letting go of more money."

They all looked at Brad. His father narrowed his eyes, and his mother simply stared.

"Interesting," Ben Cameron said. "Except that a PR campaign of that magnitude would cost a mint, and PR smells like PR no matter how you pretty it up."

"Well, you know, it depends on who presents it," Brad said mildly. "You know John Howard, don't you? From Selma; he's over at Morehouse now, I think."

"Oh, yes, I know John. Good man," Ben Cameron said. "Been a help to me in ways not many people know about. What about him?"

"I see an ongoing feature in *Downtown,* full-color, several pages a month, with Focus as the subject and a new task force tackling a new problem area every month. I see John Howard as the spokesperson for both the black community—because let's face it, that's where the problems are going to be—and sort of the official host of the series. Smoky here would write it, because she knows Howard and she's good, and a photographer named Lucas Geary would shoot it every month. You know, Focus on day care, Focus on decent housing, Focus on working conditions for city workers, Focus on health care for the elderly, Focus on Grady Hospital, Focus on street gangs—"

"I know," Ben Cameron nodded.

"All shot by the hottest young photographer in the country, the one who did that shot of Howard getting his head bashed in on the Edmund Pettus Bridge. It was a hell of a shot, ran all over the place. Geary's got carte blanche with all the big magazines now, and Matt Comfort's got him pretty much in the bag at *Downtown,* don't ask me how."

"I don't ask how Matt does anything," Ben Cameron laughed.

"It could be some of the best writing and photography coming out of the South, or the country, for that matter," Brad said. "Far out of the PR category. The fact that it's officially sponsored, so to speak, doesn't bother me a bit."

"No, just think of Agee and Walker Evans and Dorothy Stead for the WPA," I said, forgetting my shyness and whose house I was in.

"Good point," the mayor said. "But how do you know any of them would agree to do it?"

"Well, Matt would do it if Culver told him to," Brad said, smiling. "And Geary would jump at it, and so would Smoky, and I think John Howard would do it for Geary. And I think I could promise that the business community would, for the most part, like to be seen as part of the solution, not the problem. I volunteer here and now to sort of stand for the construction people. I'll bet Evan and George would agree to offer some resources from their shops. It could have a lot of impact, and even Boy would think twice if his hunting and poker buddies were on deck working with the Negro community."

There was a silence. Ben Cameron stared at Brad, nodding slowly, his gray eyes far away. The other two men looked at each other, then at Ben, and nodded, too. Ben's father said nothing, but his face was slowly purpling, and the veins on the backs of his hands were engorging. Marylou Hunt was so still that she might have turned to stone. She did not even blink. But white lines ran like a bolt of lightning from the corners of her mouth to her chin, and there were white patches on her cheeks and around her eyes.

"It wouldn't hurt to have a little chat with Culver in the morning," Ben said. "What about it, Smoky? You think it would work? You think we could pull it off?"

"I think Mr. Carnes would love to do it, for you," I said. "I think Mr. Comfort would love to do it, even if it was Mr. Carnes's idea. I don't know about John Howard, but I believe Lucas would like it, and I would absolutely adore it. I would."

"Then we'll check it out," Ben Cameron said, getting

to his feet. "Good thinking, Brad. Thanks for the idea and the offer to stand for construction. I take it there won't be any family . . . feeling . . . about your involvement."

He smiled at Brad's father and mother. It was an easy smile, but a knowing one.

"We'll do what we can, of course, if everyone else is in," Mr. Hunt said stiffly. I could see a pulse beating in his temple.

"What a strange little idea, Brad," Marylou Hunt said, ice in her voice. "However did you come up with it?"

She looked at me. I looked back.

"I had help," Brad said, and his mother smiled, the animal's smile. He gave it back to her.

"I'll bet you did," she said.

"Well, we'll be going on," Brad said. "I'm going to cook for Smoky tonight. She doesn't think I've got a domestic bone in my body."

"I'd like to see that," Ben Cameron smiled, and clapped him on the shoulder. "Make sure he wears an apron, Smoky, and don't let him con you into doing dishes."

"Oh, I don't imagine Smoky had dishes in mind." Marylou Hunt could not keep the venom from her voice.

"No, I didn't," I said. "I do windows, but not dishes. Good night, Mr. Cameron, Mr. Tarpley, Mr. Carmichael. Mr. Hunt. Mrs. Hunt. I hope I'll see you again soon."

"Oh, you will," Brad said, and gave a small wave over his shoulder and walked me off the porch.

Behind me, I heard Marylou Hunt call, softly but sharply, "Bradley, wait a minute."

"Later, Ma," he said, still not turning.

We were through the living room and back out on the veranda before he spoke.

"She hates it when I call her Ma," he said.

*   *   *

We stayed very late in the little house behind Brad's parents' big one. He did indeed cook better-than-average spaghetti for me in the tiny kitchen, and we did indeed sip champagne and eat our dinner on small tables on his pocket veranda, facing the still, stagnant swimming pool. There were crickets, and from somewhere close by the heavy, heartbreaking scent of mimosa blew in lightly. He lit candles and we toasted each other and the spring and the hopeful new Focus series. Once or twice he leaned over and kissed me softly. It was an enchanted evening, after its ugly start, but somehow I never fully relaxed and let myself slide into it. Marylou Hunt was simply too near. I could not see her, of course, but I could see the lights of what I knew, late in the evening, must be her bedroom, and I could feel her prowling near us with those extraordinary eyes. Brad's eyes.

"She can't see us," he said once, when I pulled away from a long kiss. We were lying stretched out on a chaise beside the pool, and if it had not been for the sheltering trees, I knew that anyone in the house could have watched.

"Are you sure?"

"I'm certain. I used to lie up there in my bedroom next to hers when I was a kid, and try to spy on the grown-ups down by the pool. You can't do it."

"She can see the lights, though—"

"So?"

"She'll know how late I stay."

He reached over and snuffed out the candle with his thumb and forefinger.

"No she won't. Though I wouldn't care if she did."

I did not think he would care. He was nervy and vividly animated, thrumming with a kind of interior energy, like an engine running softly, deep down. It was different from his usual loose-jointed calm, and exciting in a sharp, physical way. In another way, though, there was something just faintly—what was the word I wanted? Not dangerous, surely?—about being with Brad that night. The kisses and caresses we exchanged slid quickly from our usual long, soft, slow ones to something else, swift and hard and so insistent that by the time I finally pulled away, flushed and breathing hard, I was half undressed and we were more than halfway to making love. I sat up, heart hammering with something not far from fear.

"Stop. No. I can't. Please, Brad—"

"I want it to be tonight, Smoky."

"No. Not here. Don't you see? Not right under your mother's nose, not to . . . to celebrate some kind of victory over her—"

He sat up, too.

"Is that what you think?"

I knew I had made him angry. But this was not right, not for our first time.

"I'm sorry, but it's just not the right place."

He was silent for a time, looking out into the darkness. Through the trees the lone light still burned.

"Christ, maybe you're right," he said finally. "It makes sense. She's screwed up every other—"

"Every other girl you've been interested in?"

"I wasn't going to say that."

But I thought he had been going to say precisely that. After a moment I got up and straightened my clothing and went inside to wash my face. When I came back out again, he was standing beside the pool, scowling at the light in the big house and tossing his car keys up and down in his hand.

"Bad call on my part," he said. "Shall we try again, out of the line of fire, so to speak? One day soon?"

I was relieved that he was not angry, and felt a sudden wash of simple happiness and well-being.

"By all means," I said, and reached up and kissed his cheek.

When we finally drove away from the little pool house, the greenlit dashboard clock read two-thirty A.M. Above us, through the translucent green leaves, Marylou Hunt's light still burned, like an eye.

7

ON A STILL GREEN WEEKEND IN MAY TEDDY'S PARENTS invited the staff over for an afternoon of swimming, with a backyard picnic to follow. It was a small ritual that the Fairchilds' had established in the first year of Teddy's tenure with *Downtown*, and though Matt grumbled about having to spend a Sunday afternoon stroking Northside egos, the fact was that his was the first car there. Teddy had gone early to help her parents, and Brad picked me up at Colonial Homes. When we got there Matt was sprawled in a chaise by the oval pool with a gin and tonic in his hand, gesticulating as he talked to Oliver Fairchild and Teddy's brother, Ollie. Or rather, lectured. I recognized the note his rich voice acquired when he was in what Hank called his visionary persona.

"... in another ten years, whether you guys in Buckhead want to acknowledge it or not," I heard him say, and knew Hank was right. He regularly lectured the Club on their shortsightedness in this matter or their failure to adapt to that trend. Oliver Fairchild nodded thoughtfully, his eyes intent on Matt's sharp face. I often wondered why the Club put up with it. But they all seemed to hang on Matt's words. For a poor boy from rural Texas, I thought, it must be a real power trip.

Matt was wearing swimming trunks with an oxford cloth shirt, tails out, over it. Both were so rumpled that they looked as if he had just plucked them out of the clothes dryer. His eyes were shielded behind wire-rimmed sunglasses, and his shock of hair burned in the sun. His thin arms and legs were pale, and he looked altogether like a wizened, freckled child huddled in the deep-cushioned chaise. His feet were narrow and so white they had a bluish undertinge. I thought suddenly that he looked like some sort of tiny amphibian, blinking in the alien sunlight, except for the hair. The hair changed him altogether.

"Hi, Matt," I said, after I had greeted Mr. Fairchild and Ollie. "I've never seen you without clothes before."

He grinned.

"Hi, Smoky. I can't wait to say the same to you."

It was a nice day. After the peripatetic pace of *Downtown*'s daily routine, a day in the sun in this orderly, cloistered wedge of privilege was hypnotic. We swam and sunned lazily, listening to Ollie Fairchild's portable radio playing jazz softly and sipping the drinks that Teddy's father kept coming from the little bar under the pavilion at poolside. By five o'clock, when the sting of the high sun began to fade, most of us were somnolent and a little drunk, except for Matt, whose cheeks glowed with color and whose speech was more staccato and ebullient than when we had arrived. Matt never, I had noticed, got drunk, and the only effect liquor seemed to have on him was to make him more focused, more exuberant, more forceful.

I looked around the small group on the brick pool apron. I knew that the Fairchilds had included spouses and dates in their invitation, but with the exception of Brad, who had come with me and was in any case almost a son of this house, and Charlie Stubbs's wife, no one had brought anyone else. Charlie and the outland wife had left early, pleading another engagement, and I thought suddenly of what Teddy had said to me on a night when I had first moved into the apartment with her: "We all give up something for the magic." We had, it seemed, given up a great deal. We had literally, except for Charlie, forsaken all others. Hank had said we would.

But I haven't, I thought, and looked across at Brad and smiled. He lifted his glass to me and smiled back, his narrow face under the light, crinkled hair bronze with new sunburn.

Right at this moment, I thought, I have it all, and closed my eyes in a fugue of sun and gin and well-being.

There were two of us who were not present that day. Alicia Crowley had not come with Matt, and Tom Gordon was missing. Tom, I knew, was on a swing across the country with Lucas Geary for an editorial photo-essay dear to Matt's heart that he had only with difficulty and outright bribery persuaded Culver Carnes to allow him to do, and no one knew where Alicia was. Except Matt, and he wasn't saying.

"She had plans," he said, grinning so that you knew what plans he meant you to infer Alicia had. "Alicia has secret and private plans for this weekend. Wouldn't you like to be a fly on those walls, though?"

All of a sudden I knew, with a flash of the puzzling prescience that I sometimes had around him, that he did not know where Alicia was, and was jealous and resentful of the plans that did not include him, even though he rarely saw her after work now, except when Lucas Geary was out of pocket. I did not like Alicia, but neither did I like the way Matt Comfort spoke of her in her absence.

She had given up any private life she might have had for him, and he had ignored her except when it pleased him.

"Well, I imagine she could have her pick of plans," I said, my eyes still closed to the last of the sun.

"She sure could," Matt said. "All at one time, probably."

Something cold and argumentative had crept into his voice, and Hank said, "Matt, tell Mr. Fairchild about the piece you've got Tom Gordon and Luke off on."

Matt was silent for a moment, and I thought he was going to argue with or speak sharply to Hank, but then he laughed and said, "Great save, Cantwell. Well, Oliver, it's this . . . " and I sat up to listen, once more, because I thought the story was going to be one of the most exciting and valuable ones we would run in *Downtown*.

Lucas Geary had been in San Francisco back in January for the much-ballyhooed Human Be-In held in the Haight-Ashbury district. To me, a continent away in a city so self-absorbed by its own trajectory that news from the Outside seemed to reach it, like blown smoke, months later, the Be-In had seemed only another of the raucous and somehow exotic commotions stirred up by the legendary San Francisco hippies, who for sheer theater put our own Tight Squeeze denizens in the shade. But Lucas had come back moved and somehow changed by it, and had brought with him photographs that were stunning in their particularity and portent.

"It's different; it's the start of something else entirely," he told us at a staff meeting. Lucas was never articulate with words. But the photographs touched Matt; he seemed to extrapolate from them what Lucas was trying to say. It was always his best gift, that ability to leap, to make connections. We all felt the power of those black-and-white images, but Matt knew it for what it was.

A day or two later he announced a story idea, and we could tell he was enormously excited about it. He was fairly humming with energy, fiddling with the change from his pockets and his watch until Teddy finally reached over and took them away from him.

He wanted to send Lucas and Tom Gordon around the country, to the great urban centers, to see, as he said, what was going on with the young. They would find the pockets of activity and unrest, the enclaves in major cities like the Haight in San Francisco and Tight Squeeze in Atlanta, and do a photo-essay on them. He wanted to call it the Children's Crusade because so many of the young were very young indeed, and it was his intention that only the images and Tom's art direction of them would carry the message. There would, perhaps, be a few captions, nothing more. The story was in the young faces. He thought it would have value and pertinence for *Downtown*'s readers; send a message to the city. Culver had not thought so, but Matt had dangled the prospect of major national advertising in support, and Culver had capitulated.

"I had to promise him his choice of the next three YMOGs, though," Matt said. "Smoky, be warned."

Oliver Fairchild Senior and Junior looked at each other, and then, gravely, at Matt.

"Interesting," Teddy's father said. "And what message do you think these . . . ah, hippies . . . out there in California and in Boston and Washington and so forth might have for us down here? Except for that little nest around Tenth Street, we don't see much of 'em. Seems to me our kids are all, you know, going to school and getting summer jobs or off at camp, things like that."

Teddy closed her eyes and Hank Cantwell and I looked at each other. He hadn't a clue, then, Teddy's father. Nor, for that matter, did her brother. In their world, in

Buckhead, in the Northwest, that was precisely what the young of the great houses were doing. The world outside the boundaries of Buckhead did not, for them, exist.

Matt looked for a long moment at Oliver Fairchild, and then shrugged and reached for his fresh drink and downed half of it.

"They're what we're going to have next, Oliver," he said. "They're the future. Seems to me we ought to spend a little time with them."

"Surely, not here," Oliver Fairchild murmured, smiling. "This is a pretty simple little old world down here, when you get right down to it."

"It's going to change. All of it is," Matt said mildly, but there was a glitter in the eyes behind the glasses. I thought of Rachel Vaughn and her defiant, pitiful little wheel of birth control pills, in the IHOP bathroom. I thought of John Howard's ruined face. I looked from Matt Comfort to the Fairchilds, father and son, and to Brad. All three were regarding Matt with grave, courteous interest, their faces attentive and interested. And yet, nothing he had said had changed them.

That's the difference, I thought suddenly. They change him. Somehow, when he is with the rich and powerful of Buckhead, the people who live in these big houses and belong to the clubs, who make the policies and the rules, he is changed by them. He becomes, just slightly, someone else. But they don't. He does not change them.

And then I thought, if he can't, nothing can. Nothing will. It was a disquieting thought.

There was a small silence, like a drawn breath, and then the sun-dappled late afternoon flowed on. From the distant kitchen I could hear the clink of china and silver as Teddy's mother and her cook and butler put together trays of picnic food to bring out onto the terrace.

"There's time for one more round," Oliver Fairchild said, and rose to fetch them.

I stretched, and said, "I think I'll go get out of this wet suit. Teddy, you coming?"

"Yes," Teddy said, and at that moment, from the front of the big house, we heard the silvery claxon of an automobile horn. It drifted around through the great banks of rhododendron and Cape Jessamine down to the terrace, and rode over the flabby little slappings of the pool water like birdsong.

"Eng-a-land swings like a pendulum do," sang out the little horn, in the first line of the nonsense song that was on everybody's lips that spring.

"Shit," said Matt Comfort. "It's that asshole Buzzy," and most of us on the staff groaned.

Leo DiCiccio ("Call me Buzzy") was the cherished only son of an Italian family from Boston that had migrated South. Enzo DiCiccio, Buzzy's father, had made a fortune in used cars. His pennanted dealerships bestrewed the burgeoning Atlanta suburbs like kudzu, and his tight, dark, fistlike face dominated prime-time television hours, braying of cream puffs and deals like your mama would offer you. Everyone knew Enzo DiCiccio in one way or another. Almost no one knew Buzzy. Buzzy spent every waking hour that he could escape his father's ham-fisted domination trying to remedy that.

Buzzy was short and square and so hirsute that black chest and arm hairs crawled from his shirt apertures as if they were trying to escape. He had a low forehead and a piratical Sicilian nose, and he had been one of the first of Atlanta's young bachelors, as he called himself, to adopt the collar-brushing hair and mustache of the flower children. He looked, said Matt, whom he worshiped and emulated as nearly as possible, and who detested and regularly insulted him, like a hairy telephone booth. Buzzy worked nominally for his father, who also insulted him but made up for it with an enormous, unlimited allowance and more playthings than Howard Hughes had. But in actuality Buzzy spent his time trying to screw every wellborn Atlanta debutante he came within range of, and trying to be Matt Comfort. He was conceited in the profound way only the adored only son of an Italian mama can be, glaringly conspicuous in his manner and dress and consumption of goods and services, and underfoot at *Downtown* so often that Culver Carnes thought for a while that Matt had hired him. That was Buzzy's finest hour.

He just happened to come into restaurants where we were lunching, just happened to be at the openings of the new clubs and lounges that we were invited to, just happened to have talked his father into setting him up in the penthouse apartment at the Howell House, where Matt lived in far less splendor on a lower floor. He had, it was said, a round, satin-covered bed with a mirror over it, a new XKE Jaguar every year, a powerful inboard motor boat berthed up on Lake Lanier that he had named the *Downtown II,* and an endless stash of liquor and recreational drugs in both apartment and boat. Many of Atlanta's prettiest girls dated him—once. No one, debutante or girl Friday, dated him much more than that. There was talk about Buzzy DiCiccio, vague and gray as smoke: that he had no boundaries, went too far, had sinister friends in dark shirts and white suits with no visible means of support who hung around him, had a strange, canted streak of cruelty, a darkness in him. To know him casually was to think him simply a rich buffoon who aspired to preppiedom and who could not be insulted or driven away. To know him a little better was to know you were very wrong about that. Everyone I knew who knew

Buzzy was just a shade afraid of him under the contempt.
Everyone but Matt.

He came around the side of the house grinning and
swaggering. He wore tartan swim trunks and a blue oxford
cloth shirt loose over it, both abysmally wrinkled. He wore
tinted round wire-rimmed sunglasses. He wore, as Matt
often did, Bass Weejuns without socks. The only difference
that I could see was that a small gold cross or pendant of
some sort glinted in the mat of black hair on his chest, and
gold and diamonds winked from his short, hairy fingers.

At his side, honey hair cascading over her face, eyelet
cover-up only marginally covering a minute black swim-
suit, sauntered Alicia, hipshot and lazy.

"Well, he's finally succeeded in being you, Matt,"
Hank grinned. "Right down to the accessories."

"Bite my ass," Matt said. He did not move on his
chaise, but I could sense that his small body had stiff-
ened like a terrier's on point.

"Sorry we're late," Buzzy shouted, "but I couldn't get
this girl out of the shower."

"Buzzy, you are such a fool," Alicia said in her wispy
voice, and he grinned ferally.

"I hope you got plenty of booze, Oliver," he said to
Oliver Fairchild, who inclined his head politely toward
him. "This pretty thing has plumb wore me out."

Among his other less than endearing traits, Buzzy
continually affected what he thought to be a Southern
accent. It gave his offensive words about Alicia a cast of
slow, thick sleaziness. I am sure that I saw Teddy's
father flinch ever so slightly.

"Plenty, plenty," Oliver Fairchild said. "Let me get
you something. Let's see, I've got gin and tonic, and—"

"A double one of those for me," Buzzy said, looking
to see what Matt was drinking. "And another for this little
gal here."

"I don't believe I care for anything," Alicia said, and coiled herself down like a cat in the sun on the grass next to Matt's chaise.

"Hello, boss," she said.

"Alicia," Matt said, and nodded. He drank down the rest of his drink.

"I take it you know Buzzy," he said to Oliver Fairchild. "His daddy sells lots of cars."

"Well, I certainly know his father," Oliver Fairchild said, smiling at Buzzy. "See him at the Commerce Club sometimes. He's always talking about his boy, real proud of you, he is. Glad to meet you, Buzzy."

"Oliver," Buzzy said, nodding carelessly. But his swarthy face reddened.

We drank in the sort of silence that Buzzy habitually engendered for a small space of time, and then Buzzy said, "I was just with Ben Cameron, Matt, and he told me about the new series you're doing. The Focus thing. Fine idea; I told him so. Told him what I'll tell you: that's right up my alley. I want to be a part of that baby. I've got some dynamite ideas; I'll tell you over lunch or dinner one night next week. I could take one of the committees off your hands—"

"We're not very far along with it, Buzzy," Matt said.

I looked at him, my heart beginning to beat faster.

"Are we going to do it, then?" I said. "I mean, are you thinking about it?"

Matt looked at me silently.

"Don't I take care of you, Smoky?" Brad said.

I looked at him; he was smiling carelessly, lounging in his chair, but there was something steely in his face. Matt turned his eyes to Brad, but he still did not speak.

"Yeah, we're going to do it," he said finally. "As you probably already know. Ben Cameron went to see Culver and Dr. King the same day, and it was a done deal before I even knew about it. Ben insisted on you and Geary, and King insisted on John Howard, and Culver almost wet his knickers agreeing. It's going to be a monthly series, the Focus Report. The first one is going to cover day care; you'll get on it in the next week or so, when Lucas is back. I'm not even going to ask how you managed that one, Smoky, although it does appear your boyfriend had a little something to do with it."

He smiled at Brad. It was not a smile you'd particularly want to see again. I blushed red and hot. I knew how it must seem to him: the two major stories I had done so far had been at the behest of someone else. I thought that I would pay for Focus.

"Just a suggestion to Ben the other day, when Smoky and I were at the house," Brad smiled lazily. "He was there trying to soften my old man up to do something about Boy. It was nothing more than you and I have talked about one time or another, Matt; trying to get Focus to do something concrete, get some real teeth. I didn't push Smoky on Ben. She and he hit it off immediately."

"I'll bet," Alicia murmured.

"Actually, it's a good idea, and Ben got it through to Culver when it would have taken me a year," Matt said, and I sighed in relief. He could be fair; I forgot that sometimes. Fair and generous. I was surprised only because I knew that he did not like Brad. He tolerated him when he joined us for drinks or lunch, but he did not treat him with the affectionate, careless jibing that he accorded his staff. Brad knew it and I knew it. Brad professed not to understand it, but I did: I was one of his people, even when he was annoyed with me, as he often was. Matt did not easily allow anyone to lay a claim to one of Comfort's People.

"I'm really doing it?" I said.

"You really are. After, of course, you've finished the guide and your YMOG every month."

"All right, look, tell me what I'm going to be doing for it," Buzzy said. "Cameron all but insisted. How about this? We could use a different one of Dad's demonstrators every month to . . . to deliver food baskets down in the projects, or something. Yeah, Dad would love that, and we'd get hell's own amount of free air time—"

Hank made a stifled snorting sound and took a hasty gulp of his drink, and Teddy got up abruptly, murmuring something about helping her mother. Alicia smiled sweetly at Buzzy and then at Matt. Matt stared at Buzzy, and then said, "That's the shittiest idea I ever heard in my life, Buzzy. But—" and he held up a hand to Buzzy's purpling face, "I appreciate the thought. Tell you what: want to be the next YMOG? Smoky could interview you one night this week, or more, if it takes it. Take her to dinner; we'll pay for it. Run you in the July issue, with the flag on the cover—"

"Well, I could probably work that in," Buzzy said casually, his face suffusing with red pride. "I'll call you, Smoky."

"Do," I said. My punishment for the Focus piece, I knew, had begun.

In the middle of the next week Hank and I went out to the airport after work to meet Tom Gordon, who was flying in from Washington. Lucas Geary was staying on over the long weekend with his family in Baltimore. I don't know why that surprised me, but it did. I had somehow never thought of Lucas as having parents, a hometown, an everyday arena in a particular time and place. He seemed to exist, to me, only within the realm of my comprehension. I said as much to Hank, and he laughed.

"If Lucas Geary falls in an empty forest, will he make a sound?"

"If Lucas Geary did not exist, it would be necessary to invent him," I added, laughing, too.

Rush hour traffic was bad that evening, and we were half an hour late getting to the airport. Hank had told Tom to meet him outside the Delta Airlines baggage claim, and when we pulled up, he was there, leaning against a concrete pillar with his coat over his shoulder and his shirtsleeves rolled up his dark arms, staring at the ground. His black hair fell over his eyes, and there was fatigue in every line of his tall, loose body, but he still looked as elegant and attenuated as a fashion sketch in *Esquire*. As I always did when I had not seen him for a while, I thought what a spectacularly handsome man he was. I felt the familiar small tug of shyness, of diffidence, that the sheer physical impact of Tom could produce in me. He was as dear to me, now, as any friend I had, but it was not possible to look upon him and wonder, sometimes, what those arms would feel like around you, how that mouth would feel . . .

I shook my head slightly in annoyance, and Hank touched the horn, and Tom looked up and smiled his quick white smile, and was simply Tom again, funny and eccentric and sweet. I felt a rush of affection for him that had nothing to do with his arms and mouth.

"Going my way, sailor?" I leered out the window, and he reached in and kissed me on the forehead and threw his bag in the backseat and climbed in.

"You bet I am," he said. "You two look better to me than anything I've seen in the last two weeks."

"Bad trip?" Hank said, maneuvering the car out into the stream of Atlanta-bound traffic.

"Not so good," Tom said, and I looked around at him in surprise. Tom was an inveterate travel enthusiast; his office was full of maps and guide books and airline schedules, and he often dropped such wistful bits of arcana as, "Do you know what you'd hit first if you sailed straight out from Saint Simon's Island?"

"What?" one of us would say. "England? Ireland?"

"Madagascar."

His face was slack and his eyes were closed wearily. I thought suddenly that he would look like that when he was very old, or ill: handsome, distinguished, but depleted. Empty.

"Tell," I said.

"Not yet. First I'd like to go to Harry's and have about eight beers and a steak sandwich. Lucas has had us living off stuff like lox and bagels and gefilte fish. I've been dreaming about Harry's. Y'all got time?"

"Sure," Hank said. I nodded.

"I thought Lucas was Catholic, if he was anything," Hank said.

"He is. Go figure," Tom said.

We drove in the soft twilight to Harry's, on Spring Street, and went inside the dark, low building and found a booth. From outside you could hear, faintly, the swish of traffic outbound to the suburbs, and an occasional blaring horn, but inside, in the high, corrallike wooden booths there was only light from the guttering candles and the pink and green jukebox, and the sound of soft voices from other booths, and country music. The tabletops and the backs and sides of the booths were so crosshatched with carvings—initials, names, dates, phrases—that they were like some kind of living moss, a fur of lives frozen forever on the tundras of Harry's tabletops. I ordered a steak sandwich and a Coke and Hank and Tom had beers, and we sat back and sighed. It was a womblike darkness, warm and elemental. I liked Harry's. It was a rest from the places we usually went.

Harry's made a proper steak sandwich, with black-grilled filets, smothered in onions and doused with steak sauce. They sounded awful and tasted wonderful. When we had finished and ordered coffee, Hank looked at Tom, and said, "So?"

Tom puffed out his cheeks and exhaled slowly, and said, "So. I don't know. It . . . wasn't what I thought. Out there, I mean. The youth culture, the ones who hold the be-ins, the ones who make such great editorial photographs. They don't seem to be about anything, except dressing up and smoking pot. Drugs; Hank, I didn't know there were so many drugs out there. Nobody is . . . straight. Virtually all of 'em are stoned, on LSD, or banana peels, or Mellow Yellow, or whatever is new and cheap this week. It's this kind of mishmash of drugs and music and sex—my God, the sex, they do it everywhere, with anybody, all the time—and astrology, the I Ching, incense, slogans: Make love, not war. Turn on, tune in, drop out. Power to the people. And the rhetoric. They call it freedom, or license, love, community—but it's nothing. They don't do anything. It's not anything."

"What about the radicals?" Hank said. "What about the activists?"

"Radicals? Activists? Not in that bunch, not in the freaks and heads we went looking for. They're all too stoned. Any sense we got of radicalism, of activism, centers around the war. That's going to be mean, children. You can feel it coming, you can feel the anger and the violence building around that baby. Marches, riots, even Dr. King came out against it in New York. That's the story we probably ought to be following, if we're going to do anything national on the kids. I don't think we have a real sense down here how big and bad that war is going to get, and how fast . . . "

He paused, and drank off his coffee, and rubbed his eyes hard with his fist.

"There's something coming," he said. "Everything's

changing. Everything is about to blow. I can't put my finger on it, but it's out there. There's this song, 'For What It's Worth.' Stephen Sills. It starts out, 'There's something happening here/what it is ain't exactly clear.' Everybody's singing it out there. It's like everybody feels it . . . "

The back of my neck felt cool, as if a small wind had kissed it, passing by.

"What do you mean, Tom?" I said.

"It's so vague, just a feeling, but God, it's a strong one," he said. "You know, you've got this whole youth thing; we all know about that, the funny costumes and the music and all; it's what Matt sent us out after. But now, suddenly, there's this whole new counterculture thing springing up, that says that everybody who isn't them is the enemy, the bad guys. I mean everybody. That's us, for Christ's sake. You and me and Hank. Us. And all along we thought we were on the side of the angels. All this rage . . .

"And then, the Negroes. It's not nonviolence now, not anymore, not in the big cities where we've been. It's militance, black power, Black Panthers. Guns. It doesn't feel good to be in the middle of it out there. They don't want us, not any of us. Not even the 'good' whites, the ones who believe, who marched, who fought—I don't know where that leaves most of us. Hell, I thought we were just getting used to the nonviolent business, comfortable with that. And now there's this other. It's like the movement died before it really got going, and some kind of revolution is being born."

"God, it sounds ominous," Hank said, after a moment. I felt an involuntary shiver shake me, and rubbed the top of my bare arms with my hands. Tom looked at me, and I forced a smile and said, "Harry keeps his air-conditioning too high."

"I don't mean to sound apocalyptic," Tom said. "I'm probably just tired, and I know I'm confused. I mean, shit. You've got yippies and hippies and lovers and moth-erfuckers and draft dodgers and bra burners and pot and LSD and Black Panthers and freaks and gays and acid rock—I don't know what it all means. I can't take it in, somehow. I think maybe I'm just . . . past this. Too old."

"Don't be silly," I said vehemently. I knew that he was only thirty-one. But then, perhaps that was, now, too old. I might be, myself. Too old, at twenty-seven.

"Will you do the story that way?" Hank said. "To reflect that . . . that dichotomy? It could be good, but you'd have to add a good bit of text—"

"I don't know if there is a story out there, not a single one," Tom said. "If there is, it's damned sure not what we thought it was. It's not a children's crusade. It's not a crusade of any kind. I think about that Yeats poem, you know, 'the center cannot hold, mere anarchy is loosed upon the world.' It's more like a war. It's like the whole country is suddenly at war with itself."

There was a pause, and then he said, "I'm going to ask Matt to freelance the art direction out. Rethink it, make an editorial piece of it. The photos should be good. Lucas was excited. I just know I can't do it."

There did not seem to be anything left to say. We fin-ished our coffee and drove Tom back downtown to the Y. It was full dark, and all along Spring Street the thick, poignant smell of mimosa drifted into the open windows.

"I think urban mimosa trees can make themselves invisible," I said. "You can always smell mimosa in cities in the spring, but you can never see them. It's like they're a different species."

"It's how they survive," Tom said. "If they were visible, some asshole would cut them down and put up parking lots."

We watched him cross the sidewalk and enter the door of the huddled yellow-brown brick building. The light over the door seemed dim and mean, and I thought of the Church's Home. All of a sudden Tom Gordon seemed the loneliest man alive.

"I want him to be happy," I said to Hank. "I don't want him living in this dump. I want things to be better for him. Whatever he saw on this trip seems to be just eating him alive."

Hank was silent as he threaded the narrow streets around the bus station, and pulled onto the northeast expressway toward Buckhead. We were halfway to Colonial Homes before he said, "It's not just what he saw out there, not just the story. He . . . had somebody in Washington. They broke up. He told me on the phone last night."

"Oh, God," I said. "I'm so sorry. She must be the biggest fool in the world to let him go."

Hank was silent for another space of time, and then said, "It wasn't a she, Smokes. It was a he."

The air seemed to ring around my head, as if there had been a silent explosion. I felt stunned and stupid, unable to fit thought together.

"Oh," I said. And then, "But he was married . . . I mean, he was married, wasn't he?"

"He was. Legitimately. He tried awfully hard to make it work. It wasn't until long after they married that he found out."

"But . . . wouldn't you have some idea? Wouldn't you know somehow?"

"Are you kidding? In the early 1950s, on a farm in the South Georgia wiregrass? Hell, no, you wouldn't know. He didn't know. He's a good man, Smoky. The best I know, maybe. He wouldn't have married her if he'd had any idea. She knew before he did, that's why they broke up. She'll never forgive him, she'll never give him a moment's peace. And he'll take it all, because he thinks he deserves it."

I felt tears flood up into my eyes, and down over my cheeks. I could not speak past the cold salt lump in my throat.

"Are you going to be able to handle this?" Hank said. "I hope you are. I wouldn't have told you if I'd thought it would make a difference to you. Tom needs some friends right now. Tell me how you feel."

"I feel . . . " I said, sniffling a little, "I feel like I love him an awful lot and that will never change. And . . . I feel relieved that everytime I look at him now I don't have to wonder why he doesn't find me attractive enough to make a move on me."

Hank began to laugh, and hugged me with one arm, hard.

"That is such a fine thing to say that I think I'll buy you a piece of IHOP apple pie," he said. And he did.

"The thing for you to remember is that you need to be quiet," Luke Geary said a few days later. "Today is for looking, for seeing how it is. Let me and John do the talking. Later, if it goes okay, you can go back for some interviews. But you'll blow it for good and all if you talk much today."

"Thank you so very much, Matt Comfort," I said. "Why don't you not talk and let me shoot your photographs?"

We were in his Morgan, humid wind buffeting our faces, inching our way through early morning traffic over toward the State Capitol. I was annoyed with him. I had thought he would relish the Focus assignment, but he seemed to regard it as puffery, chamber of commerce flackery. He had been different since he returned from the swing around the country, quieter, nervier, more inward. Not nearly, as Matt would say, so bone-deep sorry.

He turned to study me from behind the tinted aviator glasses. His carroty hair and beard blew in the wind, and there were patches of peeling sunburn on his nose and forehead. I knew that he would never tan.

"Look, Smoky, nobody thinks you can't do this piece," he said. "But you don't know anything yet. You don't know anything about the people we'll be seeing, or the place we'll be going, or the way they do things there. You're a white girl in a pretty dress; that's all these folks will see. Not your talent, not your liberal sensibilities. They don't like white people and they don't trust them and they don't talk freely to them. They talk to me only because I've already gone there with John, and they love him. After they see that he's going to be working with you, get used to you, then they'll talk a little. And you know Matt said that the format will be to show existing conditions first, and then, in the next report, show what Focus has been able to do about them. You only need your eyes today."

"Not my mouth, in other words."

"You said it, not me."

I drummed my fingers on the door of the Morgan, but I knew he was right. Finally I said, smiling a little, "'I Am a Camera.'"

"Thank you, Sally Bowles."

"You can read?"

"Actually, no," he said, stretching his long, lanky body so that the bones of his spine snapped in sequence. "Somebody read it to me. In bed."

And he leered showily at me.

"Luke, you are such an ass," I said, blushing, for some reason, to the roots of my hair. I heard him laugh softly, but I did not look over at him.

He turned the little car east on Mitchell Street, past
the courthouse, the beautiful Art Deco spire of City Hall,
and the dirty marble and granite spire of the capitol
building. He turned again, past the capitol, onto Capitol
Avenue, and we slid down abruptly into the great, fea-
tureless wasteland where most of Atlanta's Negro population lived. It was a part of the city that I had not known
existed, although now, in its midst, it struck me as naive
and stupid that I had not sensed, if not known, this other
Atlanta.

One by one, silently, we ghosted through the black
communities to the south of the city's heart:
Summerhill, Peoplestown, Joyland. I could not speak.
The desolation and poverty of some of these tiny neighborhoods seemed to me as unredeemed as they were uniform. I could not tell where one left off and another
began. But Lucas Geary seemed to know. He pointed
them out by name as we passed through, and told me a
little about each. When, I thought, had he had time to
learn the geography and ethnology of these dismal black
habitats in the bowels of Camelot? I felt stupid and shy
and young. In point of fact, I was all those things.

Many of the streets in the little communities were
unpaved. In the small, snaking warrens, wooden and
cinder-block houses crowded so closely together that
often not even a driveway separated them. It probably
did not matter; I saw very few cars. Most houses sat
squarely on the streets or sidewalks, with only a few feet
of weedy concrete or hard-packed dirt for front yards,
these littered with broken toys and bottles and trash.
Most were unpainted and some had blind eyes of cardboard or newspaper for windows. I knew that there was
city water; I saw fire hydrants. But outhouses leaned
crazily in many of the backyards. Kudzu seemed everywhere, kudzu and small, stunted, virulently green trees,

and weeds. It seemed the hectic green of a jungle reclaiming a lost city. They were lost, these miniature cities. Lost, and long had been. I saw almost no people.

Occasionally we would pass a larger cross-street with a shabby grocery store, liquor store, a pawnshop or two, and a cafe. A few people, men and teenaged boys mainly, lounged here, eyes following the Morgan as it slid through. Once or twice Lucas raised a languid hand, and I would see a black hand raised in return. But mostly he kept his eyes straight ahead. I did, too.

"Where is everybody?" I said finally, in a low voice. "Where are all the women? Where are the people going to work?"

"Most of the women are already out in Buckhead, working in the kitchens," Lucas said. "The guys mostly don't have jobs. I still don't know where they go in the daytime. They're not usually around."

Driving through Summerhill, he gestured to the right. I caught a glimpse of the blue bowl of the new stadium, and heard the muted rush of traffic on the freeway.

"That used to be a neighborhood," he said.

"Where did the people go?"

"Good question. Holy Christ. The city could raise eighteen million dollars to put up a major league stadium, and the housing authority long ago pledged fifty million bucks to wipe out the slums in a decade, but they couldn't seem to relocate a single black family whose home they knocked down, or spend a penny on communities like Vine City or Buttermilk Bottom. Ben Cameron has started, but it's going to take way too long. Shit. No wonder Stokely Carmichael goes around with his fist in the air."

"Isn't there some public housing?" I said.

"Oh, yeah. Sure. There were exactly four, since about the mid-thirties, until Ben took office, and there'll be lag time till the new ones get underway. Atlanta's going to be lucky if somebody doesn't literally light a fire under it this summer."

I was silent while he piloted the Morgan through the hot, nearly empty streets over to DeKalb Avenue past the odd little white enclave of Cabbagetown, around the sprawling Fulton Bag and Cotton Mill, and into another small warren of dirt streets just past it. The street we were on was narrow and deeply rutted, and overgrown with weeds on its verges. It climbed steeply to a high point on which nothing but a small grove of tough little urban trees and more kudzu stood, and was lined on either side of its lower portion with sagging asbestos-sided houses the twins of those I had seen in the other neighborhoods. Lucas slowed the Morgan and stopped in front of one, the yard of which was planted with rioting old-fashioned sweetheart rose bushes and the latticed porch deeply shaded with purple wisteria. The smell of the invisible urban mimosa reached out again. I smiled involuntarily. The little house was shabby, but its trim was freshly painted and its dirt yard swept, and I could hear, from somewhere around back, the laughter of children.

"Is this it?"

"Yep," he said. "The official day care center of Pumphouse Hill, Mrs. Mamie Lou Roberts, proprietor. John picked her out. She's an old friend of his. There are old women like her in all the neighborhoods, community women who just take in children who don't have any other place to go while their mothers are at work, and they feed them what they can, and look after them until the women get home at night. God knows what Mrs. Roberts uses for money. I think the mothers pay what they can, but it couldn't be enough to feed all these kids, and buy mattresses and blankets for naps, and heat for

the winter. And a lot of the mothers are children themselves; young teenagers. No husbands, and their families
have kicked them out."

"Where in the hell are the fathers?" I said fiercely.

"I'm sure the mamas would like to know," he said.
"Negro men don't hang around these communities
much. If there are any jobs, they sure aren't down here."

"Aren't there programs? Doesn't the government do
something for children like these? The city, or the state,
or Johnson's new stuff?" I said, despair swamping me. I
would not have believed the communities of Atlanta's
Southeast if I had not seen them.

"I guess so, yeah," Luke said, dismissing them with a
flick of his hand. "Ben's got the promise of a lot of stuff
from Johnson. But nobody down here knows what they
are, or how to apply for them, or even what the conditions
are that have to be met before you can get the dough.
Jesus, a great many of the old women who do the most
good for the kids can't read or write, and the younger
ones, who can, are so damned tired they can't get to the
right office to apply; what government office ever kept
anything but government hours? That's one thing Ben
Cameron hopes this series can do, get the right local
agencies in touch with the right people, cut through the
damned bureaucracy and red tape. Give the problem a
human face, as ol' Culver baby so righteously said. Make
people see."

"Are we going in?" I asked, not wanting to.

"We'll wait for John. We'll be off on the wrong foot if
we don't."

We sat silently in the Morgan. The sun climbed
higher into the whitening vault of the sky. A stunted
chinaberry tree shaded us, and on the other side, in a
pool of pink dust, a thin black dog slept. It was very
quiet; the children's voices seemed to have drifted away

on the small hot wind, and I heard no traffic noise, and no birdsong.

Finally I said, "This is the worst place I have ever been. This is not even like the United States. How can this be a part of Atlanta?"

Luke sighed, and turned to me. The sly laziness was gone from his eyes, and I thought that he looked, all of a sudden, as tired as I had ever seen him.

"You saw the worst of it this morning, Smoky," he said. "I brought you through the bad ones, the flat-out ghettos, on purpose. There are better Negro communities in Atlanta, some of them okay, some of them not far from luxurious, over in the Southwest. Atlanta's got one of the richest Negro communities in the country, though nobody hears much about that. They don't want publicity. And it's got a pretty big black power structure—businessmen, clergy, the folks at the Atlanta University complex. They've worked with Dr. King and are starting to work with Ben Cameron; they respect him. He'll get a lot done through them, if time holds out for him. He's gone after as much federal money as there is up there: Head Start, Model Cities, EOA, Job Corps, urban renewal, the whole nine yards. It'll start to kick in sooner or later, and in some of the older, more stable neighborhoods, where people have lived for two and three generations, they know that, and they can hang on.

"But there are places, mainly in the Southeast, the ones I brought you through today, that haven't gotten the word. They're ghettos; as bad as anything in Detroit, or Newark. They're full of dirt-poor, hopeless rural Negroes from all over the South who came here in absolute desperation looking for something better, and didn't find it, and don't have a history with the neighborhoods, or know about the federal programs, or give a shit, or even know who Ben Cameron is. They care about where the next meal is coming from, or the next drink, period. They don't see anything out there on the horizon. They're the last ones the federal money will reach, and the ones that need it worst and first, and when trouble starts, it's going to be there. Here."

"Why didn't you show me some of the others?" I said. "Why did you want me to think it was all like this?"

"Because you don't know shit about Atlanta, although you think you do," he said. "Because you think it's all swimming pools in Buckhead and maître d's knowing your name. You have some talent and you have some guts, and I'd hate to see you waste them on what Comfort will give you."

"You take what he offers you quick enough," I said, stung. "You spend more time with him than any four of the rest of us."

"Yeah, but I've seen and done the other, too," he said. "I've put in my time in the underbelly, where things happen in the South. You need to, too. And he's not about to let you do that. I will."

I was quiet. His words made me angry, but I could feel a solid shape under them that I knew to be truth. I looked around me at Pumphouse Hill. To the west, I could see, dimly through the heat haze and smog of many dingy, low-lying industrial buildings, the skyline of Atlanta. It looked as ethereal, as unreachable, as the Emerald City must have seemed to Dorothy. As it must seem, every day, to the people of Pumphouse Hill.

"Tell me about Mrs. Roberts," I said. "Why her, particularly? What's her story?"

"Well, like I said, John knows her," Luke said. "He used to stay with her some when he first came to Atlanta. I think he preached a little at her church. Kind of an internship, and she put him up. She's got three or four children who cut out and went North and left her with grandchildren—that happens a lot here; grand-mothers raising generations of children—and gradually all the young women down here who were trying to work outside started asking her to look after their kids, and pretty soon she was kind of the local granny–day care person. Her husband died years ago, and she hasn't seen her son in years, and she needs the few pennies she gets for looking after them. John says more times than she'll tell you, she looks after them free. She loves kids. But she needs literally everything; some of the children come at daybreak and stay till after dark, and she has to scrounge food to feed them three meals, and blankets for them to roll up in for naps, and some way to keep them warm in winter. She's only got space heaters and an old gas stove. Her church helps when it can, and I know John gives her money regularly. But she's got fifteen or sixteen children at any given time, and there's never enough. Forget schooling. She can't read or write her-self, except her name."

"What will Focus do for her?" I said. My eyes stung.

"Focus will make her real to a lot of people with bucks," Luke said. "Show her face and the kids' faces around Buckhead and Ansley Park, places like that, where somebody could write one check and feed those kids for a month. John says sometimes they have cereal and water three meals a day. Let Atlanta know it's not all the Braves and the freeway down in the Southeast. Give a name to all the tired old black ladies they see waiting for the Twenty-three Oglethorpe bus. Maybe stir up the folks at the capitol to shell out some more, or at least get the city agencies to get down here and see what they can do for her. And then for other old women like her, who look after the children. It's easy to think of the people down here as 'them,' statistics, in a part of town you don't ever go, or even think about. It's harder to ignore them when they're little kids named Otis and Ivan and Patricia, looking right at you."

"And that's what you'll do, shoot the faces," I said.

"And that's what you'll do, write the names," he said.

Something swelled silently in my chest and burst, filling me out to the ends of my fingers, the top of my head.

"Yes," I said. "That's what I'll do. I'll write the names."

"Good," he said, and then, "Here comes John."

I looked up, expecting to see the dust of an automobile, but saw instead the tall figure of John Howard climbing the hill, walking easily in the middle of the road. He wore, astonishingly, overalls like the farmers in the flat country fields around Savannah wore, faded blue denim with buckled straps over his shoulders. He wore no shirt, and the sun poured a wash of bronze-red over his bare arms and shoulders. He was not powerfully muscled, but his shoulders were broad and square, and the waist that I could see, when his arms swung, through the low-cut sides of the overalls, was narrow. I thought that he was built like Tom Gordon. He was hatless and had a red bandanna stuck in the pocket of the overalls, and wore heavy work shoes on his feet. For a moment he looked absurd, like a man in costume, but then he did not. He moved and wore the work clothes as one whose primary allegiance had always been to the earth.

"Was he a farmer before he went into the ministry?" I said to Luke. "Did he grow up on a farm?"

Luke laughed. "Shit, no," he said. "He grew up in a suburb of St. Louis. His father is an OB-GYN, and his mother was his nurse. Before he went into the ministry he wasn't anything but a prep school kid and, from what I hear, an awesome stud."

"What happened to him?"

Luke looked down at me.

"I guess the movement did," he said.

I was suddenly weary of it all: the undercurrents that I alone could not feel, the innuendos I alone did not catch, the gulfs and continents of painful knowledge that I alone did not seem to possess.

"So does he just like to dress up and play Farmer in the Dell, or is he trying to impress us with his body?" I snapped.

"Any men he might run into down here are apt to be right off the farm," Luke said mildly. "It's a courtesy to them. You know, when in Rome. And then, the kids you're going to see this morning don't know any men but farmers, most of them. They don't see any men, much, except their granddaddies once in a while, and they all wear overalls like that. A man in a suit would scare them to death. A man in a suit is The Man."

"I'm sorry," I whispered. "I feel like a jerk. I should have thought. I should have worn jeans myself—"

"No, you're all right," he said. "A white woman in jeans would probably confuse the hell out of them. They'll just think you're a social worker and ignore you. That's what we want, today."

John Howard came up alongside the Morgan and slapped it on its squared-off rump.

"We ready?" he said. "Hello, Smoky."

"Hello, John," I said.

"I came by last night to talk to Mrs. Roberts," John Howard said. "Told her not to pretty things up, or try to get the kids to mind their manners. She said she wouldn't. She understands what we're trying to do: to get help for her kids, and the only way to do it is to show what she needs. It's a good time for us. She's down to grits this close to the end of the month, and those are cold. Her stove's been out for two or three days. She's been heating water to scrub the floors and bathe the children over the outdoor fireplace."

Lucas nodded and got out of the car and picked up his camera bags. I followed. We walked behind John Howard up to the porch of the little house and waited while he rapped on the screen door. It was torn, and had been patched with what looked like duct tape. The inside of the house was as dark as a cave.

"Round to the back," a low, beautiful voice called, and we went back down the steps and around the side of the house. It sat up on piled bricks off the bare earth, and the ubiquitous kudzu and wisteria vines gave it an almost exotic air, like a little jungle hut. We paused at a gate in a high wire fence, and I could smell flowers and damp-watered earth and something else, something rich and dark and wonderful, like coffee, and frying meat. The laughter and shrieks of children were louder here.

A Negro woman came to the gate and unlocked it, and stepped back, and we went in. She was a mountain of a woman, very dark and shapeless in a clean, faded housedress. It was sleeveless, and her great upper arms looked like shining, smoked sides of meat. They shook when she moved. She wore men's shoes with the toes cut out, and a bright turban wrapped around her small, shapely head. Perspiration ran down her wrinkled face, and a wide white smile split the ashy web of fine wrinkles on it. She had a gold tooth in the middle of her mouth; it caught the morning sun like a tiny flame.

"Come in here, darlin'," she said to John Howard, and hugged him hard as he stepped through the gate. "Mmm, mmm. Need to put some meat on those bones, you do. Who been feedin' you?"

"Nobody as good as you," he said, and nodded toward us.

"Mama Roberts, this is Lucas Geary and Smoky O'Donnell, that I told you about last night. They're going to help me tell folks about what you do down here, get you some help. Like I said, today we're not going to talk much. Smoky's just going to look and listen, and Lucas is going to take a few pictures. That's all. The kids should just go on doing what they always do. We won't be long."

The old woman nodded at us, gravely and politely.

"Glad to have you," she said. "We ain't got much, but it sure is more than I thought it was going to be, and you're welcome to share it with us."

"Thank you," I said, and smiled, and she patted me on the arm as if I had been a child, and turned and waddled into the fenced backyard. I followed John and Luke, not wanting to see what I knew I would.

But it was not what I had thought, not what Luke had told me it would be, not what John Howard had indicated I would find. The little backyard was full of small tables with bright paper cloths on them, and folding chairs full of chattering children. They were just finishing what I could tell, even from a distance, was a breakfast of ham and eggs and biscuits, and there were paper cups of milk and orange juice beside the paper plates of food. In one corner of the yard, under a drooping mulberry tree, was a pile of rolled-up sleeping bags. They looked bright and new. At the rear of the yard, against the fence, a big camp stove had been set up, and a young woman was turning bacon and piling biscuits on a plate with deft-handed ease. She wore a long, bright dashiki and had an Afro, glinting coppery in the sun, and on her round little cat's face were large black sunglasses. She did not stop what she was doing, did not turn when she heard our voices.

It was John Howard who finally spoke.

"Well, I see you got some other help in here, Mama Roberts," he said. His voice was flat and uninflected.

"Came this morning before light," the old woman said happily. "Heard a little knock and went to the door and here was this child, all bent over under that there stove and with piles of food all around her, and several more of 'em like her, carryin' blankets and sleeping bags and stuff. Looked like angels of the Lord, they did. Honey," she called toward the young woman, "come on over here and meet this boy and his friends. They gon' help Mama Roberts, too."

The young woman put down the plate of biscuits and turned and came across the bare earth, with its pale matted ghosts of dead grass, toward us. I could see that she was slender and small, and even behind the black glasses, very pretty. She had high cheekbones and smooth golden skin.

"Hello, John," she said. Her voice was light and soft, a Southern voice. But it was not warm.

"Hello, Juanita," John Howard said.

"Y'all know each other?" Mrs. Roberts said. "I thought this baby girl here say she was from . . . Where did you say, honey? New York? Up North somewhere—"

"We're in Philadelphia now," the young woman said. "I'm just visiting Atlanta."

"And just happened to be passing by with food and sleeping bags," John Howard said pleasantly. "Yeah, Mama Roberts. We know each other. Juanita here may be a Yankee now, but she's a Southern girl at heart. Born in . . . I believe it was Tupelo, wasn't it?"

"Yes," the young woman said, looking at him steadily. Except for the glance and a nod at Lucas and me, she never did acknowledge our presence.

"I heard you all were around," John Howard said. He turned to the old woman.

"Mama Roberts, this is not the way," he said.

The old woman looked around at the children, seemingly oblivious to us as they ate and drank and laughed, and back at John Howard, and then at the ground.

"I'll take it any way I can get it, John," she said. "They came. They had blankets and food. They cooked it. They served it. They smiled. They didn't charge me for it. They didn't ask me all kinds of questions to see did I qualify for it. They didn't say they gon' do a study and get back to me. They said they glad to do it and they gon' try to fix it so it happen every day, try to see about that before they go on back North. You do that for me, then you can come in here an' tell me this ain't the way."

"It's not the way," he said, softly, as if to no one in particular. He looked at us, then, and motioned for us to follow him, and turned away to leave the backyard.

Behind him, the young woman said, "John, have you forgotten Jonathan?"

He stopped, and turned and looked at her. I could see that his face darkened; in it, the ridge of scar down his forehead into his eyebrow stood out lividly. But his expression did not change.

"No," he said. "I haven't forgotten Jonathan. Have you forgotten the bridge?"

"Yes," she said, and there was something akin to defiance in her voice. "I didn't have a bit of trouble forgetting that."

"Well, I never will," he said, and walked around the house and out to the street. We followed behind him, not understanding, but not wanting to speak, either.

We still had not spoken when Luke had stowed his camera bags into the Morgan's trunk and I had gotten into the front seat beside him, and closed the door.

"Want us to drop you off?" Luke said, finally, to John Howard.

"No," John said. "I'm going to walk awhile. Sorry about this. It doesn't really change anything. I'll find us somebody else, and set it up. We'll make your deadline."

"Just let me know," Lucas said. John Howard nodded,

and struck off up the road toward the top of the hill. Luke started the Morgan and eased it off back down the dirt road, the way we had come.

"What was all that about?" I said finally.

"I'm not sure," Luke said. "I think I know, but I'm not really sure. I think Jonathan is Jonathan Daniels. He was a white guy who was shot and killed in the Lowndes County voter registration drive. I know he and John were good friends. I think the bridge is the Edmund Pettus; she must have been there when John was hurt. And I think she's a Panther. I know they have free breakfast programs for the kids in the ghettos, and other free stuff. And I heard they were in town. I don't know how they'd have found out about the Focus piece, but it doesn't surprise me."

"She was something to him, wasn't she?" I said.

"Might have been," he said noncommittally.

"She was," I said. I knew it was true. "Even if she's not now, she was once."

"Does it matter?"

"Well, of course it doesn't matter. I just wish I knew more about him."

"And what would you like to know about him, Smoky?" Luke said, grinning, and I knew what the slow sound in his voice meant. I was angry with him once more.

"I just wish I knew more about his women and a hell of a lot less about yours," I said waspishly.

"Well, then, want shall be your master, as the man said," Lucas Geary said, still grinning, and gunned the Morgan off the dirt road. Just before we hit the paved street, I saw a car parked on the weedy side of the track leading back into Pumphouse Hill. It was a dark red Mustang, shining new, with tan leather seats, and on the backseat there was a small pile of clothing: neatly pressed khaki trousers and a folded blue oxford cloth shirt, and polished brown loafers. I knew that it was John Howard's car, and began to laugh, and Luke began to laugh, too, and we were still laughing when we passed the capitol and drove back into the tall morning shadows of Five Points, downtown.

8

JOHN HOWARD WAS AS GOOD AS HIS WORD. HE FOUND US
another day care project to shoot for Focus, and Luke
and I went the very next day to cover it. It was in
Summerhill, a better neighborhood than Pumphouse
Hill, but only marginally. It was here, Luke told me,
that Ben Cameron had stood atop a car, trying to talk
the heat out of an impending race riot during a past
incendiary summer, and had been toppled off.
Summerhill had once been an affluent white neighborhood of large, two-story frame houses and sheltering
old hardwoods, but now it housed tiny tenements and
apartments into which some ten thousand poor Negroes
were crammed. As in Pumphouse Hill, almost all of
them were migrants from the rural South. Summerhill
was a ghetto in every sense of the word, even if it ran to
two-story tenements instead of one-room shotguns.

Mrs. Carrie Holmes lived in a downstairs apartment
off Love Street. She was a tall, thin, middle-aged
woman, almost yellow of skin, cool and formal with us.
She would not, John had said, make the impression that

the earth-motherly Mama Roberts would have, but she was fully as devoted to her children, and in a way, did more with less, since she had virtually no backyard, and her children's play yard was the sagging front and back porches of the old Victorian house, and the simmering streets around it.

"She probably won't talk to you much," John said. "Her boy was shot in Mississippi during Freedom Summer, and he still walks with a cane. She was always remote, except with children, and that didn't help the way she thinks about white folks. But she'll be courteous, and her kids are great. There's one little boy, Andre—look for Andre. I think he's your focus for this piece."

"What about Andre?" I said.

"If he's there, Andre will show you," John Howard said.

He was not going with us this time. He had, he said, some people he needed to see, and they were leaving town that afternoon. He had cleared us with Mrs. Holmes. There shouldn't be any problems.

"Will it help that I'm a crippled civil rights hero, too?" Luke said, grinning. He had brought a cane with him that day, something I had never seen him do before, and I noticed the top of an Ace bandage showing over his work shoe. He limped heavily, too. The limp came and went, but I had never seen the cane or the bandage before. I raised my eyebrow at him.

"Humidity gets to it sometimes," he said. "And the walking yesterday. It gets a lot of sympathy, too."

"It won't get you any from Mrs. Holmes," John Howard said, but he smiled slightly. "But the kids will love it. Is it bothering you much?"

"Only when I dance," Luke said. "What about your eye? Do you ever feel that?"

His tone was merely interested, as Luke's tone of voice often was. Almost everything interested him.

"Only when I laugh," said John Howard, and I thought then that it was a bond they would have all their lives, the scars of that day at the Edmund Pettus Bridge. I wondered if, many years from now, on a day of rain and heavy air, Lucas Geary's ankle would ache and he would think of John Howard, and vice versa. It gave me a strange, shy feeling, as if I were in an intimate situation with strangers. But then, that was where, I thought, I was.

Mrs. Holmes was almost silent with us, but she directed us to the back porch of the apartment where the children were having their breakfast of biscuits and weak coffee.

"Coffee?" I said, and then wished I had not. What did I know about feeding poor children?

"Church donates it," Mrs. Holmes said in a weary monotone. "It's the last thing to run out. And most of them were born drinking it. Lots of little niggers don't like milk, but they'll drink coffee."

I jerked my head up and stared hard at her. Was she taunting me? Unexpectedly she smiled, a grudging small twitch. "It's okay when we use it to each other," she said. "Just don't you do it."

"I never have," I said. I did not think that I liked Mrs. Carrie Holmes, urban saint or no.

Lucas raised the camera and squeezed off shot after shot of the children with their mugs of coffee. He could hardly have looked more conspicuous here, in this world of tiny, ragged black children, with his flaming hair and beard and his tall, boneless body, but somehow he melted into them, became a part of the furniture of the bleak porch, so that the children swirled and chattered around him as if he were one of them. Remembering his words the day before, I stood back, leaning against the side of the house, watching silently. I wore an old denim skirt and sleeveless blouse today, with scuffed loafers, so that, at least, I would not look, as he had said of my costume yesterday, like a Junior Leaguer fulfilling her service requirements.

Presently Luke dropped to one knee and began to talk to the children. He talked softly, foolishness, nonsense, and the children responded by crowing with laughter, crawling over and around him, reaching for the camera and the bright things in the camera bag, reaching out to touch his hair and beard, and the bright aluminum cane. Luke shot roll after roll of film. He did not raise his voice.

Mrs. Holmes went into the house and came back pushing a very small boy ahead of her. He looked to be younger than the others, barely toddling, and he was plainly frightened. He had a large head, out of proportion to his tiny body, and his face was moonlike, the color of shiny caramel. There were silver snailtracks of tears on his cheeks, and he looked at Luke and me out of huge brown eyes that showed a rim of white all the way around.

"Andre has been looking forward to this, but the young lady scares him," Mrs. Holmes said. "It was a white lady took him away from his mama, a little lady like that one."

She did not look at me. My face flamed.

"Why?" Luke said mildly.

"Well, his mama was beating him," Mrs. Holmes said. "He wouldn't stop shittin' in his pants. She beat him till we couldn't stand the yellin' anymore, and I called the social worker. She came and got him and put him in foster care. I went and got him, said I was his granny. He's been scared of white ladies since. I didn't know she was coming, or I'd have said no."

"She's writing this piece," Luke said. "She's a good lady and a good writer, and she's going to do these kids a lot of good. Where's Andre's mother now?"

"She's dead. She overdosed up in Pittsburgh this spring. He don't know it. He thinks she's coming back. She wasn't but sixteen herself."

I closed my eyes in pain and rage. This baby, with a dead mother herself a child, terrified now and forever of a fourth of the population of the world.

"Why in God's name would she beat a baby for messing up his pants?" I whispered.

Mrs. Holmes looked at me with ill-concealed contempt.

"He ain't a baby. He five," she said. "He just ain't never growed. Can't control his bowels. Can't speak, except to say his name. Lord knows, he says that enough, though."

"What will happen to him?" Luke said.

"I reckon I'll keep him for a while," she said. "Then maybe somebody else will take him. I don't want you to say his mother dead. I don't want this child in foster."

Luke nodded. He went and crouched down in front of the child, and touched his face gently.

"If you'll tell me your name I'll show you my car," he said in a low voice.

The child stared, and then his great face split into an enchanting smile. His eyes danced with it; his whole body seemed caught in the force of the smile.

"Andre!" he shouted. "Andre! Andre, Andre!"

"Well, come on, Andre," Luke said, swinging him up onto his shoulders. He limped heavily under the weight, but he did not stagger. He bore Andre through the dark, stifling apartment and out onto the street, where the little Morgan sat, surrounded by an honor guard of small Negro children. Luke had hired them for a nickel apiece to watch the car when we arrived.

There was a long gasp from the little boy, and then Luke set him down and he toddled as fast as his stunted legs would carry him over to the car, and hugged it. He literally hugged it, hugged the front fender and the bumper and the hood, hugged whatever part of it his short arms could encompass, and he kissed it. Luke shot swiftly as Andre hugged and kissed the Morgan, his face an epiphany of bliss.

"Andre," he crooned. "Andre, Andre."

Luke plopped him into the front seat of the Morgan and took him around the block, and as they drove away we heard his ecstatic anthem: "Andre, Andre!"

I looked at Mrs. Holmes.

"It's what he says when he's happy, when he wants to give you a present, or thank you," she said. "I told him from the first day he come to me that Andre was the most beautiful word I ever heard, and he thinks it is. He's a right happy little boy for what he's been through."

I turned away. I was determined not to cry in front of this tough, cold, loving woman.

Luke took the film straight back to his apartment and developed it, and that night we stayed late at *Downtown* and Tom and Luke and I put the first layout for Focus together. The photos were wonderful, strong black and white with a great deal of stark contrast, the faces of the children the only soft, diffused spots. We used photos of almost all of them. The lead one, a double-page spread, was a head shot of Andre kissing the Morgan, his eyes squeezed shut in rapture. I took the layout into my office and started my captions and text.

"His name is Andre," I began. "He is five years old and he can't say anything else, but he can say his name, and he shouts it aloud in joy and affirmation. Andre. His name is Andre. Remember it. . . ."

I remembered our words, Luke's and mine, the day before: "And that's what you'll do, shoot the faces."

"And that's what you'll do, write the names."

I put my head down on my typewriter and cried for a long time.

Matt loved the Focus layout and copy. He blatted the taxi horn after he had studied it, and called the whole staff in and showed it to them. He crowed and capered and grinned. He clapped Lucas and Tom Gordon on the back, and kissed me soundly on the mouth, and said that at the very least it was Peabody stuff, and maybe even Pulitzer. Then he steamed out of the office on his way upstairs to show Culver Carnes.

"This ought to buy me a fucking year of peace," he yelled back, just before the elevator bell dinged.

I went back to my office in a white dazzle of happiness and tried to get to work on captions and cutlines for the entertainment guide, but had little luck. The drumbeat of real, solid work was too loud in my blood.

Culver Carnes was ecstatic. The next day he was in Matt's office planning a press party for the venture.

"I was going to wait until we had published magazines, but that will be fall, and this is just too good to pass up," he said. "The riots in Watts and Newark and the others have had me worried; Atlanta could go up, too. We'd be fools to think it couldn't. And the Panthers have been in town, and that's not good. I took the layout over to Ben Cameron, Matt, after you left, and he asked to keep it overnight, and he's talked to Dr. King, and they both think we ought to do something with this right now. Press party, or something. Show the world what Atlanta's doing, the black and white communities together. King has agreed to let John Howard represent SCLC before the press, and said he'd see about sending a bunch of their people over—Bond, maybe, and Rosser Sellers, and some of the others who've been visible all along. He won't come himself, says it would turn into a media field day if he did, and he doesn't want to divert attention from the Focus project. I see his point. I thought the governor, and some of our civic leaders, and of course you and your staff, Smoky and this young photographer—"

Matt watched him neutrally, and I knew that he was seething that Culver Carnes had seized the piece as his own, and was hastening to make hay with it. But he was proud of it, too, and the press party would showcase *Downtown* as well as the chamber of commerce.

"Sounds like a good idea," he said. "Where did you figure on having it?"

"Well, I thought the Commerce Club. Put on a real spread, have an open bar, the works—"

"You might want to rethink that, Culver," Matt said. "It ain't exactly a bastion of racial harmony."

"Negroes have been able to eat there since 1965," Culver Carnes said.

"Yeah, but they can't join," Matt drawled. "I haven't noticed any membership drives down in the projects. I have a better idea. Let's do it at the Top of Peachtree. They've been remodeling this summer, and they're reopening next week. Let it be a grand occasion; symbolic as hell—the whole city at our feet, et cetera, et cetera. All the press guys love the Top; they spend half their time in the bar there. And Doug was one of the first owners in town to integrate, even when he didn't have to, so some of the Negro leadership go there occasionally. What do you think? They'd probably give you a real deal on the price."

Culver liked that, and so it was that on a Thursday evening in July, after a thunderstorm had whirled up out of the west and washed the city clean of the oppressive wet heat that had stifled it for weeks, Luke and Tom

Gordon and I walked across the street and around the corner in the lucent summer twilight to go to the party for our Focus piece.

Matt had wanted us all at the Top of Peachtree early, and he and Teddy and Sister and the advertising staff were already there when we got off the elevator, sitting at our favorite long table against the corner window, the rain-shined city spread out around them. I had a quick, stabbing flash of sheer community and love when I saw them: my people, in our place, waiting for me. I had never felt anything quite like it before. I had always been an outsider, I thought, even when I did not know I was. But I was outsider no more, now. I belonged to *Downtown*. I was, unquestionably and forever, one of Comfort's People.

"You all look absolutely fabulous," I said, my voice thick with joy.

They did. We all did. Matt had on a new summer-weight gray suit that set off the shock of chestnut hair and turned his eyes the color of a winter sea. It looked slightly less slept-in than his others, and he was grinning with frank satisfaction and sipping a vodka and tonic. Hank was avuncular and bankerly in a dark blue suit, and Tom Gordon looked so coolly elegant and totally wonderful in gray-striped seersucker that I felt afresh the small shock that his hawklike looks sometimes wrought in me, and thought again how utterly stupid was the lover, male or female, who could leave him. Teddy wore yellow linen and shone like the young sun, and Sister was resplendent in ruffled blue crepe up to midthigh, looking like the University of Georgia homecoming queen she had been not so long ago. Sueanne Hudspeth wore deep purple with a tiny waist and peplum and stiletto heels and looked, as Matt said, dangerous as all hell. I had a new red linen sheath and felt as vivid and glamorous as Lady Brett Ashley, whom I had always admired inordinately. Only Hank knew about Lady Brett, and as he pointed out, I had zero chance of looking like her, given my height and stubborn breasts and hips. But I loved the feeling, anyway.

Only Charlie Stubbs and Alicia were missing. Charlie almost never joined us after work now, and Alicia was on vacation with Buzzy in Nassau. Buzzy liked to gamble there, Matt said, grinning. "Guess he wanted one sure thing along," he said. I disliked the comment, but I was just as glad Alicia was not present. She would have dimmed my Lady Brett splendor.

"You look good enough to eat," Lucas Geary said, smirking so that I could not miss the double entendre. He looked astonishingly grand in an Edwardian-cut coat and narrow trousers that clung to his long legs; he even had a ruffled shirt, and his beard and mustache had been neatly trimmed around his long face, so that his wicked white grin and pointed chin showed plainly. He looked like he had stepped from a Vermeer, or a Rembrandt, with his shining red hair and beard and the dark, mannered clothes, and I was sure that he knew it.

"So do we all," I said, refusing to acknowledge the intent of his words. "Even you. You should have a Cavalier King Charles spaniel attached to you somewhere. I can think of just the place."

"Do you think of it often?" he said.

"Almost never," I said, and Matt raised his glass to me and said, "Great dress, Smokes," and the afternoon flowed on into lavender evening.

Culver Carnes had had the layout for the Focus spread enlarged and set up on easels at one end of the bar, and draped them in blue cloth. Behind the bar, where the Top's owner and manager, Doug Maloof, had had a faded mural of the potted peach trees that had once lined

downtown Peachtree Street in front of Davison's department store, another blue drop cloth hung. The bar and
restaurant had been done over in shades of deep green
and peach and white, and it looked altogether fresher and
more chic than the old gray plush and black leather. But I
missed the old; it had been like a cave hung in the sky.
Doug himself was hovering over the bar, where uniformed waiters stood at attention. A long buffet table
laden with cocktail fare stood under the far window, and
Tony, the piano player, was noodling idly at the
Steinway, playing soft jazz and a smattering of early
Beatles, his one nod to the times. Tony always said you
had to go around the corner to the A Go-Go if you
wanted to hear the new stuff.

The press came early and ate and drank like locusts.
Matt knew all of them, and they him. He was popular
with them all, but there was a nervy edge to most of
them that spoke of envy, too, either professional or personal. I thought probably that it was both. He was at his
most ebullient that night, telling outrageous stories; teasing, almost insulting, all the men; coming on shamelessly
to the women; drinking steadily and showing none of the
drinks, smoking ceaselessly. In the dim room he seemed
to shine, to give off a light of his own. I thought it must
be hard, especially for the varnished anchor men and
weather girls, to yield the limelight to a wizened, simian
little man with aviator glasses and red hair hanging in
his eyes and a suit that looked just out of a Salvation
Army bin. But yield it they did, this night.

A good deal of liquor had been drunk, the hors
d'oeuvres table nearly decimated, and the room filled up
with smoke when the elevator bell in the lobby dinged,
and the men of the Club walked in in a sort of informal
military formation. They looked so easily powerful and
so all of a piece that they might have been struck from

the same mint, as indeed, they had, and the room seemed to tighten around them. Men straightened their lounging stances and their ties; women patted their hair; everyone fell silent. Ben Cameron walked at their head, and Culver Carnes brought up the rear, much as if he was shepherding them. I looked at Matt, who was grinning.

"If he nips anybody in the ass I'm not going to be able to hold it," he said under his breath, and I giggled.

Behind them walked a handful of solemn black men, young and not so young, all in dark suits and white shirts, all looking as solid and substantial as the men ahead of them, which in all respects they were. I recognized many of the faces from newspaper and television images; knew their names from half a hundred pages of recent and terrible history. I felt the nape of my neck go cool. They looked pleasant, ordinary, unremarkable, but I knew that they were not. They were total, whole. One might even call them dangerous. Behind the small, formal smiles and nods, behind the cool, assessing eyes were marches; beatings in dark, hot country nights and mean urban noons; terror and imprisonment and bombs; firehoses and dogs and guns flashing in darkness. In the eyes, ambushed black men spun forever in their doorways; children flew into pieces in the roaring air of churches.

When I said hello to John Howard, who walked up to where Luke and I stood, my voice sounded high and silly in my throat, like the bleat of a lamb.

The men of the Club were warm to Matt and cordial to all of us. All of them complimented me on the Focus piece, with a wash of indulgent gallantry over their words that I knew they used only with women. But they all seemed to know who I was, and almost all had heard of my victory at pool over Boy Slattery, and referred to it with enjoyment. I knew that of anything I might do, it would be that that they remembered.

Drinks had been passed around and pleasantries exchanged and Culver Carnes was moving toward the draped easels to begin his presentation when the elevator bell dinged again, and Boy Slattery came into the room.

"Oh, hell," Ben Cameron said in a low voice to Matt. They were standing just behind me, and I listened unashamedly.

"Lint's not coming?" Matt said.

"This is just for you to know," Ben Cameron said, "but Lint is, at this minute, at Johns Hopkins undergoing extensive tests. He hasn't been looking at all well this summer, and we've been after him to get himself looked at, but apparently something came up right suddenly, and Hill Fraser sent him to Hopkins straight from his office. I didn't ask Boy specifically, but of course he's the man when Lint's not around—"

"How bad is it?" Matt said. His voice was tight.

"Don't know," Ben Cameron said. "You better pray for all our sakes it's not serious. Christ, how come nothing ever happens to Boy?"

Before Matt could answer, Boy paused and looked over his shoulder and held his hand out behind him, and Alicia Crowley came out of the dimness of the lobby into the room, taking his hand as she walked.

The low roar of conversation stopped dead, a collective breath was drawn, and a soft babble broke out. In it, I recognized fervent, prayerlike exclamations of "Holy shit!" and "Jesus, Joseph, and Mary!" At my side, Luke whispered, "Shiver me timbers." Behind me, Matt said nothing.

"Look what followed me up in the elevator," Boy Slattery said, a smile of stunning slyness and offensiveness splitting his broad, red face. "I think I'll keep her. May I, Matt?"

"It's the lady's call, Boy," Matt said, his voice slow and amused and lethal.

"The lady is honored," Alicia said in her little-girl drawl, and the room erupted into laughter and applause. Boy bowed, still holding Alicia's hand. Alicia smiled a small, self-possessed smile, and looked sleepily at Matt.

I have never seen a woman enter a room with the same impact that Alicia contrived that night. I'm still not sure what it was. She looked wonderful; she was tanned to a light, polished gold from the Nassau sun, and it or something had streaked her long, straight honey-colored hair with strands of pure platinum, so that it looked like a light-struck waterfall cascading over her cheekbones to her bare shoulders. She wore a short black sheath with one thin strap over her right shoulder, cut very low, and her flesh gleamed dully and without a white mark anywhere, so that you automatically wondered where her tan mark stopped, or if it did. Her eyes were a startling light blue in her tanned face, and her long, long legs were bare.

But it was more than her looks. It was as if something small and powerful and viciously, elementally female lived inside Alicia, and she had untethered it and sent it out ahead of her this night. You could almost see the darting shape of it, smell its musk, in the air around her. After she entered the room, conversation stalled and died out, and people simply stood looking at her and Boy Slattery, who kept his fat fingers solidly on her flesh all evening. He nodded to Matt and the staff of *Downtown,* said with a small, mean smile that he was ready for a rematch with me any time, greeted the Club affably and nodded to the black contingent, but he did not by so much as a nod or a look acknowledge the press. I could hear them stirring among themselves, heard derisive laughter and a muffled comment or two, but none of the reporters came up to

him to engage him in conversation. Boy was not popular
with the Atlanta press. He had maligned them to his
statewide constituency too many times.

Culver Carnes read the crowd with a practiced show-
man's eye and moved to the front. He made a short
speech of welcome, recognized Luke and John Howard
and my efforts, and unveiled the layouts on their easels.
Even though I was accustomed to them by now, the photographs leaped out at me with powerful immediacy. In
their center, four or five times as large as life, a small
boy hugged the front of a car in an ecstasy of delight,
eyes screwed shut, and my words ran in bold white type
over the dark background: "His name is Andre . . ."

The presentation was a great success. There was
spontaneous applause and cheering when the layouts
were first unveiled, followed by a tumbling spate of just
the sort of questions Culver Carnes and Ben Cameron
wanted. Microphones were held close when John
Howard, who was the appointed spokesman for the project, talked; television lights flared and flashbulbs
popped and cameras ground. We all said our few words
for the press, and Ben skillfully brought the questions
back into focus when they threatened to stray into the
overtly political, and the conference wound down in a
glow of mutual congratulations and praise. Only the
black members of the party did not participate in the
bonhomie; they stood a little apart, studying the white
faces, saying nothing, their eyes revealing nothing. His
duties over, John Howard moved to join them. Once I
caught his eyes and smiled and held up my thumb and
forefinger in a circle, but he did not respond to me. I felt
hurt, like a publicly chastised child.

Doug Maloof moved to the forefront then, and said,
"There's one more unveiling to go tonight," and pulled a
silken cord dangling from the blue drape over the bar,

and it fell away, and I gasped with pure delight, and my eyes filled with tears.

On the wall behind the bar was a great, vivid mural of this very bar, and around it were skillfully painted caricatures of the luminaries of the city. Ben Cameron was there, and most of the Club, and not a few of the news media and our more colorful local eccentrics. In the very center, in a tight circle, was . . . us. The staff of *Downtown*. Matt, standing dead in our midst with his red hair flaming in his eyes, a glass raised; around him, Tom and Hank and Lucas Geary. In front of them, seated, Sister and Alicia and Teddy and me. We were all immediately recognizable, if primitively limned, and we were all laughing.

At the piano, Tony swung into "Downtown":

When you're alone and life is making you lonely,
you can always go . . .
    downtown.
When you've got worries, all the noise and the hurry
seem to help, I know . . .
    downtown.

The room broke into a great cheer, and we all hugged Doug, and I know that there were tears on more faces than mine. Tom Gordon was wiping his eyes unashamedly, and Matt found occasion to put his dark glasses on. In my ear, Hank Cantwell whispered, "It don't get any better than this, Holy Smokes! Don't you wish your mama could see you now?"

"No," I said, dull sadness and anger stabbing through the glorious giddiness, "but I wish my father could."

The hubbub had almost died away, and the press was packing up its lights and cameras and downing a last quick drink when Boy Slattery held up the hand that was not attached to Alicia and said loudly, "Wait up, folks, I got a question for Mr. Howard here."

John Howard nodded gravely to Boy Slattery, and the cameras and microphones swung in close.

"Little bird told me some of your buddies from Lowndes County are in town, John," Boy said affably. "Hear they're lookin' to do a little organizing, and I wondered if you were helping them out some, and if so, could you share your plans with us simple folks here in the city, so we can be prepared, like? Oh, and also, if your good wife and your little boy are with them? I know the rest of the old gang's all here, including your great good friend Miss—or is it Sister—Juanita Hollings, and maybe even Mr.—or is it Brother—Carmichael . . . "

There was a long, airless silence in which I could hear only my heart hammering in my ears, even though the import of Boy Slattery's words was not yet clear to me. Then John Howard said, very softly and clearly, "I can think of very little that is less your business, Lieutenant Governor," and Ben Cameron said, equally clearly, "All right, folks, this press conference is over," and more softly, "Sorry, John. Goddamn you, Boy."

Boy Slattery held up a pink hand and said, smiling cheerfully, "Just askin', Ben."

The group of black men turned and walked deliberately out of the room, John Howard with them, and Boy Slattery followed them at a distance, Alicia still in tow. This time she did not look at him, or back at Matt. She simply followed Boy out of the room. Presently, with little more of import said, the Club fell back into formation and left, and we did, too. As I walked out of the still-bright room with Hank and Luke and Teddy, I looked back. At the bar, under the laughing image of himself on the wall, Matt sat, eyes on the starry cityscape beyond the windows. He was drinking a vodka and tonic with only Doug Maloof for company, and he was not smiling.

On the street in front of the parking lot, John Howard stood alone, waiting for his car.

"I'll get the car, Smoky," Teddy said, and vanished into the cubicle. Luke and Hank and I stood uncomfortably, saying nothing to John Howard, not knowing what to say.

Then he smiled.

It was a small smile, and did not reach his eyes, but it was a smile.

"I wish to God I'd been there to see you beat his ass, Smoky," he said, and we all laughed louder than the comment merited, in sheer relief.

"Can we give you a lift?" I said, and then blushed in the darkness. Of course, John Howard would not be going to Buckhead.

He picked up on it.

"What's a po' nigger like me gon' be doin' out in Buckhead?" he drawled.

I heard Hank take a deep, quick breath. None of us had ever heard John Howard use that word, or speak in dialect.

"Lord, I'm more a nigger than you ever thought about being, John Howard," I said. "You try the docks in Corkie before you go assigning niggerhood."

Everyone laughed again, he as loudly as anyone.

"No, thanks, Smoky," he said. "I've got my car. I'm going to stop by Paschal's."

"You got a freedom fighter suit in it?" Luke said, and I remembered the neat little pile of preppy clothes in the back of John's smart Mustang the day of the first Focus shoot, on Pumphouse Hill.

John Howard laughed again. It was a young sound.

"Nah," he said. "I wear that under my clothes. Drop into a telephone booth when the need arises."

His Mustang came squalling down the ramp and he tossed the attendant a dollar and gunned the car out of the lot, turning left toward the Southwest, toward the Atlanta University Complex and Paschal's La Carrousel Lounge.

I watched his taillights wink out of sight around the corner, and then said to Luke, "Okay, tell me what all that was about, that with Boy Slattery."

Luke paused, and then sighed, and said, "It's no secret, obviously. John and Stokely Carmichael and Juanita Hollings—the woman you met in Pumphouse Hill—and a bunch from SCLC and SNCC and some others were all together during the Lowndes County voter registration project, where Jonathan Daniels was killed. It was . . . a very intense time. I was there for a little while; I know. You get so damned close, like in a war. It was there, after Jon was killed, that a lot of them just decided that nonviolence wasn't the way anymore, that there it was time for something else. I've always thought the Panthers were born that night, really. I truly think that's when Stokely went over, and Juanita. But anyway, before that . . . well, there was a lot of fooling around. Nobody really knew whether they'd live till the next day; you can't know unless you were there . . . anyway. John and Juanita got . . . real close. Real close. We all knew it. Everybody did. It was serious enough to break up John's marriage. His wife took their kid and went back to her folks up North. She divorced him not long after that. We all thought he'd go over to the Panthers then, but he never did. He's been closer to King, and for longer, than almost any of them. I guess, in the end, he just couldn't leave the movement. But I know he's always been of two minds about it, really been pulled, ever since . . . Jon . . ."

His voice trailed off, and he looked down at me. I said nothing.

"Shit, Smoky, he may be a civil rights hero, but he ain't no saint," he said sharply, and I guessed that my face must have mirrored my thoughts. "You can't possibly know how it was in those days. If you want saints, look somewhere else."

"Yeah," Hank said, seeking to defuse the moment. "Like Luke here."

Luke snorted and moved away impatiently, and I said, sarcastically, "Mah hero," and we all laughed, dutifully.

But I realized that I did want saints, and I did want John Howard to be one, and I wished with all my heart I did not know what Luke had just told me. Anything else for that broken copper face, I thought as Teddy's car came screeching down the ramp, was simply trivial.

9

AT THE END OF JULY, BRAD ASKED ME TO GO WITH HIM to his grandmother Hunt's ninety-second birthday party on Sea Island, and I asked Matt for that Friday off. I had worked straight through two prior weekends, and I did not think he would balk at the request, but he did.

"I need you in here this weekend," he said curtly. "I sold Seth Parks at Delta a full-page inside cover ad, and promised him you'd write it. He can't get over you beating Boy at pool."

"I'm not a copywriter, you know that," I said, anger rising on a flood of red to my cheeks. "And I wish to hell I'd never seen Boy Slattery. You can't just pass me around like candy to anybody who's glad Boy got his behind beat."

"I can assign you to any writing job I see fit," he said stonily, and went into his office and slammed the door.

"Don't worry about it, Smoky, I promise you you'll get Friday off," Hank said, and followed Matt into his office. He slammed the door, too. Presently he came back out, red-faced, and said, "All set for Friday. I'm afraid you'll have to do the ad before you go, though. He knows he's wrong but he's not going to back down any further. It's not the ad, it's just that . . . you know he doesn't like anybody breaking up the team. He's scared you're going to go off and marry Brad, and he'll be out a writer and one of his people to boot. You know as well as any of us he doesn't like Brad."

"That's just too bad," I said, only slightly mollified. "What I do on my own time is my own business. Besides that, I'm not an advertising writer. I resent him dangling me like a plum to get ads, or whatever he thinks he can get."

"I know it. I told him so. Just screw up the ad and he won't ask you to do it again."

We walked out of my office and into his, where Luke Geary lay on the floor, his head on his camera bag. The bad ankle was propped on Hank's visitor's chair, and I removed it silently and none too gently and sat down. Luke lifted his camera and aimed it idly at me.

"Don't do that," I said irritably.

He clicked the shutter and gave me the shit-eating grin.

"Hear you're goin' down to the island with ol' Brad," he said. He pronounced it "ahlan," drawling it out.

"You listening at keyholes these days?"

"I have my sources," he said. "You going to marry that ol' boy?"

"Don't be an utter ass," I said, reddening. "Of course I'm not."

"Bet you do," he said. "Bet once he gets you down there on the ahlan you'll be so overcome with all that wealth and splendor and shit that you'll say 'ah do' before you know what hit you. Allow me to take the first photograph of the bride."

I jumped to my feet to flounce out of Hank's office and he aimed the camera up my skirt, and I said, "Lucas

Geary, if you touch that shutter I'm going to step on your face."

"I'd a whole lot rather you sat on it," he leered, and I stepped out of my shoe and put my stockinged foot over his face. I was balancing on the other foot, holding onto the edge of Hank's desk and scrubbing my foot into his face when I saw, from the corner of my eye, a shape go by the open doorway. I looked up to see Culver Carnes's face, blank with shocked disapproval, disappear past the door.

Hank slammed the door and the three of us collapsed into helpless laughter.

"We're all going to pay for that," I said, when we finally stopped.

"You bet your ass we will," Hank said. "But it was worth it."

"I hope you appreciate what that means," Teddy burbled gleefully, when I told her about the weekend at Sea Island.

"What?" I said warily.

"It means you're as good as engaged," she said. "It's practically an Atlanta tradition, getting engaged at Sea Island, and going there on your honeymoon. I know maybe ten girls from Westminster alone who did it. And old Mrs. Hunt's birthday party to boot. Yep. You're as good as gone."

"I'm not going at all if you're going to talk like that," I said. We were sitting on her bed, drinking milk and eating cookies, as we sometimes did late at night. We seldom had a chance to talk intimately except at times like these. I loved them. They had an MGM, best-friend, big-sister quality I had dreamed of all my life.

"I'll stop," she said. "But seriously, it's really something, that birthday party. Everybody from here goes down for it. And she's really something. Do you know anything about her?"

"Only that Brad says she lives down there year-round, with a companion and some servants, and that she's a little . . . foggy these days."

"Foggy! She's crazy as batshit," Teddy crowed. "I saw her when we were down there last summer—everybody goes by and pays their respects, like she's the queen mother, which in a way she is—and she thought it was right after Pearl Harbor and we'd come to pick her up and take her to the Red Cross to roll bandages. Got madder than hell when Mother told her that it was twenty-five years later and we'd won the war. She practically threw us out. She's a mean old biddy. And she hates Brad's mother like poison."

"What a lovely family," I said. "Does anybody in it like anybody else?"

"Brad and his brother and sister like each other. And of course his mother really likes Brad, as I'm sure you've noticed. That's about it, except when you're a member of it they'll all like you. Of course, you may have a little problem with Marylou."

I ignored that.

"Why does his grandmother hate his mother?" I said. "Not that I blame her."

"Nobody really knows. She just always has, from the minute Mr. Hunt married her," Teddy said. "I've always thought it was because Marylou is so beautiful, and Grandma looks . . . exactly like Brad's father in a wig. It would be hard to lose your favorite son to a woman that drop-dead gorgeous when you were, to say the least, a tad homely, and Mr. Hunt is the absolute apple of her eye. Or was, until she got older and queer enough to say whatever came into her head, and started insulting Marylou. Mr. Hunt got on her about that, so she got mad at him and transferred her affection to Brad. Now he can do no wrong in her eyes, and she won't even let Marylou spend the night under her roof. When his folks go down there they stay at the Cloister. Marylou's been itching for years to get her hands on that house; it's really a fabulous old place. Huge and pink and kind of Spanish, with wrought iron balconies and loggias and verandas, and this wonderful old Spanish tile pool and cabana, and about a million rooms, right on the ocean. It's terribly rundown now; the old lady's way past spending any money on it, and couldn't care less, anyway. She and her companion, who's almost as old as she is, live in one or two rooms upstairs. The beach has eroded until the ocean is practically up to the doorstep at high tide, but she won't put in a sea wall, and Marylou won't let Brad's dad put a penny into it, because—get this—the old lady's leaving it to Brad. Said that common daughter-in-law of hers would never get her claws on it, and wrote out a new will naming Brad as sole heir of the place, and made sure it would stick. Grayson Venable drew it up. Marylou pretends she hates the place, but everybody knows she loves Sea Island, and would kill for that house. Nobody else in her crowd has to stay at the Cloister when they're down there but her—not that it's exactly hardship duty. It's just that most of her friends have houses. It's hard on Marylou because Sea Island is her kind of place. She hates Highlands and she wouldn't be caught dead anywhere as simple and rustic as Tate. You'll see when you get down there. Sea Island is just her."

"Teddy," I said in simple wonderment. "How do you know all that stuff?"

She looked at me in astonishment.

"Everybody knows that," she said, and turned her attention to the problem of my wardrobe.

"Your red linen will be good for Friday night, but you'll need something long for Mama Hunt's party and dinner afterward—it's always in the Spanish Lounge at the Cloister, and the Hunts take her to dinner in the dining room afterward. That's formal on Saturday night. And you'll need bermuda shorts and a bathing suit with boy legs, and sandals, and maybe something white for tennis, and a Lilly would be good—"

"Stop," I said, holding up my hand. "Right now. I do not now and have never owned anything long except my First Communion dress, and I look like an elf on a goofy golf course in Bermuda shorts, and a horrible little boy with boobs in boy-legged bathing suits, and I can't play tennis and don't intend to learn, and anyway I don't have any money, and as for a Lilly—"

"This is not the time to haul out your principles," Teddy said. "We're talking about the rest of your life here. I'll grant you the tennis and the Lilly, but you absolutely have to have the other stuff. You're going into the heart of Ward and June Cleaver country, that is, if they were rich. Let me see what I can do."

We said no more about it, and I went to bed determined to go to Sea Island with the few distinctly urban, inexpensive clothes that I had and no others. But the following night Teddy came home late, having "run by" her parents' house, and dropped an armful of clothing on my bed, still swathed in dry cleaner's plastic.

"Lucky my mother never throws anything away," she said. "She's been waiting for me to lose fifteen pounds for years so I could get back into these, but that's not going to happen, and she was tickled to death that you might be able to wear them. She thinks it's wonderful about the weekend. She and Dad will be at the birthday party, as a matter of fact. She says to wear these and look pretty for Brad, and that she's keeping her fingers crossed."

I shot Teddy a look, but her round face was suffused with such genuine, unaffected interest and joy at my good fortune in capturing Buckhead's most eligible and elusive bachelor that I just shook my head and turned to the clothes. I could, after all, simply leave them hanging in my closet. Or, that is, the closet of Brad's grandmother's guest room. He had said we would be staying at her home.

Most of the clothes had labels from Atlanta's best shops, and a few were from New York, and they were all straight out of the fifties. But it was a fifties that I had never been privy to, and I examined each piece with something akin to hunger. Even if I would never choose them, the clothes were all pretty, and wonderfully made. There was a straight, floor-length white piqué with spaghetti straps and little embroidered flowers scattered over it that had a long pink satin sash. It was only a size larger than I wore, and I knew that I could cinch in the sash and it would be perfect for the formal party and dinner afterward. There was a white, fringed silk shawl that would go over it, and also over my red sleeveless linen, and there were white satin sandals with tiny Cuban heels that looked as if they, too, would fit.

"I wore those to my coming-out party," Teddy said.

"If you'd rather I didn't—" I began.

"Oh, no," she said hastily. "They killed me all night. I hated them and the party, too. I'm not sentimental about anything from that period of my life."

I would have liked to ask her about that time in her life, but something in her manner stopped me. Teddy always could, without seeming to move a muscle in her sweet, round face, hang up a "no admittance" sign there. It was in place now.

"Thanks, then," I said, and held up the next article, a two-piece bathing suit in gray-striped, white-piped seersucker cotton, with little-boy legs.

"The waist is elastic," she said, "and if you don't take a deep breath you won't fall out of the top. It'll give you terrific cleavage. I used to stuff stockings in there to get it. Brad will salivate, and Marylou will die. It's perfect."

I laughed, and picked up the knife-creased plaid madras bermudas and matching pink T-shirt and the little plaid wrap skirt that completed her offering.

"If nobody mistakes me for Gidget it won't be your fault," I said wryly. "Thanks, pardner. I'll try to be worthy of them."

And I reached over and hugged her.

She hugged me back, hard.

"I really am happy for you," she whispered. "It really is a special place, and it . . . means more than you think."

I drew back, beginning to protest once more, and she clapped her hand lightly over my mouth.

"Give it a chance, at least," she said. "Now. Do you need stockings?"

Brad and I left at six A.M. on Friday, and by eight were past Macon and nearing Perry, where, he said, it was a family tradition to stop for breakfast in the coffee shop of the New Perry Hotel. He was driving his sober sedan, and I was glad, for once, not to be in the gull-winged Mercedes. His brother would be driving that down the next day. The sedan had an air-conditioner, and we already needed it. The air outside had turned as thick and hot and humid as if we were in the tropics.

"Got your protective coloration on, I see," he said, nodding at the wrap skirt and sleeveless blouse that I had, after all, put on that morning. "You look like a proper little Buckhead postdeb. Didn't we meet in dancing class?"

"You almost got me in a bare midriff and bell-bottoms, so don't push your luck," I said. "If it weren't for Teddy I'd be doomed before I started with Sea Island."

"Have you ever been?"

It was a nice touch. He must know that I had not, not to stay.

"Well, I saw the Cloister once," I said deliberately. "We went down there from Corkie when I was about five, in my father's old La Salle that he bought second-hand from the foreman on his shift before the war. It was just after V-J Day; I think we were celebrating being able to get gas again. Anyway, the car was full of us kids and all over road dirt, and my father was in his undershirt, and when we went past that gatehouse thing I remember that they stopped us and asked my father if we had business over there, and Daddy said he just wanted to show us the Cloister, and the guard said for us to make the circle in front and come right on back out. I never forgot that. We went past the Cloister so fast that all I remember is a blur of light stucco and red tiles, and Daddy cursing. It made a big impression on me."

"Arrogant sons of bitches," Brad said, and his voice was so hard and tight that I glanced over at him. His face was pale under its tan, and his mouth was set in a thin line. I felt a surge of affection for him, and a warm wash of safety.

"Don't look like that," I said, putting my hand on his knee, and he covered it with his own.

"That will never happen to you again, Smoky," he said. "Not here and not anywhere. Not as long as I'm around."

"Well," I said mildly, "it probably wouldn't happen again anyway; I've cleaned myself up some, and learned a few manners. But thanks, anyway."

"I didn't mean that the way it sounded," he said. "I just meant—"

"I know. I really meant thanks," I said, and we drove on for a time in silence, holding hands.

I told him about the press party for the Focus piece, and he was interested and complimentary, and suitably appalled at Boy Slattery's behavior. He laughed outright at my account of Alicia leaving on Boy's arm after electrifying the crowd of reporters, but then the laughter trailed off, and he said soberly, "I wonder if Buzzy knew she was going to that party."

"I think so," I said. "I think I heard her tell somebody he was still in Nassau because some friends of his were coming down from Las Vegas to gamble, and he didn't want to break his streak. He told her to go on. I doubt if he knew she took up with Boy, though."

I smiled at the memory, but Brad's brow furrowed.

"I hope to God not," he said. "Buzzy can get downright ugly when his women indicate a preference for someone else."

"Lord, Brad, what's he going to do, beat her up?" I said, amused at the thought of silly, puddinglike Buzzy in the throes of a grand passion such as jealousy.

"No, it's more his style to have it done," Brad said matter-of-factly, and I simply stared at him.

"You're kidding," I said finally.

"I wish I was. I've heard some pretty scary things about some of Buzzy's ex-girlfriends and those white-tied Cro-Magnons he travels with. Nobody knows for absolute certain sure, you understand, and the girls themselves sure ain't going to talk, but I've heard that there's a sort of marginal plastic surgeon on the West Coast who occasionally does a little cosmetic work for a few of Buzzy's ladies. I hear he gives them such a deal."

I felt cold, colder than the air-conditioning warranted.

"That's awful," I said. "That's . . . terrifying."

"Well, it just might be a kind of urban legend," Brad said. "They spring up like weeds around Buzzy. Alicia ought to watch it, though. At the very least, Buzzy is to be taken seriously."

"Should I tell her? Should you?"

"Christ, no, don't you go telling her anything she could spill to Buzzy. Let me talk to Matt. You forget about it."

But I did not think that that would happen.

At breakfast I told him about Pumphouse Hill and the beautiful young woman whom Luke said was a Panther, and about the shoot at Mrs. Holmes's apartment in Summerhill, and about Andre. I still found it hard to speak about Andre without quick tears sabotaging me, and this time was no exception. He looked at me sympathetically.

"You can't help him by crying for him," he said. "What you did for him will help him far more than tears. Him and a lot of other little kids who don't know their last names. Good job, Smoky."

"You just don't know how good it felt to do some serious work for a cause that means something, for something bigger than yourself, outside yourself," I said. "Or at least, you probably do, but I never did. It . . . changes things. It makes me look at myself differently."

"How?" His voice was intent, interested.

"Well, it makes me think that I might make some kind of difference to the world one day. That it's not impossible that I could . . . count for something as a writer, make people look at things differently—"

"You've got the gift for it, no doubt about that," Brad said. "It might make you feel good to know that you make a big difference to me right now."

I touched his hand, lightly. "It makes me feel terrific," I said. "Now if Matt could just see me that way—"

"Your job means a lot to you, doesn't it?"

I looked at him. He was not smiling. All of a sudden I felt tentative, cautious, uncertain, as if I were walking on mined earth. What was going on here? He knew how I felt about *Downtown;* he had always known that. I talked often of it.

"You know it does," I said.

"Does it mean everything?"

"I don't know how to answer that," I said. "Why should it have to mean everything? I mean, you talk as if I have to make some sort of choice, my job or . . . everything else—"

"No choice," he said. "I wouldn't ask that of you. No reason why you shouldn't have your job and . . . everything else."

Back in the car, he said, "What's next for Focus? You doing the next piece, too?"

"Right now it's my baby, mine and Luke's and John Howard's," I said. "Ben Cameron saw to that, God bless him, or I'd still be the subhead queen of Atlanta. Next is, of all things, a convention of Negro disc jockeys. It's a big convention, and one of the oldest around, but all of a sudden no major hotel in Atlanta can find room for them. They're all mysteriously full up, and the deejays have had to go to this dinky little motel way out on Stewart Avenue. To a string of third-rate motels, as a matter of fact. Nobody will say that it's because they're black since the Public Accommodations Act passed, but Ben Cameron says it's the first time in his life he can remember such a shortage of hotel rooms in late summer. I mean, it isn't exactly the height of the tourist season. Ben says if it were true, Atlanta would be the richest city in the country, at least for that week. He's really steamed about it. Public Accommodations is his baby; he testified before the Senate for the bill. Kennedy asked him to do it. And we were doing pretty good down here, he says, until this summer, when all of a sudden all these big-shot hotels are turning up full for the black deejays. He's sure Boy and his crowd are behind it, but he can't prove anything. We're going to do a photo-essay on them, show who they are and what they do, and show how hard it is for them to do their business stuck out there in a string of substandard motels on Stewart Avenue—"

"Y'all going after Boy?"

"Not directly. Not in so many words. We're hoping that just the exposure, just showing that these are average guys trying to have a business convention and not being able to do it right, here in the premier city in the South, will open a few eyes and make a few faces red."

"I wouldn't count on making many faces red," Brad said. "It's an awful long leap from little black kids kissing cars to big black deejays in earrings and high heels and all that. I mean the guys. These are not just your run-of-the-mill blue-collar working stiffs, Smokes. These guys are weird. There's not apt to be a lot of sympathy for them."

"Well, the point is, you don't have to have sympathy for them," I said. "You just have to give them equal treatment under the law of the land. All the problems Focus will tackle can't be about cute little children. Ben thinks the diversity, the contrast, will be good, and Matt loves the idea. It'll be a wonderful human interest feature. I'm looking forward to it."

"Well, go to it," he said. "But let me give you just one little word of advice. Don't talk about it this weekend. It's going to be bad enough when the Andre piece comes out with your byline on it. The people who go to Sea Island, especially the ones who'll be at Mama Hunt's party, aren't your typical *Downtown* readers. You won't exactly be making new friends talking about the problems of the Atlanta Negroes. What with Andre, and now the black deejays, a lot of them are going to look on you as the appointed 'black' writer."

"So what if they do?" I said, stung.

He held up a propitiatory hand.

"Hey, don't shoot the messenger," he said. "You have to realize that the only Negroes most of them know work in their kitchens. Their hearts are in the right place—most of them, anyway—but it's going to take a long time."

"Well, let's get them started, then," I snapped.

He shrugged. "Do what you think is best," he said coolly, and we did not speak for a long while after that. I was determined not to apologize, or sound as if I were, and apparently he was not, either. I solved the matter by putting my head back and falling asleep. When I woke, dry mouthed and stiff necked, it was with my head resting on his shoulder and his arm lightly around me, and the rusty, stinking smell of the paper mill in Brunswick curling in through the tightly shut windows.

"Almost there," he said, and it was as if the small coldness between us had never existed. I stretched and looked around, seeing the great, flat, green waterworld of the marshes of Glynn County flash past me as we crossed the causeway onto Saint Simons Island. All of a sudden my mouth was dry with more than heavy sleep, and my heart began to beat fast and light. The landscape was almost eerily like that you passed through going into Savannah and Corkie, but it was not Savannah and Corkie ahead of me. It was one of the creamiest, plushest bastions of old money in the United States of America, and I was going to the birthday party of its unchallenged social doyenne, taken there by the grandson who would one day inherit her kingdom by the sea.

"I think I'm scared," I said.

"I can't wait to show you how little you have to be afraid of," Brad said, and smiled, and I smiled back. Safe. Yes. That's what it was, or a large part of it, that warmth that he gave off, that wrapped me close whenever I was with him. With him I was, among many other things, safe.

It was such a new feeling for me that I had not known its name.

We bowled past the gatehouse on the Sea Island causeway that I remembered, and a guard raised his hand in salute to Brad. Brad waved back.

"I did remember it," I said. "Where are the arrow slits? Where are the gun emplacements?"

"There," Brad grinned, and we passed, on the left, the low, shrub-shaded Sea Island Gun Club. Even in the swaying, cobralike heat, a man and a woman stood, erect in their khaki canvas jackets, guns raised, aiming out across the shimmering marshes.

"Pull," I heard one of them cry, faintly, and a gun cracked.

"Is it open season on Irishmen?" I asked.

"Not on my watch," Brad said, and then we were across the Black Banks River and on Sea Island proper, and plunged instantly into a deep, cool, permanent semigloom of monstrous old live oaks and silvery, shrouding moss, and masses of brilliant semitropical flowers and perfect sweeps of velvet lawns. After the blinding, searing white light and heat of the coastal plain and the marshes, it was like tumbling out of purgatory and into paradise, or into the jewellike waters of the Great Barrier Reef. In that instant I felt my temperature drop ten degrees.

On our left, the elegant old dowager Cloister slept in its garden of flowers, under its arching canopy of ancient oaks. Only a few people were about in this hot noon, walking their bicycles over the paths that bisected the hotel's deep green lawns, or ambling in spotless whites back toward the tennis courts or toward the ocean and the beach club, off to our right. I saw two or three black, white-coated waiters on bicycles, trays of snowy, covered food balanced in one hand, pedaling toward the lushly planted cottage clusters that fringed the blue Atlantic. Down the long, straight, moss-curtained main road that ran alongside the cottages and the beach club, a few more people strolled or rode bikes. They were, without exception, much older couples or young women with children in tow.

"Where are all the men?" I said.

"Most of them come down on weekends," Brad said, raising a languid hand at one young mother and her tow-headed brood. The young woman waved and smiled at him and stared at me.

"The people you see around on weekdays are mainly retirees or out-of-staters on vacation, or women and kids who have houses down here. Some people stay here year-round; when you say 'cottage' down here you don't exactly mean like Hansel and Gretel had. But it's fullest in summer, when school's out. Everybody will be having lunch at the beach club about now, or maybe taking naps. In the mornings they play golf and tennis, and in the afternoon they hit the pool and the beach. Drinks start about five, and dinner around eight. There's probably a cocktail party at every other cottage on the island on any given night, during the season."

"Sounds like a lot of drinking," I said. I could think of nothing else to say. We were passing the first of the big private cottages now, and I had not been prepared for the sheer size and splendor of them, or the lushness of their grounds. And I knew that the ones over on the beach, down the short cross streets, were even more splendid still. Teddy had told me that. It did not seem possible to me that normal people leading normal lives would lead them from these houses.

"Probably no more than you all drink on an average day at the magazine," Brad said. "I don't think I've ever seen many drunks down here."

"You've come here every summer?" I said. I knew that he had, but the implications of that were stronger now.

"That I can remember," he said. "Except for a year or two in the navy. Until I finished school and went to work, I spent most of every summer down here with Mama Hunt. It sounds grim, and it'll seem even grimmer when you meet her, but I was almost never in the house. It seemed like everybody I knew back in Atlanta was down here. We had enough to do to keep us out from dawn to way past dark every night."

"Like what?"

"Oh," he said, "You know. Island things."

I did not know, but did not say so, for we were turning off the main road onto a short, private street and then pulling in between the gateposts of a great, pale-pink brick fence overgrown with tumbling bougainvillea, and stopping in a cobbled courtyard before a pink stucco house as lovely and graceful as a tall ship under full sail, and, "Here we are," Brad said.

A dignified black woman in a gray uniform and white apron met us at the great door. She wore horn-rimmed glasses and had her wiry graying hair back in a bun, and, with the glasses and her handsome, aquiline face, looked altogether like a college professor.

"Hi, Sarelle," Brad said, and hugged her, and she gave him a smack on the bottom and said, "Hi, yourself, Mr. Brad. We been waitin' for you."

Brad introduced me and Sarelle smiled and said, "We're gon' put Miss Smoky in the yellow room upstairs, the one on the end. You have your old room. You take them things on up and then come down to the sun porch. Your grandmama and Miss Isobel out there. You hurry up, though; she didn't sleep good last night and it's past her nap time. She's all stirred up over this party; you might find her a little grumpy."

"Christ, that means she's loaded for bear," Brad said, and I followed him through a vast, two-story entrance hall paved in black and white marble, up a circular stair-case carpeted in faded, sour-smelling green wool and railed with beautiful wrought iron. The railings were rusted and dim, and I had noticed that the marble tiles were dim and pitted, too. The lower part of the house was in gloom, floor-length drapes drawn against the blinding white noon, but I could see that the drapes were faded too, as well as the upholstery and pillows on the rattan couches and chairs in the downstairs rooms. The house was done in what I thought of as Palm Beach traditional, an impression garnered solely from old movies on television: wicker and rattan, green and pink floral chintzes, white mouldings and woodwork. I knew that it must have been very chic and grand once, but the miasma of forlorn decay was as thick as fog in the high-ceilinged rooms, and age and illness and disuse clung in corners and bobbed at the pierced tin tray ceilings. There was dust everywhere. Whatever Sarelle did did not, apparently, run to housekeeping. Melancholy settled heavily on my shoulders. I wished that we did not have to spend two nights under this beautiful, desolate roof.

I trudged down a long, dim upstairs hall after Brad, seeing only more faded carpet and closed, carved doors, the line of them broken only by an occasional massive Spanish table holding an old iron lamp, and by a floor vase full of dusty pampas grass. The odor of mold and dust was stronger here. I counted six doors before Brad pushed open the last one on the left. I followed him in, and gasped with pleasure.

It was a large, airy room, with a white-beamed ceiling and white stucco walls, and butter-yellow shag carpets laid down over gleaming dark hardwood floors. A narrow, tall tester bed with a yellow chintz canopy sat against the wall, piled with pillows in yellow and green and coral, and there was a huge mahogany wardrobe and a dressing table, and a tall chest of drawers. The old wood shone, and the smell of lemon polish blew lightly on the wind from the sea. The wall opposite the bed was a length of French windows and doors, open onto a balcony overlooking a long, parched front lawn and the fabled Spanish tile pool and poolhouse, and beyond that, the gray-blue Atlantic, glittering in the high, hard sun as if a handful of diamond dust had been thrown down on it. The tan beach was empty, and the tall, half-dead palm trees on the lawn rustled and clattered in the wind. The smell of the sea was glorious, and I rushed out onto the balcony and threw my arms wide as if to embrace everything I saw.

"Sarelle's fixed it up nice for you," Brad said behind me. "Polish, and fresh flowers, and a good airing. I've always loved this room. It was Mama Hunt's when I first started coming down here; Papa Hunt had the one just like it at the other end of the hall. She closed them both after he died, though, and moved to the one she has now, in the other wing. It overlooks the courtyard in back. I always thought this was the best room in the house, but she finally admitted that the ocean made her nervous, so she moved to the other one. You should thank your stars for that. She's a whole wing away from you. I, on the other hand, am just across the hall from her and the lovely and talented Miss Davison. I guess she figures she needs to keep an eye on where we sleep, and she can do it easier to me than to you."

"It's glorious," I said. "I can't wait to lie in bed and look at the stars over the ocean. What do you mean, keep an eye on us? Does she think that we're going to—you know—in her own house?"

"Stranger things have happened," Brad said gravely, and I felt a sudden stab. It stood to reason that he had brought other women here, to this house that was his summer home; he was, after all, thirty-one years old. I wondered who, before me, had lain in the tester bed and waited for the old carved door to open and let him in.

"I would never abuse her hospitality like that," I said primly.

"I would never ask you to . . . abuse her hospitality," he said, and I caught the laughter in his voice, and grinned unwillingly.

He left me to take his bag to his room in the other wing, and I went into the bathroom across the hall to freshen up. It was as dim and musty as a cave, with a floor of tiny black and white tiles and a huge, bulbous, claw-footed bathtub, and outsized wash basin and toilet. Nothing here had been modernized, and the full-length mirror on the back of the door was wavery and speckled. My own image shimmered in it, flesh glowing whitely, like a drowned woman at the bottom of a pool. The air in the room was still and hot, and the overhead light was dim, but there was a pile of thick, fresh white towels laid out on the counter, and Sarelle or someone had put a small bouquet of zinnias on the dressing table. I peered at my image in the mirror, leaning close, and thought of the night, scarcely eight months ago, when I had stood peering into another mirror, in the Church's Home for Girls, feeling almost exactly as I did now: expectant, a little frightened, more than a little lost.

"What a long way you've come," I whispered to the girl in the mirror, and she swam to the surface and grimaced back at me. I washed my face and hands and brushed my hair and straightened Teddy's madras wrap skirt and blouse and ran lightly and in dread down the stairs where Brad waited to take me to his grandmother.

The two old women waited for us on a narrow, glassed-in porch that ran alongside the house, facing the courtyard on one end and the lawn and sea on the other. They sat on opposite ends of a flowered rattan sofa, both so bent and small that their feet scarcely touched the floor. I thought of children sitting gingerly on grown-up furniture. A glass and rattan table before them held a pitcher of what looked to be orange juice and a tray of glasses, and Sarelle was just uncovering a plate of tiny sandwiches skewered with frilled toothpicks. From the litter of frilly toothpicks on the tabletop, I judged that the two old ladies had not been able to wait for us. Two empty glasses sat there, too.

I had no trouble telling which of the ladies was Brad's grandmother. Teddy had been right; the smaller of the two looked precisely as his father might look in thirty years or so, wearing one of the ghastly, frowsy Beatles wigs that sold briskly at novelty stores. She was bent almost double, and propped up with pillows and bolsters, and she sat with chin on liver-spotted bosom, eyes closed and mouth agape.

I had the idiot thought that she had died, but Sarelle smiled and made pantomimed snoring motions, and the other old lady giggled and whispered, "She's asleep again. She's fallen asleep three times since we got up this morning."

She was vastly fat, and short, with thin white hair cut in a Dutch bob through which her pink scalp showed, and had a big, powdered face in the middle of which all her little features sat. I thought of Humpty Dumpty, or a balloon in the Macy's Thanksgiving Day Parade. But so old, so frail—how could this desiccated dumpling of a woman be an effective companion to the other? And then I understood the shabby state of the house and grounds: Sarelle, hired to be a housekeeper, was instead a nurse and attendant to not one but two very elderly women. I sent Sarelle a smile of what I hoped she would recognize as sympathy and understanding. Her answering smile was polite and bland.

"I am not asleep. You're a hopeless fool, Isobel," said the other old woman, in a midge's whine, and her eyes opened, and I thought of a malicious old bird of prey. They were filmed with cataracts and pouched in crepey, wrinkled flesh, but wicked living coals burned in their depths.

"I probably am," the hapless Isobel simpered, and speared another sandwich. "Hey, Braddy. Let us meet this pretty girl."

Brad kissed his grandmother and whispered something in her ear, and she cackled, witchlike, and peered at me. I smiled as prettily as I knew how, feeling every inch of rebellious breast and hip as if they were naked and jiggling. This ruined, elegant house called for height and slouching slenderness, and cool composure. But then, Marylou Hunt had those things in abundance, and she was not welcome here.

Sarelle vanished into the dark house and Brad sat on a hassock drawn up to his grandmother's side. I sat on a facing sofa, so overstuffed that my own feet barely brushed the floor, and smiled and smiled. Miss Isobel Davison kept up a barrage of birdlike chatter, and ate and drank steadily, and the glitter in her eyes told me that there was more than orange juice in the pitcher, but Mama Hunt did not say another word. She simply sat on her sofa on the stifling hot sun porch, her bird's legs agape so far that one averted one's eyes from her lap, and drank Mimosas and stared at me. For perhaps thirty minutes, while Brad talked lazily of home and the coming party and Miss Isobel giggled and I smiled, she said nothing at all.

Finally she put down her glass and said to me, "What kind of a name is Smoky?"

"It's a nickname," I said. "I got it when I was a little girl. My real name is Maureen."

"O'Malley, or some such," she said.

"O'Donnell."

"From where?"

"Savannah," I said, waiting. I did not wait long.

"Ah," she said. "Your folks are on the docks, then." It was not a question.

"Yes."

"And you're aiming to marry my grandson, am I right?"

Brad started to speak, but I overrode him.

"No," I said. "I absolutely am not aiming to marry your grandson."

"Don't tell me you're not. All of them are. Every one of them he brings down here takes one look at this house and sets their cap for him. It's going to be his, you know. They all know that. Don't try to tell me you're any different. Except for being shanty Irish, I mean. The others have been a little better bred."

"That's enough, Mama Hunt," Brad said, making as if to rise.

"I won't try to tell you anything, Mrs. Hunt," I said, anger making my voice shake. "Except that I love Atlanta and I love my job and I wouldn't trade either one for a million houses like yours."

"And what is your job, missy?" she said.

"I write stories about Negroes for an Atlanta magazine," I said.

She stared at me for a long moment, and then began to shake all over silently. A terrible wheezing sound came from her lips. I thought she was having some sort of attack, but then I realized that she was laughing.

"I'll bet Marylou absolutely despises you, doesn't she?" she wheezed.

"Absolutely," I said.

"Well, I like you," she said, and poked Brad in the ribs. "I like her," she said. "I think she'll do just fine. You sleeping with her, Brad?"

I thought that he colored under his tan, but his blue eyes were mild and amused.

"No, ma'am," he said. "She won't have me."

"Well, let's let your mother think you are. I'm sure she already thinks that. It's all she understands. Meanwhile, Smoky, or whatever your name is, don't you be so prissy with this boy. I can name you a dozen girls prettier than you who'd be glad to—"

"Okay, Mama Hunt," Brad said, getting to his feet. "You're snockered and you're out of bounds. We're on our way to lunch with Mother and Dad at the beach club, but we'll be back to change before we go to dinner. If you're still up we'll look in on you. You ought to get a good night's sleep, though. Big doings tomorrow."

"I hate these damned parties," the old lady said. "Marylou only gives them to show off. You bring this girl back to have a drink with us before supper, you hear?"

"I will," Brad said, and I took the withered, dry old hands and said, "It was nice meeting you, Mrs. Hunt."

"You know you're lying," she said. "I'm a mean little old thing, and I can be meaner still. You ask that trashy daughter-in-law of mine how mean I can be."

She cut her eyes at Brad and he rolled his and held

out his hand and I took it, and we started back upstairs to change into our bathing suits.

I had gotten to the door of the sun porch when she shrilled at me, "You've got a good bosom, girl, and a good, wide bottom. You Irish are good breeders. I'll bet there are five more like you at home. You could fill Brad's house up with little Irish brats. Marylou would love that."

"Actually, there are six more of us at home," I said, my cheeks burning. I had never been one of those who thought viper-tongued old ladies were cute. "But you're right about the breeding. We Irish pop 'em out like champagne corks."

Behind us, like an evil benediction, I heard her terrible old laugh.

"I guess there's no use asking you what you thought about all that," Brad said wryly. "I'm sorry. It was awful."

We were walking hand in hand down the beach, just at the surf line. When we had started out the air and water were almost alike, so still and thick and warm that it was like wading in warm blood, but we had not gone far over the scorching sand before a strong little wind had sprung up, and everything changed. The air cooled and the gentle surf creaming in around our ankles was charged with bubbles, and the sun that poured down over our bare heads and shoulders mellowed. His hair burned on his head like a gilt helmet, and drops of sweat glistened on his shoulders. I could not see his eyes for the sheltering dark glasses. I could read the amusement and consternation in his voice, though.

"I thought Tennessee Williams did it better," I said, and he laughed.

"She is kind of like a Tennessee Williams gargoyle, isn't she? I forget just how terrible she can be sometimes."

But I could tell he did not really think she was terrible. People possessed of monstrous relatives often succeed in telling themselves they are merely quaint and eccentric.

"The whole thing is Tennessee Williams," I said. "That beautiful old wreck of a house, and the heat, and the booze, and the strange old companion, and the enigmatic servant—what about Sarelle, anyway? Who helps her out? What kind of life does she have down here?"

"I don't know," he said, sounding faintly surprised. "She's been with Mama Hunt a long time. She has a house in Atlanta, in Vine City, I think, but she comes down here when Mama Hunt does, and lives in. That's most of the year. I guess nobody helps her out now, from the looks of the house. There used to be a couple that cooked and drove for Mama Hunt, and a gardener who came in from the island, but the couple left and Mama Hunt got mad and fired the gardener, and she won't let Mother and Daddy hire anybody else. Says they're trying to bleed her dry of her money. She has enough to last several lifetimes, of course, but try telling her that—"

"I can't imagine what sort of life a middle-aged Negro woman from Atlanta would have on Sea Island," I said. "Especially if she's left her own family behind. Who could her friends be down here? Where could she go on her days off? Not, I'm sure, the beach club or the tennis court."

"I guess I've never thought about it," Brad said.

"I guess not," I said, feeling contentious and holy. The sheer decadence and waste of the big, decaying house and the spoiled old women in it; the oiled and bejeweled bodies I fancied were waiting for us at the beach club, lying in the sun; the whole sybaritic island, all conspired to make me cross. It was too soon after Pumphouse Hill, too soon after Andre.

"I'll try to talk Grandma into hiring some extra help,

and ask Sarelle what she needs," Brad said. "You're right, it can't be much of a life. Meanwhile, try to enjoy it as much as you can. It would please me if it pleased you. Let's get wet, shall we?"

"Let's," I said, feeling like a spoiled child myself, and followed him into the surf.

It was wonderful, cool and dark green in its depths, sun-hot and dancing on the surface. We went all the way under the small waves and rode them into the beach, and ducked each other, and shouted and laughed and tumbled like puppies at the water line. When finally we came out, shaking the salt water from our bodies, I was sodden and seal-haired and red-eyed and breathless, and realized that I had neither comb nor cover-up with me. Far down the beach I could see people in deck chairs on the sand outside the beach club, and sitting under umbrellas on the terrace and around the pool, and crowding around a line of small beached sailboats, red sails luffing slightly in the freshening wind. All the people seemed, from this distance, tanned and beautiful and gotten up in smart sun hats and cover-ups.

"I've got to go back," I said. "I look like a drowned rat, and I don't even have a jacket."

"You don't need one," he said. "We'll eat outside on the terrace. I think you look sexy as hell, dripping like that. Here."

And he dashed up to the lawn of one of the big houses and twisted a hibiscus blossom from a bush, and brought it to me, and thrust it behind my ear.

"Now you look like Sheena, Queen of the Jungle," he said, giving me a hug. His wet body felt warm against mine. And so it was with salt-stiffened hair and Teddy's bathing suit clinging wetly to my body and a sun-pinked nose and a red hibiscus behind one ear that I went to meet Marylou Hunt on her own turf.

*   *   *

We sat late at dinner that night. There is only one long sitting in the Cloister's graceful old dining room, and guests keep the same table throughout their stay. The one at which we sat was, Marylou Hunt said, the one the Hunt family had had for many years. It overlooked a dramatically lit little walled garden, but commanded a premier view of the room, too. From it, Marylou could both see and be seen.

Looking back, I remember it as a pleasant evening, even an exhilarating one, though at the start of it, I could not have said why. It should have been excruciating; I was in a virtual holy of holies from which my entire family had once been barred, and all of Marylou's exquisite little sharp knives were out. They had been since we sat down at the terrace table with her for lunch, at the beach club. I was outclassed on every side the entire day, and knew it, and she knew it, and Brad did too, probably, though he never indicated by so much as a raised eyebrow that he did.

But somehow, on that strange golden day, nothing that Brad's mother did seemed to touch me. I ate lunch, lay in the sun, made polite conversation, swam, went home and changed and came back to meet the senior Hunts in the Cloister's lounge, went down the elegant little shop-lined hallway and in to dinner, nodded to a great many people and spoke with some, ate wonderfully well, and drank a great deal of wine in a hermetically sealed, impenetrable bubble of power and well-being.

It was not until we were walking out of the dining room and down another long corridor to the lounge for a nightcap that I saw our reflections in an ornate mirror over a little mahogany side table, Marylou Hunt's and mine, and realized why.

I was not looking in the mirror, merely looking idly about while Marylou and I waited for Brad and his father to catch up with us. But I raised my head and saw in its depths a woman so beautiful, so starkly and powerfully commanding, that I gave a small, silent gasp. Only after I had stared at the image for a long second did I realize that I was looking at the image of Marylou Hunt, who stood behind me, and that she was staring, not at herself, but at the image of me in the mirror, and on her unguarded face was not the barely concealed contempt that I had fancied I had seen all afternoon, but naked, hungry envy. It was a primitive expression; powerful, somehow pure. It was more than the animosity of a mother toward a younger rival for her son's affections. It was somehow murderous, all-consuming, and yet so nakedly vulnerable that I shut my eyes involuntarily.

When I opened them she had looked away, and her face was back in the chiseled ivory mask that it always wore, overlaid now with a careful wash of sheer gold from her morning's perfectly calibrated sunning. Her eyelids were shaded a delicate pewter, and her wonderful, deep blue eyes were fringed with long, silky lashes, and her deep red lipstick had burnished gold overtones that echoed the serene gilt of her hair. She was as whole and perfect as a Fabergé egg, or a Chinese porcelain, and as incomparably beautiful. She wore wide-legged white silk palazzo pants cinched with a gold mesh belt, and the sheer artifice of her at that moment was breathtaking.

But I had seen that other face, and everything changed in that moment. I saw myself in front of her, juxtaposed against her, flushed with wine and red-cheeked with sun and wind, black hair an unruly tangle of curls from the humid night wind, red linen slightly rumpled, shoulders and neck and bosom glowing with heat and sunburn, eyes sparkling from alcohol and a kind of reckless triumph. I was raw and unfinished beside her, but totally and unconquerably young.

That was my power. Only that, but it was for that moment enough. I could run nearly naked on a hot, windy beach and plunge without care into a running diamond sea; roll on the sand and fling my arms wide to the sun and still be what I was, that she could never again be: young. Her beauty was a triumph of wonderful bone and great art and much, much money, but it was a fragile triumph, needing to be tended and lacquered and shaded and guarded. My beauty was nothing next to hers, but I had the vitality and spontaneity and the supple flesh and the sheen of youth, and it was, to her, a terrible weapon.

I stood still, staring into the mirror, my head ringing with the realization of it. And then joy flooded in, swift and exultant. I would use it, then; she could not touch me. I had won everything, I saw in that moment, everything that she wanted: her son, the big old house down the beach, the right of succession to the life she led in her big Buckhead house. I knew that I had won them. I did not stop to think whether I wanted them. I simply stood in the dim hallway of that consummately elegant old hotel and rejoiced in the power I had that night. That it was fleeting; that I would as surely lose it as she had lost it; that it was a small and cruel power, did not occur to me in that moment. All that did was that I had come into enemy territory feeling helpless and vulnerable and had found, after all, that I had come armed.

When Brad and his father reached us, I took his arm and said, "I don't think I want a drink, after all. I'd really like to just go back and go to bed. We were up awfully early, and tomorrow's a big day."

I laid my head lightly on Brad's shoulder when I said "bed," and smiled at Marylou and his father.

She flushed.

"I told the Thorntons we'd see them in the bar after dinner, Brad," she said, looking narrowly at her son.

"Lucy's with them. Her divorce was final last week, and they thought a little rest would be good for her. She's awfully anxious to see you."

"Not tonight, Ma," he said, ruffling my hair. "Smoky's right. She's had a long, hard day."

"Well, then, I'll tell her you'll see her for tennis in the morning," his mother said. In the dimness her blue eyes flashed. "She said she hoped you'd give her a game. Remember how you two used to play tennis all day long down here?"

"Ma," Brad said, smiling, "In the morning I'm going to sleep until noon at the very least, and then I'm taking Smoky sailing. Tell Lucy I'll see her at Mama Hunt's party. Or if not there, I'll catch up with her back home."

Marylou Hunt lifted her carved chin.

"I thought at the very least you might give me a hand with the party arrangements in the morning," she said. "I've got that whole lounge to get into shape, and the flowers to be brought—"

"Since when have I ever helped you with that party?" he grinned. "What has the Cloister got a florist and a staff for? Let up, Ma. Smoky's going to think you're a nag, and she's already gotten a broadside from Mama Hunt."

Marylou smiled silkily.

"I do hope she wasn't too awful, Smoky," she said. "She has a terrible tongue. I tried to get Brad to put you up in one of the cottages, but oh, no, it had to be that old wreck—"

"The old wreck is looking pretty good," Brad said. "And Grandma was positively taken with Smoky. They hit it off like gangbusters, didn't you, Smokes?"

"She's really something," I said.

"Yeah, her last words as we left for lunch had to do with, ah, Smoky's remarkable reproductive potential," Brad smiled. He watched his mother.

Two hectic red spots appeared on her cheeks.

"It would be hard to miss that, wouldn't it?" she said, and turned and walked down the hall. Brad's father looked at us, shrugged helplessly, turned his red palms out, and trudged off after her.

Brad chuckled softly.

"That was rotten," I said, leaning back against him. I could feel the soft, steady thrum of the lazy power in me, like a tiny engine. I thought that he could probably feel it too, under his blue blazer.

"Not nearly rotten enough," he said, and I could feel him laugh softly. "She asks for it. Over and over, she asks for it."

"Well, she gets it," I said. "You ready?"

We decided to walk home down the beach. I went into the ladies' room and took off my panty hose and put them in my purse, and Brad tossed a folded bill to the parking valet and asked him to garage his car, and we walked through the silent, torch-lit gardens over to the beach club and down the terrace steps and out onto the sand, to the edge of the water. Behind us, on the upper pool terrace, colored lights uplit the great oaks, and the strains of soft rock drifted gently, but the wind was off the sea, strong and fresh, and we could not hear the music clearly. We took off our shoes and walked in the edge of the surf. It was sun warm, birth-warm. After a few minutes the cluster of lights faded, and except for a few lone yellow-lit windows in the big, far-apart houses, the night was almost totally dark. There was no moon at all, and a faint silver peppering of stars hardly showed through the scrim of high cloud. The sea itself seemed to give off light, a spectral, colorless light that was more like the sea's breath. I could hear the splash of Brad's feet beside me, and feel the warmth of his hand on mine, and the soft exhalation of his body heat, but I could hardly make him out at all. The night was soft and thick and black and warm as velvet, silky on my skin, smelling of iodine and salt and crape myrtle and that ineffable, skin-prickling saline emanation that says "ocean" to me whenever I smell it, hundreds of miles inland. It always moves me close to tears, so visceral, so old and tidal is its pull. I have often thought that it is the first smell we know, the amniotic smell of our first, secret sea.

After a while, Brad said, "You're handling the Hunt women awfully well. I'd say today and tonight were yours on knockouts."

"Well, it strikes me that you could get a little tired of fighting after a while," I said.

"You wouldn't have to fight long. Grandma's already on your side. Mother will be, too, when you're . . . you know, part of her world. When she knows you're a long-term thing. And you are, you know. If you want to be."

"I think that your mother will be on my side about as soon as your grandmother was on hers," I said. "I'm not saying it makes a lot of difference, not to me. I can live an astonishingly full life without your mother in it. But I think it would eventually make an enormous difference to you."

"You're wrong," he said. "I love my mother, I guess, but I don't like her. What she thinks about my . . . woman is simply not a factor."

"Brad," I said, still wrapped in the languid, dreaming state in which I had left the hotel, "of course it's a factor. What do you think all this stuff is about, anyway?"

He did not answer. He pulled me closer into the curve of his body and we walked slowly, kicking the glittering foam, our arms around each other's waists. Languor wrapped me like warm water. Marylou Hunt simply did not matter. Very little did, but the sensations of this night.

"Can you live with all this family business?" Brad said. "I'll try to keep it apart from us, but some of it will spill over. We're not an easy family, but I'd try to make us easier to take than we have been."

"You haven't seen a messed-up family until you've seen mine," I said. "I've learned to live pretty close inside myself. Families aren't a major factor with me. I always thought I'd have my own family, and the rest of them could just . . . work it out."

"So when will I meet yours, then?"

"There is a very good chance that you won't," I said, and stopped and turned to face him. "I told you when we first met what they're like. That isn't going to change. If we . . . if we should get together, it would not be a matter of rejoicing to them. On the contrary, the bitterness and resentment would just get thicker. I've seen it start to happen already. I don't plan to go home again, Brad, unless somebody dies, and then it will be alone, and for as short a time as I can decently manage. One thing your mother will not have to contend with is a pack of wild shanty Irishmen."

"It's your call," he said. "Although I'd give a lot to see my mother tackle your father. What you've told me of him anyway. We'll be virtual orphans, then, if that's what you want."

I knew that he was speaking of marriage, speaking more directly of it than he ever had, and that very soon now I must throw off this delicious torpor, this tiny, effervescent fizzing in my blood, and answer him. Soon, I said to myself, drifting down the night beach in the circle of his arm. Soon. But not just this second.

Presently we were opposite the big pink house, and started across the beach up to the steps and the lawn. The tide was very far out, so that we walked for some time. At the dune line, just before the whispering stands

of sea oats and dune grass began, the sand was as damp
and cold as the skin of a snake under my feet. We picked
our way through matted sand spurs and small, broken
shells to the path that led between the dunes, and then
up the sandy marble steps and onto the stiff, dew-cold
Bermuda grass of the lawn. When we drew even with
the cabana that lay alongside the pool, Brad said, "Let's
sit out awhile. I think there's some scotch in the cabana
that I left there last year, and I'll put on some music.
You're not ready to go in, are you?"

His voice was low and rough, as if it caught in his
throat.

"No," I said, around the breath that was soft and
thick in my own throat. "I'm not."

"Be right back."

He disappeared into the little bougainvillea-clad
cabana and I dropped down on a wrought iron chaise
and stretched out. It was damp with dew, and my bare
legs and feet recoiled from the wet chill. I sat up again,
wrapping my arms around my bare legs, and looked up
at the house. No lights broke the great sweep of its
facade. It was so dark that I could scarcely make out the
line of the flat tiled roof against the sky. Even if Brad's
grandmother or her companion or Sarelle were awake
and looking out, I thought, they could not see us. We
might be the only two people on all the length of this
beautiful beach. Alone under the sky, in the wind, beside
the sea. I shivered. The entire inside of me, from my
throat to the dark, secret core of me, began to tremble,
such a small, silvery shivering that it made me think of
the beating of hummingbird wings, of moths fluttering
in the warm dark. The smell of bougainvillea was heavy
and sweet.

Brad came out of the cabana carrying a bottle, and
inside, I heard the mechanism of a record player lift and

thump, rustily, and Frank Sinatra began to sing, softly, of April in Paris.

Brad handed me a glass and said, "Here's looking at you, kid," and I took a long, burning swallow of scotch and felt it track its way down the tunnel inside me to where the trembling had settled.

He dropped down on the lounge beside me and pulled me against him. The hand that rested on my shoulder traced the line of it, down inside my red linen, to where the fresh sunburn felt as if it were glowing. I felt my skin flicker as if a fly had lit there.

"What are you thinking?" he said.

"I'm thinking . . . that I've forgotten all about Andre," I said, surprising myself. "I have. I've lost him entirely—"

He kissed the top of my head.

"Smoky, you can have Andre and all this, too. Don't you see that? You don't have to lose Andre. Keep him, keep all your Andres and your . . . your YMOGs, and whatever else you want to keep. You can still have this. This house, this island, all of it. I'm not asking you to give anything up when you take this on."

I took a deep breath and skewed around so that I could look at him. I could only see the glimmer of teeth, and the white of eyes.

"Brad, what are we talking about?" I said.

"You must know that we're talking about getting married. Do you want me to ask you formally, on my knees? I will. I thought you understood that's what I've been talking about all day."

"So . . . when would you want to do it?" I said. My voice sounded as if it belonged to a stranger.

He was silent for a moment, and then he said, "I'd like to give you a ring at Christmas and get married in June. And I'd like to come down here for a couple of weeks. I didn't think I was going to care about the whens and wheres, but all of a sudden I do. That's the way my crowd has always done it, and that's the way I want to do it, too. Unless you want something else—"

"No, no . . . I don't care. I mean, I never had any special plans about how I'd do it. I didn't even know if I would—do you mean, stay here in the house with your grandmother?"

"Jesus, no," he laughed. "One of the big cottage suites right on the water, breakfast in bed, lunch in bed, dinner in bed, fresh oysters and champagne at midnight—"

"Well," I said, my ears ringing, "That sounds good to me. Christmas sounds fine."

We looked at each other, or at least, where each other should be, in the darkness.

"It sounds as if we've been negotiating a merger," I said, laughing a little and hearing my voice break.

He got up from the chaise and pulled me up after him. Behind us, in the cabana, I heard a record fall, and then the smoky voices of the Four Freshmen:

Angel eyes, that old devil-sent,
they glow unbearably bright. . . .
Need I say, that my love's misspent,
misspent with angel eyes tonight. . . .

"Dance with me, Smoky," Brad whispered, and I went wordlessly into his arms, and we swayed together on the dark apron of the still pool, its surface throwing back moon-scud and star-pricks, while that most sensuous and limbic of ballads spun out into the soft air. By the time it ended, we were standing still, bodies pressed so hard together that we seemed to be part of each other, and the kisses that had begun on the side of my face and my closed eyelids had turned into such long, deep, seeking, blinded things that I had no breath left, felt nothing but the heat and pressure of his body and his hands on mine, and the simple, crushing need to be separate from him no longer.

He jerked his head back and took deep, ragged breaths of air.

"I don't know if I'm going to make it until Christmas," he half-gasped, half-laughed. "Does this answer your question about negotiations?"

I stood still, blinded, body humming all over, as if every inch of me had been scorched that day by the sun.

"Let's go swimming," I said, and could scarcely make out the words in my own ears.

"Smokes—"

"Let's do it," I said, and stepped back hastily and reached behind me and unzipped my dress and let it fall to the concrete. I stepped out of it, and unfastened my bra and let it fall, and then the little nylon bikini panties that I had bought at J.P. Allen, with Peter Max whorls and stars on them. I stood naked in the dark, burning, shaking, looking at Brad, and then I went to the edge of the pool and let myself down into the dark water. It was like slipping into sun-hot silk, black and enveloping, lapping warm at my breasts and thighs, covering me, as warm as the blood inside me, as dark as the night outside.

I held up my arms to him.

"Come in."

He made a small, strangled sound, and I heard his clothing rustle and fall, and then he was in front of me, holding me against him, the firm, rubbery feel of flesh against mine all the way down the length of me, nothing held back now, no barriers, cradled in the buoyant water as in other arms. I wrapped my arms and legs around him in the dark water, and held him close, and closed my eyes.

He maneuvered us against the side, so that he had purchase on the bottom of the pool, holding me above the surface. If he had let go I would have gone completely under; he was inches taller than I. But he did not let go. He moved against me in the dark, warm water, murmuring things that I knew on my skin and in my mouth, instead of hearing with my ears, rocking gently, rocking.

"I shouldn't," he said into my wet hair. "I didn't mean this yet—"

"Yes," I said fiercely. "I want this now. I do, Brad—"

"How long has it been since . . . the last time, Smokes?" he whispered, not stopping the rocking. I was nearly mad with it.

"Never . . . I thought you knew that—"

"No, I mean . . . since your last period. I don't have anything with me—"

"It's okay," I said, feeling my nails biting into his back. "It's okay. It was just a few days ago—"

"Ah, God!" he cried softly, and went into me.

At first I could not get a deep breath, and when I could, I thought that the pain would rob me of my voice. With the pain came a silent explosion of fear and despair so black and profound that it felt, simply, apocalyptic. When I could cry out, it sounded like the mewling of a kitten.

"Stop! Oh, Brad, stop—"

The pain stopped abruptly and he hung on the side of the pool beside me, gasping for breath.

"Oh, God, I'm sorry, Smoky! Jesus, I should have been gentler, I should have gone slower. . . . Are you hurt? Did I hurt you bad?"

"No, no, it's all right," I whispered, but even in the pool I could feel sweat pouring off my face, and the tingling around my mouth that meant the blood had drained away from it. I had never felt anything like it before, neither the pain nor the blackness. I put my hands up to my face and began to cry.

He pulled me gently up out of the pool and found a big towel and cradled me in it, drying me gently and whispering to me. He was so contrite and so worried that I tried to reassure him, but I could not stop the ridiculous blubbering.

He rocked me against him until some of the weeping stopped.

"It won't be like that again," he said. "There are ways, things I can do. . . . I rushed you. I should have thought. . . . Next time will be a whole different thing. We have all the time in the world, Smokes. I'll get you some pills, and then we won't have anything at all to worry about."

"It wasn't you," I said, sniffling, trying to hold on to him. "It wasn't you. I'm all right, it doesn't hurt now. But Brad . . . I can't do that again. I just can't. Not until . . . not right away—"

"I know. I said we wouldn't, until you have the pills and there's the right time and place to take it slow. It's my fault—"

"No. It's not you. It's . . . I'm sorry. This sounds so damned Catholic. But . . . I think it's the Church. Right at the time we were—right when it happened—it was like every muscle in my body turned to iron, and something in my head just screamed No! No! Do this and you are—I don't know—lost. Just . . . lost—"

I began to cry again. I sounded demented, even to myself.

He took in a long breath and let it out softly.

"I had no idea you felt that strongly about the Church, Smoky," he said.

"I didn't, either," I said. "I don't. I haven't thought about the Church since I left home. I haven't even been to church. I don't know what's the matter with me. I wanted you to do that—"

"It's all been too much," he said, pressing my face into his bare, wet shoulder. "My mother's been at you since day one, and then Grandma, and this afternoon, and that business at dinner, and the goddamned party hanging over both of us—you just panicked. You're tired, and I pushed you too fast. We'll cool it, sweetie, for now. Until Christmas. We'll just . . . take cold showers and keep our hands off each other and think pure thoughts, and then see where we are when you have the ring and it's all settled. That okay with you? Would that help?"

"Yes," I said, kissing his shoulder and tasting salt and chlorine. "Yes, it would. I'm sorry. I just feel like a . . . you know, a tease—"

"Nobody was ever less one," he said. "But I want you to start on the pills, anyway. I think they take awhile to work. Come on. Let's get you to bed. Tomorrow we'll start over, fresh. I'll even get down on my knees and propose to you."

We dressed and went quietly up the dark stairs and down the hall to my room. He opened the door for me, and switched on my bedside lamp, but did not come in.

"I will not be responsible for my actions if I do," he said, and kissed me lightly on the forehead, and closed the door behind him.

I meant to take a long hot bath, but I did not, after all. I just skinned into my nightgown and crawled into bed and turned out the light. Remembering that I had wanted to lie in bed and look at the stars over the sea, I turned on my side to face the window wall, but it was blank, dark. The wind had fallen, and the chintz drapes hung limp against the screens. Only the small ticking of night insects against them broke the thick silence. I slept almost immediately.

During the night I woke with a sharp, stinging pain between my legs and a dull headache. I got up and went into the bathroom for an aspirin. When I got back into bed, I saw that there was a small, damp blot of blood on the silky, yellowed old percale sheet. I started back to the bathroom for a cold, damp washcloth, to scrub it out, but stopped midway. The hell with it. I did not think that there had been the stains of life and love on these sheets for fifty years, only, perhaps, the thin, sour spillings of medicine and weak tea. Let Mama Hunt make of it what she would.

I got back into bed and pulled up the sheet and was asleep before my head hit the pillows.

Teddy was waiting for me when I climbed the last steps of the apartment—gingerly, for the pain between my legs still bit and stung—and dropped down onto the sofa.

"Well?" she yelped. "Did you?"

I looked at her for a moment, and then shrugged, and said, "Yeah. I guess I did. Sort of."

"Oh, fantastic! Tell about it! How was it!"

"Teddy . . . does it always hurt like that?"

She stared at me, and then began to laugh and make small noises of distress at the same time.

"Oh, sweetie! I meant did you get engaged! But I guess you did, if you did that. . . . Oh, no! It doesn't hurt at all after a while. It gets to be wonderful, it really does. But it almost always hurts the first time. . . . Damn Brad. He shouldn't have rushed you . . . but, oh, Smoky! So when will you get your ring? When will you get married?"

"Christmas, I think, for the ring," I said. Here, in the city, it seemed simply impossible that she and I should be having this conversation, about rings and weddings. I shook my head.

"And the wedding? Can I be in it? I demand to be your maid of honor, on pain of death. . . . Oh, Lord, but Marylou will simply shit, isn't it wonderful?"

"Brad said something about next June," I said. "But nothing's set. Please don't tell anybody, Teddy. I . . . I have to get used to the idea first. It all feels so strange. Lord! And then, we have to make all those plans—"

Fatigue washed over me like tepid water. The plans hung ahead of me like a line of alps on the horizon. I did not see how I could cross them.

"Oh, all right," she said. "But I can't wait to see Matt's face. Are you sure I can't tell just a few people?"

"I'm sure. Really. Please don't. I'll tell you when."

"You're the bride," she said, coming over to hug me. "Sit down. I'll make coffee. So tell me, how was the party?"

"Just like your folks' Christmas party, only with palm trees," I said.

10

AFTER THAT, EVERYTHING WAS DIFFERENT, AND YET IT was not. I still went to work each morning and came home each evening, often very late; I still jockied with Matt for stories with teeth in them and often lost; I still laughed at Tom Gordon's whimsical foolishness and often noticed, behind it, the new aloneness in his eyes; I still bantered affectionately with Hank and Teddy and often was submerged in pure joy at my affection for them. I still stepped over Lucas Geary, and more than once stepped on him. I was still inundated, at odd, unguarded moments, with a tidal wave of delight and incredulity at my good fortune for having been cast out of Corkie and into Camelot.

But I did it all, now, with the subterranean knowledge that I was a semiofficial part of Brad Hunt's life, and would, in four short months, become an official part of it. And six months after that, would become myself a Hunt. I felt, obscurely, as if a clock had begun to tick.

I could not give a name to the confluence of feelings that swept me when I thought about Brad. Pride, certainly;

I could not look at him without feeling that, nor think of all that the name Hunt connoted without it. The mere thought of the lovely, shabby old house on Sea Island made me giddy with joy; it did not seem possible that soon it would be mine. I thought far more about it than the house where Brad and I would live, for I had no idea, yet, what it would be like, or where. Brad had said he would start looking around Buckhead, and when I said that there were some wonderful old houses in Ansley Park that I liked, he smiled.

"Out of my orbit, but I'll look," he said.

I know that I felt physical desire for him, despite the abortive ending to our first attempt at lovemaking, on Sea Island. He was simply too masculine, too assured, too handsome for me or any woman not to respond to him. The lovemaking would ultimately be wonderful, transcendent. Teddy had said so, and I did not doubt her.

And he was, I thought, a good man; he felt strongly about the right things. His sympathies were mine. I would always be proud of him. He would be a real factor in the life of the city. In those early, tentative days I did not doubt that I loved him.

But there was something else, something. . . . Somehow I could not imagine my life after the wedding ceremony at St. Philip's Cathedral. Try as I might, I could not imagine what my days and nights would be for all the years ahead of me. I could imagine a future centered around *Downtown*; it was as vivid and palpable to me as if I had already lived it. But somehow I could not bring Brad into it. Try as I might, I could not imagine getting up in our house in Collier Hills or Brookwood Hills— proper starter-house neighborhoods for Brad's set—and going to work for Matt Comfort's magazine. The two worlds simply did not seem malleable enough to mix.

And yet I knew that he wanted me to continue on the staff. He had said as much, over and over. There was no reason I could not be both Smoky O'Donnell and Mrs. Bradley Hunt III. But I kept wanting to ask him, over and over, if he was serious about that. I did not know why.

I did not ask. I did not talk much with Brad about being engaged or being married the following June. I felt shy about it, almost, for some reason, embarrassed. And he did not push it. We simply went about our lives as we had done before, going out two or three times a week, talking on the phone daily. Teddy did not push it, either. She bit her tongue daily, I knew, but she told no one. For a time after we returned from Sea Island, it was as if we had never been, Brad and I. It was altogether a strange, suspended time, though I do not remember it being an uncomfortable one. Just . . . suspended.

In late August he took me to dinner at the Coach and Six, out Peachtree Road toward Buckhead. We sat in a black leather booth and drank daiquiris and ate wonderful, flaky spinach and cheese puffs and perfect lamb chops in little white frilled paper panties, and afterward he gave me a small gold-wrapped box.

For some reason my heart began to pound. Not yet, my mind said, clearly and silently.

"What's this?" I smiled at him.

"It's sort of a going away present," he said. "Dad wants me to go over to Huntsville and bid a job. It's a big one, a complex for some new rocket thing at Redstone Arsenal. I've never bid one completely on my own before, and there'll be a lot of larger firms in the running. It could go on for several weeks. I ought to have the experience if I'm going to take over the company one day, but it's a hell of a time to have to leave you—"

"But it's a big thing for you," I said, knowing that it was. Brad's father was reluctant to let go of the reins of the business he had built, and I knew that Brad often chafed about that.

"I'm so proud," I went on. "Aren't you at all excited?"

"Yeah, I have to admit I am," he said, and his blue eyes danced in the light of the small shaded table lamp. "I really am. I love this part of the business, and it's going to be a real fire fight. But I'm going to miss you like crazy. I'll get home one or two weekends, but it's not going to be much fun."

"Well, it's not as if it'll be forever, or very far away," I said. "Maybe I could come over for a weekend."

"Jesus, you'd hate it," he laughed. "It's like boot camp, all posturing and testosterone. You'd probably get raped walking to the Coke machine. Stay here and work hard and let me think wet-sheet thoughts about you."

I reddened and he laughed and squeezed my hand.

"Open your present," he said, and I did.

Inside was a small black velvet jeweler's box. It was not new; the velvet was worn down to the matte backing in spots, and it smelled faintly of dusting powder and cedar. I opened it. A thin gold bracelet lay on a bed of yellowing white satin, a simple circle of old, pinkish gold, glowing dully in the lamplight. In it were set a row of rubies, so dark that they flashed red only in their hearts. It was old-fashioned and very beautiful.

"Oh, Brad," I said, looking up at him. It was obviously a family treasure. I felt for a moment as if I had been given something so intimate and personal that it was forbidden, something stolen, spoils in some sort of war.

Perhaps, I thought, I had.

He clasped it around my wrist. I held it up, watching the lamplight dance on the burnished old gold.

"It's absolutely beautiful," I said.

"It was my great-grandmother Hunt's," he said. "There's a tradition that the newest of the Hunt brides-to-be gets it, until it's time to pass it along. Mother never especially liked it; it's been in the safe for a long time. It's kind of a pre-pre-wedding thing. Not on the level of an engagement ring, but a statement of policy, anyway. The ring is great-grandmother's, too; rubies and emeralds. You get that at Christmas. There are some terrific diamonds, a necklace and bracelet and earrings, but you don't get those until the wedding. The family pearls come when the first baby is born."

I sat turning my wrist this way and that. I had never even imagined such things as he sat talking of, family jewels that came on state occasions, to mark the passages of life. In Corkie, jewelry was purchased on the installment plan, and ran to the sentimentally religious: crosses with modest diamond chips, and rosaries with pearls. But in Brad's family, rubies came with understandings, diamonds rained down on weddings, pearls flowed when the babies came.

Babies . . .

"Babies?" I said stupidly to Brad.

"You know. Wah wah? Diapers? Talcum powder? You do want children, don't you, Smoky?"

I had never once since I had met Brad Hunt, from the time he had told me I had eyes the color of rain in Teddy's parents' game room to now, when he sat talking of rubies and diamonds and pearls, thought of children. I could not seem to take the words in.

"What would I do about my job?" I said. Even in my own ringing ears, the words sounded ridiculous.

"Well, I don't mean immediately," he said. "Not for maybe two or three years. I'd want us to get settled in a house first and have time to get used to each other. Wait awhile until we have to lock the bedroom door. You'd work right along until then, of course. But you'd want to be home with them for a while, at least, wouldn't you? We could get a nurse or a nanny or something later, but right for the first few years, I mean, you'd want to do that, wouldn't you? You could always do some freelance stuff. Lots of girls . . . women . . . I know do that. Snake Cartwright's wife writes a column for the Marietta *Daily Journal,* and she has three kids. Dottie Findlay does catering with her college roommate, and she's got two. You don't have to stop working entirely, not ever."

I sat still, images darting and pecking at me like birds. Small, tow-headed children capering on the beach at Sea Island. Small black children at rickety tables on a tiny, dismal back porch in Summerhill. A small black child, his face radiant with joy, hugging the bumper of a little English car . . .

I was nowhere in the images.

"Smoky?"

I shook my head and smiled at him.

"Of course I want children," I said. "Every woman does—"

"But you could still work. You could still write. If it stays important to you," he said, smiling back at me. "Sometimes things change when children come."

"I'll always want to, Brad," I said.

"Then you shall. Now. Look down under the layer of satin."

I did, and pulled out a small vial of pills and a folded prescription.

"A head start on not having any, until we want to," he grinned. "A head start on things being better for us. I got them from Pom Fowler. He's doing his residency at Piedmont this year, in OB-GYN. Says take them for a month according to the directions. I thought we might as well do this while I'm gone, so when I get back I can stop taking cold showers every time I think about you. By the time I'm back from Huntsville, we should . . . be in business."

I looked at the pills and the prescription. I looked up at him. In the lamplight he looked so impossibly handsome that it was as if I were seeing him for the first time.

"I don't want to wait, Smoky," he said in a low voice. "I keep thinking about you in that pool. About the way you looked and felt . . . "

Out of nowhere the blackness struck again, a swift rush of such lightlessness and despair that I could only close my eyes against it and hold my breath.

Oh, God, don't, the thought came, spontaneous and terrible. Don't. I haven't done it again. I'm not going to, not anytime soon . . .

The blackness ebbed and I opened my eyes and looked at him. I knew that he had noticed nothing.

"We said we'd wait—" I whispered.

"And so we will, if we have to. But this is just in case . . . we can't. I want to show you how good it can be, Smoky. I want you to forget about that other."

I tried to smile, but the memory of the blackness was like dark water over me.

"But if I wanted to wait until we were married? Would that be so awful?" I said finally.

"I guess not. Not if you really wanted to. I thought, the other night, down there . . . I thought you wanted it, too."

"I did. I really did. I do. It's just that—you'd have to be raised Catholic to understand it, Brad. I know I don't go to church now, and I don't want to make a point of it, but all those years of being told no, wait, don't, it's a sin, you'll be punished—it's hard. I didn't know how hard it was going to be."

He raised his hand. "If that's what makes you comfortable, Smokes, that's what we'll do. Jesus, and I thought the sexual revolution was here. But will you take the pills anyway? Just so you'll be used to them when the time comes? Pom says sometimes you have to change dosages or brands before you get 'em right. He says when you've finished this batch, come see him before you get the prescription filled. You ought to have an OB-GYN anyway, and he's going to be one of the best."

"Yes, all right," I said, thinking I'd rather die than have one of Brad's dancing school friends poking and prodding around in that secret darkness, where, it seemed now, God waited like a coiled snake.

"Good girl. Want some chocolate mousse?" he said.

"Why not?" I said, smiling, looking at my bracelet and feeling in my palm the shape of the pill vial, like an amulet.

Like a stone.

I lay awake a long time that night. There was a huge, sullen white moon, and it seemed to me that I could feel the hot weight of it on my body. The air-conditioner labored and the green glow of the digital clock bathed the bedside table. In it, I could see the little bottle of birth control pills. There was, now, one less pill in it. I lay waiting for the enormity of swallowing it to crash down over me, for the black emptiness that seemed, obscurely, to be the voice of the Church, perhaps the very forbidding voice of God, but it did not come. It did not matter. I had felt it twice now, both times in conjunction with making love to Brad Hunt, and it had made its point.

In all my years in the Church, in all my endless years of parochial education, I had never taken seriously the nun's dictum that sinners were swiftly and directly punished for their sins. I thought, if I thought of it at all, that they meant that sooner or later, you would suffer the consequences of this sinful act or that, and invariably come to repent them. I had not imagined that the Church spoke directly and terribly in your heart at the moment of your sin, much less at the mere contemplation of it.

I still did not think so, not rationally. It was too simplistic, too pat. I would have heard about it, my friends would have spoken of it. Surely there were, among their number, greater sinners than I. But I did not know what the terrible, empty despair meant, and down in the place inside me where no rationality lived, the Catholic place, it frightened me. I lay awake a long time thinking of it.

I would have liked to ask someone what it meant, but could think of no one, not in Atlanta, this newest and most pragmatic of cities. Not among the sunlit people who were now my people. And then I thought, Sister Joan. I can ask Sister Joan. If it happens again, that's what I'll do.

The morning after Brad left for Huntsville, Matt called me into his office.

"Brad called me last night," he said, without preliminaries. "He's worried about you doing the black deejay piece. He doesn't think it's quite seemly, and he thinks it might even be dangerous. He's worried about all the rioting. Thinks the deejays are going to go on a rampage, I guess."

He tilted back in his desk chair and peered at me over the wire-rimmed glasses. He looked especially rumpled this morning, as if he had been doing more in his clothes during the night than sleeping. His long fingers played restlessly with the ever-present pile of coins and the watch.

I was literally dumbfounded. I could feel the heat rise in my face and knew that the red stain was climbing behind it.

"I can't believe he'd do a thing like that," I said finally.

"Yep. Right adamant about it, he was," Matt said. "Said little black kids in day care was one thing, but black musicians and their camp followers in a motel on

Stewart Avenue was another. Camp followers; been a long time since I've heard that. Seemed to think there was going to be right much . . . ah, controlled substance use among the conventioneers. Can't imagine why he'd think a thing like that."

"He had no right," I said. My mouth was numb.

"He seemed to think he had every right. Is there something you're not telling us, Smoky? Are congratulations in order here?"

He grinned.

I shook my head silently.

Matt's smile faded and he leaned back in the chair and put his small feet on his desk, and laced his fingers behind his head.

"Thing is, he could be right. The country's in a shitty mood. Everybody's mad, and the young Negroes are the maddest of all. I've heard a rumor that the Panthers will be back in town, and if they are, you can bet your ass they'll be at that convention. It's too good to pass up. And they're packin', baby. I don't need you anywhere around any fucking guns. We've got the war thing, too; ever since Dr. King joined that March in April, the war has gotten to be a big Negro thing. And the mess in Newark and Detroit . . . we pretty much forget about rioting and violence down here, because our particular focus is Dr. King and the nonviolent business, and Atlanta never did give much of a shit about what was going on anywhere else. But you can bet the deejays are going to bring it in here. And drugs, sure there'll be drugs. Every kind you ever heard of. These guys invented drugs. I hadn't really thought all that through when I assigned this convention for Focus."

"And it was Brad who was so kind as to point all this out to you?" I asked incredulously. I had never heard Brad concern himself with events outside the city.

"No. Matter of fact, it was Luke. He's concerned about taking you along. He knows the smell of things as well as anybody I know. He's not really worried about any of it except the Panthers. Nobody really knows what these mothers'll do after they stormed the California assembly toting rifles last spring. I don't feel like messing around with those cats."

"Matt, you promised me Focus," I said, foolish tears beginning to well up in my eyes. I did not know why I was so insistent. I should have been alarmed at his words, and indeed, a part of me was. But a larger part felt betrayed, and furiously angry. How dare Brad do this to me? How dare Luke?

"I promised before I thought, Smoky," he said. "I'm not a fool; I know better than to send my people where there's danger. I ought to cancel the whole business. Thing is, the convention PR people have already announced that we'll be doing an in-depth photo-essay. We'd look like assholes if we reneged. Like we were cowards. I called John Howard on this, and he said he didn't think there was any danger involved. There's going to be too much media there, and most of these guys—they're musicians, they're lovers—they just aren't political. The Panthers are, of course, if it's true they're back in town. But he doesn't think there'll be any trouble from them. I gather he knows the ones who're apt to be there, and he says their whole thing nowadays is to show people how much better their way is than the old nonviolent way. He thinks they'd be the last ones to start trouble. Real bad PR."

"So what are you saying?"

"I'm saying you can go, and I'm probably a fool to let you. But you work well with Luke, and Howard likes your style. The day care story was a fine piece of work."

I looked at him, beginning to grin.

"Thank you, Matt."

"You're welcome, Smoky. Now git. And tell Hank I want him in here."

I paused in the doorway and looked back at him, but he was already bent over his desk. Then he lifted his head, bared his teeth at me like a wizened wolf, and gave three raucous blats on the taxi horn.

"Don't go shining your behind yet," he said.

"I won't," I said, and left his office, heart high.

From the outset, it was clear that the meeting of black disc jockeys was not much of a convention, and the story was probably nonexistent. When we pulled up to the Santa Fe Plaza Motel at dusk on a hot, still Friday evening of the Labor Day weekend, we might have been pulling into a tourist court in the Florida wiregrass in the early 1950s. There were not many cars in the spaces behind the motel, where the sad, straggling urban woods threatened to take back the weedy asphalt parking lot. I could see few at the adjoining motels, either. They lay like tarnished, badly strung necklaces on either side of Stewart Avenue. The avenue itself was tarnished, far past its prime and slightly menacing in the motionless twilight. Pawnshops, nude dancing clubs, convenience stores, package stores, aluminum bus stops, phone booths with the phones torn out, mom and pop groceries—Stewart Avenue was, simply, banal and badly used. It lacked the gut-wrenching drama of the horrific ghettos to the east, and had none of the sheen of affluence that lay on the neighborhoods to the northwest. There was a continual stream of traffic along it, and along the broken sidewalks beside it, but it was aimless, desultory. None of the faces I saw was white.

"Where is everybody?" I said, looking around the motel parking lot. "I thought there were at least a couple of thousand deejays at this thing."

"Deejays don't like the light of day," Luke said, unloading his cameras from John Howard's trunk. "They're like vampires. Only howl when the sun has set."

"Yeah," John Howard said, locking the Mustang. "I bet if we went inside we'd find 'em all in their rooms with the lights off and the shades down, lying in coffins."

"No," I giggled, "Hanging from the shower rods upside down, like bats."

"They'll be hanging from the shower rods by tomorrow morning," John said. "Hung up and hungover."

I laughed outright.

He was different this evening. For one thing, he looked different. He did not wear the Ivy League shirts that were his habitual daytime dress, and he did not wear the ridiculous overalls he had worn on Pumphouse Hill, either. Tonight he wore bell-bottom blue jeans and a shirt of some silky black stuff, open almost to his waist, with a peace medal bumping against his smooth red-brown chest, and something that looked like an African fetish, of feathers and bone, on a leather thong. With the remarkable feral yellow eyes and the slanting scar through his eyebrow, he looked splendid, exotic, dangerous in a seductive way, like a jaguar, or another of the big cats.

"Lord, John, I wouldn't get in an elevator with you," I had said when he picked Luke and me up at the Commerce Building curb in the Mustang.

"Lawsy, Miss Smoky, I just a po' darky tryin' to git along," he had drawled, scowling at me, but I saw the amusement in his eyes. Since the night in the parking garage after the press party, when I had given him back his mocking banter, I was no longer in awe of him. But I was aware, still, that he had let me in only a very short way, and that I would not likely be allowed further.

The other difference in him was that he was ever so slightly nervy, just the least bit on edge. It was noticeable only in the barely perceptible increase in the pace of his words and movements, a kind of lithe jitteriness to him, and he laughed more than I had ever known him to do. Of course, I had never really known him any way but the way he appeared in the Focus meetings: grave, pleasant, assured, almost totally detached. Any change leaped out as if he had been boisterous. Laughter and joking about vampires and hangovers was, in John Howard, tantamount almost to hysteria.

"You look good," Luke said to me. "Look like you're ready to swing all night."

"I am," I said, and did a little bump-and-grind in the empty parking lot. I wore skin-tight, low-riding blue jeans with belled bottoms over a pair of Teddy's see-through vinyl boots and a turtleneck poor-boy sweater, sleeveless and cut high so that a wedge of midriff showed. The sweater was tight enough, Teddy said, to be trashy, and I agreed, but did not change it. I had glued on, ineptly, a pair of dime-store false eyelashes, and had a thick frosting of Carnaby Coral on my mouth, and wooden dangle earrings that almost brushed my shoulders. Lavender granny sunglasses completed the ensemble. I looked, Teddy had said when I left the apartment to meet Luke and John Howard, as tacky as gully dirt.

"But great," she added. "Slutty and go-to-hell and absolutely great. I wish Brad could see you."

"Yeah, that would just about do it," I said dryly. I was still angry at him for calling Matt about the story, and determined to tell him so when he called me on Sunday, as he had promised.

"Do that again," Luke said now, and I repeated the bump-and-grind and held my hand out to John Howard, and he took it, and we did a few exaggerated, hip-swinging, frug-like steps on the gritty pavement. Luke swung the Leica up and shot.

"Y'all are sure enough by-God goners now," he said, letting the camera bounce off his chest and ambling toward the motel office. "Cross me and I'll circulate that in Corkie and the SCLC."

"Corkie wouldn't know what it was," I said.

"You can see worse than that any night at Paschal's," John said. "And you have."

"Not from you, bro," Luke grinned, and we went into the motel to find the convention.

We found, instead, an empty lobby with burn-scarred Naugahyde furniture and overflowing pedestal ashtrays and a long plastic rubber plant that someone had decorated with round gold foil-wrapped condoms. Behind the desk an enormously fat white man sat, licking his index finger and paging through a cheap Bible. Over his knees was a broken shotgun. On the desk was a small American flag stuck upright in a coffee cup. At our approach the fat man looked up.

His look of weary inquiry changed to hostility when he saw me. He looked slowly from me to John Howard and then to Lucas Geary. He had small, slitted light eyes and white brows and lashes, and the heavy smell of stale sweat reached out from him to where we stood.

"Got no vacancies," he said, staring narrowly at my chest.

"We don't want a room," Luke said in an ineffably gentle drawl. "We're looking for the convention. The black disc jockeys?"

"You a disc jockey?" the man said to John Howard. He pronounced it dee-isk jawkey, drawing out the syllables insultingly.

"No," John Howard said.

"Look like one, got up like that," the man said.

"We're here to do a story on the convention for *Downtown* magazine," I said in what I supposed to be an authoritative voice. I saw Luke swallow a smile, and knew I was once again sounding like a Junior Leaguer.

"We have press passes," I added idiotically.

"Do you now," he said, leering and looking pointedly at my breasts and midriff. "You want to show me your . . . press pass, sweetie?"

"Are you the manager?" John Howard said pleasantly. His face was still.

"Night clerk. Manager ain't here. I'm runnin' 'er tonight," the man said. "Somethin' you wanted . . . sir?"

His tone said, "boy."

"We've got a legitimate appointment to do this story, and I'd appreciate it if you'd tell us where the delegates are," I said, my face hot. "I'd hate to have to tell my editor we got no cooperation from you."

He got up and started around the desk, waddling cumbrously.

"There's some of 'em down on the end, to the back," he said into my face. "And a few more upstairs in the rooms by the ice machines. Them's passed out, I think. Ain't heard that goddamned caterwaulin' in a while. The live ones are likely around back. Think I heard 'em throwin' coconuts at each other whallago. But I tell you one thing, girlie, you ain't goin' back there. White girls ain't gon' drink and party and I don't know what all with coloreds while I'm on duty. Two of 'em already gone back there early this afternoon and they ain't come out, and I ain't going back there lookin' for 'em, either. I told the manager wasn't no good going to come from letting coloreds carry on in this motel—"

Luke laid down his cameras and ambled up to the desk clerk. He reached out and took the man's fleshy cheek gently in his hand and twisted it. The man took a deep breath and reached back for the shotgun. John Howard went around the desk as quickly and lightly as a cat, and picked the gun up and held it behind him. I stared.

"We are from the *New York Times*," Luke said softly and merrily into the man's gobbling, outraged face. "All three of us have identification if you require it, and you should know that there are four or five more of us on the way. If you'd like to change your mind about directing us to the convention delegates, we'll go on back. Otherwise, I'm going to make one quick phone call and every newspaper and wire service in this country will have a stringer out here before you can change your britches. Your decision, friend."

The man wrenched his cheek out of Luke's grasp and retreated into an inner office and slammed the door. We heard the lock click into place.

"After you, Harrison Salisbury," John Howard said, bowing slightly to Luke, and we got halfway down the sour-smelling, smoky hall before we collapsed against the wall in silent, helpless laughter.

The back wing of the motel, where the fat man had said the convention delegates would be, was hot and dark and smelled powerfully of marijuana and liquor, and seemed to me as abandoned as a newly discovered Egyptian tomb. Walking down the shabby corridor was eerie; I felt the back of my neck prickle, and thought of every bad horror movie I had ever seen. We looked into one filthy, disheveled room after another: tangled bedclothes and strewn underclothing and empty plates and glasses said that life had been here, but the silence and the buzzing of flies said that it had gone. I waited, teeth clenched, to come to the room where the bodies were piled.

"It ain't exactly the Hyatt Regency, is it?" John Howard said grimly.

"For God's sake, don't pull back any shower curtains," Luke muttered. He had the Leica to his face, shooting one empty, terrible room after another. I knew that we could make something of the accommodations these visitors were forced to occupy in our article, if we could find faces to go with them.

We turned a corner into another long, stifling, shadowy corridor and heard music, faraway and insistent, the percussion first. It sounded as if, in the farthest rooms, someone was playing jungle drums.

"Man is in the forest," Luke said.

About halfway down the hall we pushed in a half-opened door and looked into the room. Grunts and squeals were coming from it, and a pounding, squeaking rhythm that I could not identify. Then I saw that a man and a woman were having sex half-on, half-off the sagging mattress, and that the sounds were coming from them and the mattress. Both were black and naked; she sat astraddle him, and at that moment they jackknifed off the bed and the woman shrieked and the man howled like a wolf.

I jerked my head out of the room and whirled away, face flaming.

"Whoa, 'scuse me, brother," Luke said under his breath. He did not lift the camera; I would have slapped it out of his hand if he had.

"People will do it," John Howard said. His face was calm and even a bit amused, but there was an involuntary lift to his upper lip, and a slight flaring of his nostrils, as if he could not disguise his disgust. I walked stiffly ahead of them both down the hall, the images of the sweat-slick black bodies contorting on the bed and John Howard's rictus of fastidiousness burning behind my eyes. Both were disturbing. Neither should have been, really.

At the end of the hall two doors were flung wide open and a powerful barrage of sound boiled out into the hall. It was Motown, a big, prowling wail of sound from an obviously good sound system. I recognized Aretha Franklin hammering out the ending of "Respect," and then, with no pause at all, the beginning of Otis Redding doing Fa-fa-fa-fa-fa. John Howard went into the nearest of the rooms, and Luke and I followed him.

It was completely dark; no lamps were lit, and the drapes were drawn tightly, but I don't think we could have made out anything of substance if the room had been floodlit. The sweet, acrid smoke of marijuana cigarettes was too thick. I choked on it, and coughed until I had to back out of the room. When my eyes stopped tearing and I went back in, someone had switched on a dim lamp, and I saw that John and Luke were standing just inside the door talking to an impossibly thin, yellowish man in a gigantic Afro and a silver lamé jumpsuit, who was lying on one of the beds smoking. Next to the man, in the crook of his arm, a heavyset black woman in only a loosely draped towel lay, smoking and drinking from a bottle of sweet wine. As my eyes grew accustomed to the murk, I saw that the other bed and the floor were occupied by couples in various stages of undress, all smoking and drinking, and that they had probably been at it for some time. Everyone had the stunned, loose-limbed beatific demeanor that I had come to associate with pot. Moreover, the bedside tables and floor corners were piled high with takeout food boxes, and half-eaten pizzas and gnawed chicken wings competed with empty wine bottles and overflowing ashtrays for floor space. Food and sweet smoke: no hard drugs here. I relaxed slightly.

The thin man uncoiled himself from the bed and stood, swaying slightly, to give me an exaggeratedly courtly bow. Behind him the woman stared levelly and insolently at us, and let the towel fall away from her great breasts. Luke grinned and raised the camera, and she pulled it up. The insolence gave way to dull anger.

"Allow me to present Lord Byron Playboy, from Scranton, Pennsylvania," Luke said, and the thin yellow man said, in a perfect Liverpudlian accent, "Chawmed."

"Likewise," I said, smiling. Lord Byron smiled back, and I saw with simple disbelief that his front teeth had been filed to sharp points.

"The better to eat you with, my dear," he said. I said nothing.

"I've explained to these folks what we're about, and Lord Byron here says it's okay by him if we take some shots," Luke said. "Seems like the rest of the folks are either . . . napping or over at La Carrousel. Horace Silver's in town. He also tells me that there's a big barbecue tonight over by AU for the delegates, thrown by none other than our little friends the Panthers. So the pickings here are pretty slim as far as the story goes. No offense, my man."

He nodded to Lord Byron Playboy, who had collapsed back on the bed. Lord Byron nodded back affably.

"'Fraid y'all stuck with jes' us no-'count, spaced-out niggers," he beamed. "Gon' have to go to the bobbycue to git the in crowd. Ought to be worth it, though. Them Panthers look real pretty in them little Panther suits. Make good pitchers, they would."

He looked over at John Howard, who stood leaning against a wall, studying him with courteous interest.

"You ain't one of 'em, are you, brother? Seem to me like I know your face from somewhere."

"I ain't one of 'em, no, brother," John said mildly.

"You with this magazine then?"

I knew that Lord Byron Playboy was parodying the rough dialect of the uneducated black man, and guessed that he meant it as a taunt to John Howard. But his smile was still brilliant and lazy and startling, with the vulpine pointed teeth.

"No," John said. "I'm with SCLC when I'm with anything. These are friends of mine. I'm just along for the ride."

"Whooee," Lord Byron said. "SCLC, FBI, NBC— Lord Byron don't know nothin' 'bout no initials. You mean you along to ride shotgun, don't you, brother? Keep this nice white girl and boy from gittin' set upon by savages?"

"You don't look too savage to me . . . brother," John said lazily. "Despite the Secret Squirrel teeth. What did you have in mind?"

"Why, bro, no mind at all," Lord Byron said, laughing mightily. "Go on and take your pictures, and then we give you a little somethin' to puff, or sip, or maybe a snack, if you fancy chawin' a bone."

He waved his hand loosely at Luke, who grinned and lifted the camera and shot around the room at the bodies on the beds and floors. No one moved, except to follow the camera with bloodshot, half-lidded eyes. Otis Redding segued into Ben E. King: "Stand by me, ohhhhh stand by me . . ."

Someone began to giggle, and I looked around for the sound, a smile tugging at my lips. A giggle was better than nothing. The sound went on and on, and then I realized that it was not a giggle at all, but sobbing, that got louder and louder until it was a wail, sick and hopeless, dreadful to hear. It broke off into vomiting, and then the whining sobbing began again. I thought that it was coming from behind the closed bathroom door. I looked around at the people in the room, but no one was paying any attention. I looked at Luke and John, who were looking at each other. The sobbing began to rise again, and I went quickly across the littered floor, literally stepping over couples, and opened the door into the bathroom.

A woman lay on the floor, curled in a fetal position around the base of the toilet. The bathroom was indescribable, unspeakable, filthy, hideous smelling. The woman lay with her head buried in her thin arms, and I could not see her face, but I saw that she was white. The desk clerk had said that two white women had come into the motel earlier; this must be one of them. There had to be something terribly wrong with her. The room reeked of vomit, and there was vomit caked in her hair, and on her arms and legs. Why the hell wasn't someone doing something for her? I took a deep breath and leaned over her.

It was not until I had gotten her turned over and half-propped against the wall and was squatting beside her, dabbing at her encrusted face with wet toilet paper, that I realized that she was Rachel Vaughn. I was so shocked that I rocked back on my heels and sat down heavily on the filthy floor.

She looked as if she were dying. Dying at that moment, of illness or starvation or perhaps physical abuse; she was so thin that I could almost see the bones through her slack, dirty gray flesh, and she was all over yellowing bruises. Especially on her bare arms and legs; they were so discolored that they did not look as if they belonged to a living human. I did not think that they would, for long. I really did think, sitting there and staring at her, my head whirling, that she would die under my eyes.

Her little fox's face, once sly and somehow charming, was edematous, swollen and discolored almost beyond recognition, but I knew her. The swelling did not seem to be that of physical abuse, but of illness. I could not define it. There were deep, near-black circles under her closed eyes, and her blazing fox's brush of hair had faded to hacked, pinkish-dyed straw, tangled now with her vomit. She had stopped crying for the time being, but she was breathing in deep gasps, as if she would vomit again, and I got up off my buttocks and tilted her head back and wiped her face gently with wet toilet tissue. There were no towels or washcloths at hand. Perhaps, I thought furiously, the sated and stoned women in the bedrooms were wearing them all.

"Rachel," I whispered. "Rachel. Can you open your eyes? Rachel, it's Smoky. Smoky O'Donnell. You remember me, from Our Lady?"

She did not open her eyes, but her puffed lips made a silent shape: "Smoky."

I found a filthy glass that had rolled under the washbasin and filled it, and held it to her lips, and she drank greedily, and then vomited it up, all over herself. The vomit was clear and thin; there was nothing left inside her. I turned for the roll of toilet paper, and when I turned back for her, her eyes were open and she was looking weakly at me.

"Smoky," she whispered.

"Let me clean you up," I said, dabbing furiously, "and then we're going to take you out of here."

She began to shake her head weakly, back and forth, no, no.

"Rachel, you're sick, you can't stay here. Oh, God, what on earth are you doing here, anyway?"

"What are you?" she said, and tried to smile. It was a terrible thing to see.

"I'm working," I said distractedly, and she stretched her mouth farther.

"So am I," she said, and all of a sudden I knew that she had come here as a prostitute, to make money. Sorrow and a terrible anger began, far down inside me.

She had never gone back to Our Lady, then.

"Well, you can't stay here. You're sicker than a dog. I'm going to get you to a doctor—"

"No." Her voice was stronger.

"Rachel—"

"No, goddammit, Smoky! Shit, I haven't even . . . scored yet. I got ahold of some bad stuff, and I've been puking ever since. I've still got my panties on." She tried to laugh, and it turned into a retch.

"Bad stuff. You mean food? Liquor?"

She shut her eyes and rolled her head on her neck.

"Stuff, Smoky. Shit. H. Heroin. Guy in there said he had some of the absolute best, but it's bad. . . . Oh, fuck it, you're impossible. You always were. Just get on out of here and let me alone."

"I'm not going to do that. You look like you could die—"

"I'm not going to die. I know the signs; I've had this before. It's just bad stuff. It wears off. I've got to score. I'm broker than shit—"

"I have some money. We have some with us—"

"No." Wearily.

"Well, then . . . Sister Joan. Let me call Sister Joan. You know she'll help, and she'll do it with no questions asked, not like those others. . . . Let me do that, Rachel."

"No. Christ. What's Sister Joan going to do, sing 'Blowin' in the Wind' to me? Go on, Smoky. Get out of here."

She slumped back onto the floor and covered her face with her hands. I scrambled to my feet.

"I'm going to call her," I said, and started out of the room.

"*Nooooooooooo!*"

It was a great, animal howl of illness and despair. It froze me in my tracks.

The door burst open and the heavy black woman was on me like a wildcat before I could move, clawing and scratching and spitting, literally spitting. I could feel her spittle hitting my face along with her fists, feel her hands in my hair, pulling my head straight back.

"You get out of here and leave us and our people alone, you white cunt," she screeched. "You got no business in there botherin' that girl! She came in with us!"

She jerked sharply backward, off me, and I saw that John Howard had her from behind, pinioning her flailing arms. He was holding her up off the floor, and her black legs were kicking at him and me alike. She was stark naked, and as wild and furious as a captured animal.

"Fucking cunt!" she screamed into my face, her face contorted. I felt my own go out of control with rage.

"You were going to just let her lie here and die, you bitch!" I screamed back, my face inches from hers. I had never been so angry in my life.

Luke came in, then, and he and John wrestled the thrashing woman back into the bedroom. Lord Byron Playboy got lazily to his feet and gave her a smack across the face, so hard that she staggered with it, and fell back onto the bed. She did not make another sound, but lay there, naked and heaving, staring murderously at me.

"Might be y'all will want to mosey on, now," Lord Byron said softly, and I saw that one or two of the men on the floor and the other bed were beginning to make as if to rise, slowly, and John said, "We'll be doing that," and before I could protest, he and Luke had marched me out of the room and were trotting me down the hall.

"But . . . Rachel . . . You don't understand, that girl in the bathroom, she's sick, she's had bad heroin, I know her. . . . Luke, she was at the Church's Home for Girls with me when I first got here. I just can't go off and leave her, she could die—"

"You can't help her, Smoky," John Howard said sharply, and pulled me out into the lobby. "You stick around and you'll get her hurt, as well as yourself. Lord, we never should have brought you—"

"I didn't start that," I said, wounded. My ears were still ringing, and my face stung from the black woman's blows. I tasted something metallic, and knew that the inside of my mouth was cut.

"I didn't say you did," he said. "I just said we shouldn't have brought you. You and Luke go on out to the car. I'll make a call and get her some help."

"Oh, John, not the police—"

"No. There's a doctor in SCLC I know who'll come."

"But she's white—"

"He's a good doctor, Smoky," John Howard said.

"I didn't mean it that way," I whispered.

"I know," he said, and went off to phone. Luke and I walked slowly toward the Mustang. The parking lot was still deserted and hot, but lying in full darkness now. The moon was almost full, but it had not yet risen. I took deep gulps of the fetid air.

A fine trembling began in my arms and legs, and my knees wobbled. Luke slipped his arm around me. We sat down together on the Mustang's hood.

"You okay?" he said. "Jesus, Matt was worried about race riots and drugs and what we get is rednecks with shotguns and one pissed black lady. It just goes to show you."

"Show you what?" I said. My teeth were chattering.

"I don't know. Wait, you're drooling blood. Shit, Smoky, but you're a mess," he said, and pulled my head down on his shoulder. I leaned there, taking deep breaths. Presently the trembling slowed and stopped.

John Howard came out of the motel and walked across the parking lot to us. As he did, a neat, dark

Chevrolet pulled up alongside him. He was near enough to us so that I could see that the driver was the pretty young black woman with the Afro who had been at the first day care center we had visited, on Pumphouse Hill. Juanita Hollings. The woman for whom John Howard had left his wife and son, or, perhaps, vice versa. . . . The lady Panther. Or so Lucas had said.

She stopped the car and leaned out, and we could hear what she said:

"Hello, John."

"Juanita. We meet again."

"We do. I came by to tell you that some of us are having a barbecue over at AU for the deejays, and we'd like it if you could join us. We're going on to Paschal's afterward. I left word with the desk clerk but I guess he didn't tell you."

"No," John Howard said.

"So come on by."

"I don't think so, thanks," John said. "I've got some folks with me."

She looked in our direction.

"Luke," she said.

"Juanita," he said back.

As she had before, she nodded slightly to me, but did not speak. She turned back to John Howard.

"Lots of people there you haven't seen in a long time. Paul is there. Terry's there. Terry would like to see you, John."

John Howard said nothing, and then he said, "Maybe I will, after a while. Tell Terry . . . Is Terry okay?"

"Terry's fine. So . . . we'll see you, then?"

Finally, he nodded.

She nodded, too, and put her head back into the car's window, and then backed out.

"Keisha's there, too, Luke," she called.

Luke nodded, but he did not speak.

John got into the car and said, "Doctor's on his way, Smoky. They'll see she gets medical attention and a place to sleep tonight, and they'll call this Sister Joan in the morning. Will that do?"

"Thanks, yes," I said. "Sister Joan will get help for her. Oh, Jesus, poor Rachel. She was pretty once, she really was."

"That's bad stuff," he said.

They were both silent on the drive back to the Commerce Building garage, and John Howard said only, when he dropped us off, "If you didn't get anything tonight, Luke, we might try the rally on the capitol steps tomorrow. It's not what you wanted, but it should be . . . colorful."

"I'll see what I have when I develop 'em tonight," Luke said, and we got out of the Mustang and went up to the ticket window to get the Morgan.

"What rally?" I said. "I didn't know there was going to be a rally."

"Me, either," he said. "The Panthers, I guess."

He was silent on the way to my apartment, and I simply did not feel like talking. My face ached and my mouth hurt and I was completely out of adrenaline, as if I had run a marathon. But my mind teemed with questions. Questions and images. Oh, Rachel . . .

We were almost to the Colonial Homes turnoff on Peachtree Road before I said, touching my tongue to the inside of my mouth where the stinging was, "He's going to meet her tonight, isn't he? He's going to go back together with her. I can tell. Who is Paul, Luke? Who is Terry?"

"People he knew in Lowndes County. People who were there when Jonathan Daniels was shot. I told you a little about that."

"Panthers?"

"I don't know," he said. "Maybe."

"And Keisha? Who is she?"

"She was there, too."

"Is she a Panther?"

"I don't know, Smokes."

"You're going to Paschal's, too, aren't you? To see her?"

He looked over at me.

"For a girl who just got her ass whupped, you sure do talk a lot," he said, and I was silent.

We did not speak again until he had walked me to my door and I had fished my key out of my purse and put it into the lock. Then he took me by the shoulders and leaned me against the door and bent over and kissed me. It was not a short kiss, and not a brotherly one. When he lifted his head I stared at him.

"What was that for?" I said, tasting him on my mouth.

"How can you not kiss somebody who's got her eyelashes hanging on her belly button?" he said, and I looked down and saw that one of my false eyelashes had come off and was stuck to the nubby fabric of my sweater, dangling over my bare midriff.

"What would you do if they were both hanging over my belly button?" I said.

"Stay tuned," Luke Geary said, and ambled off into the darkness, grinning to himself.

Sometimes—not very often, in any life—there come days so perfect and seamless and golden that you remember them always. Almost everyone has them, though some, I think, have more than others. It just isn't given to everyone to simply love a day for its own sake. But they are the very coin of memory, and you can pull them out over and over again and fondle them, and spend them, and they are never depleted. That Labor Day was one of mine.

In accordance with Matt's policy of making a small holiday for the staff after each issue was wrapped, we spent that Labor Day on Culver Carnes's houseboat up at Lake Lanier, celebrating the wrapping up of the November issue and the publication of the September one. Matt had pulled another editorial article out of September and rammed the Focus piece through, and the day care story was now out. It would be on the stands on Tuesday. He had a small pile of advance copies on board, and champagne on ice to toast them. We all knew that the Andre piece, as it had become known around the office, was special. We started the day with the jauntiness of talented but fallible people who knew they had not, this time, fouled up.

Even the weather shone for us. After the muzzy heat of August, a little out-of-season tornado had spun up from the Florida panhandle, nipped at a trailer park or two, and departed, leaving the air crystal and sweet and the dusty, used leaves sparkling. The lake surface was a diamond-dusted, dancing indigo, and there was a smart enough wind so that the Thistles in the regatta setting out from the Lanier Yacht Club down the lake were all flying taut, fat spinnakers. The wind and water were cool and the sun hot, and even before we left the dock we were laughing.

"What's so funny?" I said, as Teddy and I stepped aboard. We had come up in her car, lugging barbecue from Harry's and an angel food cake from her mother.

Matt was laughing so hard that he could only point at Tom Gordon, who sat slumped in a canvas deck chair on the little stern deck, looking like a collapsed runner from

Marathon, drinking beer and grinning broadly. Matt was usually the perpetrator of the best jokes; I don't think I had ever seen him so helpless with laughter. It was infectious. Teddy and I began to laugh, too, even before Hank spoke.

"We got lost," Hank said, wiping his eyes. "Tom was driving and Matt was navigating, which as every fool knows is precisely backward, and the directions Matt got from Culver just didn't seem to make any sense, so we stopped at this little filling station way the hell out in the country, and this midget comes out."

"I don't believe this," I said, beginning to laugh harder.

"Swear to God. I was in the backseat," Hank said. "So anyway, Tom tells the midget they're looking for the Holiday Marina, and the midget says that's easy, just turn around and go way on back the way we came, till we see a signpost laying on the ground, says Marina— somebody knocked it down this weekend and they haven't put it back up yet. So Tom thanks the midget and turns around and starts back off down the road and the midget yells after him, 'It's a long way, now.' So we drive and drive, and we don't see any sign laying on the ground, and then before we know it we're back at the Interstate. So we turn around again, and finally . . . finally, almost back at the filling station, not fifty yards from it, we see the sign. Matt wants to go in and cuss the midget out, because you could have spit on that sign from where he was standing, and he told us it was a long, long way. But Tom says, 'Naw, Matt, let it go. I guess that is a long way to a midget.'"

It should not have been funny, but it was. Teddy whooped and I doubled over, clutching my stomach. As soon as one of us stopped laughing, another would say, "Guess it is a long way for a midget." I knew even as I gasped helplessly for air that we would repeat it to each other as long as we were together. It was a long time before we could stop laughing enough to get the houseboat underway.

It was a small group. Matt had an edict that few outsiders came along on these excursions, not even husbands and wives, and few did. They were mostly pure Comfort People, and the ones of us who were not wholly drawn into that usually did not appear. Sueanne rarely did, and none of the advertising staff. Sister often did but she was not present today. She was visiting her gout-ridden land-baron daddy this weekend, I knew. Sister would pay for that with merciless teasing from Matt tomorrow.

Alicia was not present, either. No one asked why. Buzzy had his own expensive toy berthed at the lake and usually spent holiday weekends on it with whoever was current in his life and bed. Alicia still was. I wondered if Matt thought about her, Alicia with her honey-satin hair and skin and long, smooth legs, only a lake away. I knew that he had another friend, as Hank put it, now, a sleek, supercharged brunette who handled public relations for the local Playboy Club.

"Nothing so crass as a bunny for Matt," Hank said. "But I hear she was promoted straight from the hutch. He's the best I ever saw at having his cake and eating it too. You should pardon the expression."

"It would be hard to top Alicia," I said, and winced.

"You should also pardon the expression."

And we laughed together. But they had been a couple for a long time, and she had been at the very epicenter of Comfort's People. I thought Matt must feel her absence, even if he did not lament it.

When I went into the dim, cool main cabin to dump the food in the galley and change, I found Luke Geary sprawled on one of the long, royal blue sofas, fiddling with his cameras. He wore faded old plaid madras trunks with a Baltimore Orioles T-shirt over them, and his long, knobbly limbs were so freckled that he looked tanned to a burnished copper. His legs stuck out before him into the room, and I saw that his left ankle was a lunar relief map of shiny white scars and cratered keloidal tissue. I winced inadvertently.

He saw it, and smiled.

"It gets me into more sacks than you could imagine," he said. "I go barefoot whenever possible. Are you moved to lustful pity, Smoky, or perhaps pitiful lust?"

"I'm moved to ask you to move it," I said. Then I flopped down beside him on the sofa.

"Did you get any good stuff from the other night?"

"A little, I think. I'll show you some contacts tomorrow," he said. "And I want you to sign a release; your back is in some of them. But I doubt Matt will want to use them. There's just not enough. John knows a black minister in Mechanicsville who's set up a soup kitchen in the church basement, and it sounds like it might work. I'm going to go look at it this week. We've got time. Andre will carry us a long way."

He paused, and then looked at me.

"You okay? No shiners? No fat lip?"

"Nope. But I wondered what you'd heard about Rachel. Or if you had. I called Our Lady Saturday, but Sister Joan wasn't in and I didn't want to talk about Rachel with the other sister . . . I forget her name. She could have run the Inquisition single-handed."

"Rachel split," he said briefly, and I stared at him.

"John's doctor friend went to pick her up and our gracious host Mr. Playboy said that she suddenly felt better and left. John said he couldn't imagine how she got out of there, there's no bus line near, and he couldn't see any of that bunch calling her a cab, or paying for one."

"Oh, Lord, we're going to have to try and find her—"

"Let it go, Smoky," he said, turning back to the cameras. "You did what you could. You'd never find her; you wouldn't know where to look, and you couldn't do anything for her if you did, if she didn't want you to."

"She's sick, Luke—"

"She's an addict, Smoky. She'll get clean or she won't. You don't figure in that stuff. Believe me. I've seen too much of it. It's all over Atlanta, if you know where to look."

"Maybe we ought to do something on that for Focus," I said. "It could be awfully powerful."

"Culver Carnes would shit bricks," he said. "There's no percentage in druggies. Community outreach ain't going to cut it there. What, you want to do a photo-essay on a junkie kissing a car?"

I was silent. Then I said, "Maybe that's just what Atlanta ought to see."

"Forget it," he said, stretching until each separate vertebra in his spine popped. "This is my day off. Pop a beer and come lie in the sun and let me shoot your body. I came up here to shoot oiled female flesh, not talk about the underbelly of this great country. Go suit up and I'll put you in *Cosmo*."

Suddenly I was tired of grimness and crusades. I wanted sun and laughter and music and food and the flatout, breakneck, no-holds-barred being of simply what I was: young. I jumped up off the sofa and sashayed into the big bedroom at the back of the boat, hips swaying.

"Get that little Hawkie-Browneye ready, buster," I called back, and Matt, who had been fiddling with the controls of the boat, turned the key and it roared into life and gave a mighty backward lunge, and somebody dropped the arm down on Teddy's portable and the

Doors bellowed out "Light My Fire" and we were off across the lake and into that golden day.

I remember it chiefly as a string of vignettes: a small, secret cove in green-black pines that Tom Gordon knew about, where we dropped anchor and plunged, one after another, into water so clear and cold in its depths that it was like swimming in ginger ale, trailing bubbles; lying on the deck as supine as a beached fish, stunned with sun and beer, feeling the boat rock under me as it bobbed at its anchor and seeing only the red of the sun through my closed eyelids, listening to the drumbeat of the music, sun-weight as heavy as another body on every inch of my skin; eating prodigiously and choking with laughter at something Matt and Hank had going; swimming again, this time in a satiny wrapping of alcohol and too much sun, going far down in the silent green underwater and thinking that if I wanted, I never had to come up; coming out of the water, finally, with the sting gone out of the sun and the light turning, for the first time that year, to the thick gold of the coming autumn, and twilight drawing on, pulling on Luke Geary's sweatshirt against the first chill of evening.

By the time we started home, the boat wallowing sedately across the gunmetal lake, the sun had gone, and most of us were frankly tight. It did not seem to matter. I was nearly comatose with contentment and affection for Comfort's People.

I climbed the little ladder up to the tarpaper roof of the houseboat to clear my head a bit, and found Luke sprawled on his back on a towel, a straw planter's hat over his face.

"Can I join you?" I said.

He patted the towel and I plopped down beside him and lay back and closed my eyes. Wind poured over my drying skin; I could feel it everywhere, even on my closed

eyelids and in my hair. The air smelled of sun on pine
and the fishy breath of clean lake water, and the boat
rocked and chugged steadily, and all my consciousness
seemed to draw out of my body and into my mind. For a
moment I lay there all mind, all perception, existing only
in the space behind my closed eyes.

I thought about the blackness then, and sat up swiftly
and opened my eyes. I simply would not allow it here.
Not here, not now.

"You're a Catholic, aren't you, Luke?" I said after a bit.

"Was," he said from under the hat, not moving.

"Well, then you still are," I said. "You don't just
decide not to be one."

"I did."

"Why?"

"The only answers it had didn't fit my questions," he
said drowsily.

"Luke did you . . . have you ever felt anything that
you thought might be—I don't know—the voice of God,
or the voice of the Church, or something like that?
Something that just came over you all of a sudden when
you were . . . maybe starting to do something you'd
always been told not to . . . and felt completely black,
awful, like a kind of death?"

He did not move or answer, and I was suddenly terribly embarrassed.

"No. I don't think I ever did, not like that," he said
then, and his voice was merely serious and interested, as
it often was.

"But I've heard the Church can get you like that. I
think Graham Greene wrote a good bit about it. What's
the matter, Smokes, you been stealing from the poor
box?"

"No," I said, and was silent. I wished I had never
mentioned the blackness. I could not imagine why I had.

"Sweetie," Luke said from under the hat, "There's nothing you could do bad enough for God to light out after you like that. It just ain't in your makeup. It's a lot more likely that what you feel is your own good sense telling you not to sleep with YMOGs."

I gave a silent gasp, or at least I thought it had been silent. But he raised the hat off his face and looked at me.

"No offense intended," he said, and smiled sweetly. It really was a singularly sweet smile. There was nothing of his customary lazy malice in it.

Suddenly the heavy memory of the blackness took wings and flew straight out of my mind and into the air and was gone. I knew, without knowing how, that it would not be back. I began to laugh.

From below, Matt's taxi horn blatted and he bellowed, "Gather round, chirrun," and Luke and I looked at each other, he smiling, me laughing, and then we scrambled down the ladder and into the main cabin of the houseboat. Matt sat on the blue sofa, holding up a dripping bottle of champagne. Everyone was circled around him, pinked with sun and walleyed with beer. Matt himself was just a trifle unsteady, and held in his other hand a half-empty tumbler of something deep amber.

"I have in my pocket a handwritten note whose author I will not yet disclose, but whose letterhead says Sixteen-hundred Pennsylvania Avenue, congratulating us on Andre," he crowed. "An official proclamation from the undersecretary of something or other will follow. Names are named and congratulations tendered, and I can assure you that copies of this document will be circulated to every chamber of commerce in the free world by Culver Carnes, who is doubtless at the Xerox machine as we speak. I would expect maximum media coverage. So I would like to be the first to lift a glass to

Smoky O'Donnell and Lucas Geary, and say, Well done, guys. Your jobs are safe for another month."

He popped the cork and the champagne fizzed out over the bottle and down his arm, everyone cheered, and Hank handed out glasses, and I began to cry.

"I love you all," I sobbed. "I love you every last one."

Behind me Teddy dropped the phonograph arm down and Petula Clark roared out, "When you're alone and life is making you lonely, you can always go . . . Downtown!"

At the wheel, Tom Gordon gunned the houseboat and it took off across the sunset lake, wallowing and creaking, churning along with a large pink and gold wake behind it, and we capered and hugged and danced with each other, and we sang:

> *Listen to the rhythm of the gentle Bossa Nova.*
> *You'll be dancing with 'em, too, before the night is over,*
> > *happy again . . .*
> *The lights are much brighter there, you can forget*
> > *all your troubles, forget all your cares, and go*
> *downtown . . . where all the lights are bright . . .*
> *downtown . . . waiting for you tonight . . .*
> *downtown . . . You're gonna be all right . . .*
> > *now!*

11

WHEN WE GOT HOME FROM THE LAKE, BRAD CALLED from Huntsville to say that he had to come back to Atlanta for the day on the following Friday to consult with his father on estimates, and would like to meet me downtown somewhere for lunch.

"I can't stay over," he said, "but at least I can look at you and grope your knees under the table. Unless you'd like to go for a nooner at your place?"

"I'll meet you at the Top of Peachtree," I said. "Boy, have I got a bone to pick with you about the black deejay story."

"Uh-oh. I know what that's about," he said. "How'd it go?"

"It went so smoothly that there's not even a story," I said. "Luke didn't get anything newsworthy. We're going to do a church soup kitchen instead. So you could have saved yourself a lot of worry."

"I should have told you I'd talked to Matt," he said.

"No. You shouldn't have talked to him at all. This is my life, Brad. I can take care of myself."

"You're my life now, too, Smoky," he said. "You can't blame me if I worry about you sometimes. You're awfully quick to go in harm's way."

"I can't blame you for worrying, but I can blame you for making me look like a fool with Matt. He and I can decide what's harmful and what's not when it comes to my work."

"Okay," he said. "Truce. Can we take this up Friday?"

"You bet we can," I said, slightly mollified, but still determined to clear the air once and for all about my *Downtown* assignments.

"See you then. I love you."

"Me too," I said, and felt a warm rush of happiness and the new sense of safety, and thought, well, after all, what's so awful about a man worrying about his wife-to-be? Wouldn't you worry about him, if you thought he was going to do something dangerous?

Only then did I realize that I would not. I could not conceive of Brad in a situation that he could not handle. That, I knew, was where the safety sprang from.

On Thursday afternoon Luke came into my office looking slightly sheepish and grinning the shit-eating grin. I laughed aloud. He looked for all the world like Tom Sawyer caught in a misdeed by Aunt Polly.

"You been whitewashing fences?" I said.

"Whitewashing wouldn't be a bad idea," he replied. "I have a feeling a bucket of whitewash would serve me well before long."

"Why?"

"This," he said, and pulled a folded piece of paper from his camera bag. He handed it to me and stood silently, arms folded over his chest, as I took it and unfolded it.

All of a sudden the air around my face felt charged and thick, as though there had been a silent explosion. My face and lips tingled with it, and my ears rang. The paper was a page proof from *Life* magazine, and the photo on it was an extreme close-up of me and the young black woman in the bathroom of the Santa Fe Plaza Motel, face thrust into furious face, screaming silently at each other.

Her face was full on, and in it you could read years, centuries of corrosive rage and impotence. There was such venom in her contorted mouth and slitted eyes that even here, in my silent, sunny office, I flinched away, feeling again her clawing hands and nails. My own face was in profile, skin very white against her black cheeks, eyes looking pale and ghost-gray and somehow eerie, mouth opened in what I knew to be angry shock but what looked to be spitting vindictiveness. Even in profile, it was undeniably me. Even untitled, the photograph pulsed and shimmered with power and particularity. It was impossible to look away from it. Some small, clear part of my mind knew that *Life* would run it uncaptioned and full-page bleed. It spoke for itself: the rage of race against race, the swift, menacing new fury of the young. Even in my beginning anger and outrage at Lucas Geary, that same part of my mind applauded *Life* for its editorial sensibility. It was a stunning photograph.

After a very long time I whispered, "Luke, how could you?"

He shook his head, as if he did not himself understand.

"How could I not?" he said.

I sat down heavily in my desk chair and stared from the page proof to him. He was not smiling, but he did not look unduly guilty, or chagrined. He merely looked very focused, and very interested, the old Luke look.

He waited, not speaking.

"It makes me look like a terrible racist," I said, tears beginning to prickle in my eyes. "Can't you see that?

You know I'm not. You know I'm not! Oh, Luke, every-thing that Matt was beginning to let me do, all the Focus work, this makes it all . . . just a joke!"

He shook his head.

"Not to anybody who knows you. Not to anybody who knows me, or John Howard, or Matt. This photo-graph isn't about you, Smoky. Don't you see that? It's about now, about the times—"

"Everybody will see it. They'll see it in Corkie, Brad's family will see it—"

"Well, from what you say, it ought to earn you big points in Corkie and with Brad's family," he said, begin-ning to grin, and my tears spilled over.

I turned away from him and stood looking blindly out my window. The white-hot September sun glinted off the gold dome of the Capitol. It danced and wavered through the salt blur in my eyes.

Behind me he said, "I didn't think it would hurt you, Smoky. It won't be captioned; you won't be identified. They promised that. No names. You did sign a release . . . "

His voice trailed off, and I knew that he was embar-rassed at last. He knew and I knew that I had thought the release merely a formality. But he must have sus-pected all along what he had in this photograph.

"When will it run?"

"Be on the stands Monday. I brought you this so you could get used to it and . . . you know, alert anybody it might take by surprise."

I knew that he meant Brad.

"I guess there's no doubt that it's going to run?"

"No. I couldn't stop it now if I wanted to. And I don't. Smoky . . . just look at it. Look at it again, and pretend it isn't you."

I simply stared at him. Pretend it was not me? That ugly rictus of rage, not me? But then I thought, that's

Lucas. That's what he is, that's how he sees things. He is a camera. Matt was right. He is . . . dangerous.

I looked back at the proof spread out on my desk and thought, for just an instant, what a spectacular photograph that is.

He saw the thought register, and said, "See?"

"I know it's good," I said. "I know it's powerful. I guess I'd run it too, if I worked for *Life*. But Luke . . . this is *me*. This hurts *me*. Don't you care about that?"

He screwed up his eyes as though he were concentrating very hard. "I care a lot if it really hurts you," he said. "But I can't see why it would. Everybody who knows you knows you're not a racist; anything but. Who gives a shit about the rest? You don't, do you? I didn't think you'd care—nothing's going to change, Smoky. It isn't going to hurt Focus. Christ, if Hunt gets his drawers in an uproar over this he doesn't deserve you—"

"He's not going to get his drawers in an uproar," I shouted angrily. The tears receded. "He's just going to be madder than hell that you've made me look like a damned Ku Klux Klanner! What do you think he is?"

"Good question," he said mildly. "So I guess you're pissed, huh?"

"I'm . . . oh, I don't know what I am! Go away and leave me alone, Luke. And don't come near me anymore with that damned camera. I don't trust you worth . . . I don't know what."

"I never meant for you to feel bad about it, Smoky," he said, his voice subdued, and started out of the office.

"Has Matt seen it?" I said after him.

"Yeah."

"What did he say? That I got into trouble after all, and that he told me so?"

"Nope. Just said it sure wasn't your best side," Luke said, and shut the door softly behind him. I sat for a long

time, staring at the page proof, and then I put it into my
top drawer and shut it firmly. I would, I thought, think
about it later.

And I did. All that afternoon, and all evening, and
until early into the morning hours, I lay thinking about it,
the black and white faces burned into the space behind
my eyes, wondering whether to show it to Brad, wondering how to behave about it if I did, wondering what, if
anything, I should say to them back in Corkie, before the
photograph ran. In the end, I crammed it into an envelope and took it with me to the Top of Peachtree to meet
Brad for lunch the next day, my eyes burning from lack of
sleep, dawdling along the hot, crowded sidewalk in my
indecision about whether or not I would show it to him.

In the end I did. Lunch went so wonderfully well that I
simply forgot I had ever doubted I would. In the powerful
lamp of Brad's obvious delight in seeing me again, and the
tumble of things we had saved to tell each other, and
the laughter we shared, and the cold white wine, and the
shrimp salad and lemon mousse and the soft pressure of
his knee against mine under the table and the sheer, proprietary pride I felt looking at him across the table—how
handsome he was; it was always a small shock when I saw
him afresh—I forgot my apprehension of the day before.
Just before we rose to leave, I to go back to the office and
he to drive back to Huntsville, I said, "Oh, I almost forgot.
Look what Lucas Geary has done to me," and pulled out
the page proof and handed it to him. For a long moment, I
sat watching him across the table, smiling slightly, waiting
for the rueful grin and the snort of annoyance at Lucas.
Above him, behind his gleaming blond head, the mural
shone in the gray-tinted dusk of the bar, and my own face
seemed to look back at me, smiling. Smiling.

He lifted his head from the proof and looked across the
table at me. His face had whitened while I was smiling at

myself in the mural, and there were scarlet patches on each cheekbone. His lips were bloodless. Even his eyes looked paler, somehow bleached, like lake ice at the end of winter.

"It's not that bad," I said, smiling at him.

He did not speak.

"He didn't mean to make me look like a racist," I said. I was warmed by his obvious anger at Luke, but I did not want a serious quarrel between them.

He still did not speak. But he took a deep breath, as though he meant to, and then let it out again. He was obviously struggling to control himself. I had never seen him so angry. I had never, in fact, seen him angry at all. Not really.

"Don't be mad at him," I said. "He's a photographer; it's what he does. It's what he is. He can't help it. It won't jeopardize my work. Matt made a joke of it."

"Did he now."

It was not a voice I knew. I fell silent, looking warily at him.

"You said," he said in a precise, dry voice, as if he were reciting from memory, "that there wasn't a story. That you didn't get—and I quote—'anything newsworthy.' Apparently *Life* magazine didn't agree with you."

"Well, I didn't know Luke was shooting," I said uncertainly. "He didn't say anything until he brought me this, yesterday. *Downtown* isn't running anything—"

"Oh, well, then, everything is all right," Brad said, and his voice cut me as if it were the lash of a whip. I simply looked at him.

"You've been a busy girl, haven't you, Smoky? Busy, busy, busy. First your picture on the wall of the busiest bar in town, and then why, my goodness me, look ahere! Here's ol' Smoky in the flesh, spitting like a cat at a darky in a dopehead motel, close up so all America can see."

His voice was so like that of Marylou Hunt that I could not speak. He was, at that moment, no one I knew even remotely, no one I had ever known.

"So what's next, Smokes?" he said, in a ghastly caricature of joviality. "Starting a riot at the Saint Paddy's Day Parade? I bet I know. The Blessed Virgin is going to appear to you in the ladies' room mirror; your typewriter will develop a stigmata—"

"Shut up."

I could taste tears in my mouth, but I could not feel them running down my face. For the second time in two days, I felt in the air that terrible silent explosion.

His ashen face flushed and he dropped his eyes. It seemed to me simply idiotic that I would notice and admire the way his thick gold-tipped lashes shuttered them, but I did. Part of me did. The other part was frozen, dead.

"I'm sorry," he said. "But there's something in you that just doesn't know when to quit, Smoky. You don't have any . . . any boundaries; you don't know what the limits are."

I was silent, and he raised his eyes. They were slightly wild. I thought that perhaps there was a sheen of tears in them.

"You go too far, Smoky," he said in the new, cold, level voice. "It's beyond . . . courage, or spirit. I don't know. . . . It's so—"

"It's so Irish. Isn't that what you were going to say, Brad?" I said. My voice was very steady. I was amazed at myself. I could feel the tears now, a regular runnel of them on both cheeks. I did not raise my hand to wipe them away.

"You said it. I didn't. But since you did . . . " he said, and looked away from me. In profile, he was Marylou Hunt. I wondered why I had never seen it before. All that separated them was her long hair and his gilt stubble of beard.

I got up from the table and crumpled the page proof into a loose ball and tossed it into his dessert plate. I slid the gold bracelet off my wrist and laid it on top of the proof.

"For your mother," I said. "She's going to love both of them."

I turned and walked out of the dining room and slipped into the elevator just as the doors were closing. I thought that I heard him call "Smoky!" just as they slid shut, but I was not sure, and in any case, the roaring in my ears made exterior sound suspect. I rode down with a carful of loud, well-fed strangers, eyes fixed on the changing floor numbers, face stiff and hot, ears ringing, and walked back to the office. By the time I got there, the fierce heat had dried the tears on my face, but it felt soiled and scummed and sore, as if I had been slapped hard on both cheeks, and so I went into the ladies' room and washed my face and reapplied my makeup. I gave my face a last quick survey, remembered his poisoned words, whispered "Last chance," to the Blessed Virgin, and walked out. There was no sign from the Virgin. There was none either, all that afternoon, from Brad. Even as I told myself he would call to apologize and I would refuse to talk to him, I knew that he would not. Marylou would not have. Neither, now, would her son.

I Scotch-taped a sign on my door that said, "Captions and subheads due 5:00 P.M. Do not disturb," and shut it. I phoned Sister and asked that she hold my calls and visitors unless Matt needed me for something really important.

"You okay?" she said. "You came steaming through here like a bat out of torment."

"Fine," I said. "Just way past deadline on the guide. Can you keep the screaming crowd at bay?"

"You betcha," Sister said. "This dog can hunt."

Sister might look like a Mary Quant poster girl, but the South Georgia wiregrass regularly booby-trapped her speech. I had to grin, and felt a little better. A little.

"Thanks," I said, and bent to the piled up cutlines and subheads. And I learned, really for the first time, something that I had not known before: work could save me. Work would save me.

I did not look up, and I did not think about Brad Hunt until my door opened abruptly hours later and I looked up to see Luke Geary standing in it, and the miserable lunch at the Top of Peachtree came flooding back over me. I blinked away sudden tears, and swallowed past a huge, cold salt lump at the base of my throat.

"You busy?" Luke said.

The tears and the salt lump made me angry; if anyone was hurting from the noon encounter, it should be Brad, not me. He was the betrayer, the ambusher, not I. I took it out on Luke, thinking even as I spoke that perhaps I should have gotten angrier at him earlier. It seemed important to me that somebody pay for the ugliness of that lunch besides the victim. I would not think of myself as anything else.

"Whatever the hell made you think I was busy? Could it possibly have been the sign and the closed door?" I said furiously.

"Ah," he said, as if something had come clear to him, but he did not speak. He stood for a moment, leaning on the door, looking boneless and lazy, as he always did.

"The *Life* thing," he said presently. "I'm still on your list."

"It will no doubt grieve you deeply to learn that I have not thought about you or the *Life* thing for a substantial number of hours," I snapped.

"Good," he said. "Because I came to take you over to Paschal's. Ramsey Lewis just came in town. John and some of the others are going to be there. I thought you might . . . want to show the flag a little."

"Oh, sure. Go waltzing right into La Carrousel when that damned photograph is about to hit the stands, let everybody get a good look at little whitey turncoat—"

"Smoky, there is a very good chance that not everybody in the universe reads *Life*," Luke said. "Most of those guys stopped fooling with the popular media years ago. But if there's the slightest chance you think they're going to think you've joined the Klan or something, you ought to go meet a few of them and let them get to know you a little. You may need some contacts among them one day. After they meet you, it won't be a problem. I promise that. You'll be with me, and I know a lot of them, and John knows the rest, and . . . it just won't be a problem. It's the least I can do—"

"Oh, well, thanks, Lucas, but I don't think I want to be your duty date for the prom," I said. "Don't worry about it, okay?"

"It's not a duty date," he said. "I thought while we were at it I'd make a serious pass at you. While the cat's away, and all that. Warm you up with a little Ramsey Lewis, ply you with drink, invoke the spirit of the young heroes of the movement, and then, while your delicate senses are reeling—kapow. As they say."

"No thanks. As they say."

But I felt the corners of my mouth quirk. Damn him, he was unconscionable, outrageous. . . .

"King's going to be there."

And prescient. As long as I had been in Atlanta, I had yearned to meet Martin Luther King Jr. He was, to me, a hero of epic dimensions. But there seemed no way that I ever would. I could not imagine that our paths would simply cross.

"You don't know that."

"Yeah. I do know that. I know that for a fact."

I sat looking at him, and he looked back, grinning slightly.

"Make a good photo-essay for somebody," he said thoughtfully. "King and his lieutenants kicking back. Heroes at play. I thought I'd take along a camera. Of course, somebody would have to write it, and to do that, they'd have to be there—"

"You are beyond shame," I said, finally and unwillingly smiling a little, and got up and fished my purse from the bottom drawer, to go into the ladies' room and fix my face.

"But not beyond reach," he said, ambling after me as I went out of the office. "I may not be a pushover, but I can be had. You, for instance, could have me if you played your cards right."

The pain of lunchtime; the enormity of what we had done to each other, Brad and I; the violent wrenching away of the fragile new safety; the sheer humiliation, took me suddenly, along with the held-back tears. They spewed up into my throat and hung there. I took a deep breath, and willed them back savagely. I literally willed the sickening pain away, willed my mind and heart white and empty. Emptiness came. I waited, and took a long, tentative breath. Emptiness held. All right, then. I would make my own safety.

"Lucas Geary," I said, "we are going to start with several—several—drinks at an oasis of my choice. Not a cheap one. And then we are going to go to the Coach and Six and I am going to have wine and double lamb chops and maybe two desserts. And then I am going to have a stinger, a white crème de menthe one. And after that maybe—maybe—we will go and listen to Ramsey Lewis until the last cent you will ever have is gone. And we will leave only when it is. Do you read me?"

"Loud and clear," he said. "Go fix your face. Your lip-stick is all over it. I'll meet you at the car."

I went into the ladies' room and fixed my face and added a great squirt of Ma Griffe, something I usually forgot to do. I started out and then went back and squirted a jet of it down into my bra, just where the swell of my breasts started. It felt cold, silken, sensuous.

"Really last chance," I said to the Blessed Virgin, but she said nothing, and I ran out of the ladies' room and onto the elevator and rode down to meet Luke Geary in the dying day.

We did indeed have several drinks, or at least I did, at the Top of Peachtree. I wanted to get back what it had always been to me; I wanted to lose the ugliness of the lunch hour and reclaim the lovely, lavender twilight full of laughter and sovereignty that it had always meant. After the drinks, I did. When you have a choice between laughter and wounding, ferocious pain, laughter will always win. It is when laughter is not an option that pain will kill you. I think that Luke Geary saved something very real in me that night, because he kept me laughing. The liquor helped.

He sat across from me, looking as threadbare and disheveled as if he had passed the night in a mission for the indigent; unlike Matt, his disorder did not include expensive clothes and careful barbering. But somehow he looked fine to me that night, arresting, comforting. Luke was never handsome, but he was as appealing to look upon as a raw-boned Irish setter puppy. It was a completely misleading appearance, belying his complexity and cynicism and the odd distance in him. But I took pleasure in it, as I did the cold gin and tonics that he kept coming, one after another. I noticed somewhere along the way that he was drinking beer, and not a lot of that, but it did not matter to me. On this night I did not feel that I had to impress Lucas Geary with my gentility, restraint, or anything else.

He told me funny stories about himself, stories about his boyhood and the people he had encountered and photographed since he had left Sewanee. He had graduated from college the year I had; that surprised me, faintly. He must be almost exactly my age. I had thought he was older.

"You've been around enough for several lifetimes already," I said, after listening to his adventures photographing the Civil Rights movement in Mississippi and Alabama and now Georgia. He made all of them scurrilously funny. No one, freedom rider or klansman, escaped the honeyed acid of his tongue.

"Only after school," he said. "Before that I was the proverbial fly in amber. You ain't seen amber till you've seen Baltimore and Sewanee, Tennessee."

"How did a good Irish Catholic boy end up at Sewanee?" I said. I slurred it a little, I think.

"Scholarship," he said. "I applied for every scholarship they knew about in the guidance office in high school. That was the biggest one, and when I won it, my father suddenly developed an Anglican turn of mind. He'd given up on me playing football for Notre Dame, but I think he still had something at Georgetown in mind. But Sewanee's stipend was too good to turn down. It was fine with me; I was real taken with the Fugitives at that time—you know, the Agrarian Manifesto—and Andrew Lytle was teaching at Sewanee then. It was while I was there that I found out about photography."

"Was your family very poor?" I said, feeling that I could say anything, in this envelope of glowing intoxication, to Luke Geary.

"No. They were very rich. They still are," he said matter-of-factly.

I goggled silently at him. I had always assumed he was a child of poverty, and had clawed his way up out of it via his camera.

"It's the clothes," he grinned. "Plus the fact that I guess I look like po' white trash. Daddy said I did once; said I looked like I had chronic hookworms. After that there didn't seem any sense in ties and starched collars. I loved it when the flower chirrun came along. Now we all look the same. Don't judge a man by his clothes, Smoky."

"Rich," I said wonderingly. "Everybody around me turns out to be rich. Lord. First Brad, and then you tell me John Howard's folks are well off, and now you—I need to get out of here and find some proletariat."

I slurred that, too, and he laughed again.

"That sort of explains you and John Howard," I said. "Two little rich boys in the middle of a poor folks' movement. No wonder you get on so well."

"Maybe," he said. "I always thought we got on because we're both outsiders. I always felt like I was a slum kid who got adopted into a rich family, or something; the way we lived in Baltimore never seemed to fit right. Nothing did until I found cameras and the Civil Rights movement. And John was not only well off, he never really realized he was black. They lived in a white neighborhood, and he went away to a mostly white prep school. His father was adamant about that. His dad was light; he could have passed, John said, but he didn't want to do that. His practice was among blacks, and he couldn't have made any money trying to practice among white folks. But John always thought he wanted his only son to pass, because from the time he was born they raised him like he was a white kid. The result was, of course, that he never felt like he fit in anywhere. He went to an all-black theological seminary when he was barely seventeen because no white one would take him and then on to Howard Law School because his father insisted on a law degree, and he said it was only in those places that he found out he really was black, and these blacks weren't exactly run-of-the-mill. He's still not really used to it. I think it's one reason he got so deeply into the SCLC and so attached to Dr. King. They made him feel like he truly belonged, somewhere, for the first time in his life. He'll do anything for them; I think it's why he put himself in the line of fire so often. He'll never forget his loyalty to them. When we first met, during the Washington march in nineteen sixty-three, it was like we knew each other from the cradle. Inside two hours we were making jokes about the way we were raised. Two outsiders trying somehow to pass."

He paused. Then he said, "It's why you're so easy with him, isn't it? I think it is; I think it's why he's comfortable with you. Otherwise he simply wouldn't be around you. You're an outsider, too. And you just never had a thing about Negroes. You can't, if you're raised really Irish. I know about that. If you're brought up with the hard-core Irish thing, there's just not any time or room to single out the Negroes. They're only an incidental part of the bigotry you learn about everything that isn't Irish."

I had not thought about this before. Finally I said, "My father hated the Negroes. He thought they were taking jobs that ought to belong to the men in Corkie. He tried to organize a rebellion against them; it eventually got him fired. He never had anything good to say about them after that."

"Ah, but that was because they took something from an Irishman," Luke grinned. "He'd have hated the

Lutherans, if he thought they'd taken Irish jobs. He'd have hated anybody who did that. You have to understand that with the Irish, hating is a reaction against a threat to the Irish. With your garden-variety Southerner, it's hating for the blackness that counts. People say that white Southern prejudice is a matter of economics and culture, that whites hate Negroes who threaten their jobs and their little bit of social supremacy. But there ain't no hate like a rich white Southerner for a nigger, baby."

Suddenly I was tired of it all.

"White, black, Irish, not Irish, rich, poor," I said. "The hell with all of it. I'm hungry. I want lamb chops before your money runs out."

"It's not going to," he said. "I'm putting it all on Matt's tab. Figure he owes you."

"How can you do that?"

He shrugged.

"I don't hang around *Downtown* strictly for the honor of shooting photo-essays for Culver Carnes," he said.

"Then why?"

"Let's just say Matt finds a way to disguise my occasional, ah, indulgences, in the new business development budget. Don't look so shocked, Smoky. Half of what Matt does is trade-off or write-off. He couldn't run the magazine on the budget the chamber gives him. They know that."

"Then I'm changing to surf 'n' turf," I said.

"Let the good times roll," Luke said, and he paid the check and we left for the Coach and Six.

We did have lobster, though not the ubiquitous surf 'n' turf that dominated Atlanta menus then. Luke had broiled stuffed lobster and I had a silken, elegant Thermidor, and white wine like a kiss of air, and something many-layered and chocolate sporting thin shavings of darker chocolate from the dessert cart, and the white crème de menthe stinger I had coveted. By then the evening was beginning to slant oddly, canting in and out as with the tide, and the pain that lay like jumbled razor blades around my heart had dulled down. Laughter nibbled at my lips like tiny fish in warm water, though it frequently shivered on the edge of tears. When we walked out to wait for the Morgan, I was unsteady on my feet, and Luke put a casual arm about my waist that served somewhat to keep me erect. He put the Morgan's top down, and by the time we had ridden in the warm, rushing air through downtown and into Southwest Atlanta, I was fairly clear again. I did not think I wanted to go home for a very long time.

Luke found a parking place on the street a block and a half down, toward the Atlanta University complex, and we walked the weedy, deserted no-man's-land back to Paschal's in silence. It was nearly ten-thirty, and there was no one else in the street in front of the unprepossessing two-story motel and restaurant that was the unofficial epicenter of the Civil Rights movement. I had walked without real fear in Pumphouse Hill and Summerhill, but somehow this shabby, lunar street left me uneasy. I was acutely conscious that my skin shone white in the pale light from the few unbroken streetlights. I looked around me as we walked.

"Relax," Luke said. "Put away your blowgun. We're not exactly going into the heart of darkness. Most nights this is the center of the civilized world. They've had Basie, Hampton, Don Shirley, Red Norvo, Gillespie—you name it. We probably won't be the only white faces, if that's what worries you. Matt and I come here a lot. We've never been the only ones."

"I'm not worried about that."

"Then what?"

"I don't know. I guess it seems very real to me all of a sudden. The movement and all . . . "

And it did. I felt acutely conscious, on every inch of my skin, that I was walking into a place that often drew together the members of something whose passion and purpose paled, with its simple human significance, anything my small life had known. I might even be, for a short time, in the presence of one of the great and luminous legends of my time and any other. My residual drunkenness fled, and so did the scraps of the pain, as well as the tremulous laughter.

We went inside, threading our way through the close-crowded, small tables, pushing through nearly palpable planes of smoke lying motionless in the air. Luke looked around for John Howard, who had promised to hold a table for us. I followed him, head held high, a silly feeling, unmovable smile on my mouth. I knew that a part of me was searching the room for hostility as a wolf would sniff the wind.

But I felt none, and felt little curiosity. It was a quiet crowd, with only the sinuous, seminal flow of the music winding through it like a joyous heartbeat. Luke slouched along, nodding here and there to people he knew, and I stumbled along behind him, rigid to my eyebrows with the simple desire not to appear as if I were slumming. I was consumed with a ridiculous desire to let everyone in the room see how delighted I was to be there. I caught myself smiling right and left, and felt myself redden in the darkness.

"Will you stop nodding like somebody in a bad play?" Luke whispered over his shoulder. "You look like Queen Elizabeth reviewing the troops."

I stopped.

We fetched up at a table against a far wall, and slid into chairs. John Howard sat on the far side, chair tipped back against the wall. Beside him, on his left, Juanita Hollings sat. John had a half-empty beer glass in front of him, but there was nothing on the table in front of her. She sat quietly, her shapely small head bound tonight in a bright African kerchief, gold hoops in her ears. She wore, instead of the djellaba, a simple white blouse and blue jeans. Nevertheless, she looked exotic, nearly feral, in the smoky gloom. Her bone structure was extraordinary; I thought she would be beautiful in whatever she chose to wear. The thought flashed into my mind that she would be even more beautiful in nothing. I looked from her to John Howard, and they both nodded to me. Only John smiled.

"Hi, Smoky," he said.

Juanita said nothing.

John hit Luke's shoulder lightly with a balled fist and held up his hand for a waitress. When one came, he ordered beers all around. He did not ask me if I preferred anything else, and I would not have said I did for anything on earth. I wanted only to sit very still and try to melt into the smoke and gloom. My whiteness seemed to wink rottenly beside all the rich shades of dark flesh around me. Not even Lucas Geary seemed so blindingly white. He looked, in fact, somehow as black as the blacks around him. It was amazing.

A young black man leaned forward out of the shadows beside Juanita, someone I had never seen before. He had been tipped back against the wall; I had not noticed him in the gloom.

"Introduce me to your friends, John," he said, in a thick, slow voice, and at first I thought he might be drunk, but there were no empty glasses around him, and I realized that he was, with the exaggerated, gentle drawl, mocking us very slightly. I flushed again.

"Smoky O'Donnell and Luke Geary, this is Sonny Pickens," John said. "An old friend of Juanita's, in town from Berkeley. He's never been to Atlanta, and we're softening him up with some barbecue and Ramsey Lewis."

Luke grinned and nodded affably, and I smiled, too. Sonny Pickens gave us both a wide white smile that looked, in the murk, more like a shark's demeanor than a smile. His voice might be slow, but he himself was thin and quick, with nervous, jerky movements. I thought of something small and darting, quick to bite. A fox? A weasel? His face was pointed and his cheekbones high and sharp, and his Afro was larger even than Juanita's. He was yellow rather than brown. I thought that he might well be someone you would want to soften up. I also thought he was years younger than John Howard, though not, perhaps, Juanita.

"How do you like Atlanta?" I said politely.

"I think I'm going to like it right well," he said. His voice, though slow, was not Southern. "It's got everything Juanita said it did. Good folks, good food, good music," he nodded toward the band. "Really good . . . connections. Just looka here, this very room is full of heroes. Why, I'm sitting at the table with a real live hero . . . "

John Howard looked unreadably at him.

"Don't be an ass, Sonny," Juanita said. Her voice was light and sweet, but there was steel under it. Sonny grinned and leaned back against the wall. He folded his arms across his thin chest and closed his eyes, rocking slightly with the music. Like Juanita, he wore a neat, unremarkable white shirt and blue jeans, but also like her, there was something powerfully electric about him, as though he were a young monarch masquerading as a commoner. A sense, I thought, of being something other than he appeared.

The music swarmed through the room like a loosened hive of bees: a playful piano weaving in and out around bass and drums. The very walls throbbed with it, a teasing rhythm now bright as a school of minnows in sunny, shallow water, now as glistening dark as viscera, with a heavy blues beat and a skittering counterpoint. I swam into it instinctively, my feet tapping with it, my face turning to it of its own volition. The pianist, a crew-cut young man in horn-rimmed glasses who might have been an accountant, raised a cheerful hand to us, and John and Luke saluted back. I began to relax, very slightly.

Luke looked down at me.

"Like it?"

The trio slid into Duke Ellington's "Come Sunday" and I smiled at him. "It's wonderful. They're terrific. I'd like to have some of their stuff."

"I've got it all," he said. "I'll lend you some. I'll introduce you, when the set's over."

He looked at John Howard, across the table.

"Dr. King here?" he said.

"Might be. He's here a lot. We just got here ourselves. I see some of our folks over there at the table by the bandstand. I'll ask."

He beckoned toward a large table in the opposite corner of the room.

Two men rose and came across the room and stood behind John Howard, looking down at us. The short, pudgy one was Tony Willingham and the taller, blacker one Rosser Sellers. I knew their names from half a decade of news accounts, and their faces, vaguely, from the press conference for the day care story. I knew they were, like John Howard, SCLC—King's men. I knew that both had demonstrated and marched with him; gone quietly to shabby county jails with him; been beaten, bitten, kicked, gassed, shot at. Rosser Sellers had, I knew, been hit, though I could not remember where, or how badly. Self-consciousness thickened my tongue to silence, which was, I knew, just as well. I felt the Irish brogue hovering just behind my lips. It was not exactly just what we needed tonight.

When John introduced me, both of them smiled. They were small smiles, but I thought that they were genuine.

"Good work with the Focus business," Tony Willingham said. "I hear there's some money about to shake loose because of it."

"Good work with the pool, too," Rosser Sellers said, and they both laughed, and I felt pleasure light my face like a lamp. There was no shade of patronization here, no polite indulgence. Reserve, certainly, but nothing else.

"I don't know what felt better, maybe doing a little good for kids like Andre or beating Boy Slattery at pool," I said, and everyone laughed again, except Juanita and Sonny Pickens. Somehow I did not think I was going to win smiles there.

"And who knows which will pay off bigger in the long run," Tony Willingham said.

Only then did they acknowledge the two out-of-towners at the table.

"Sonny," Rosser Sellers said neutrally, nodding to him. "Juanita. Long time."

"It has been," Juanita said, smiling slightly. Lord, but she was beautiful. In the dim, smoky room she looked like a priestess, like a carved deity.

"Seems like yesterday," Sonny Pickens said. The sharklike smile widened. No one spoke for a moment.

"Sit with us," Juanita said then, smiling, and they looked at her for another moment, and then dropped into vacant chairs. John raised a hand for the waitress, but they both shook their heads.

"Well," Rosser Sellers said. "Y'all just catching up, or doing a little scouting?"

"Guess you might say some of both," Sonny Pickens said, the strange parody of glee on his sharp face once more. I saw that there was no mirth behind it; he probably did it unconsciously. A smiling man whose smile promised nothing.

Juanita looked levelly at him, and then at the two newcomers.

"It's a free country, brothers," she said lazily. "But of course you know that."

"Doin' any good?"

Tony Willingham did not look at her when he spoke, but at John Howard. I saw John's face tighten, though his expression did not change.

"I'm always willing to listen, brother," he said, with an accent on the "brother." "I remember when y'all were, too."

"Oh," Willingham said, rearing back against the wall and smiling a smile I did not like. "I think it depends entirely on what you're being asked to listen to. Don't you . . . brother?"

John Howard did not respond. Juanita laid a hand lightly on his arm and smiled at Tony Willingham.

"Be surprised what you can learn if you just listen . . . brother," she said.

Beside her Sonny Pickens snorted, but he did not open his eyes. He seemed lost fathoms deep in the music.

What is going on here? I thought. Obviously they're all old friends, or at least acquaintances. They know each other from earlier times; they've been through a lot together. But they're beating each other over the head with this brother business. And all this cold, awful smiling. They're like dogs, sniffing and circling. Who has betrayed who? If Sonny and Juanita are Panthers, what are they doing hanging out in the very backyard of everything they say they despise? I wish I'd never laid eyes on Juanita. I wish she'd go back to wherever they go and leave . . .

I realized that I was thinking, leave John alone. In the darkness I blushed as if I had thought something indecent.

"How you doing, Luke?" Tony Willingham said to Lucas. "I don't think I've seen you to talk to you since the sit-in at Rich's. Christ, you must have still been in school then; trying to grow a beard and mustache and not having much luck. What's it been, six years? Seven?"

"About," Luke grinned. "It's taken me that long to grow the beard. I remember one of the first shots I ever got printed was that one of you I took that day, with that little old lady whacking you with her umbrella. I never could figure out if she was one of the segs, or she just didn't like your style."

Tony Willingham laughed hugely. "Those were some kind of days, weren't they?" he said. "There must have been fifteen hundred folks on that picket line at one time. It circled all downtown Atlanta. God, there were shuttle buses to take people down there and back, and we had two-way radios and special signs that rain and spit and worse wouldn't wash off, and special coats for the girls so they wouldn't get spit on . . . and worse again. Man, we thought we were hot shit. And we were. We were."

Everyone laughed but Juanita. Even Sonny Pickens cackled mirthlessly. Juanita sat carved and golden, still as an idol, her hand on John Howard's arm.

"So, is the Lord here?" Sonny Pickens said. He still did not open his eyes.

"Sonny," Juanita said softly, menacingly.

"The Lord?" I said.

"King. We heard he might be," Sonny Pickens said.

"He's in the dining room," Rosser Sellers said, looking narrowly at Sonny Pickens.

"Good move," Pickens said lazily. "Least he knows he can get served. That ain't always true everywhere, you know, even in these enlightened days. It's like John Lewis was telling—wasn't it brother John? Talking about Nashville, I think. Somebody said, 'Well, you know we don't serve niggers here,' and somebody else said, 'That's okay because we don't eat 'em.' Quick mind, brother John. Goin' with the times, though maybe not far enough."

There was a silence. Then Tony Willingham said, very softly, "Something on your mind, brother?"

"Just thinkin'; the good old days don't look so good to me anymore," Sonny Pickens said, and opened his eyes, and gave the table a smile stunning in its white ferality.

"And you got a better way," Willingham said even more softly. It was not a question.

"Oh, yeah. We got a better way. I'd be glad to tell you all about it, but ol' Juanita here is our designated spokeswoman, so best I shut up and let her spokes," Pickens said. The smile did not falter. It did not reach his eyes, either. He thrust it around the table like a flung gauntlet.

"This is not the time, Sonny," Juanita said, and her voice was not soft now. Neither was her face.

"It past time," he said. He was not smiling now, either.

Rosser Sellers looked from Pickens and Juanita to John Howard. John met his eyes steadily, but I knew that he was disturbed. The scar that ran down into his eyebrow was livid, had whitened. The knuckles of his clasped hands were lighter than the skin around them.

"What do you think about all this, brother John?" Sellers said.

"I think there's some things we need to look at again," he said. "I think we'd be fools not to look at everything."

The silence this time was freighted, seeming to beat with invisible wings. Sonny Pickens gave his high, cracked laugh, but no one else did. The music wove its separate strands around us. Tension crackled. My skin crawled with it. I wondered how soon we might leave, and where the ladies' room was, and if I dared cross the charged room to find it. I could not feel Luke's presence beside me and I did not know the taut stranger with John Howard's face, and the others were as alien to me as if they came from another planet. I felt primally, abysmally alone.

Another figure was beside the table suddenly.

"Do your mamas know you boys are out?" said a voice that had a dream, had stirred a nation, preached love and gentleness from a hundred besieged pulpits and a score of jails. My breath seemed to stop. I looked up. He stood there wearing a cardigan sweater against the chill of the air-conditioning, and a white shirt with an open collar, and khaki slacks, looking as inevitable as a mountain, larger than any of us, preternaturally solid and focused, and *there*.

We were on our feet in an instant. I almost upset my chair as I scrambled out of it, and Luke reached out to steady me. So did Martin Luther King. I simply stood, feeling my mouth curve into a smile, staring at the dark moon of his face, the full lips, the slanted, faintly Mongolian eyes, the solid set of his shoulders, the good hands. He smiled back.

There were introductions all around. He did not linger. His eyes rested as gently and knowingly on Juanita and Sonny Pickens as on his young lieutenants, not now so young. He nodded affably to Luke and patted John Howard briefly on the shoulder.

To me he said, "It was fine work you and Luke and John did on the day care piece, Smoky. It was maybe even finer work when you whipped ole Boy Slattery at pool," and he chuckled and touched my arm softly, and then he was gone into the crowd. The trio broke gleefully into "You Been Talkin' 'Bout Me, Baby," and Luke pushed his chair back and said, "We need to get going, Smoky. I've got film to process."

I stood, and picked up my nearly untouched beer, and drained it. I was dizzy with alcohol and the undercurrents at the table and above all the head-spinning exhilaration of meeting Dr. King. Me, I kept thinking to myself. That was me, talking to Dr. Martin Luther King Jr., who knows my name and likes my work. Me.

All of a sudden I wanted desperately to tell my father, and to have him understand. I knew that it wouldn't happen. I hooked a full beer off the table and carried it with me as we left the room. Behind us, Tony Willingham and Rosser Sellers followed Dr. King into the sacrosanct back room of the club, and John Howard sat still at the table, his eyes fixed on something faraway that I could not see. Juanita sat beside him, tracing her long red nail over the back of his hand. It left white traceries on the bronze skin. Sonny Pickens leaned against his wall, eyes closed again, smiling, nodding in time to the music.

"Thanks for the evening," I called softly back to John Howard, but he did not appear to have heard me.

Out on the hot, empty sidewalk, I realized suddenly that I was very drunk. I did not feel drunk; I felt wonderful, giddy and floating and chatty, aware with every atom of my being of the thick, soft air on my bare arms and the grit of the sidewalk under the thin soles of my shoes, of the somehow good, gasolinelike smell of vanished traffic hanging over the streets, of the weight of my hair on my neck and cheek.

But I knew that I must be drunk. I could not walk straight, even though I felt that I could have danced and sung my way down the street like Cyd Charisse. My knees kept buckling, and I kept listing into Luke. Halfway to the car he put his arm around me and half-carried me, and I leaned into him, liking the hardness of his arm around my waist and the way my head fit into the hollow of his shoulder, just where it joined his neck. His beard tickled the top of my head when he leaned down to talk to me, and I liked that, too. He was, I thought, a little taller than Brad. Somehow I did not bump awkwardly into Luke, but fit as though we were designed to walk in lockstep.

"We fit," I said dreamily, burrowing my head into his neck. "Feel how good we fit."

"We fit when you're drunk as a skunk and I'm all but carrying you," he said. "'Scuse me for not having noticed before."

"I am not drunk," I said. "I may be a little high, though. Oh, Luke, I don't want it to be over. I loved that, I wanted it to last. You could just feel, in that room, what the movement was all about . . . the power. Didn't you feel it?"

"I felt power, all right," he said soberly from above my head. "I'm not sure where it was coming from, though."

"Well, from Dr. King. John. Tony and Rosser. You know what they are better than most people—"

"I know what they were."

"What do you mean?"

"I don't know. I really don't know what I mean exactly, Smoky. I didn't much like that little scene. I don't like those two . . . brothers. Brother and sister, rather. I know what they are, but I don't know what they're doing there. It's not their scene. They don't believe in mingling with the nonviolents anymore than they believe in fraternizing with whitey. Ordinarily they wouldn't be caught dead anywhere near you and me, but there they were, making nice. Or at least, trying to. And I didn't like seeing them with Dr. King. It reminded me somehow of . . . of hyenas circling a wounded lion, or something. Gave me the willies."

I did indeed feel a small shiver pass through him, and pressed myself closer to him, as if to warm it away. I wanted suddenly to make things good for him. The thought was so ridiculous that I giggled.

"What are you laughing at?"

"I wanted to comfort you for a minute there. It's the silliest idea I ever had."

"You don't think I ever need any comfort?"

I felt rather than heard him laugh.

"Let's get you home," he said.

Dull sadness descended so suddenly that I stumbled under its weight. Sadness, and the pain that had lain dormant since early evening. It waited. I knew then that it did. When he was gone and I was alone in my bed it would strike. I was silent until we had almost reached the Tenth Street exit of the freeway, and then I said, "Can I watch you develop film for a while? Teddy's spending the night at her folks', and I don't feel like being by myself yet."

He looked sidewise at me.

"You okay? You feeling sick or something? You had an awful lot to drink."

"I'm not sick. I just . . . feel lonesome."

"Ol' YMOG ought to get himself back over here," Luke said, but he turned the car onto Tenth Street, headed, I knew, for Ansley Park and his apartment. The pain receded a little, growling.

"He was here today," I said. "I had lunch with him. He had to go back, though."

"Ah," he said. "Did you show him the *Life* thing?"

"Yeah."

"And does he think you're a foaming racist?"

"No. He doesn't think that. I don't think it even crossed his mind."

"Well, I underestimated him, then. My apologies."

"None needed," I said. But I said no more about Brad. I was taking no chances with the pain.

"You got anything to drink at your house?" I said.

"Not for the likes of you, little Nell," he replied. "I'll give you coffee or some hot chocolate, but no more booze."

"It's Friday."

"I don't care. I don't want you throwing up on my film. You really can't drink worth shit, Smoky."

"Well, it's not like I do a lot of it," I said, and gave a loud, completely involuntary hiccup.

"No it's not. I wonder why you did tonight."

I did not answer. As we bowled through the dark, quiet warren of leaf-hung streets in Ansley Park, a new and unpleasant sensation began in my midriff. I swallowed hard, but it did not go away.

He pulled to a stop at the curb, below the big old brick house whose carriage house he occupied, and came around to open the door for me. My head swam, and a horrid buzzing began in my wrists and fingers.

"I think I'm going to be sick," I said, and was, violently, and repeatedly, in the gutter, while he held me around the waist from behind.

When I stopped, I was weak and wobbly-kneed, but much clearer-headed. I was also mortified. Tears of embarrassment stood in my eyes. I did not want to turn around and look at Lucas Geary.

"I'm so embarrassed," I whispered. "Lord, how gross. I'm sorry, Luke. I've never been sick in public before in my life."

"It's not exactly public," he said. "Don't worry about it. You'll feel better now. I threw up for two days the first time I got that drunk. You ought to try grass. It's a lot easier on your system, and you don't get sick. Come on, let's walk a little."

He slipped his arm around me and I leaned gratefully against him once more. I did not need the support now, but his body felt good, familiar somehow. With his other hand he reached over and smoothed the tangled hair off my face. It was a gentle touch, as if I had been a sick child.

Across from the sleeping houses there was a little park that ran the length of the short street, a deep-shadowed ravine now, where I could hear the sighing of a little wind in the tops of the old trees, and the silvery plink of running water. We crossed the street and went into it, and down a little rock path to the far end. A small creek ran over a man-made rock waterfall there, and into a deep little rock-lined pool. Ferns were thick around it, and the ground was carpeted with soft moss. We sat down at the edge of the pool and took off our shoes and dangled our feet into the water. It was surprisingly cool, almost cold. The air down here was sweet and heavy with damp, secret growing things, and the sense of isolation was magical. It was like being in a hidden glen out of some childhood fairy tale. Overhead, through the canopy of green leaves, I could see a faint silver peppering of stars.

I reached down into the water and splashed a handful on my hot face. It felt wonderful.

"It's cold," I said. "Where does it come from?"

"Underground spring, or artesian well, or something, my landlady says," Luke said. "In the daytime this park's full of kids and dogs and mommies and nannies, and some nights it's full of heads and freaks doing whatever they can't do on the street in broad daylight. Tight Squeeze isn't far. Don't look too close on the ground around you."

I remembered the walk through Tight Squeeze on my first day in Atlanta, with Rachel Vaughn, and the used condoms on the streets. I did not look around me. This was too lovely, too perfect.

Luke took a loose, spilling white cigarette out of his shirt pocket and lit it, and the air turned sweet and pungent. I wrinkled my nose.

"Pot?" I said. I knew it was.

"Yep. It's my vice of choice. I don't do a lot of it, but there are definitely times it's called for, like a good cigar and brandy after dinner."

He passed it to me and I hesitated, then took it and inhaled deeply from it, feeling as if I had just leaped off a cliff into utter nothingness. I coughed from the acrid smoke, but felt nothing else.

"I don't see what everybody thinks is so great," I said, and passed it back to him.

We shared the cigarette. I felt curiously disappointed that it had no effect on me. If I was going to sin, I wanted to know that I had.

Finally he ground it out and flipped it into the darkness.

"No sense trying to save that one," he said. "It's a done deal. Come on. I'll make you that coffee now. And I've got some lemon cheesecake my landlady brought me. You hungry?"

"No," I said dreamily, though I realized suddenly that I was, very hungry. "Don't let's go yet. This is so pretty. I never really noticed how pretty stars are over a city. And the frogs sound so nice, and the moss is . . . wonderful. Don't you think the moss is wonderful, Luke?"

Silvery glee, delight, a kind of subterranean, Christmas-morning feeling woke inside me and licked at my consciousness. I felt the soft, velvety air on every inch of my skin.

"I feel like there's bubbles in my blood," I said, giggling. "So do you. I can feel every bubble in your blood, Luke."

I ran my hand along his cheek, down his neck and under his shirt along his shoulder. I traced the long line of his arm down to his wrist and over his fingers, one by one. It seemed to me that I could feel every separate atom and platelet of him, every nerve ending, every long fiber of muscle.

"You're like an anatomy lesson," I said, holding his hand up to my mouth and putting my tongue out to touch it. His skin tasted complex and wonderful, somehow like sweet, dried grass with sun on it. "There was a model of a man without his skin in my biology class in high school. You could see how he worked right down to his bones. Can you see how I work down to my bones?"

He lifted my hand and kissed it, back first, and then the palm. Fire leaped along the veins that ran up my arm. I drew a little shallow breath.

"Do that again," I whispered, and he did, to the other hand. More fire, and again, the light shallowness in my breathing. I put my hands out and took his face in them, and held it, feeling the sharp angles and bones under my fingers, feeling the individual hairs of his beard and mustache, at once wiry and silky. I pulled his face down to mine and kissed him, feeling my lips melt and part and merge into his, feeling the fire, sweet and molten, surge deep inside me like lava. He sat stone still for a moment and then pulled me to him hard, and kissed me again and again, until I had no more breath and was all sensation, sensation on every inch of flesh, sensation even at the roots of my hair and the bottoms of my wet bare feet. I could not seem to get close enough to him, could not seem to stop my body moving against his.

"No, don't," I whispered fiercely when he pulled away.

He held me loosely against the grass, where I had lain back and pulled him down with me, and propped himself on one elbow. His face was large over mine, it shut out the trees and the prickling stars. I could see it very clearly. It was gentle and serious, and I thought he was very beautiful, medieval, with the long lines of his head and the pointed beard and soft mustache. I reached up and traced the line of his eyebrows with the tip of my finger, and then his mouth. He bit my finger gently and then took my hand and ran his tongue over it, as lightly as a butterfly, back and palm and fingers. I made a small sound in my throat and tried to pull him down again, but he resisted.

"You're feeling the pot, you know," he said. His voice was thick, and he cleared his throat.

"That's not all I'm feeling," I said, stretching voluptuously. "Don't tell me it's all you're feeling. I can feel . . . what you're feeling."

He made a wry face and shifted a little so that he did not press so hard against me.

"I've got no secrets from you, Smokes," he said.

"You want to do this, don't you?" I said into his ear, puffing my breath a little so that it tickled his ear and cheek.

"Jesus Christ, of course I want to do this," he said into my hair. "I've wanted to do this for longer than you know. But I don't take advantage of pot first-timers, and I don't move in on other guys' territory."

"And I thought you were the lover of the Western world," I said, moving a little so that my body was under his. The parts of my flesh that did not touch his felt cold, hungry, bereft.

"Oh, I am," he said. "But I don't rustle in other guys' corrals. It's the only rule I've got. Shit, Smoky, stop it."

"The other guy's corral is empty," I said into his neck.

I felt his body stiffen slightly.

"What do you mean?"

"We had a most unloving little scene today at lunch. I walked out on him. I'm not going back."

He was silent for a long moment, and then he said, "The *Life* thing."

"Yes."

There was another long silence, and then he propped himself up on his elbow again and looked down at me. His face was troubled.

"So that's what's been eating you all night. I guess I ought to say I'm sorry, Smoky, but I'm not. I mean I'm sorry if it hurt you, but I'm not sorry if it ran him off. If he thinks less of you because of that fucking picture, he doesn't deserve to touch the ground you walk on. What did he think, that it was unseemly, or something?"

"Or something. He thought it was exceedingly Irish. He said I didn't know when to stop, that I didn't have any sense of boundaries, no limits. He turned into his mama right before my eyes, Luke."

Luke began to laugh, softly.

"I know about the old Irish appellation. In some circles it's worse than nigger. What a fucking prick," he said. "He's right, though. You don't have any limits. You don't know when to stop. Got no boundaries at all. You'd be an awful liability at the Driving Club for a former YMOG. But it's what makes you a writer, Smokes. It's what I saw in you when I first met you. It's what Matt saw. Christ, all the time you were with Hunt I used to just chomp my teeth thinking what he and his family were going to turn you into."

"What?"

"A robot. Or no, a little wild thing in a cage. Pretty soon your fur would lose its shine and your eyes would lose light, and you'd forget how to run free even if you ever got out. I think sooner or later I would have just grabbed you and run off with you."

"How do you know that?"

"Because I watched it happen to my sister," he said. "I watched the Baltimore version of Bradley Hunt the Umpteenth and his family turn a vivid, wild young painter into a nervous woman who does covers for the Junior League follies and drinks too much at the country club. A guy can live that kind of life and still do his own thing, but I've never seen the woman who could manage it. I don't know why the hell the YMOGs are drawn to the wild birds, but they are. You can see the results in country club bars and fancy nuthouses all over the South."

I laid my head back on his arm and looked up at him. The big pink house on Sea Island, the neat starter house in Collier Hills, the tow-headed children, the stately white wedding at the Cathedral—they all wheeled over my head and his and spiraled up into the opening in the trees that held the stars, and were gone. They might never have been. Only his face was real now, only his body. I reached again for both of them.

"I want to stay with you," I said against his lips. "I want to stay tonight."

"You sure it's over? You sure, Smoky?"

"I'm sure. I gave him back his bracelet."

Then I began to laugh. I felt his lips curve against mine with answering laughter.

"What's funny now?"

"I didn't give him back his birth control pills."

He snorted. "Then come on," he whispered. "Come on and let's go inside."

He pulled me up off the grass and held me hard against him, and we began to walk back up the path toward the street and the dark house above it, and the carriage house behind that. At the bottom of the steep driveway I stumbled, and he swung me up into his arms as easily as if I had been a child. I put my arms around his neck and kissed his face and hair as he walked, carrying me.

"Aren't you afraid this is going to be a rebound . . . you know?" I whispered in his ear. "Aren't you afraid that afterward I'm going to think it was the night and the wine and the music and all that, and not you at all?"

He kissed the top of my head, and traced the line of my breast with his finger. I shivered with the sensation; it set my entire body afire once more. I moved against him under the fire's touch.

"You probably will," he said into my hair. "But not for long."

The next day, when I finally went back to the apartment, Teddy told me that Brad had called several times from Huntsville to apologize. But by then it was far, far too late.

12

HAVE YOU COMPLETELY LOST YOUR MIND? HAVE YOU flipped totally out? Breaking up with Brad and taking up with Luke Geary all in the same day? What were you drinking? Did you take anything?"

At seven o'clock the following night I was sitting on the sofa in clean pajamas with my wet hair wrapped in a towel, eating ham and potato salad from Teddy's mother's kitchen and watching Teddy pace back and forth across the living room, waving her arms as if she were conducting an orchestra. The casement windows were open to the warm September evening and I could hear the sound of car doors opening and closing, and laughter, and music pouring from many phonographs. Saturday night in Colonial Homes.

Teddy had to shout over the sound of the Ramsey Lewis album Luke had lent me. She was in her shortie Peter Max nightshirt with her dark hair in huge rollers; Teddy stopped short of orange juice cans, but only just. She looked like a fierce little woman warrior in an Ionesco play, and I smiled. I had been smiling ever since Luke brought me home. I was very happy.

"I drank about a zillion drinks and then I smoked grass," I said. "Neither one was very much fun. But the other was . . . incredible."

"Well, that's it, then. You were high. Surely you can't think that getting high and screwing is the way it always is. I mean, the way screwing is when you're not high—"

"Yes, I can," I said.

When I woke that morning, in Luke's waterbed in the small bedroom off the big living room of the carriage house, I stretched voluptuously with well-being, realized that I was naked, remembered the night before, and whipped myself into a fetal ball, waiting for the blackness to crash down over me like a tidal wave, waiting to drown in shame.

Nothing happened. Behind my tight-squeezed lids I still felt wonderful. I was aware of small pullings, tightenings, soreness in places I had never felt before, a great, voluptuous soreness between my legs. Even as I felt my face flame, I moved slightly to better feel it. Warmth spread out from it through my legs and stomach like slow fire. I felt myself smile, even with my face pressed into the pillow.

I put out a hand to touch Luke and found only empty space. Before I could sit up, before I could even assess his absence, I heard his footsteps and looked up at him through the fingers I had clamped over my eyes.

He stood over the low bed, wearing only a knotted towel, holding a tray. He had been in the shower; I could see droplets of water still clinging to his beard and mustache, and there were damp comb tracks in his thick, water-dark red hair. The furze of fine red-gold hairs on his arms and legs sparkled with water, too, and he smelled of damp towel and soap and hot coffee. He smelled wonderful. He looked wonderful. Why had I ever thought Lucas Geary was too thin? His narrow body was as supple and smooth as the trunk of a young tree. I wanted to touch it. I wanted to run my hand lightly over it, from his wide, sloping shoulders down his torso and legs to his feet; to touch the scarred foot with my fingers; to trace the long bones and skeins of muscle. He had a body like a swimmer's. I realized that I did not know if he swam or not. I did not, in fact, know what he did at all, except what we had done together in the dark hours just past before, finally, we slept. I felt my face and chest redden, and shut my eyes again. I had been abandoned past anything I had ever imagined.

"Coffee first, then bagels," he said, and put the tray down on the floor beside the waterbed and flopped down on it. He reached over and pulled my fingers away from my face and studied it, and then laughed.

"You have a hickey the size of a chrysanthemum on your neck," he said. "Stop being coy and sit up and talk to me. Are you embarrassed about last night?"

I nodded.

"Did you feel that black shit? Did it hurt?"

I shook my head.

"Cat got your tongue? I didn't think you did. Listen, I bet you think it all happened because you were high, right? And that in the cold light of morning everything is different?"

I nodded again.

"Then," he said, unknotting the towel and drawing me to him very gently, "I think we better do it again. Just to put your mind at ease."

And we did. And again, just, as he said, to be absolutely sure. By the time we both lay, sweating and emptied, on the undulating surface of the waterbed, the coffee was stone cold, and I was throbbing in every nerve and sinew with a wild, loose sweetness and laughing with what felt very like elementary, primitive triumph.

The laughter started low in my throat like a growl, and my head fell back on his arm with it. I rolled it on my neck luxuriously. I don't think I will ever feel as utterly and simply female again in my life as I did in that moment on Luke Geary's waterbed.

"So what's your pleasure?" he said, stretching mightily and leaning over to kiss me between my damp breasts. "Breakfast? A shower? A trip to the moon on gossamer wings?"

"Breakfast," I said. "I'm starved. And then a shower. And then maybe we could do it again one more time, just to be absolutely sure that it wasn't . . . you know, the grass and the booze and everything."

"Jesus, I've created a monster," he laughed. "I'm good, but I'm not that good. Could you wait until lunchtime, do you think?"

"Just," I said, and bit the tip of his shoulder, where the freckles flocked so closely that he looked made of copper.

"But . . . Luke?" Teddy said, her brows knit with the effort to understand. "Looks aside, what on earth could he possibly have that's better than Brad Hunt? Besides, I thought you didn't much like Luke. He's always on your case."

"Brad . . . can hurt you," I said slowly. The effort to talk about Brad tired me. I knew that I could not make her understand. But this was Teddy, and I wanted to try.

"Brad did hurt me, at lunch yesterday. He did it deliberately, and it hurt a great deal. I think he was sorry afterward, and maybe he didn't entirely mean what he said, but he did it on purpose, and he meant enough of it. He probably doesn't do it a lot, but he can do it, and he will. I'd never know, after that, when he was going to do it again. I don't think Luke would do that. He might do it unintentionally, but he wouldn't just think about hurting you and then do it. He would never set out to simply hurt somebody. Not me and not anybody else. I really believe that."

"Nobody's that saintly," Teddy said.

"I didn't mean he was saintly. I just meant that it isn't the way his mind works. He's entirely up front about things. He doesn't play games."

"Brad wasn't playing games with you," Teddy said. "He was going to marry you."

"Are you kidding? He was playing one long game with his mother, and I was the prize," I said. "He may not have been aware that he was, but he was. It had to hurt me sooner or later. I don't know why I didn't see it before."

"And Luke Geary isn't a game player?"

"No," I said positively. "He isn't."

I thought of the *Life* photograph then, and of the permission that I had signed after he had told me it was just routine. Had that been a game? I did not think it had. I thought that Luke honestly could not imagine I would have any objection to being part of something as powerful and telling as that frozen moment. He had thought that I would see, when I saw the photograph, how necessary it was that it exist and be seen. And I had. Even at my angriest and most shocked, I had seen the necessity for the photograph. It had been one artist in communion with another. He had been communicating with the thing in me that, even now, he saw more clearly than I did.

I thought of something he said this afternoon, too. It was after we had had bagels and cream cheese and lox and wonderful, strong hot coffee spiked with cinnamon that he had gotten from what he called the one decent deli in Atlanta, and were sitting on the minuscule deck that jutted out into the very treetops above the wooded backyard of the widow's tall brick house, lost in leaf dapple, dressed only in damp towels. Music was booming softly from his complex sound system; silvery, skittering jazz. He had put on the Swingle Singers doing "Going Baroque" and followed that with the Modern Jazz Quartet's haunting "No Sun in Venice."

"I don't want you to feel hemmed in," I said. "I don't want you to feel like I'm making demands on you. I'm not going to do that."

"You should," he said. "I'm going to make demands on you. You should make them on me. I know you've heard that I'm a great swordsman, or whatever it is you've heard about me and women, and that's true. I love women. I always have. But it's always one person at a time, and I always try to get the terms defined right at the start. All relationships are not the same; you know right from the start that some are not going to be long-term. At least, I usually know, and I assume the women do, too. And so I say so. When there needs to be an end to things, I say that, too. And I ask my—partner, I guess—to do the same."

"So where's the end to this?" I said, feeling my heart squeeze with dread. I could do this, I knew; I could keep this volatile, spinning, shimmeringly physical thing going indefinitely, but I could not do it lightly. Had I been wrong in sensing that he felt that way, too? I had, after all, literally no experience in reading this sort of thing.

"I don't see an end to it," he said. "I want to be with you now. I will be with you. When I don't have to be away on a shoot, where I'll be is with you. When I can, I'll take you with me. I'm going out tonight with Matt and John, to hear Ramsey Lewis again, and I'm not going to take you with me because it's been planned like this for a while. But that's all. After that I want us to be together. I'm going to tell Matt that tonight. All this is presupposing that you want that, too."

I nodded. I knew that I did. It was just what I wanted. Perhaps it had always been what I wanted.

"No making up with Hunt? No running back to Sea Island? No juggling me and dinner at the Driving Club?"

"No. None of that. Okay, so how long do you want us to be together, then?"

"I don't know. You can't possibly know, either. Like I said, I don't see an end. I'll tell you if I do. I want you to promise the same thing. And if you ever want things to . . . change, I want to know about that, too."

I knew what he meant. He meant that he knew that the day might well come when I would want more, when I would want permanence, a long commitment. Wasn't it what we all wanted, we young women of this time in the world? Despite all the popular cant about love and freedom, hadn't all our lives been about that; hadn't we been drilled and groomed and programmed for just that?

I sat at his side in the early afternoon sun and realized with surprise that I did not want that, and perhaps never had. Maybe, I thought, that was the source of the blackness after all, not the Church, not guilt, not God. Maybe it was the very heaviness of the rest of my life hanging over me. I did not want the rest of my life to be decided now. I wanted only this moment. I wanted this moment to go on endlessly, without the elephantine weight of St. Philip's Cathedral hanging over me, of the starter house in Brookwood Hills, of the huge pink shadow of the Sea Island house. If I saw anything ahead of me at this moment it was this moment, stretching out to infinity. Work; laughter; music; talk; Matt and his great, mercurial talent and his quicksilver mind and his blatting Bahamian taxi horn; Tom with his gentleness and his beautiful body and dry sweet smile; Teddy with her staunch, loving heart; Hank with his buoyant constancy; bylines and honors and opening nights and long lunches and blue cocktail hours full of preening and laughter; the bite and shine of *Downtown;* the days and nights of Lucas Geary; his eyes and my voice together, making life-changing wholes: images, words. His and mine. Just now. Just this.

There was nothing in any of it to hurt me. Nothing in all of Lucas Geary that could hurt me as Brad Hunt had hurt me with a half a minute's worth, yesterday, of words.

"So what else did you do?" Teddy said. "Besides fuck like minks, I mean?"

We laughed longer at that than it warranted. Then I said, "Oh, Teddy, everything. Nothing. But it was a wonderful day. I think it was the best day I ever spent."

"Oh, shit," she said. "You're going to be absolutely impossible in love. Some people are."

I had spoken the truth. Luke and I had, essentially, done nothing; and yet I still remember the first day we were together as if it were burned into the cells of my brain. There was a clarity about it like bright water; everything shimmered with import. After lunch we had sat long on the little deck, watching the angle of the sun change in the blue bowl of the sky above us, drinking the half bottle of cold white chablis we had found in his small refrigerator, and talking. We talked as if we had been talking together all our lives; there was no sense of beginning in our conversation. Always, Luke's and my words to each other have been more like continuations to me. I learned more about him and he did about me, and yet, that long, slow afternoon, they did not seem new, but like things we had only, for a little while, forgotten about each other. Under the talk the secret, tickling tug of the new physical wanting lay like a living thing.

"Who is Sonny Pickens?" I said.

"I'm not really sure. One of the new ones, one of the Berkeley bunch that wasn't around at Selma and Lowndes County. I've heard of them, but I've never met one. Real sharp. Real angry. Real black. Into black power in a big way; the guns and the leather jackets and the berets and the salute, the whole nine yards. A hundred and eighty degrees away from the movement in the South; nothing nonviolent about these cats. Want to take the reins from the SCLC and even the moderate blacks in SNCC and CORE. Want to throw all the whites, even the most liberal ones, completely out of the loop. I know they've been recruiting big time in the North, in the places where the riots have been the worst and the war is heavy. What I don't know is what guys like Sonny are doing down here. If they're trying to enlist some of King's guys they'd do better to let the ones like Juanita have a crack at them. At least she's got a history with the troops down here. She was a proper little freedom rider and a support sister before she turned militant. And she's got contacts."

"John, you mean."

"Yeah. But they all remember her from Selma and Lowndes. She was one of the best before she went over."

"You think she's trying to get John to be a Panther? From what you tell me that's a losing battle. At least, if he's all that loyal to Dr. King."

"He is," Luke said. "It's just that . . . he thinks some things that should be happening aren't. Or aren't happening fast enough. Or maybe never will. He's really vulnerable right now. I wish to hell she'd go on back to wherever her home base is. I think old Sonny was a bad mistake and she probably knows that. Never should have brought that dude into the epicenter of the movement. She'll probably take him and go on home now. Get him out of Dodge."

"I wonder," I said. "It looked to me like she had more in mind than turning John into a Panther."

"Like what?"

"Oh, Lord, Luke, don't be dense. You've got eyes. Didn't you see how she was hanging all over him? Like getting him back into bed."

"That would be the lesser of several evils," Luke said.

"Maybe not," I said thoughtfully.

"Listen, I've got some champagne," he said. "You want some? Let's drink a little, and then I'm going to go develop some film before John comes by. Can you find something to do, read or listen to music, or something?"

"Or something," I said, and reached over and ran my fingernail down his stomach to the top of the towel.

"I'll develop fast," he grinned, and went and got the champagne. It was lovely, silky, tingling stuff, in a beautiful dark green bottle with a red wax seal. I did not know the brand, only that it must be expensive.

"Where'd you get it?" I said.

"My landlady. I fixed her transmission. Or her transition, as she calls it."

He got up and went into the small darkroom off his minuscule kitchen, taking his glass with him. I dressed and combed my hair and sat, bare feet tucked under me, on the big velvet sofa in his living room, sipping at the champagne left in my glass and looking around the place where he lived.

It was not like any of the singles' apartments I had been in in Atlanta; it had about it, in the pale afternoon sunlight, a feeling of age and a kind of elegant oddness that struck me as exotic, foreign. I remembered then that his landlady the widow had furnished the little house with her own pieces, and that she had been born in Vienna and was said to be wealthy in the fusty, dark, mittel-European way of many Viennese. The carriage house looked it, with its tall glass bookcases and enormous, dark, carved armoires and wing chairs and its many faded, tasseled silk pillows and its large, dark, gilt-framed paintings of deep-bosomed women and bearded men. Bits of decorative china and glass were scattered everywhere, and I knew that they were not Luke's, but somehow the overall ambience of the place suited him. The hundreds upon hundreds of books and records and the sound equipment and a few pieces of African sculpture were, I knew, his additions. Oddly, they did not clash with the widow's things. The place spoke of Luke Geary even with little actual physical evidence of him.

I was stretched out on the sofa listening to *Carmina Burana* and reading Walker Percy when a light rap on the screened door broke into my mindless contentment and I looked up to see John Howard standing just outside it, on the cottage's doorstep.

"Come in," I called, and he did, and stood looking at me, squinting his yellow wolf's eyes against the gloom.

"Hey, Smoky," he said, as if he was accustomed to finding me alone in Luke's living room. "Luke around?"

"Processing film," I said. "He'll be done in a little while. Want some champagne? We opened a bottle and didn't drink much, and it's just sitting there going flat. It's lovely stuff. Let me get you a glass."

"Well . . . yeah. Thanks. Champagne sounds just right for a September Saturday," he said, smiling, and I padded out to the kitchen and came back with the bottle and a clean, stemmed glass. It had small flowers etched on the bowl, millefleur, I thought they were called. The widow again.

Luke called a greeting from the closed door of the darkroom and John Howard yelled back affably, and raised his glass to me.

"Cheers, Smoky," he said. "To Andre. And don't worry about the *Life* thing. Luke said you were. It's not going to have any repercussions. Nobody much reads it in my crowd."

"Little do you know," I said. "But thanks. John, I loved last night. Meeting Dr. King was something I'll never forget. There's just such—I don't know—goodness about him. It must mean a lot to work with him. How did you get hooked up with him, anyway?"

He laughed. It was a rich sound, relaxed. He looked elegant and remote sitting across from me in the widow's wing chair, sipping the champagne. He wore jeans and a neatly pressed blue oxford cloth shirt, the sleeves rolled up on his bronze forearms. It was like having a Remington statue for cocktails.

"I guess you might say I ran away and joined him like you would the circus, because I was mad at my daddy," he said.

"Tell," I said.

I knew I would not have said that to John Howard the day before. The woman who did it now was not the girl who had gone to lunch yesterday and watched her future crumble at her feet. I did not know what had changed me, not precisely, anyway. Of course, I had crossed the great Rubicon that had always separated girls from women, at least in Corkie; was now someone who had done what had been known in my parochial circles as the Dirty Deed or the Black Act. I had passed over. I could never again be someone who did not know how it was. But I could not think that was why, suddenly, I felt easy and equal with John Howard. Nevertheless, I did. Perhaps it was all simply a part of the vivid, crystal-edged day.

"Well, I was just out of law school and trying to decide what I wanted to do with my life," John said. "I was twenty-six years old and I'd been in school one way or another since I was seven. I'd thought I wanted to preach, but somehow the call I thought I had when I was a teenager had sort of faded out; with everything going on in the early sixties preaching just seemed kind of sideline stuff to me. I don't think I was ever touched with the fire. And to tell you the truth, I think the ministry was always more a way to get at my dad than a real calling. He really wanted me in one of the professions that made some bucks, wanted me to have what he called a decent life out of the ghetto. I don't know why he thought I'd end up in the ghetto; none of my family ever even saw one. But anyway, I went on to Howard to law school more to make peace with him than from any burning desire to practice law. And, of course, to put off preaching. I've done some of that, enough to know that I'm no leader of men, much less a pipeline from God. So I got my degree and went on back to St. Louis that spring to look around some, see where I might get a job. But all the time the Civil Rights movement was pulling at me; it seemed indecent somehow to just sit it out in St. Louis. I thought I ought to go somewhere and get a little taste of it, see what it was all about. The march on Washington came up that summer, and I decided to go. My father went straight into orbit. The last thing he said, as my bus rolled off for Washington, was 'I hope you get arrested.'"

"Shit, that's just what my old man told me when my bus left Baltimore," Luke said, coming into the room. He slapped John Howard on the shoulder and walked over and dropped a kiss on the top of my head. I felt myself color. I looked obliquely at John Howard, and he smiled back at me and nodded slightly, as if he was conferring a benediction, but he said nothing.

"Y'all met there," I said. Luke had told me that much.

"Yeah, we met very elegantly standing in line for one of the outdoor toilets SCLC had put up behind their headquarters," Luke said. "We noticed each other immediately. There we were, two skinny kids in seersucker suits and madras ties and brushcuts, standing in line with all the overalls and work shirts and peace pendants and sandals. We looked at each other and started laughing, and I pulled off my tie and he did his, and we balled them up and threw them over behind the toilets and tied our coats around our waists and rolled up our shirt-sleeves, and walked over and shook hands with each other. Pulling that tie off and slinging it behind a Porta Potty was the biggest act of liberation I'd ever made in my life, besides getting on the bus in Baltimore. I think it was for John, too. After that we went to hell pretty fast."

"After King's 'I Have a Dream' speech there wasn't any doubt that I was going to follow him," John said. "I didn't even call home. I got on one of the buses that was going back to Atlanta from Washington and Luke came with me. I didn't know what to do with him; here was this skinny kid so white his face shone like new money on a bear's behind, as somebody said about him on the bus, dragging his little Samsonite suitcase and all these cameras around his neck. I liked him, but I didn't exactly think he was an asset on that bus. But he was like a stray dog; I couldn't lose him. When we got to Atlanta I went on down to SCLC headquarters and found Dr. King—he was always accessible when he was in town; I just walked into his office—and told him I was a new lawyer and I wanted to work for him and he didn't have to pay me anything until he saw whether he could use me or not. Luke was right behind me, saying the same thing. Turned out they could use a photographer a lot quicker than they could a lawyer; Luke went out immediately with a bunch of them to cover voter registration in Mississippi, and I got stuck in Atlanta doing pro bono scutwork. It was a year before they even let me get anybody out of jail. I ended up doing some assistant stuff over at Atlanta University, and some tutoring; it gave me a little money and a place to live. I still do that, and I've still got that student apartment. Luke, as you know, went on to fame and fortune by getting his foot stepped on by a police hoss in Selma. And the rest is history. As they say."

"Yeah," I said, smiling. "It literally is, isn't it? And you got as close to Dr. King as anybody ever has. Why you, John?"

It was a presumptuous question, but I did not intend it that way and he did not take it as such.

"I think," he said, leaning back and holding his glass up to the light, so that the pale gold bubbles danced and swirled, "it was because he knew a penitent little elitist when he saw one. He'd been one himself. He wasn't always a quote, man of the people, you know. He was raised a lot like me; he was sheltered and educated and pretty cultured. He literally made himself over so he could talk the talk and walk the walk; he became the ultimate common man so he could touch and move his people, do something for them. It must have taken an enormous act of love and will. And it changed me to be around him. I'll never have his total empathy with the rank and file of the movement, but I've learned from him that they're what it's all about. They're the important ones, the so-called little people. The poor folks. This is their fight. Martin's given himself to them utterly, and I've tried to follow in his footsteps. I haven't totally succeeded, but it's given me myself in a way nothing else ever could. Being with him did that."

We were quiet for a spell. It was an extraordinary speech, I thought. The most extraordinary thing about it was that he had spoken it so openly and naturally in front of me. I was moved nearly to tears, but said nothing. To have spoken would have been, somehow, both arrogant and callow.

"So," Luke said. "How'd the rest of the party go last night? Didn't look like Tony and Rosser took to ol' Sonnyboy too well. Who is he, exactly, John?"

John Howard made an impatient gesture.

"One of the new young ones that took up with Huey and Bobby out at Merritt, in Oakland," he said. "I don't know much about him beyond that. I think he was at Berkeley for a year, and then he got in on the hoohaw at the California state legislature. There are a bunch like him coming along; never been South, never marched, never sat-in, never did any jail time, never did have the foggiest notion what Martin is talking about. They're too young and they're all mad as shit. They like the guns and the tough talk and the uniforms; it's like playing war. Nothing's real to them yet. I'm afraid by the time it is, they're going to have done a lot of damage. Things got really ugly last night after y'all left. I had to frog-march the little bastard out the back door before somebody beat the shit out of him."

"What happened?"

"He said some bad stuff about Martin. Hell, that's not unusual, nowadays. It's just that he picked the wrong place to say it."

"I thought last night the vibes were bad," Luke said. "I told Smokes Dr. King reminded me of an old lion surrounded by jackals, or something."

"The king must die," I said, thinking of a seminar in classical mythology I had had in college. "You know, the myth that the king had to die, to be sacrificed ritually, and another had to take his place to insure that the crops came in and life went on. Almost all cultures have it in one way or another. I thought about it when Kennedy was shot."

John Howard looked at me somberly.

"Yeah, well, that's almost exactly what Sonny said, although I'd bet my boots that dude wouldn't know classical mythology from cat piss. What he said was, 'King is dead, you know.' Sat right there and said it as Martin was leaving the room with Tony and Rosser. I don't know if Martin heard him, but the other two were back there like a shot. Asked him what the hell he meant, and he just smiled that jackass smile and said, 'He was dead when Stokely raised his fist in Greenwood and the crowd hollered "Black Power!" He's walkin' around dead, only he don't know it, and you all don't, either. That was the beginning of the end for the old movement, brothers.'"

Luke's indrawn breath hissed, and I shivered.

"Greenwood?" I said.

"Mississippi," Luke said. "When Stokely Carmichael got arrested for pitching his tent in Greenwood during the Meredith march, there was a big rally. He came straight from the jail. Everybody was mad; it was a chickenshit arrest. He made what everybody thinks is the first black power salute that night. And some folks think that night was the first time 'Black Power!' replaced 'Freedom' as a rallying cry. Not that it really matters."

"What a horrible thing to say anytime, but especially last night," I said, thinking of the sense of joy and exaltation I had had last night at La Carrousel. "That's his place. Dr. King's. The nerve of that little—"

"Yeah, I thought Rosser was going to kill him," John Howard said. "He had him by the back of the collar and was fixing just to kick the shit out of him, but Juanita apologized and we pulled him out of there. She knows it was a bad thing for him to be there. She didn't bring him. He just showed up. I think he's trying to ride on her coattails. She's got a lot of friends in the movement still, and I think he'd love to recruit them."

"Apparently she does have friends," Luke said, and smiled mirthlessly at John.

"I'm not apologizing, Luke," John said. "She's a hell of a woman, no matter what side she's on. She was one of the best we ever had. You can't just write that off. And besides, they're not all like Sonny Pickens. Most of them were us once. I try not to forget that."

"They seem to have forgotten it," Luke said. "You're not going over are you, old buddy?"

"You know I'm not. All I'm saying is that maybe it's time to listen to what they're really saying, the meat below the posturing and the slogans. It may not be so far from what we've been saying all along. The end is the same. The means are different, that's all. And they get things done. They accomplish things you can see and touch and point to. It's not outside the realm of possibility that if we got closer together we could learn from each other. Christ, Luke, our way isn't working. I believe with all my heart in our way, but it's like all of a sudden it's just stopped working. It got a lot of legislation in place, but nobody's enforcing it. It's like we're walking in molasses. Ever since the White House Conference last year people have been mad; a lot of the foot soldiers came home from that disillusioned and cynical. It's pretty obvious Johnson is just using the movement. Before that, I think we were mad about different things, the North and the South. Up there, they were mad because the promises haven't been upheld. Down here, there just weren't any promises being made. Now we're both mad about the same stuff. Now the promises have been made, and we're seeing that nobody in the government is doing shit to get them enforced. Don't you see? That makes all the . . . all the marching and beatings and jail and the shooting and the dying for nothing. Just for nothing, if they resulted in only promises that nobody means to keep. So yeah, I think we do need to look at what works. We could work it out about the means."

"You really think the SCLC is going to find something it can use in the Panthers' camp?" Luke said. "You think Dr. King and the rest of them are going to get guns and black berets and leather jackets and scarves and march around?"

"Don't be a fool. Of course not. But you can't deny that they've got an impressive organization. They've got this hot breakfast program going in virtually every major city they're in, and day care, and black studies programs, and employment programs, and food banks, and they're teaching inner-city blacks how to organize for better breaks in their jobs, and better treatment from the police—"

"And they're showing little kids how to shoot Magnums and they're saying all the whites should butt out entirely, and they're advocating armed insurrection—"

"I never said they had all the answers," John Howard said. "Not even many of them. A lot of what they say is bullshit. But I think even they know that. It's saber-rattling, to get attention. You can't do anything without the attention. And they've flat got it, especially from the media. We don't have that anymore. With an organizational structure like theirs, and with the press they've got, if we could just move closer together instead of separating into factions like we have—Jesus, SCLC never did have more than a few thousand folks, and never much money, and now that SNCC and CORE have pulled away, we're like David going up against Goliath, only without the slingshot. All I'm saying is that their side has things we can use, and ours has stuff they need. We need to let them show us what they could do for us. We need to at least listen. We can say no to the guns; they don't really use them, anyway. I don't think they'd even push it; I think that's just bait. I think we may be closer together than we think, them and us."

"Wow," Luke said. "She's better than I thought."

"She never left us that far behind," John Howard said levelly. "One reason she was down here was to see if there wasn't some middle ground we could meet on. To see if we could talk. She hasn't forgotten the Delta, she hasn't forgotten Lowndes County. They're not all Sonny Pickens, like I said. Most of them aren't."

"So what are y'all planning to do to bring everybody together?"

"She's not planning anything," John said. "She left this morning to go back home. She's got a little girl in one of their day care programs in Philadelphia, did you know that? Kimba. She's three. Her father's long gone. Juanita's got more to think about than infiltrating us down here, no matter what some of the troops think."

"Well, then, what are you planning?"

"Nothing. I don't know. I'm going to talk to Martin about it, though. One thing's for certain, he'll listen. That's more than I can say for Tony and Rosser."

Luke stretched. "It seems like such a long time ago. All of it. Like it happened to somebody else. Doesn't it, to you? Christ, I don't ever want to be shot at or hosed again, but the spirit in those days—it was something, wasn't it?"

"It was something," John Howard said. The golden eyes were far away. "It was something, that's for sure . . ."

There was a soft tapping on the door, and Luke got up to answer. He opened it and a short, square young black woman came in carrying a crystal platter with a pound cake on it. It was still warm; fragrant steam wafted from it.

"Miz Strauss sent this for y'all," she said. "She says save some for your company, Luke."

Luke took the platter and put it in the kitchen. The young woman—hardly more than a girl, really, I saw on closer inspection—stood looking at us shyly. She was very black, and her head was wrapped in a bright cotton scarf with an African print, as Juanita's had been last night. There were dark seed beads around her neck, and big wooden hoops in her ears. She wore bell-bottom blue jeans and a peasant blouse, and had sandals on her stubby, sturdy feet. She could not have been long past her teens.

"This is Luella Hatfield," Luke said. "She helps Mrs. Strauss out and does entirely more for me than I deserve. I think she gets extra hardship pay for keeping after my place. I'm teaching her photography and she's teaching me to sing."

"A lost cause," John Howard said, smiling. "He sings like a forty-dollar mule with the colic. It's good to meet you, Luella. I'm John Howard."

"And this is Smoky O'Donnell," Luke said.

The girl gave John and me a sweet, shy smile.

"You done the Andre piece," she said. "Luke showed me. I know you from Selma, Mr. Howard."

"No kidding," John Howard said. "Were you marching? You look too young."

"No. My daddy wouldn't let me march till I was sixteen and I wasn't but fifteen then. I was singin'."

"Luella was a Freedom Singer," Luke said. "You remember Bernice Reagon's bunch? Those great spirituals and movement songs? She had a bunch she took around the South just to sing, and God, sing they did—I never heard such music. They sang us all across that bridge in Selma. This gal can flat sing; Aretha Franklin hasn't got anything on her. Folks think there's an earthquake when she lets go."

"I remember," John Howard said, smiling. "It was the best singing I ever heard. So did you come up here to sing, or what?"

"Well, I just came up here after Selma because it was where Dr. King and all y'all were," she said, ducking her head. "My daddy wanted me to try to get a scholarship and go on to study somewhere, but I knew I had to be up here where y'all were. So I came on up here with my cousin."

"Where do you live? Are you studying?" John said. "You ought to be training somewhere—"

"Not much call for singin' now, don't look like," the girl said. Her smile was sunny and without regret. "And my cousin got married and moved to Columbus. I got a job with Miz Strauss right after that. I live in with her. She's real good to work for. She gives me money and her daughter's clothes and all the time off I want. She's trying to see if somebody in the orchestra can get me some training. Her husband used to be the boss of it, you know."

I felt my heart squeeze. From the valiant verges of the Edmund Pettus Bridge, from the ranks of the best and bravest young voices in the country, to a spare room in a white woman's house and the cast-off clothes of a white girl. It did not seem much of a trade-off.

I felt my eyes fill. Luke must have seen them. He caught my attention and gave me a stern look and shook his head slightly. Aloud he said, "A person could do worse than work for Mrs. Strauss. She's a fire-breathing liberal and a soft-hearted romantic at the same time. Luella and I both reap the benefits of that."

"Sho do," Luella said.

"I'll ask around at AU. I think maybe we can work out some training for you," John Howard said. He smiled at her with no suggestion of patronization, no sense of the difference between them. "What was your favorite song? Did you have one?"

"I always liked 'Eyes on the Prize,'" she said. "You remember that one?"

"Do I not," John Howard said. He was silent for a moment, still smiling, as at some lost memory, and then suddenly he closed his eyes and threw his head back and began to sing:

The only chain that a man can stand
Is the chain of hand in hand.
Keep your eyes on the prize,
Hold on, hold on.

He had a voice like a great bronze bell, dark and strong and full of the ancient resonances of Africa, the red clay of Southern fields, that gave the spirituals and the songs of the movement their poignance and power. It was a rich voice, timeless, compelling. I stood with my breath held.

Luella Hatfield clapped her hands and took it up:

We're gonna board that old Greyhound,
Carrying love from town to town.
Keep your eyes on the prize,
Hold on, hold on.

I have never heard a voice like that since that afternoon. It swelled and soared until it filled the room and spilled out into the waning afternoon; it was honey, smoke, crystal, fire, wind, water, earth. My hair stood up at the base of my neck. My spine crawled.

John moved close to her and put his arm around her and they sang together:

The only thing we did wrong,
Stayed in the wilderness a day too long.
Keep your eyes on the prize,
Hold on, hold on.
But the one thing we did right
Was the day we started to fight.
Keep your eyes on the prize,
Hold on, hold on.

When they stopped, neither Luke nor I spoke. The two intertwined voices seemed to hover in the room like the breath of gods. The silence spun out. From outside, down on the street, came the sound of clapping.

We clapped too, then, and John Howard and Luella Hatfield hugged and laughed, and she ducked her head and slipped out the screen door.

"Pleased to meetch'all," drifted back.

"'But the one thing we did right was the day we started to fight,'" John Howard said softly to Luke, and Luke lifted his palms and said, "Who am I to argue with destiny?"

"'Scuse me," I mumbled, and went into the bathroom and shut the door and ran the water so that they would not hear me cry.

13

I THINK THAT SOMETIMES THE GREAT CHANGES IN OUR LIVES, the ones that divide time, happen so deep down and silently that we don't even know when they occur. I've never been good at sensing them. Only with hindsight can I see clearly that yes, this was such an event, that was such a time. It frequently happens that the seasons of the greatest change are the times that feel the most tranquil, the most suspended, the most . . . timeless, I guess. But if you could read them, as if on some interior seismograph, you could see the sharp peaks and valleys that marked the tiny, silent earthquakes. I suppose it would save everybody a lot of grief if those seismographs were actual, but of course that's not the way life works. Not mine, anyway.

That fall was one of those times. Earthquake season. Miniature earthquakes, of course; largely personal ones, but upheavals, certainly. Alterers of lives. But I did not feel them. I wonder if any of us did, really, in that glorious bronze autumn. Just as I will remember the fall of 1967 as the time that the change began, so will I remember it as the loveliest autumn I have ever seen.

I think it was because it was my first real autumn. We do not have them in Savannah, not really. On the coast of Georgia and the sea islands of the Carolinas, we get a change of seasons, but it would be hard to think of it as conventional autumn. It is too subtle, too slow to ripen. It stays warm for one thing, though the great, suffocating wet heat of summer withdraws. The sea and sky go deep blue and seem to widen, and the sun turns from white to gold, and the light on the marshes becomes strange and luminous, as tawny as the marshes themselves when the green of summer fades. It is lovely and magical, but it is not, to me, autumn.

Fall in the foothill country just below the Blue Ridge Mountains is another matter entirely. That year the heat left swiftly, overnight. A gust of cold air from some faraway Canadian peak swept in at the end of September, driving a great rainstorm ahead of it; a wind that first tickled and shivered, then lashed the pallid, dusty trees, summoning from them a booming shouting chorus they—and we—had almost forgotten. Rain then, in buckets, sheets, shrouds, waves, that drenched the matted ghost of grass in the park across the street from Luke's apartment, and filled the little stream so that it poured over the waterfall in a flood of tea-brown water. Luke and I were caught in it, coming home from the Atlanta Falcons camp on Black Mountain, North Carolina, where he had been photographing the team at practice, and by the time we got the top of the Morgan up, we were soaked and shivering and laughing with the exhilaration of the promise of fall.

And the next morning, there it was. Waking pressed together in the waterbed, chilly for the first time since I had been sleeping there, we heard the furnace come on in the carriage house, and smelled the familiar, evocative smell of dusty heat. You forget that smell from autumn to autumn, but it means fall to me as surely as the smell of sweet smoke from burning leaves, and the perfume of cold winesap apples bought at roadside stands in the mountains.

In a few weeks the great sea of hardwoods from which Atlanta is carved was wildfire. Early frost bit the leaves to scarlet and yellow and bronze, and they skirled down like flaming snow all over the city. The air was clean and bronze-blue, and the sky was a color I had never seen before. We could not seem to get enough of the outdoors. On weekends we took the Morgan and packed lunches and drove into the flaming foothills, or simply took sandwiches and thermoses of coffee into the little park across the street and lay on our backs on an old blanket of the widow's, the air chilly around us but the high sun lying like thick honey on our closed lids. We went to football games, we went to craft shows and folk fairs and flea markets. The Southeastern World's Fair wheeled by in a Technicolor blur of sawdust and cotton candy; we went to the freak shows and the nude revues and rode everything, and Luke won me a truly dreadful Barbie doll look-alike dressed up like Scarlett O'Hara. It was the worst prize he could find in the entire hideous pantheon. When we made love that night, burrowed deep under the nest of blankets and quilts that covered the waterbed now, that smelled of smoke from the fires that we never quite made properly, the Scarlett doll simpered at us from the corner of Luke's bureau until he got up and draped his shorts over her.

"Lawdy, Miss Scarlett, you don't know nothin' 'bout no fuckin'," he growled into my neck, and I laughed with joy and a kind of happiness that was deeper and quieter than joy. They say that spring is for lovers, but to me autumn will always be the very living country of love.

Love? Dear Lord, but I was in love. Teddy had been right; I was impossible. I had thought I had loved people before, but I simply had not known what the word meant. I could not even remember what I had felt for Brad Hunt, and I had thought, for a time, that surely I loved him.

He had called several times while he was in Huntsville, unable to believe that I would not forgive him that single lapse and I could not think what to say to him that would not hurt him. Finally I had said, badly and without preface, that I was in love with Luke Geary, and he had said that that was quick work even for a couple of micks, and hung up on me. I felt a kind of dim, generic regret, but mostly relief. Nothing, now, stood between me and Luke.

Teddy said more than once that fall that many people went all their lives and never felt what I felt for Lucas Geary, and did very well, and maybe, in the long run, better with lesser passions. It was her fond but exasperated contention that I had turned as stupid as a sheep with my feelings for him, though I tried very hard, when I thought about it, not to allow this consuming new emotion to affect my work. I suppose it did, though; how could it not have? I was not at all the same person I had been before the night at La Carrousel, not even remotely. That person was untouched. This one was used, involved, consumed. It had to show.

I did not see him nearly as much as I had before, certainly not every day. We soon found that there had to be, as Kahlil Gibran said in *The Prophet,* spaces in our togetherness. Otherwise I think the intensity might have burnt up something vital and healthy in both of us. It certainly would have annoyed the people around us badly; almost everyone in *Downtown*'s orbit knew about Luke and me, and almost no one seemed sanguine about it. No one wished us ill, I don't think, except perhaps Matt, who openly disliked the relationship. But it seemed to unsettle everyone who was a part of that tight, shining entity known as Comfort's People. Everybody in the inner circle grumped or teased or laughed about Luke and me. I remembered what Teddy had said, in one of the first talks we had ever had together: that Comfort's People did not have interrelationships, but were faithful to the whole. I had not paid a great deal of attention at the time; it had not, then, occurred to me that I would ever want to be anything but one of Comfort's People. Now, I wondered peevishly, when Teddy rolled her eyes or Hank jibed at me or Matt bellowed in frustration when he needed Luke and found him in my office or gone entirely, why it was not possible to be Luke Geary's person as well as one of Matt Comfort's. We had both begun as Matt's people. But the part of me that was not drowned in Luke knew, wearily and well, that it was not. I realized many times that fall that we had broken the code, but it was beyond me to care.

Unlike me, Luke did not seem to change at all. Luke was so inalterably Luke that Luke in love was indistinguishable from Luke not in love. In the office he did everything he always had: he lounged on office floors and shot lazy, lewd photographs of female underpants; he baited Sister and bantered with Hank and went to lunch with Matt and let him pick up the check; he grinned ostentatiously at Culver Carnes and photographed Culver's stiff, furious, retreating behind when he steamed out of the office on yet another unsuccessful mission to catch the Caped Cupholder Crusader in the act; he signed Culver's name to several more luncheon checks for Francis Brewton and the lank, wild-eyed young gospel preacher on the corner of Spring and Peachtree Streets; he borrowed endless dimes from petty cash for stamps and coffee and candy bars, and never paid them back.

But at night, and on weekends, he was solely and wholly with me.

How could I have known anything like it existed? Not many people get in a lifetime what I had with Luke in those first few weeks, I don't think. Or perhaps they do, and handle it better. But I don't see how a great many could, and get the world's work done. It was more a tribute to Luke and his insistence on workaday normalcy that I got mine done, than to my own powers of concentration. I was, in those days, purely drunk on sensation.

We made love all over the place and a great deal of the time. In Luke's dim little bedroom on the rolling waterbed; in the big living room before the fire, on the smoky blankets; in his tiny kitchen; once in his bathtub; outside on the frost-silvered grass beside the little pool, under the cold radiance of a great white moon. We made fast, silent love or slow, shouting love, or every shade and experience of love in between. Each time I learned a new and shuddering dimension of sensation, and almost always, we laughed. To make love with Luke Geary was to dive down, to sink, to drown, and to rise again in joy. In those few weeks I had become almost entirely a creature of flesh and abandon. He had only to touch my arm in the office and look at me, and my knees went slack and I had to stiffen my muscles against the need simply to close my door and lie down with him. I had only to say his name, "Luke," and if we were in the apartment, he stopped what he was doing and came to me and we came together. My limbs were always loose and heavy with either wanting or completion in that time, and my eyelids felt perpetually heavy and at half-mast. Sometimes I thought that smoke must come off me like steam off hot water on a cold day.

"I'm going to have to stay away from the office for a while," he said on a very early occasion, when we had come so close to doing it on the elevator going down after work that we were both white faced and shaking when the doors opened and disgorged us into the home-bound crowd in the lobby. "If I don't they're going to start turning the hose on us, and Culver will catch us screwing on the Xerox machine or something, and you'll lose your job and I'll forget how to take pictures. Matt's already pissed enough with us. I'll look in once or twice a week, but there's no sense in making things worse for you. He's being an asshole about it, but it's you who'll take the heat if we get too—what would Culver say? indiscriminate—around the office."

"Is Matt really mad at me?" I said in honest conster-nation. I had not noticed. But then, I had not noticed much of anything at all, except Luke.

"Yeah, he is. I think he'll get over it if I make myself scarce and spend a little time with him one or two nights a week, but for now I'd work twice as hard if I were you, and show him your mind isn't entirely in your crotch . . . or mine."

"He's not being fair."

"Who ever accused Matt of being fair?"

"What does he think, that I lured you away from him? Broke up a set? Doesn't he have anybody to play with after school?"

"I don't think he's thinking, Smokes. He's always had a special man friend to run around with; you know he doesn't make friends of his women. The Playboy chick is for late nights. I was the Huck Finn to his Tom Sawyer, and now I've defected. Since he doesn't like women worth a damn except to screw, it's you he'll blame for breaking up his buddy act. Only he won't think of it like that; he'll think he's being righteously indignant because you're diluting the integrity of the *Downtown* unit, or some sanctimonious shit like that. Give him some time and space. He'll fall back in with Hank and Tom, and everything will ease off."

And so he stayed away from the magazine for the most part, and I missed him as though there was a hole in the universe, but it did seem easier to get my work done, and most of the teasing and grumbling slowed and stopped.

In the new clarity I looked around me and saw with surprise that there had been erosions in the infrastructure that supported us all. So fast; they had happened so fast. Out in the world, in that vast place that had always seemed to me a grassy, naked plain outside the fertile biosphere of Atlanta and *Downtown,* the little tremors had been coming fast and thick, and they felt ominously to me, sensitized as I was now to nuance, like foreshocks for something huge and cataclysmic. I thought of Tom Gordon, and what he had said to Hank and me the night he had come home from his trip with Luke. And yet, the fissures were not of themselves particularly telling. In San Francisco, the disenchanted flower children who had staged the World's First Human Be-In last January held a mass funeral for "Hippie, the devoted son of Mass Media," and began to leave the city in droves. But then, they always were a mercurial subculture, flocking like birds, flowing lemminglike away on a whim.

In Mississippi, a federal jury investigating the murder of three Civil Rights workers acquitted eight codefendants and failed to reach a decision on three others. But that, after all, was Mississippi.

In Washington, after more than a hundred thousand young people marched to protest the war in Vietnam, many placed flowers in the soldiers' gun barrels facing them. Radical elements in the group tried to storm the Pentagon steps and violence broke out. Some thousand demonstrators were arrested. But after all, it was no more than had happened in many besieged Northern cities during the terrible summer of 1967. Only Washington was not North . . .

And Alicia Crowley left *Downtown*. After that, it was not possible to pretend that nothing had changed.

She had not looked well that early fall. I had not noticed until Teddy mentioned it, but after that I did. She was pale, her glorious tawny sheen gone, and her spill of honey hair seemed dry and lusterless, and sometime over the summer she had lost weight, so that the elegant length of leg and arm became stretches of bone. Matt, who had treated her largely as he might a temporary from the secretarial pool since she took up with Buzzy, teased her a little about emulating Twiggy. Alicia laughed her husky laugh, but there no longer seemed to be secrets and promises in it. Poor Alicia, the one for whom she kept her secrets and made her promises had gone coldly away from her and shut his office and apartment door.

When Teddy said she thought Alicia must be sick, Luke said no, she was in mourning for her place as Queen Consort. He was lying on his back in front of the fire watching Teddy and me ladling out vegetable soup she had brought from home, and I looked over at him to see if he was being funny. But he wasn't.

"Well, she abdicated when she took up with that turd Buzzy," Teddy said. She had liked Alicia Crowley even less than I, with perhaps more reason. I still remembered Teddy's embarrassment and pain when she said, on the first night I spent with her in our apartment, "Matt doesn't stay over."

"Not until he dumped her to run off with Luke and John Howard," I said. Why was I defending Alicia? "She'd never have gone near that creep if she hadn't been trying to make Matt jealous. Then he takes up with that ice queen from the Playboy Club, for God's sake, when Alicia is ten times better looking than anything in the bunny hutch. It really wasn't fair to Alicia. She had her whole life tied up in Matt, not to mention that apartment. I wonder he's kept her on there."

"He's not totally without honor," Luke grinned. "He knows he acted like shit to Alicia, even if he'll never admit it. And she's still here because she's a damned good assistant and a big part of what keeps Culver Carnes out of Matt's hair. Haven't you ever noticed that whenever there's a visiting muckety-muck in town Culver baby finds a reason to trot him by Alicia? I think she goes out with them right regularly, too."

"How can she?" Teddy said indignantly. "That's the same as selling yourself for a great apartment."

"What else has she got?" Luke said, and I felt a cold little wind of uneasiness, almost sadness, on the back of my neck. For some reason, my terrible last image of Rachel Vaughn sprang into my mind.

Alicia did not give the customary two weeks' notice, and she did not say good-bye. There was no farewell celebration at the Top of Peachtree, where she glowed the brightest of all of us in the dusky mural. She was simply gone when we came in on a Monday morning in October, her little cubicle next to Matt's antiseptically bare.

"Buzzy wanted her to quit and cruise with him," Matt said crisply when we asked. "It came up right sudden, I gather. He's spending a couple of months in the Caribbean with some of his, ah, business associates, looking to buy into a casino, I think she said. He was right insistent, I hear. Lucky for Alicia she thinks ol' Buzzy is hot shit, otherwise I expect she'd be sleeping with the fishes if she turned him down. Get that look off your face, Smoky; I didn't fire her. She can come back whenever she wants to. I ain't looking for her, though."

The next day Sueanne Hudspeth moved into Alicia's office and a plump, beehived woman with the avid demeanor of a hungry grackle, sent down by Culver Carnes, took Sueanne's desk, and the office was a place no one knew. Mary Kay Crimp, as the new woman was improbably but aptly called, was silent and industrious, but Matt's bellowing and horn-blatting made her flinch and Lucas outraged her so with his invasive camera that a formally written edict banning it came down from Culver Carnes, and we knew then that Mary Kay Crimp was a direct pipeline to him. Somehow she managed to do her work and watch, too. She watched us constantly. Teddy said she could turn her head all the way around on her neck like an owl. Hank maintained the great, lacquered black beehive concealed a periscope. I stayed as far away from her as possible. I knew that it was me and Luke she watched most of all.

It was as if cloud shadow had fallen over *Downtown*. The office was silent and very nearly decorous. Not so many visitors streamed in and out. Mr. Tommy T. Bliss did not come to stand on his head for us much anymore, and after one particularly fragmented and malodorous foray into Mary Kay's territory another edict came down and Francis Brewton did not come, either.

I did not like what we had become, and did not know why we did not simply band together and drive out the cuckoo in the nest as we surely would have done in other days. Matt had never cared about Culver Carnes's memos and ultimatums before. But now he shut himself into his office and did nothing. One move from him, one prank, one merciless session of teasing, one siege of the taxi horn and he could have routed Mary Kay Crimp, or, if he had chosen, simply charmed her into becoming one of Comfort's People. But he did neither, and none of us quite dared to undertake an ouster that he did not lead. What Matt did in those days he did in his office with his door closed, or in brisk, no-nonsense meetings, or on the phone. The rest of us took to shutting our office doors, too. Whenever we looked out, there were the bright, avian eyes of Mary Kay Crimp. Watching.

Later I would say to Luke, "Alicia was the first rupture, wasn't she?"

"No," he said. "You and I were the first."

It was not long before I realized that he was right.

Andre's story won the honors we had thought it would, followed quickly by a wonderfully photographed spread on the Soup Kitchen. The expected commendation from the blue-ribbon senatorial committee and the attendant media flurry over the personal letters of congratulations Luke and I got from the White House clinched matters. *Downtown* was named the best city magazine in the country at the association's autumn banquet. Culver Carnes preened like a tom turkey, letters and phone calls poured in to Matt from the Club, and Matt took Luke and me out to dinner. But it was a perfunctory affair, almost as Luke said later, a duty dance. Matt drank too much and got, for the first time I could remember, frankly drunk, so that we put him, mumbling and lurching, into a taxi and sent him home, feeling like embarrassed servants who had had to put the master to bed after a bad night in the drawing room.

"I feel about that like Mark Twain's story about being tarred and feathered and ridden out of town on a rail," Luke said afterward. "If it hadn't been for the honor of the thing, I'd just as soon have walked."

I laughed, but I had not liked the night, either.

"What more could he want?" I said. "We're number one in the country. Everybody from the president on down to the janitor is praising him. It's more than that stupid Crimp woman; he could get rid of her if he wanted to. What's the matter with him, Luke?"

"He misses the old gang, the way we were," Luke said. "Things changed on him before he could control them and he can't get back the . . . the whole, the unit that we used to be. And he can't seem to go on and make a new one. He misses Alicia."

"Too bad," I said sarcastically. "He's the one who ran her off."

"He'll always do that, to whoever gets closest to him. I've heard about some of the others who did, before," Luke said soberly. "He can't help it. I'd love to know what his early life was like. He's drinking way too much, or at least it's getting to him like it never used to. That worries me more than anything. He goes out a lot at night by himself, when what's-her-name at the Playboy Club has to work, and just drinks till it's time to come home and go to bed. Hank hears about it, and I do, too, a little. They're really worried about him at the Top. Sometimes Hank goes out with him, but Tom doesn't, anymore. Hank says he doesn't talk much, just drinks. Occasionally he'll have a good night and the old vinegar and shine will be back, but not often. Hank asked me to talk to him, but I don't know how to reach Matt anymore. When he does go out with a bunch, it's usually that stupid Playboy crowd. Jesus Christ, can you imagine? Matt Comfort, the big keyholder?"

"I hate this," I said in a small voice. I was near tears.

"It'll probably pass," Luke said. "Tom said he went through something like this early on, when the magazine was just getting started. Pulled away from everybody, drank a lot, kept his door closed. It didn't last very long. Tom says he's always thought Matt ought to be on lithium or something. We ought to just lie low and wait it out. But you need to learn to put down shallow roots, babe, so you can roll on when you need to. You've got too much of yourself invested with Matt. The time will come when you need to move on. It always does. You're not cut out to stay in Atlanta working for a local maga-zine."

I looked at him in surprise.

"Where would I go?"

He smiled. "There ain't no telling where you're going, Smokes."

"But . . . with you, right?"

He reached out and mussed my hair. "We're too good a team to break up," he said.

Luke left in the middle of the next week to go to Chicago for *Life*, to cover what was purported to be the largest antiwar demonstration so far in the heartland. I was anxious and unhappy about it; antiwar demonstra-tions did not seem to be bound by the same tacit rules of peace and nonviolence that marked the few protest gath-erings I had witnessed around Atlanta. Luke was right; Atlanta was virtually untouched so far about the bur-geoning war. I tried hard to be upbeat about his going, though. I had said I would make no demands on him, and I intended not to. But he was so restless and preoc-cupied before he left that I finally said, "For God's sake, go on and have a good time at the demonstration. I know your place is where things are happening. I'm not worried about you. It's not like you were heading for Saigon."

"I may need to do that before it's over, babe," he said.

"Well, so do it," I said, and smiled at him, and he finally smiled back at me. I could not have spoken again for the pounding of my heart.

"Thanks for understanding," he said. "It just seems like the war is getting awfully real all of a sudden. I need to check it out."

"Don't thank me. I knew you for the no-good ambu-lance chaser you are when I took up with you," I said.

"You think the action is in the war now, and not in the movement?"

"It's not that simple. There's action still in the movement. But the heat right now is in the war."

And I knew what he meant, and did not press it further. But I felt still and cold and small, like a bird when the shadow of the hawk is on the earth, the entire time he was in Chicago.

Just after he left a man called George Barber called me from *Look* magazine and asked me if I would like to do a small piece for them on Andre, just a brief, personal update. He had found the Focus piece very moving, he said, and Andre still haunted him.

"You mean a photo-essay?" I said. "Is Lucas Geary shooting it for you?"

"No. An opinion piece. Geary's first rate, but it's your words we want," George Barber said. "We can't pay you much, but we'll give you a nice fat byline."

I was in Matt's office so fast that I stumbled on his rug.

"Sorry," he said. "It's a nice offer, but I just can't afford to let you do outside work right now. Culver's going around telling everybody about his prize girl reporter, and he'd have my ass if your byline turned up in *Look*."

"But . . . " I whispered incredulously. "You've always said it reflected well on us if staff members did national stuff—"

"That was when we needed the ink," he said, looking down at the clutter on his desk and not at me. "We don't need it now. They need us, or they wouldn't be calling you."

He looked mussed, pale, papery-skinned, tired. The chestnut fire on his head was peculiarly ashen, dried. The fingers that fiddled with the pile of coins and the watch trembled. I was almost, for an instant, more alarmed than I was angry, but only almost. Disappointment and rage flared through me like wildfire.

"You're punishing me for something and I don't know what it is!" I cried softly.

"I'm not punishing you," he said irritably. "I can't spare you. We've been shining our behinds with show-off stuff so long that the meat and potatoes of the magazine is backed up. In fact, I'm pulling you off Focus for a while to concentrate on YMOG and a new thing Culver's got going. He's asked specifically for you on it. It's a monthly roundup of chamber of commerce doings in the five-county metro area. It's going to take a lot of time setting up a format. I'm asking Claire Degan at the *AJC* to take over Focus for a few months."

I stared at him, my head buzzing.

"Why are you doing this?"

"I told you—"

"Why are you doing this?"

"All right, goddammit," he shouted. "Since you ask, it seems that you've fucked *Downtown* as well as Lucas Geary, the way you've been carrying on. I've gotten some bad heat from Culver about you. Apparently you two are being less than discreet in some very public places, and it's getting back to the chamber. I don't care who you screw, Smoky, but you can't do it in public and expect nobody to notice . . . "

I could not even speak. I simply stared at him. Then I whispered, "We have never—"

"Somebody saw you doing it in the parking lot at the Lion's Head the other night," he said, and picked up his papers as if to dismiss me.

I remembered it then. We had stopped off after a movie at the little English pub, one of the first of a score that had sprung up in Atlanta like mushrooms after rain, for drinks before the fire. The firelight and the brandy did their magical work; we could not seem to keep our hands off each other. The long, dark room was largely deserted, but still, we had a rather wobbly rule that we would not paw each other too much in public. Sexual revolution or not, it was distasteful to both of us, not what we were about. When it became obvious that we could not stay apart much longer, Luke tossed some crumpled bills onto the table and we left.

The potholed parking lot behind the building was long and unlit, and overhung with trees. At its end, where the Morgan sat, there were no other cars and the blackness was almost total. When he walked around to open the passenger door for me he simply stayed there, leaning against the car, and pulled me against him, and before either of us really knew what we were about, we had slumped into the passenger seat, me on his lap, and the dirty deed, as Sister called it, was done.

"Lord," I said, shaking my head to clear it and pulling my skirt down. "Now that's tacky, in case you ever wondered. Do you think anybody saw us?"

"No," he said, starting the car. "There's nobody around. But I wish there had been. Who'd ever believe that was possible in the front seat of a Morgan?"

But someone must have. I thought of sharp bird's eyes in the dark, like anthracite under a black beehive; mincing stiletto heels on broken gravel, a fussy sweater drawn tight around a plump body against the chilly night. I would never know. I would always wonder, but I would never know.

I said nothing, only looked at him.

"I got the word to tell you to back off that stuff," he said coldly. "I trust you can do it."

"Did you tell Luke to back off, too?" I said furiously.

"Luke isn't the one who looks like a slut."

"I'm not doing a damned thing that you and every

other guy on this magazine doesn't do practically every other night," I cried. "What's the matter with you?"

"That's enough. I've said what I had to say. Get caught humping again and I can't save your ass," he said, and got up and came around the desk. "No, don't say another word. The whole office probably heard you, including motor mouth out there. Close the door when you leave."

I did, slamming it so hard that heads appeared in doorways all the way down the line. At the front desk Mary Kay Crimp smiled creamily and picked up her ringing phone.

"Good afternoon, *Downtown* magazine," she sing-songed. "How may I help you?"

"By eating a shit sandwich," I muttered under my ragged breath as I went into my office. It was the worst thing I could think of to say; I always cringed when Matt said it, but I laughed, too, then. I was not laughing now. Impotent tears were pressing close under my anger.

I told Luke about it when he got back that weekend.

"You ought to quit," he said.

I waited, but he did not say anything more. He was unpacking his camera bags in the darkroom and drinking a beer. He was keyed up and distracted at once. I knew something in the Chicago shoot had affected him powerfully. I would ask him when the strange mood had passed. Meanwhile, I had expected more from him about the scene with Matt than "You ought to quit." But he did not say more.

"I thought you'd be madder at him," I said finally, when he was done in the darkroom and had showered and we were sitting down to a late dinner.

"I'm plenty mad at him. He's a prick. He doesn't care whether we screw at noon in the middle of Five Points. It's what I said, he's getting at you because you're with me. Somebody probably did see us, but that's the kind of thing he'd think was funny. He knows better than to say anything to me about it."

"You're not going to say anything to him, are you?"

"No. It's your fight. You're the one who needs to settle it."

"But he could fire me—"

"He'd be stupider than I think is possible even for him, but yeah, he could. So what? Go work for *Look.*"

"You really think I could work for a national magazine? Be that kind of writer?"

"They're already asking for you, Smokes. I wish you'd told this Barber guy yes and told Matt to stick it. I'd be very surprised if he fired you."

I shook my head. "I just can't take the chance right now—"

"You mean because of me? Of us?"

"No. Well, maybe. . . . I just don't want things to change yet, Luke. I want us to go on—"

"We will go on. But I can't have you letting me hold you back from the kind of work you should be doing. I'd leave, if I thought you were doing that."

"Would you really? Would you really leave me now?"

He sighed. "No. I wouldn't. Whatever else, it's not time to change things. You're right. But you need to know that one day the time will come for you to leave, because it will be time to make your move, and I don't think you can stay with Matt Comfort and do it. Don't worry about leaving me behind; I'm nothing if not mobile. I can go where you go."

We said no more about it. When I slept that night, it was a troubled sleep full of shards of dreams and alarms, and I could not seem to get warm.

Toward the end of the next week Matt called me into his office and motioned to me to shut the door.

"I'm putting you back on Focus," he said.

I said nothing, looking at him, waiting.

A little smile jerked the corners of his mouth. It was the first time I had seen him smile in a very long time. I smiled back, tentatively.

"John Howard won't work with anybody else," he said. "I got a snotty little letter from him this morning that said he would be forced to withdraw from the project if the team was broken up. I had to give Claire Degan her choice of the next three sandwich features. Y'all better make this next one good."

"What is this one?" I said efficiently. I was not going to thank him, or shout with exultation as I wanted to.

"He's got some little black country gal with a world-class voice, wants to do something on how she's been working as a maid for a white lady and trying to be a singer. She was at Selma, used to be one of the Freedom Singers. John's gotten her a tutor and a place at AU to live, and thinks a piece in the magazine could get some tuition money for her. I think he's right. We need to focus on some individuals, and it would be good to get the arts in on it. He says you know the girl."

"Yes, I do," I said pleasantly. Then I shouted, "Yes! Oh, Matt, yes! What a good idea, what a wonderful story, oh yes—"

The small smile widened into the old, wonderful, world-lighting Matt Comfort grin. He threw the shock of hair off his forehead and laughed aloud. It was one of the best sounds I have ever heard. Matt was back.

He grabbed the taxi horn and gave three sharp blats on it. Doors popped open and faces emerged from them, smiling. There was laughter where there had been none for days and days.

Matt grabbed me up and waltzed me out of his office and down the aisle. My head was exactly even with his, and he held my eyes with his as we capered and whirled. I could see why no woman seemed able to resist this mercurial little scrap of a man. The power of his smile and his eyes was enormous.

"'Hey there, toots, put on your dancin' boots, and come dance with me,'" he bellowed. "Top of Peachtree in five minutes flat. Everybody. All of you. Chop chop. Nobody leaves till I say they leave. Mary Kay, dear heart, you will be a precious muffin and stay here and cover our asses, won't you?"

"Mr. Comfort, I can't—" Mary Kay Crimp said, flinching away from Matt and the taxi horn.

"Well, then, tell Culver when you call him that I said to BMA," Matt said, still whirling me around. "He'll know what I mean."

We were still laughing, all of us, when the office door swung shut behind us. Mary Kay Crimp was indeed reaching for the telephone, her face swelled up like a turkey gobbler's. Not one of us cared.

Matt was back.

Thanksgiving weekend was bright and very cold. Neither Luke nor I went home. We would, we told each other, do something about meeting the respective families later, maybe at Christmas. Or maybe not. Everyone else had scattered; Hank to his brother's family, Sueanne and Sister to their own, Tom Gordon to New Orleans to visit friends. Matt was having dinner with "the Playboy family" at the club. It was held, Luke said gravely, for those bunnies who could not, for one reason or another, go home for the holidays.

"Hard to get those tails on Delta in tourist," he said, and we both collapsed in laughter. The idea of Matt Comfort eating turkey and cranberry sauce with "the Playboy family" was almost too ludicrous to contemplate.

We went, late in the afternoon, to have dinner with

Teddy and her family. When we got back, around nine, the moon was so huge and white and magical that we bundled into jackets and scarves and walked. Traffic was light and the wind whispered along the corridors of midtown, and it was like wading in liquid diamonds: cold, pure radiance. I could not remember that the entire winter last year had been this cold, but I did not mind.

We walked a little way into Tight Squeeze. It was practically deserted. The litter of the street people eddied in the wind; homemade cigarette butts, faded banners hawking the Maharishi Yogi and *Sgt. Pepper's Lonely Hearts Club Band,* Peter Max posters for myriad rock concerts; posters proclaiming "Make Love, Not War," "Do Your Own Thing," "If It Moves, Fondle It." But except for a few bundled figures scurrying along the sidewalks, there were no street people.

"I walked here the first day I was in Atlanta, just about one year ago," I told Luke, "and the street was wall-to-wall freaks, and you had to jump over used condoms. Not a freak or a condom in sight tonight, though. 'The times, they are a'changin.'"

"More likely it's the weather," Luke said. He aimed his camera at a torn banner whipping across the deserted, lunar street; "Power to the People," it read. He put the camera away and we walked on.

"Nothing worse than a fair-weather freak," Luke said. "Where did you think you'd be this Thanksgiving, when you were here that first day?"

"I didn't have any idea. Probably still at the Church's Home, trying to sneak in late past the sisters. Still wondering what it was like to lose your virginity."

"You've come a longer way than I think you know," Luke said.

Back in the carriage house we built a fire and made coffee. Luke sprawled on the sofa and I was in the kitchen slicing the half pecan pie Teddy's mother had sent home with us when I heard the doorbell. I stopped, listening. No one ever rang this late unless we were expecting them.

I heard Luke's voice, and another one, frail and child-like, and then Luke called, "Come in here, Smoky," and I went, still holding the pie. Alicia Crowley sat on the sofa, her head down on her chest, looking up at us through strands of honey hair. It was so matted and limp that I almost did not recognize her. Nothing else about her was familiar, either, except the beautiful blue maxi coat she had gotten for Christmas last year. I remembered that we had all speculated that Matt had given it to her, but Alicia never said. The coat was spotted, and one of its military brass buttons was gone. Alicia was shivering so hard that the sofa shook with it. At first I thought it was because she was cold, for she wore no gloves and only shower clogs on her narrow blue-white feet. But the shivering was worse than mere cold; it was profound, seemed to rack her entire body. Her face was dead white, but two hectic circles of red burned on her cheeks. She wore no makeup, and her lips were chafed and bitten raw. She looked ghastly.

Luke dropped a quilt around her shoulders and said, "She came in a taxi. I'm going out and pay him. Get her some brandy or something and see if you can warm her up. I don't think she can talk. Something's bad wrong."

He went quickly out the door and I dropped down on the sofa beside Alicia and put my arm around her. She looked at me with eyes that were glittering and opaque, hot-looking eyes. They filled with tears, and she dropped her head again.

"Tell me what's the matter," I said. "We'll help you, but you have to tell us. Did something happen with Buzzy? Did he hurt you?"

She shook her head and tried to speak, but could not. I filled a glass half full of bourbon and held it to her lips, and she got some down. The rest went down the front of the coat.

"I'm sick," she whispered finally, the words chattering past her teeth. "I'm real sick, and I can't go to a doctor, and I'm scared to death."

Luke came back in and knelt in front of her, and took her hands.

"Tell us," he said. "There isn't anything so bad that we can't fix it. Tell us, babe."

She leaned against the sofa back and closed her eyes.

"I got pregnant," she whispered after a long time. "I thought everybody would have guessed. When I told Buzzy he had a fit. He said it wasn't his, but of course it was, and he knew it. Finally he gave me some money, this huge wad of bills, and told me to be on a street corner in Tight Squeeze at five-thirty a few mornings ago, that it would be taken care of. He said . . . he said not to come back to his place, not to try to get in touch with him. And he said if I told anybody where the . . . the doctor was, or what had happened . . . something would happen to me. It's illegal, you know. Having an abortion is illegal. Can you imagine Buzzy worrying about that?"

She laughed, and it turned into a sob, and I tightened my arm around her and looked at Luke. His eyes were slits, and the skin around his nose and mouth was white.

"So I waited in the dark on the street corner, and this humongous limousine pulled up and the driver said my name, and I got in, and we drove and drove. . . . I think we drove to Tennessee somewhere. I didn't pay any attention to the road signs. I was scared to death. The limousine had shades over all the windows and a panel behind the driver I couldn't see through. He never said another word to me until we were back in Atlanta.

"He dropped me off at this place, it was awful, down in the Negro part of town, although the doctor and nurse were white, and they . . . did the abortion. It hurt like nothing I could have imagined. They didn't give me anything. When I left, the doctor gave me some antibiotics and pain pills and told me that if I had any symptoms, I should get to a doctor here real fast, but that if I told where I had been I would be awfully sorry. And I knew he was telling the truth. Buzzy . . . Buzzy could do that. When we got back here the limousine dropped me off at the TraveLodge Motel over on Spring Street. Buzzy had paid two weeks on a room. I knew I was going to have to do something about getting my job back, or getting another one, and finding somewhere to stay, but somehow I just couldn't go to Matt right then. I looked so bad, and I felt awful, and I didn't know what Buzzy might have told him. And then I got really sick, with fever, and chills, and bleeding, and I knew that I had an infection, but I was just too scared to go to a doctor. I don't know any doctors. I've never been sick . . . "

Her voice faded out as if she were simply too exhausted to go on. She lay against the back of the sofa, eyes shut, and I thought for a moment she had dropped off to sleep. Then she made a great effort and whispered, "Please help me. I think I might be dying."

Luke sprang to his feet and put his arm around her.

"Help me get her into the bedroom," he said. I supported her on the other side, and we raised her to her feet. There was a dark blot of blood on the sofa where she had been sitting. The enormity and reality of it hit me then. I began to tremble, too, a fine, silvery fluttering in my arms and legs. I could scarcely support Alicia's long, knobbly length. And yet, she weighed practically nothing. It was like carrying a bundle of dried twigs.

We got her down on the bed and Luke propped her feet up with pillows and packed blankets around her.

"Give her some more whiskey," he said, "and put a towel under her. I'll be right back."

"Where are you going?"

"To make a phone call."

"Luke, no! You heard what she said, Buzzy will . . . do something to her if she tells people, and if she sees a doctor she'll have to tell; they'll know. Jesus, you can't be going to call Matt!"

"No. I know what to do. Get the whiskey, Smokes."

I got the glass and went back to Alicia, straining to make out what he was saying on the telephone, but I could only hear the sound of his voice, low and urgent, not his words. The whiskey dribbled out of Alicia's mouth and she lay with her head turned into the pillow and her eyes closed. I thought she looked as if she were dead, and kept putting the back of my hand to her mouth to see if I could feel breath on it. I could, light, stringy breathing. I was terribly, terribly afraid. Under the fear anger rode, cold and mature.

Luke came back and sat on the other side of the waterbed and took her wrist in his. He looked at me a couple of times, but mostly he stared at a point beyond me, at the wall. I could not read his face. I started once to ask him who he had called, but he simply shook his head, and I did not ask again.

After what seemed a very long time, there was another ring at the door, and he rose and went into the living room and came back, followed by John Howard. John looked remote and elegant in a blue three-piece suit and a white shirt, and I wondered what Thanksgiving celebration Luke had called him from. He nodded to me, but did not speak. He and Luke lifted Alicia off the bed and walked her, stumbling and muttering, into the living room. Luke picked up her coat, but her knees buckled and she slumped toward the floor. John Howard picked her up in his arms and Luke covered her with a blanket and they started for the door.

"We're taking her to John's doctor friend," Luke said over his shoulder. "He's waiting for us at his clinic. You remember, he came when we called him about your friend that night at the motel. He can help her; he's a good doctor. And he sure isn't going to talk. Be back when we can."

"Wait, I'm coming with you," I said, but he shook his head.

"The fewer white faces the better, babe," he said. "You'd only be a hindrance tonight. Wait here and I'll call you and tell you what we need to do. That'll help more than anything."

And they were gone out the door.

I meant to straighten the apartment, wash some dishes, clean the blood off the sofa, put away the food we had brought home with us, maybe make some soup or something Alicia might be able to eat, but in the end I did nothing. I sat on the sofa and stared into the fire and drank the rest of the whiskey in the glass I had filled for her, and thought of nothing at all that I can remember. I knew that the great wind of anger waiting deep inside me would come out soon, and with it grief and outrage at the sheer, awful wrongness of this thing, but it could not get through the white stillness in me yet. Eventually I fell asleep on the sofa. It was very late, near morning, really, when the phone rang again and I heard Luke's voice.

Alicia had a bad sepsis. The doctor had had to do a D&C, and did not know yet if more surgery would be necessary. He did not think so. He had pumped Alicia full of intravenous antibiotics and fluids, and she would rest there in the clinic until midday, when he could tell whether the antibiotics were working. The doctor and his nurse would stay with her. So would John Howard. They were sending Luke home.

He was so white and exhausted when he got there that I simply drew him into bed and held him. I said only, "You're sure the doctor isn't going to tell?"

"No. He's done a lot of this, cleaned up after bad abortions. You can imagine he'd get a lot of it in the projects. He does some, too; good surgery, careful stuff, for women who need it. He's illegal, so of course he's not going to report it. Not all his patients are black, by a long shot."

"He's a good man," I murmured into Luke's neck.

"He's a goddamned saint," Luke murmured back, and was asleep almost before the words were out of his mouth.

Alicia did well on the antibiotics, and could be discharged a day later provided she had somewhere to go and nursing care for a week. She did not; she had no more days left at the motel, and so Luke and John brought her back to the carriage house and we put her to bed, taking turns sleeping on the sofa and in Luke's filthy old sleeping bag before the fire. She drank the soup and juice we brought her, and took the pills, and let me give her a sponge bath and comb her hair, but she did not talk much. She slept, and slept, and slept.

I went back to work the following Monday morning, and left Luke in charge of her. I did not know quite why, but I was so angry with Matt that I simply could not talk to him. I hid in my office for two days with the doors shut, feigning backed-up work. Hank and Sister and Teddy looked at me in puzzlement, but I don't think Matt noticed. He had come back from the holiday weekend taciturn and remote once more. His door was as firmly closed as mine was.

By the end of the week Alicia was much better. Thin to bone, pale as a cave fish, but with a faint wash of color along her elegant cheekbones, and the sheen restored to her hair. She washed the clothes Luke had bundled hastily into her bags at the motel, after paying her last night's rent, and pressed them, and said that the next weekend she was going to get another motel room until she could find a job.

"I can't impose on you all anymore," she said. "I owe you everything. I'll never forget it. But I can't stay here."

Luke and I together only had enough money, after our own expenses, to pay for a few days' lodging for her.

"What are you going to do for money until you find a job?" Luke said. "Can your family help?"

She merely laughed. It was not a mirthful sound.

"What I'm going to do is go talk to Matt," she said. "He said I could have my job back if I wanted it. If he wasn't just talking, it'll solve a lot of problems."

"You really want to do that?" Luke said.

She lifted her shoulders and let them fall in a slight, eloquent shrug, and smiled faintly. The old, enigmatic Alicia was back; she seemed untouched by the past awful week. But I knew she wasn't, could not be.

"I'd rather do anything else in the world," she said. "But I can't think of anything."

She came into the office that afternoon, looking otherworldly and altogether stunning in her new thinness and the strange luminosity that illness gave her skin. She wore a black miniskirt I had not seen, and black heels. Her legs looked a yard long in fine black mesh stockings. She smiled and nodded at everyone like a duchess reviewing her staff, and went into Matt's office and closed the door.

She came out half an hour later with her head high and two circles of pure red on her face, saying nothing to anyone, sailing out of the office as if borne on water. That night she moved her things from Luke's apartment. We had gone to a movie; when we got back, she was gone.

She left no note. We did not know where she went.

Neither of us would have asked Matt for the earth, and he volunteered nothing. His door was closed almost all the time now.

It was almost a week later that we learned that Matt had called his Playboy PR lady friend and gotten Alicia a job as a bunny at the Atlanta Playboy Club. Hank had seen her there when he took his out-of-town brother for drinks and dinner. Alicia was, he said, the best-looking bunny in the hutch and had more keyholders clamoring for her services than all the others put together. She fended them all off with her cool little smile and said little to them, Hank reported. If she had seen him and his brother in the room she showed no sign. She was not assigned to their table.

"I guess it solves her problem," I said to Luke that night. "But I hate the very thought of it. It's just . . . not right. There's something awfully, awfully wrong about it. I'm not sure what I mean. She didn't have to take it if she hadn't wanted it."

"She had to," Luke said briefly, in the tone of voice that meant he didn't want to talk about it anymore. "Don't kid yourself. What else can the Alicias do?"

"He said she could come back to the magazine—"

"He's full of shit. He wasn't going to take her back after Buzzy. I don't know which of them I'd rather kill first."

I dropped it, but the image of Alicia Crowley in black satin tights and mesh stockings, folding her long legs into the bunny dip and stepping deftly away from the hands reaching for her tail, was a terrible one to me. I could not seem to lose it. I thought of it often, and of the slanted, beautiful eyes above the black satin. In my mind's eye, they were lifeless. I wondered if Matt still went there, and if he did, if Alicia brought him his drinks.

The thought was, somehow, insupportable. But Matt never said.

14

WHENEVER I THINK BACK TO THAT SUSPENDED TIME between Thanksgiving and Christmas of 1967, I think of Matt and *Downtown* as a sort of juggling act. I have the notion that the magazine then was a gilded sphere that contained all of us on the staff and our habitat: the city, the ethos of the times, the people who swirled around us and formed our tribe, our clan. Matt was the juggler. He had, for some reason, stumbled, and the sphere had wobbled and skewed dangerously on the end of its pole, and indeed had spilled out one of us. I knew that Alicia was lost to us. And I knew that in his deepest heart Matt thought that Luke and I were, too.

But I think he could have righted himself and kept the sphere spinning smoothly, after a blackly comic series of contortions and near-falls, except that Tom Gordon told us all, on a morning in early December, that he was leaving the first of the year and going to New Orleans to become art director of a new city magazine there. The sphere smacked the earth then, and though we all dashed to pick up the pieces, and worked feverishly to glue them back together, the entity was never again whole and shining.

We were accustomed, once or twice a month, to going across the street and around the corner to a little nameless, hole-in-the-wall cafe that served the sort of breakfasts Matt delighted in.

"Texas breakfasts," he said more than once. "Not an egg Benedict in the place. Fried in lard and ten miles wide. Quantity is all."

The cafe had a big sign on the dingy mirrored wall where the booths were that said, "You are what you eat," and inevitably Matt would crow "Ah'm an aig," and Tom Gordon would follow with "Ah'm poke sawsidge," and Hank would yell, "Ah'm grits an' redeye." I was appointed to be oatmeal, because Matt had some idea the Irish ate a lot of that, and dismissed my attempts to tell him about porridge with a sneer. Luke was biscuits, mainly because he said once a biscuit that wasn't made with hog lard was not a biscuit at all, but a bleached turd. The nameless cafe's biscuits were most assuredly made with lard. It probably ruined the cholesterol level of a good part of downtown Atlanta before it closed with the decade.

The food charade was funny to no one but us, most especially not the counterman and the waitress, both of whom had been there forever and seen all there was to see of downtown eccentricity. On a scale with Francis Brewton and the street preachers and the old lady who wore a white sheet, togalike, and carried a flashlight which she held aloft like a torch, people who called themselves eggs and pork sausage were small stuff indeed. But somehow the ritual of food-naming never ceased to be hilarious to us. We had just finished the litany, cackling crazily, when Tom told us.

No one spoke. I heard a swift inhalation of breath and realized that I had made it, and a little soft grunt from

Matt that sounded like someone had hit him in the stomach. But no one said anything.

"I feel like a bastard at a family reunion," Tom said finally. "Maybe I should have told you first, Matt, and then everybody else, but I wanted to do it when we were all together. I guess I thought it would be easier. For me, I mean. I don't think I can go through this more than once."

"Ah, shit," Matt said softly, and I saw with incredulity that tears stood in his eyes for an instant. Then he closed them briefly. He looked defeated. Nothing else. Just . . . defeated. Tom had been the first person he had hired for *Downtown*. Far under my shock and grief, fear flickered.

Then he opened his eyes and they were flat and still. I had seen that look before. The round glasses magnified it. It meant that he was angry in the cold, implacable way that was worse by far than the more frequent bellowing rages. After the cold ones, people suffered.

"I gather you're going to tell us why?" he asked politely. "It will help when I tell Culver that his prize-winning art director is jumping ship just when the magazine has won every honor in the fucking country. Probably not much, but it will help."

Tom looked down at his plate, where the remnants of his breakfast cooled greasily. In the merciless fluorescent light his strong hawk's face had a greenish cast, as if it had been done in marble. Even then, with awfulness and sorrow settling down over me like a cast net, I thought yet again how wonderful he looked, and how I would miss simply looking at him. Then he looked up, and the black-brown eyes were liquid with tears. My own tears overflowed and slipped down my cheeks. I would miss his sheer goodness more than anything. We all would.

"Yeah, I'll tell you why," Tom said. "It's not anything you don't all know. But I'll say it if it'll help. I'm going for two reasons. One, I just can't stand any more change. I don't necessarily mean at the magazine, though that's going to come, too; it has to. I mean . . . in the city. In the country. It's out there; it's coming in on us . . . and I don't think I can change with it. Something was left out of me; I've always thought I should have lived in one of those times when everything stayed the same generation after generation, and you could count on the world, even if it was awful. New Orleans is one of the few places I've ever been that feels . . . timeless. The tempo now is essentially the same as it was a hundred years ago. That sweet old decadent Creole world—nothing can crack it, not in the old parts, not in the Quarter. It changes the world, not the other way around. You may eventually drown in it, but it isn't going to blow apart on you. I need that like I need to breathe."

I stared at him intently, trying to understand, to feel the thing that he was obviously feeling. I remembered how he had talked after his trip around the country with Luke, photographing the peripatetic young. He had hated the trip, been badly unsettled by it. The children's crusade was set to run in the February issue. Tom would not be here to see it. I blinked furiously, and swallowed around the cold salt lump in my throat. Still, no one spoke.

He looked down again, took a swallow of his cold coffee, and looked up. His eyes held each of ours, one by one, and then he said, "The other reason is that I'm gay, and I need not to try and live any other way any longer. I'm sick of pretending. I'm past it. I have a friend there . . . a close one. We're going to live together in the Quarter. He's a painter. He knew about the magazine starting up, and got me an appointment with the chamber people down there. They know about *Downtown,* of course, and that helped me. What helped most was they don't seem to give a damn about the gay part. We didn't talk about it, but you could just tell that it didn't matter. It doesn't, down there. I don't have to tell you that Culver would fire me in a New York minute if he found out, no matter how many prizes we won. You know that's true."

He looked away, out through the windows to the gray street beyond. The cold weather had held, and the people hurrying past had their heads ducked against the wind, and coat collars pulled up around their ears. I could not imagine what this talk had cost Tom Gordon. He was the most emotionally fastidious man I have ever known.

"Back to work," Matt said after a while, and we all stood. One by one we hugged Tom, and when we walked out, Matt walked beside him, his arm through Tom's. No one looked at anyone else. I think we all would have wept, if we had.

I did cry that night. Luke and I went to see *Bonnie and Clyde* and I began to cry at the end, when the two outlaw lovers began their grotesque, jerking dance of death in the bullet-riddled car. I got up and went out of the auditorium and into the ladies' room and mopped my face with wet tissues, but it didn't help much. As soon as the tears stopped, they began again. Finally I found my sunglasses in the bottom of my purse and put them on and went back out into the lobby. Luke was leaning against the counter, eating popcorn. When he saw me he came and put his arm around me and led me out onto the icy street.

"Bad scene, wasn't it?" he said as we trotted the freezing two blocks to where the Morgan was parked.

"What? The movie? Yeah, it was. I'm sorry. I can't seem to quit crying. I think it's Tom and not Bonnie and Clyde."

"That's what I meant," he said.

Back at the apartment, in bed, lying in the curve of Luke's arm, I began to cry again. He brushed the hair off my face and said, "It's really the best thing for him, babe."

"I know," I sobbed. "I know it is. I don't know what's the matter with me. I love him; I want what's best for him. It's just that . . . it seems like he's going to die, not leave. It feels like somebody just said they were going to die."

"Well, Tom's finally going to start living. We can go see him; we will. I think what you're feeling is that *Downtown*—or what we know of it—is going to change. And it will. It won't be the same without Tom; he was probably the best of us. But it isn't going to die. There'll be a new art director and Matt'll make him part of the team within a week, and we'll still have *Downtown*. It'll just be a little different. *Downtown* won't die until Matt lets it."

"You think not?"

"I know not. We're all special people, I think, the ones who are part of it, but he's what pulls us together, and the . . . the sum of us won't scatter unless he pulls out of it. Can you see Matt pulling out of *Downtown*?"

I could not. But still, the grief I felt for the perfect, soaring, spinning comet that *Downtown* had been when I came to it a year before was real; it was profound. It followed me through the dark-bright days along the path toward Christmas like a sad and faithful beast.

On the surface, not so much changed. Matt was still distracted and distant, but no more so than he had been before Tom told us he was leaving. He was abrupt and curt and often downright churlish, but I remembered that he was often so, to a lesser degree, around holidays. Matt hated holidays, for reasons that no one ever really ascertained.

"It's because he wants to be God or president," Teddy grinned ruefully when Matt had snarled at Cecelia

Henley, the pretty little new receptionist he had hired to replace the vanquished Mary Kay Crimp, about the gigantic, ceiling-brushing Christmas tree she had dragged in on her lunch hour. "He only hates the official holidays. The ones he organizes himself, like the lake last summer, he adores. Don't take it personally, Cecelia. He almost blew me out of the water one year when I put a wreath on his door, but he didn't take it down."

And he didn't order the tree out of the office. When we had gotten it decorated it looked very pretty indeed, and was much admired throughout the chamber. In fact, the artificial silver and blue tabletop tree that had skulked in the corner of the chamber lobby upstairs for years, Teddy said, disappeared after Culver Carnes saw ours, and a live one, even larger and more elaborately dressed, went up.

And the great Christmas War began. Whenever we added a bauble the chamber added three. Our mistletoe bunch became, upstairs, garlands and masses of it. Cecelia strung up tinsel; the chamber offices looked like the web of a great silver spider. After a weekend in mid-December, the chamber staff came in on Monday morning to find their tree wearing, in addition to its expensive new baubles, the chamber's entire complement of cupholders. Culver was in Matt's office, the door closed, within minutes of the discovery, and we could hear him shouting all the way to the water cooler outside our offices. But in the end nothing came of it. All of us had demonstrably been somewhere else over that weekend; work slowed to a sludgy trickle around Christmas, and no one stayed late or worked on weekends. Matt himself had been in Gatlinburg with the Playboy PR woman, skiing. I have never seen an angrier man than Culver Carnes when finally he left Matt's office. He was so red of face and short of breath that we could hear him breathing as far as the elevator lobby. We waited until the bell dinged before we collapsed in grateful laughter.

We never did find out who did the Christmas tree job, though I sometimes thought that Hank and even Matt himself were the culprits in the other coffeecup capers. Matt stoutly denied culpability.

"If he doubts I was skiing at Gatlinburg he's only got to ask about a hundred people who saw me ski straight down the slope and into the side of the lodge," he said, grinning. It was a real grin, one of the few famous Comfort grins we would see for the rest of the year. Victory over Culver Carnes could always do it.

"Did you really ski into the lodge?" Hank said. "I'd have given a good deal to see that."

"I did. I knew you were supposed to yell something when you couldn't stop on skis, but I couldn't remember what it was. So I yelled, 'Fore!' Didn't help a goddamned bit. I still ran over two assholes in those little French racing suits."

It is an image I still cherish, a vastly rumpled little gnome of a man in borrowed ski wear two sizes two big, chestnut hair spraying out like a wind-torn bird's nest, windmilling down a frozen slope bellowing "Fore!" Over the years it has made me smile in the face of many things.

Luke and I talked about going to his parents' home in Baltimore for the holidays, but in the end we decided not to. His sister and her husband and three children were going to be there, he said, and while he was fond of his sister, he could not abide his brother-in-law, nor stomach what he had made of his small niece and nephews.

"He's a fat little fascist in a three-piece suit and a Rotary button," Luke said. "He's a smug little professional Catholic and a rabid Republican and such a bloodthirsty hawk that his poor little kid told me last time I saw him that he thought we ought to bomb everybody in Vietnam until we sank the island. I think Johnny's teaching them geography, as well as politics. He thinks I'm a communist pothead, and says so, though not to my face. He married my sister because my old man has money, and I think he's pissed as hell because the old man won't die and leave it to her. He thinks I'm out of the running, and he's probably right. But he sucks up to Dad until even the old man gets sick of him. I've learned to stay away from him; it hurts too much to see what Sarah has turned into. She used to have paint under her nails all the time, you know? Now she has perfect nails and her face is just dead. I said we'd come in the spring, maybe. You think we ought to go see your folks?"

"No," I said. "I called my father on his birthday and told him I'd like to bring someone home at Christmas for him and Mother to meet, and he said he wasn't interested in meeting any of my Atlanta paramours. He said paramours, Luke. I'm not going home after that. I was going to ask him to put Mother on the line, but I could hear her start crying in the background, and all of a sudden I just . . . it just made me so tired, and so sad, and so angry. There's no reason for him to talk to me that way. There's no reason for her to cry all the time. I don't want to go home. I don't care if I never do again."

He rubbed my back absently.

"The Irish and their damned, sad, awful anger," he said. "It's always under there, isn't it? Though I guess you could call me a paramour if you wanted to, come to think of it. It has a nice seventeenth-century ring to it. So what do you want to do about Christmas?"

"Have our own tree. Maybe . . . maybe go to midnight Mass at Christ the King. You know, we could even have a little party. Have some eggnog or something, and ask a few people to come by. I know Matt's going to Texas to see his mama, but Teddy will be around, and Hank, and I don't think Tom is going to New Orleans since he'll be moving there right after New Year's."

"There's something else we could do," Luke said. "I've been thinking whether to tell you about it or not. I'm not supposed to tell anybody, but I don't think that includes you."

"What, for goodness' sake?"

"We could go to the Spelman-Morehouse concert. It's the weekend before Christmas. Do you know about it?"

"I've heard of it. With the combined college choirs? Teddy says everybody goes, black and white; it's a real old tradition. She says you never heard such singing. Her family has gone for years. I forgot about it, but I'd love to go. Why shouldn't you mention it to me?"

"John's bringing the Panthers in," he said.

"What?"

"My reaction exactly, when he told me. He's got a . . . what, a cadre of them, I guess, coming in, kind of to show the city that we can all get along together, that they can be a part of the city without disrupting anything, that nobody should be afraid of them, I guess. That they don't shoot honkies on sight. They'll be in full regalia—you know, the leather jackets, and the berets and all. The deal is no guns, though. I guess that would be a little much, sidearms at a Christmas concert in a chapel. John is really high on it."

"But you aren't?"

"I don't know. On the face of it, what's the harm? They'll march in and sit there and sing and all and march out again; nobody's going to make a real fuss in a chapel. I can't think of a safer place for them to show the flag, if that's what they want to do. All that peace and love and reverence built in, black and white together, all that stuff. But still, the public perception of them is just not good. I think it could scare shit out of some people."

"Whose idea was it, anyway?"

"I don't know that, either. John didn't say. It sounds like Juanita baby to me. And I can't figure out what her motives are; surely she ain't looking to recruit the liberal white folks. I guess it's to clinch things with John. Get him in the fold once and for all. Shit, maybe they really do want to hold out an olive branch to the SCLC, to the King camp. That would be the place for it. I wouldn't have said that was on their agenda, but stranger things have happened."

"Does Dr. King know about it? Any of his people?"

"I don't think so. Not from John, and ostensibly not from the Panthers. The surprise is the thing, you see. I'll be surprised myself if somebody doesn't get wind of it, though. Somebody always knows when those cats are going to be in town. I thought I'd go and get some stuff for *Life*; it's going to be a real coup. Can't you see it? The Panthers singing carols? Little white kiddies with their eyes full of leather jackets and Afros? Buckhead matrons in their minks, side by side with dashikis or whatever?"

"You couldn't keep me away with a ten-foot pole," I said. "Maybe Matt would let us do something for *Downtown*."

"Are you kidding? Culver would have his ass before an issue hit the stands. Panthers at Atlanta social and cultural events? In a chamber of commerce magazine? Tell you what, though; I'll see if *Life* wants some words from a journalist who was on the scene. They ought to jump at it."

"Then Culver Carnes would have *my* ass, Luke," I said. He shrugged.

"You're going to have to decide what you want some

day, Smokes," he said. "Maybe this is the time for it. It would be a real feather in your cap."

Oh, not yet, not yet, I cried in my heart, but I did not say it aloud.

"Can I just go with you and decide later?" I said. "I'd love to hear the concert, no matter what we end up doing about it."

"Yeah," he said. "But don't say anything about it to anybody. John was adamant about that. Any media at all and Boy Slattery will run them out of town before they've set a foot in Sisters' Chapel. Or try to."

"Why Boy Slattery? You know Governor Wylie wouldn't, and Boy would have to go through him."

"Haven't you heard?" Luke said. "I guess you haven't. You were at that meeting with the theater people when Matt told us. Ben Cameron told him at the Commerce Club at lunch. Lint Wylie is at Johns Hopkins having treatment for some kind of lymphoma. It was sudden; he collapsed in his office late yesterday afternoon. They aren't releasing it to the media until probably in the morning, depending on what the word is out of Baltimore, but it means that Boy is acting governor for the time being. With all attendant powers, like calling in the state police or the national guard, or whatever crosses his tiny little mind. He'd just mortally love to mix it up with Panthers."

"Oh, God, Luke. Do you think John ought to cancel it?"

"No. I think that would look like he's scared of Boy, and he's not. But I think the longer he can keep it quiet the better. I personally don't think he can, but maybe he can keep it from getting to those assholes around Boy. It'll help that it's Christmas and all. It would likely get to Ben Cameron first, and he's not going to tell Boy."

"Oh, Lord, how awful," I said, meaning it. "Boy Slattery sitting in the governor's seat. How bad is it with Governor Wylie? What happens if he . . . if he dies?"

"I don't know how bad it is," he said. "I don't think some lymphomas are as bad as some other kinds of cancer, but it's never good. If he dies, we're stuck with Boy until there can be a special election, I guess. At least until the end of January, when the legislature convenes. I don't really know how Georgia does it. I think the best thing to do is pray for the worst winter in a hundred years."

It looked as if it might be. The bitter cold did not abate. Worse, the winter rains that usually set in in January and February came early, and ice storm after ice storm swept in from the west, sent, the newspapers said waggishly, by Birmingham, just to trim Atlanta's sails a bit. The media was having a field day with the inclement weather; huge black headlines that read BRRRRRRR or ICE NOT NICE dominated the front pages of both the morning and afternoon papers, and television weathermen kept their sleeves rolled up and their ties askew for weeks at a time.

Atlanta usually gets one or two fairly substantial snows a year, and they are the stuff of municipal rejoicing, but the more frequent ice storms are not nearly so welcome as the fickle, pretty snows. Power lines go down, plunging whole sections of the city into cold and darkness; road conditions are hideous and made worse by Atlanta motorists' homicidal determination to drive on them no matter what; fractures and sprains proliferate; the incidence of house fires caused by faulty space heaters and malfunctioning fireplaces soars, especially in the miserable ghettos and public housing projects. That year Ben Cameron kept the city's fire department on alert, and petitioned his peers in other cities for extra sand and power trucks. The phone company all but gave up.

In Ansley Park, where Luke's carriage house was, the combination of huge old hardwood trees and aging power lines meant that we were without power more often than not. At first I did not mind; weather has always been the stuff of festivity and exhilaration in the Deep South, and I had never seen an ice storm before. The big living room fireplace roared day and night, kept blazing from the dwindling woodpile behind the widow's garage. She herself went to her daughter's new house in Dunwoody, where the power lines were prudently buried. Luke had a campstove, too, and kerosene lanterns and fuel. We found an elderly kerosene heater in the garage and he cleaned it up and lugged it in, and between fireplace and heater and the kitchen's gas stove, we were fairly warm, and could have hot meals.

We were luckier than most and I knew it, but when day after cold, dark day went by, I began to yearn for light and music and a deliriously long, hot bath. I longed to zip down Peachtree Road to work in the Morgan again, instead of the wallowing, sliding, perpetually late 23 Oglethorpe bus that I had to trudge two long, frozen blocks to catch. I got to know and fear that peculiar, raw wet smell in a night sky that means ice is on the way, and the flashing "We interrupt this broadcast to bring you an emergency weather bulletin" signs on the newly restored television set sent me nearly frantic. On several days the office was closed because no one could get in, and Luke shut himself into the darkroom and developed film for hours, catching up on the ever-present backlog. I read by lamp and candlelight until my eyes ached, and slept a great deal in his old sleeping bag, in front of the fire. I never thought I would tire of the hollow hiss and snicker of an open fire, or the sweet smell of burning fatwood, but I did.

On the last week before Christmas the weather loosened its grip somewhat, and the swollen gray-white clouds thinned to reveal segments of tender, milky blue, and a penitent sun came sidling out. The staff met in the

Downtown office like survivors of an arctic whiteout. Tales of hardships endured mounted in sheer awfulness until we had to laugh at them, and the renewed excitement of the looming holidays made us manic. We were out of the office more than in it, scurrying out to buy Christmas presents, nipping back to answer our mail and return phone messages, going for long lunches, phoning old friends, making dates with new ones. Little Cecelia Henley had an unexpected talent for gift-wrapping, and we shamelessly browbeat her into wrapping our packages. Soon the office was strewn with mounds of beautiful, glittering gifts, and Sister and Sueanne came in each day with another batch of divinity or Christmas cookies made from old family recipes.

"Sister, have these things got liquor in them?" Hank said, biting into a cookie from a new batch.

"Old family recipe," Sister said. "I knew you put bourbon in 'em, but I couldn't remember how much, so I just dumped the rest of the bottle in. Do you like 'em?"

"Oh, yeah," Hank said, rolling his eyes. The cookies were gone by midmorning.

It was, I remember, a lovely, manic, foolish, shiftless time, that week of my second Christmas at *Downtown.* Very little work got done.

Matt did not come into the office for four days.

"He's doing some work at home," Hank said on the second day, when we noticed Matt's absence and began asking.

"Sueanne talked to him yesterday and he said to hold his calls and take messages, that with Christmas and the weather, it was a good time to get some planning ahead done, and catch up on his column. He'll see us before the holidays."

But he sounded doubtful somehow, and I said, "Hank?"

"That's all I know, Smokes," he said. "God knows we need the column. I'll call him tomorrow if I haven't heard from him."

No one heard, and late that next afternoon Hank called Matt at his apartment.

"Has a bad cold," he said briefly. "He does sound bad. Says he'll be fine by Friday, though, and to tell everybody he'll take us for lunch at the Top and then let us go home early."

"And you think he's really okay? I mean, just a cold?" I said. I was brushed with unease. Matt was never sick. He never went out of the office unless it was on unavoidable business, and then with bad grace. "Goddamned froufrou," he called the speeches and fund-raising sorties that were often required of him. I could not imagine him languishing in bed with Vicks salve on his chest and chicken soup on his bedside table.

"That's what the man says," Hank said, and went back into his office and closed the door.

"You think it's more than a bad cold?" I said that night to Luke.

"I think it's more likely a bad hangover," he said.

"Oh, Luke!"

"He's been drinking way too much, babe. And I know he does it sometimes at home by himself. I've been over there in the mornings and seen his empties. I've never known him to miss work, though."

"Is it Alicia, do you think, and Tom? What?"

He shrugged. "Don't know. He's got a darkness in him. Tom and Hank have told me about some times before, when he just sort of . . . went away. I don't think he ever actually went out of the office though. If he's not back tomorrow I'm going over there."

But he was. On the Friday before Christmas Matt was in his office when we all came in, drinking coffee and spitting orders into his dictating machine, rattling his change and watch, bellowing obscene verses to the cloying Christmas carols that seeped from the Muzak. He seemed to me thinner than ever, and there were purse-like bags under his eyes, and an unhealthy flush on his sharp cheekbones. But he was freshly shaved and smelled of some piney new aftershave, and the chestnut hair was combed wetly in place, and the miserably wrinkled blue oxford cloth shirt still had a price sticker on the collar. The office bloomed again, like the Christmas rose the treacly tenor on the Muzak was singing about. Matt finally threw a cupholder at the speaker just outside his office. It was, I noticed, a yellow one, one of the chamber's. Sueanne dodged it and grinned and got up and turned the Muzak down.

We did indeed have lunch at the Top of Peachtree, the whole staff, boycotting the chamber's Christmas party upstairs. When Sueanne questioned the wisdom of that, Matt said, "Which had you rather do, get drunk on champagne at the Top with the most fascinating people in town, or stand around up there drinking Kool-Aid and lime sherbet punch and eating those goddamned mouse turds the secretaries bring in, watching Culver in a Santy Claus hat handing out fruit baskets?"

"Sorry I asked," Sueanne said, grinning.

"Will we get any flak from Mr. Carnes?" I asked Matt.

"You won't," he said. "Only me, and I don't give a happy rat's ass. Anyway, I can guarantee that he'll have forgotten it when we come back from Christmas."

"How do you know?"

"I know."

And so we went to the Top of Peachtree, and drank a great deal of champagne, and ate until our sides ached, and laughed, and wished each other Merry Christmas, and kissed each other fondly, and at last started out into the elevator lobby, laden with the gifts we had chosen for each other, full of champagne and joy.

Matt stayed behind at the table.

"I'm meeting somebody," he said. "Guy couldn't make it any other time. Y'all go on. Merry Christmas. Bah, humbug."

When we went out of the room I looked back over my shoulder. Matt was lifting one finger for the waiter.

Luke caught my look.

"Don't ask," he said, and I did not. But some of the joy seeped out of the day. Downstairs, on the street, the sky was overcast, and the raw, wet smell was back in the air. The clouds had come in fast.

"Oh, no," I said. "Ice. And the concert's tonight."

Sleet had begun to fall when we got to the Atlanta University campus, but it was not sticking to the pavement. It rimed the campus grass and shrubbery, though, looking pretty and festive with the lights from Sisters' Chapel spilling out onto it. The weather had not thinned the crowd. Cars were everywhere, and when we reached the chapel, jogging to escape the needlelike sting of the sleet, it was clotted with people, streaming in from the cold or settling into their seats like brightly feathered birds. The beautiful chapel blazed with candles and smelled gloriously of the pine and cedar boughs that decorated the altar and choir loft and the edges of the pews. I noticed too, the smell of dusty hymnals and worn plush carpet that seemed indigenous to all the churches of my childhood, and the somehow exotic smell of wet wool and perfume. Only the bass note of the incense was missing. It seemed strange.

It was a quiet crowd, hushed, as was proper for a church at this holiest of seasons, but a pleasant one, friendly. There were more black faces than white, but not so many. Whole sections of the auditorium were given over to white families. Most blacks and whites were dressed for church, in sober suits and bright holiday silks, but there were sprinklings of African dress, too: dashikis, djellabas, beads, batiks. And there was more of the plumage of the hip young than you would have expected to find in a church: miniskirts, smock dresses, turtlenecks, here and there a Nehru jacket. Here and there, also, you saw bell-bottom jeans and ragged vests, and furs—mink, persian lamb, raccoon, orange-dyed rabbit—were everywhere. It was a truly eclectic crowd, just the sort, I thought, that you would get on a college campus in any large city. I felt ecumenical and integrated and very pleased with myself and the night. But I noticed that the wedges of black and white faces, though they nodded and smiled pleasantly to each other, were not intermingled.

We were a little late, and the auditorium was largely filled. Down at the very front, a small section of seats was vacant, as you would see at a wedding, waiting to be occupied by the bride's and groom's families. On the row behind it there were only a few people. John Howard was one of them. Luke moved down the aisle toward him, and I followed, and when we reached his row I saw that the empty block in front of him was corded off with red velvet ropes.

I slid in beside Luke. On his other side, John nodded remotely to us, but did not speak. He wore the blue three-piece suit I had seen at Thanksgiving, and except for his nod to us, he looked steadily ahead at the empty choir loft. I thought that he could easily model for *Esquire* or *Gentlemen's Quarterly,* the way he looked this evening, except there was something coiled and forbidding in the sharp-planed face, something unsettling and near dangerous. And the scar. . . . No. John Howard would not sell many suits.

"How'd you manage that?" Luke whispered to him, gesturing at the roped-off seats.

"Said I had some out-of-town VIPs," John said briefly.

"Christ, I bet they're looking for the editorial board of the *New York Times*," Luke whispered back, grinning, and John Howard gave him a reluctant grin in return.

"Surprise, surprise," he said.

"You saving this row, too?" Luke said.

"Just for some of the sisters, if they decide to come," John Howard said. "There won't be many of them, if any. They don't march. A few are here, but I'm not looking for them. Don't be surprised if they don't embrace you with open arms, though, if any of them do show."

I wondered if Juanita was in Atlanta. I thought she probably was.

"I have a feeling not much is going to surprise me tonight," Luke said.

"Probably not," John Howard said. He looked at Luke's coat, draped over the back of the seat.

"You got a camera?"

"Yeah, but it's just a little one," Luke said. "Don't worry. I'll look just like all the folks who've come to take pictures of their chirrun singing."

"Yeah, right," John Howard said. He smiled again, briefly, and turned his eyes back to the choir loft. He did not look at us again. He might, I thought, have been a bronze statue; his skin shone in the flickering candlelight, and he was very still.

I stood up once, to shed my coat, and Luke reached up and helped me out of it, and laid it over his. Before I sat back down, I looked around at the crowd behind me. In the sea of faces I saw, as if my eyes had been drawn to them by a magnet, Brad Hunt and his family, sitting about halfway down on the aisle. Beside Brad was a blonde girl with long, smooth hair drawn back into a blue satin bow. She was indistinguishable from many of the girls I had met in Atlanta who were Teddy's schoolmates at Westminster, and I knew that I had not met her, but knew her anyway. She would be an executive secretary in a bank, live at home, do volunteer work for the Junior League, be good at tennis. She looked at me and dropped her eyes. So did Brad, a long, unreadable look, before he dropped his own.

On his other side, Marylou Hunt, stark and shining in black, did not drop hers. Triumph fairly radiated from them, and she smiled, a small, V-shaped smile such as you see on archaic Greek and Roman statues. It must be a real occasion of triumph for her; vindication. Here I sat, her avowed enemy, in the company of a dangerous-looking black man and a wild-bearded hippie. I smiled back and sat down. My heart was pounding with simple shock. I did not care if Brad and his family attended the Spelman-Morehouse concert, but I had not expected to see them. It stood to reason, though, I thought, smoothing my sleet-mussed mop of curls off my face, that sooner or later, in this intimate city, I would run into Brad Hunt. I hoped, I think genuinely, that the girl beside him was a serious friendship. I still felt vaguely guilty about Brad, though it made little sense.

The choir was late coming in, and the crowd rustled and whispered restlessly. Coughs peppered the silence. The house lights flickered once, then, and the crowd settled back in their pews like a flock of birds coming to earth. There were many smiles in anticipation of the choir's marching in.

And then there was the sound of the closed auditorium doors opening, and a great wind of sound started up in the back of the church and swept down toward the front: whispering, in-drawn breaths, more movement. And the Black Panthers came in.

They came two by two, in military formation, grouped according to height, in perfect silence. They wore black leather jackets and turtlenecks and black pants and black boots, and the familiar, yet exotic, berets crowned sculptured Afros. Most wore wire-rimmed sunglasses and they all wore bandoliers, and though there were no guns in sight—Luke had said there would be none carried—the sense of them was as cold and steel-heavy as the reality of them would have been. They made no sound and looked neither to the right nor left, and they seemed to swallow sound as they came down the center aisle, so that, behind them, they left a trail of perfect silence. I thought that they looked somehow beautiful and terrifying at the same time, in the flickering candlelight and the trailing silence. They broke ranks to file into the two rows ahead of us, still in perfect formation, and remained standing until all of them were in place. Then, at a nod from the tallest, they all sat. They did not look around at John Howard, nor at the crowd, nor anywhere at all except toward the empty choir loft.

There were no women with them or behind them.

"Holy shit," Luke breathed, and lifted the little Leica to his eyes and began to shoot.

I did not reply. It was difficult for me to get my breath. Behind us, the church was as silent as if the audience had drawn in a single great breath and not released it.

The conductor came in then. He stared for a long time at the two rows of blacks in front of the church, then at John Howard, and then nodded at the piano player and organist, seated at twin instruments below him.

The great, golden strains of "Come, All Ye Faithful" crashed out, and the choir came marching in from the wings on either side of the risers set up for them, singing as they came: "Oh come, all ye faithful, joyful and triumphant, oh come ye, oh come ye, to Bethlehem . . ."

The voices filled the auditorium and soared toward the icy skies outside, and my skin crawled, and tears came into my eyes. They were transcendent, the perfectly joined voices of these young black students in their festival robes, with a dusky richness, a resonance, a deep loneliness lacking in even the most cultivated white voices. Another collective breath was drawn in the chapel, and then I knew that it was going to be all right. The young voices owned the night; they had a power beyond any that might be generated from the crowd below them, even the double row of darkness at the front. In their seats, the Panthers did not move. They kept their eyes on the singers. I wondered what they felt. I did not think that they could possibly be unmoved.

It was not a long concert. There was no intermission. We sat silent as they sang traditional hymns, spirituals, folk songs, African anthems, solos. I was entranced; I did not even notice as Luke shot and reloaded, shot and reloaded. There was the soft lightning of many flash-bulbs behind me in the audience. The young singers had friends and family in abundance. I recognized the music critic from the *Atlanta Constitution* sitting across the center aisle from us, scribbling busily. Beside him, a press photographer shot unobtrusively, too. I was sure that the Panthers were getting by far the most film, but they gave no sign that they noticed. They were perfectly still, perfectly quiet, perfectly attentive. It was almost possible to forget they were there. Almost.

The next to the last song listed in the program was simply "Solo," and a spotlight followed a small, sturdy figure in a simple black evening dress out onto the stage. With a shock of joy I saw that it was Luella Hatfield. She stood alone in the spotlight, hands clasped loosely in front of her, head bowed. And then she lifted her head and sang, without accompaniment: "Go tell it on the mountain, over the fields and everywhere. . . . Go tell it on the mountain . . . that Jesus Christ is born. . . ."

The crowd gasped and broke into spontaneous applause. It went on and on. Her voice was as I had remembered it: a pure and stunning element of nature. She stood quietly smiling until the applause stopped and then went on. The piano and organ swelled behind her. When she finished, the audience was on its feet, clapping, whistling, shouting. It was a most unchurchlike reaction, and the only one possible for the voice of Luella Hatfield. In front of us the Panthers stood and clapped too, as hard as anyone. Flashbulbs bloomed.

"Oh, John," I whispered, tears trembling on my lower lashes. He did not turn to look at me, but I saw the corners of his mouth lift in a little smile.

After that the chorus led the audience in "Silent Night," and then, without a pause, segued into "We Shall Overcome." I don't know why it took me so by surprise. I imagine all concerts in black churches and halls ended with it in those days. I stood holding Luke's hand, his other hand linked in John Howard's, and swayed with the crowd, and felt my heart rise out of my body and my tears spill over as we sang: "Deep in my heart . . . I do believe . . . that we shall overcome some day."

What if I had never come up here from Savannah? I thought. What if I had never had a chance to do this? I will never forget this moment as long as I live.

In front of me the Panthers stood at respectful attention, but they did not clasp hands, and they did not sing.

Over it all the joyous voice of Luella Hatfield rode like a great golden flute.

When the last note had faded, lying like smoke in the still air, no one moved in their seat. It was as if no one wanted to break the tender, perfect skin of the night. Everyone sat silently for another moment, and then the

Panthers rose in a unit and filed out of their rows and back up the aisle, two by two, tall and black and royal in their silence. Not one of them, I thought, had made a sound the entire evening, except to clap.

Only then did the crowd rise from their seats and reach for their coats and begin to laugh and chat with their neighbors. It was as if a cadre of great black birds of prey had hovered over a woodland for a time, done no harm, and moved on. Only then did life come back into the forest. By the time I had risen and turned to face the departing audience, the Panthers were nowhere in sight, gone out the great double doors onto the porch.

"Well, it went off pretty smoothly, didn't it?" I said to John Howard. "Where will they go now?"

"Back to their bus," he said. "They'll be riding all night. They've got to be in Montgomery in the morning."

"What for?"

"Going to do a Bar Mitzvah over there," he said, and I stared at him before I realized he was teasing me. He smiled a little, but he did not take his eyes off the door and the crowd moving toward it.

"Do you think you got anything?" I said to Luke, as he helped me into my coat.

"Not a lot. Maybe some good stuff of faces—" he began. The first sound broke in then.

It was a confused babel of sound, like a crowd scene in an old movie, spotty and inconsequential, but definitely not the sound of an ordinary crowd leaving a concert. Then shouts rang out, and the thumping and rustling of many feet, and a shrill female scream, and then others. I turned to ice; I could not move.

The double doors burst open and the crowd, that had been streaming out into the night, stampeded back into the church. Men shouted hoarsely; women screamed; here and there the silvery shriek of a small child tore over the other sounds. The crowd eddied and swarmed like a living thing, surging back down the aisles toward us, away from the outside. I could see lights out there, brighter than anything I could imagine, seeming to bounce off the spinning wisps of fog and ice that fell steadily into the light, and a deep, monotonous chugging, like the beating of a great inhuman heart. Ringing, metallic shouts rose over the noise of the crowd. It was only long seconds later that I realized someone was using a bullhorn.

Luke leaped onto the pew and strained to see over the milling crowd.

"That motherfucking Boy has called out the troopers," he said in a strangely calm voice. "They've got a goddamned riot going on out there. Holy Mother of God, somebody should shoot him."

He leaped down off the seat and took off up the aisle without looking back. I started after him, screaming "Luke, Luke, don't! Wait, don't go out there . . . "

He could not have heard me. Without a backward look he was swallowed up into the crowd trying to press back into the safety of the auditorium. I stood numbly, hands pressed to my mouth, staring at the place he had vanished. As if in slow motion, as if in the clarity of a dream, or a drugged state, I thought, this is only the first time. All my life, if I spend it with him, I will stand in a crowd watching him rush away into danger, without ever looking back at me. . . .

Beside me John Howard stood stone still, and I turned to him.

"John, go get him," I said in a silly small voice. "You can get through. I'm afraid something's going to happen to him. . . ."

He did not look at me. He did not move. He stood staring toward the door. His face was as gray as dead ashes. His mouth was open. His eyes looked as if he had been blinded.

We heard the shots then, first one and then a stuttering stitchery of them, and more screams, and, far away, the first shrill keening of an incoming siren. John Howard's body jerked as if he had been hit by the bullets, and he gave a great, guttural wordless cry and started forward, clumsily, as if he could not make his arms and legs work properly.

I grabbed him around the waist; I all but tackled him and dragged him to the floor. I held on with all my strength, my face buried in his back, screaming, screaming.

"Don't you dare!" I screamed. "Don't you dare go out there! Damn you, John Howard, don't you dare go out there and get yourself killed; I can't stand it! I won't let you! What the hell is the matter with you. . . ."

Even as I screamed, even as I held him with all my strength, feeling the muscles in his back and legs straining away from me, feeling the wool of his suit coat scrubbing into my face, I thought, I can't stop Luke now, but I will die before I let John go. I will die before I do. And I held on, and I held on, and I sobbed.

Abruptly the tension went out of his body and he slumped down onto the seat. I fell backward onto it, too, and sat gasping for breath and staring wildly at him, shuddering with my terror. He sat quietly for a moment, his hands pressed together in front of him as if in prayer, and then he began to cry. It was a terrible crying; a grotesque, choking weeping; an anguished sobbing wrung from a man whom you knew had not wept for a very long time, and never in public. He sat with his hands raised in front of him like a child, his mouth squared away from his teeth in a rictus of grief, his eyes blind with tears. They left opaque silver tracks on his bronze face. He made an awful sound, a keening, but it was very low.

"I never meant this," he gasped. "Before Christ, I never meant this. . . ."

I slid over on the seat and put my arms around him and drew his head down on my shoulder, and he slumped against me, and we sat like that for a long time, both of us weeping, he by far the hardest, his sobs racking me as if he had taken my shoulders in his hands and shaken me. I could feel every ragged breath he drew; feel his face hot and wet in my neck; feel the muscles of his body contorted against my hands. We sat like that for a long time. I do not remember how long.

In the pew behind us, a white woman in a fur coat, her hair mussed and her dress over her thighs, massaged her crushed instep and said over and over, "This is ridiculous. We only came because our chauffeur's boy was singing. This is absolutely ridiculous."

It was not much of a riot, really, as riots go. The icy rain defused it. The Panthers melted away like ground mist and were, as Luke said, halfway to Montgomery before Boy Slattery's hastily summoned state troopers got their bearings. There was no threat at all in the concert crowd. There had never been; the Panthers had been nothing if not orderly. But the ring of troopers and the television lights and cameras, and the chugging generators, and the spinning lights, and the city police screaming in soon after, and the screaming spectators and the students running from the dormitories to see what was going on, all gave it the immediacy and menace of yet another of the awful scenes we had all seen during the summer before, burning on television screens from half a dozen cities. It was the students, confused and furious, who had thrown the first rocks at the troopers, and it had been the cold and panicked young troopers, first one and then another, who had shot into the crowd.

No one was killed. Only a few were injured. One Buckhead attorney had a bullet in his shoulder; he had been treated at Piedmont and released. A small black boy, brother of one of the singers, had been shot in the foot, and was in Grady Memorial Hospital, resting after surgery. There were some sprains and fractures. Two or three troopers had stone and brick injuries, and many of the crowd were treated for minor cuts and abrasions suffered in the backwash of the panicked retreat into the chapel. An elderly woman had a heart attack and died in the projects after she got home from the concert, but no one could positively link the attack with the riot. She was very old. Her great-grandson had been singing.

For Atlanta, however, the City Too Busy to Hate, it was a stinging, shameful blow. It was a fiasco of a riot, a joke, a laughing matter: the fat, racist lieutenant governor of Georgia had gotten wind that the Panthers were attending a concert of Christmas carols—Christmas carols, for God's sake—and called in the state troopers and the media, the troopers managed to shoot a rich lawyer and a little black boy, and then the lieutenant governor holed up in his office under heavy personal guard. Ben Cameron was grim and furious in the newspapers and on television news the next day, denouncing Boy Slattery and calling for calm heads to prevail. Don't go down to Atlanta University looking for trouble, Ben said. There is no trouble there in that fine institution. The trouble sits barricaded in the governor's office, laughing with his racist cronies and counting his votes in the next gubernatorial election. Don't compound his dirty work, Ben said. Let this sorry thing die.

And it did. The Panthers were long gone to Montgomery or wherever. They had no comment; never did. The university was quiet under a blanket of debris and ice. The ice rained down all the next day, and Atlanta's sad, silly Christmas Carol riot was history. Luke barely got enough good shots for a spread in *Life*.

John Howard left Atlanta the day after that.

Luke had gone by to see how he was doing, and found him packing his Mustang. He was silent and stricken and would not tell Luke, at first, where he was going. But he did, finally. Luke told me that night, tears in his eyes for the first time I had ever known him, that John was going to try and make some sort of peace with his wife in Detroit, and to see his child. It had been a long time since he had tried. His wife had never let him before, but now he wanted to try again.

"He needs a family," he had told Luke. "Everybody needs that. I should have done this long before."

"Did Dr. King make him leave?" I said.

"No. He says not. He says Dr. King wanted him to come on back to the SCLC office and get on with things. He doesn't blame John. I think a lot of the other guys do, though."

"Do you think he'll ever come back?"

I was beginning to cry now. I could not bear the thought of John Howard driving, in his sorrow and pain, out of town alone in the flashy Mustang.

"I really don't know, babe. Want to go see him off?"

"Yes. Yes I do, Luke."

And so the next morning, before full daylight, Luke and I stood beside the icy curb on the Atlanta University campus as John Howard slammed the trunk of the Mustang on the last of his bags and few belongings. Ice glazed, crazily, an old electric fan; roped piles of books were covered with it. He turned to us.

"I'll be in touch," he said to Luke, and hesitated, and then hugged him, hard. Luke hugged him back, and hit him lightly on the bicep with his fist.

"Smoky," John Howard said, and looked down at me. I said nothing, only looked up at him, trying not to cry.

"You always go the distance, don't you, Smokes?" John Howard said softly, and smiled, and touched me on the cheek.

And then he got in the Mustang and drove away, traveling, as he always had, alone.

15

On the second Sunday of January, Luke and I went over to Teddy's apartment to watch the pro playoff game with her and Hank. It was still nominally my apartment too, I suppose; my name was still on the lease, and what little mail I got came there. But I had paid no rent since I had moved in with Luke in the weeks after we had begun our relationship. Teddy would not allow it. She had a trust fund from her grandmother that made rent a small matter, she said. Better I pooled my share with Luke. And it did make a difference to us. Movies and an occasional dinner at an Italian restaurant and even one or two budget weekends in the Georgia mountains were not out of range now.

I never thought about it being a duplicitous arrangement. Many young Atlanta women were, I knew, keeping nominal apartments in one place and living with their young men in others. I wonder how many mothers were fooled. It was, if not the first wave of the new permissiveness, the last gasp of the old nonpermissiveness. The pill was a great enabler in more ways than one.

It was good to get out of the dark apartment in Ansley Park for an evening, good to sprawl on the familiar old furniture laughing and jibing with friends, good to mooch about the tiny kitchen, laughing helplessly as Teddy's and my attempt at a cheese soufflé fell flatter than an old inner tube. Luke and I had not been out to speak of, except for work, for a long time. The Spelman-Morehouse concert had been the last significant event we had attended. Even Christmas we spent by ourselves, eating the smoked turkey Matt had given us, along with everyone else on the staff, and drinking Rhine wine from the widow. New Year's Eve we spent at Johnny Escoe's restaurant on Peachtree Road in the company of raucous, half-drunk strangers, a belated decision made when Luke said, about four o'clock on the dark afternoon of New Year's Eve, that we ought at least try to kick-start the New Year out of the Slough of Despond. It was a bad mistake. We liked Escoe's, but we both hated it that evening.

"Never again," Luke said, when we got home and collapsed gratefully on the floor in front of the fire. "I will never again spend New Year's Eve anywhere but at home. The Slough of Despond is better any day."

"It hasn't been so bad," I said, curling up with my head in his lap. "It's been good to just be home with you. That won't happen again until the next Christmas holidays. And you just can't imagine how much better this New Year's Eve is than the last one."

Even thinking of the cold, bitter holidays at my parents' house in Corkie the year before was oppressive. I had thought then I would never really go back; now I was not only sure of it, but I knew where, if I were permitted to follow my delirious star, I would go from here. I would go where Luke went. Or rather, stay where he stayed. I realized, as 1967 slid into 1968 and we toasted each other with white wine, that despite the darkness than hung over my familiar landscape now, where I wanted us to stay was Atlanta and *Downtown*.

Somehow I was reluctant to ask Luke if that was what he wanted, too. He had not said differently, but the reluctance was peculiarly strong. It was not, I realized, anything I was ready to probe. So far, this new year was for waiting.

Teddy had said Hank would be joining us, but when we got to Colonial Homes I realized that it was more than a casual presence. He was in the kitchen mixing Bloody Marys when we got there, and when he came out to greet us he kissed me on the cheek and Teddy, lightly and with a sweet familiarity, on her lips.

I followed Teddy upstairs when she took our coats.

"You and Hank?" I said, flopping on the twin bed that had been mine. It was pushed close to the other to make a large bed, and the whole was rumpled. I grinned at it, and then at her, and she blushed.

"Well, I guess so," she said.

"When did all this happen?"

She stood in front of the mirror over her bureau, fiddling with her hair, and then she turned and smiled at me, joy blazing out of her face. My own smile deepened. No one could have failed to smile at Teddy Fairchild on this day.

"It's been happening all fall, if you hadn't been blinder than a bat and deafer than a post over Luke. Ever since you and Luke, as a matter of fact. Hank finally decided you were a lost cause and looked around, and there I was. Boy, you bet there I was. I've been waiting for him to get over you for a solid year."

"Lord, Teddy, that's not so," I said, honestly shocked. "Hank Cantwell? Me? He had never said. I had never thought—"

"Oh, yes. He's been in love with you since college. I'm not even sure he really knows it, but anybody with half a brain could tell. He never did think Brad was going to last, you could just tell he didn't. But Luke was a different matter. He gave up then. It didn't take me long to move in on him. Nature abhors a vacuum, you know. I cooked for him, and took him home to Mother and Daddy, and helped him fix up that disaster area of an apartment, and one thing led to another, and . . . here we are. It's right, Smoky. I always knew it would be. He is a very, very good man."

"Yes," I said, tears stinging my eyes, "he is. And you are a very, very good woman. I love you both. I hope it lasts for three lifetimes."

"It will," she said, her face a lit candle, and I hugged her. One way or another, I thought, Teddy had been in the wilderness a long time.

"Do your parents care that he's not . . . you know, Buckhead? All that stuff?"

"I think my dad may, a little, but he really likes Hank and he's coming around. It would be silly to worry about whether or not Hank'll be able to support me in the manner to which, blah, blah. I'll have enough, one way or another, for us to live almost anyway we want to. Hank's being stubborn about that, but he's not stupid. As for Mother, she's so grateful I'm involved with anybody at all that she's walking on air. She's had the Cathedral and the Driving Club reserved for a month."

"Teddy! Is it that far along?"

"No. Not to anybody but Mother. But it could happen, I guess. I don't want to think any further ahead than now—"

"I know," I said. "I feel that way, too."

"You want to talk about that?"

"I don't think so. Not right now. After a drink, maybe."

When we went back downstairs Luke and Hank were sprawled in front of the television set, and a frantic preppy in a pre-freak brush cut was starting the pregame countdown, or whatever it was called. Hank looked up at me as I came into the room.

Is it okay? he said silently, with his lifted eyebrows and a small, questioning smile.

"Okay for you, Hank Cantwell," I said aloud, and went over and kissed his mouse-fur hair. I noticed that it was thinning just a little, on the very top of his head. Somehow that wrung my heart.

"You be happy," I whispered in his ear. He reached back and squeezed my hand.

"You be, too," he whispered back.

At halftime we ate the collapsed soufflé and drank the wine Luke and I had brought, and we talked of Matt. It had not been a good January. After Tom Gordon left, Matt spent more and more time out of the office, spending longer and longer at lunches that we no longer attended; coming in smelling of whiskey and almost, but not quite, lurching when he walked; saying curtly that someone had to court the assholes that bought the double-page spreads, make the speeches that kept Culver Carnes happy, guide the chattering flock of freelancers who were doing, now, as the magazine grew larger, more and more of the editorial assignments. When he was in the office, he spent the time with his door closed. We had long known that he kept a bottle of Cutty Sark in his credenza; now, Sister reported worriedly, she fished his empties out of the wastebasket every two or three days. The work of the magazine went forward; Matt had not, so far, stinted on that, but it went forward in solitary segments, and without much of the cartwheeling seat-of-the-pants joy that we were used to. We still went out for lunch together and sat under our mural at the Top of Peachtree and Tony still launched into

"Downtown" when we entered, but we entered, now, without Matt, and the song, already bittersweet to me, gained a new poignance, as if Tony were trying, with its chords, to conjure the old Matt Comfort whose anthem it was. The new Matt had no music in him. The lights, for him, no longer seemed brighter downtown.

"Is it Tom, do you think?" Teddy said, giving up on the soufflé and drinking wine. "I know I miss him awfully. I can't even stand to look in his office and see the new guy, and he's a nice guy. He's a good art director. He's trying so hard to be one of us. But it should be Tom in there—"

"Partly," Hank said. "It's partly Tom, and partly Alicia. Partly John Howard, I think, though Matt was never all that close to him. It's mostly the fact that the unit got broken. For some reason that just outrages and appalls him. He could have made the new guy one of us in a day; poor bastard came here full of Comfort legends and the old *Downtown* magic, and what does he get? Closed doors and whispering and so much gloom we might be an actuarial office. Probably wishes he'd stayed in advertising. I'm trying to bring him into the gang, but there's not much gang to bring him into. I wish you guys would open up to him a little."

The new guy was Whit Wilkerson, a talented young art director recruited from a hot new advertising agency. He was funny, unpretentious, street smart, sweet-tempered. Tom Gordon had picked him as his successor, and he was doing a fine job at editorial art direction. But you could tell he was lost and disappointed. *Downtown* had promised him, tacitly, Matt Comfort and Comfort's People, and he had gotten a morose recluse of an editor and a silent staff who kept their doors closed and talked, when they did, in hushed monotones. I had meant to do something about making friends with Whit; I think we all had. But I had simply not had the energy. Now I promised myself that on the very next day I would take him to lunch and ask the others to join us, and we would make him laugh and reassure him that the arctic winter emanating from Matt's office would end. That it always did.

I hoped I could reassure myself as well.

"Speaking of John Howard, have you heard from him?" Hank said to Luke. Luke was lying on his back with his feet propped on the sofa and a can of beer balanced on his chest. He did not lift his head. I looked at the top of it, thinking how I loved the small whorl on the crown where a cowlick was concealed in the thick tangle of red curls. I traced it, in my mind, with my fingertips, as I had a hundred times before. All of a sudden I wanted to be in bed with him, in a darkened room, the shades drawn, the world shut out, clocks stopped, time stopped. I swallowed and looked away.

"He called Friday," Luke said, and I looked back at him. He had not told me he'd heard from John. I started to speak, and then did not.

"Has he worked it out with his wife and kid?" Hank said.

"Nope. He sees the kid twice a month now, but that's all she'll let him do. From noon to six on Sundays, twice a month. She still won't speak to him. She's not ever going to forgive him Juanita."

"Not even after what happened at Christmas? She must know that's torn him up," I said, anger flaring.

"I don't think he told her," Luke said. "I don't think he got a chance. He's not going to stay in Detroit. He's going to New York in a week or two. There's some kind of Civil Rights project at Columbia that wants him to edit one of a series of books they're doing, and they've offered him a lectureship that'll pay him enough to live on. He'll be close enough to go see his kid twice a month, and this'll keep him busy for a semester or two. After that, he doesn't know."

"Why didn't you tell me?" I said. "I've been missing him. I've been worried about him."

"I was going to," Luke said. "He asked about you. I was thinking over a proposition he made me, and I wanted to decide about it before I told you."

The back of my neck prickled slightly.

"What proposition?" I asked, keeping my voice level.

"They want to start over on the photographs for the book, do all new stuff. He thought I might want to take it on. It would mean about six weeks or two months around the country, shooting, and then another month or so in New York, editing. The pay's good."

"So what did you decide?" I said in the level, pleasant, silly voice.

He tilted his head back so that he was looking at me upside down and grinned.

"I decided I didn't want to do it. The pay's not that good. I don't like New York. I was afraid if I left you'd move somebody like Buzzy into the apartment. And I just can't work up a hard-on about Civil Rights anymore. It just feels like the heat's gone out of it. The Christmas thing kind of did me in; it felt like the last gasp of something—passion, or purpose, or just plain sense. I don't know what I mean. The movement isn't over, I know. But like I told you before, it's not really where the heat is now."

"You mean it's in the war," Hank said.

"Yeah," Luke said. "I guess that is what I mean."

He's going, I thought. Sooner or later, probably sooner, Luke is going to go shoot that damned war. It isn't going to be long at all. Desolation swamped me.

"Let's get this miserable soufflé out of sight. It's depressing me," I said to Teddy, and scrambled to my feet and began gathering up plates and glasses. Luke reached out and touched my leg as I passed him.

"You okay, babe?" he said.

"I wish you'd told me," I said. Idiotically, I felt as if I was going to cry.

In the kitchen, Teddy scraped plates as I filled the minuscule sink with hot water.

"You two going to get married?" she said casually, not looking at me.

"Oh, Teddy, I don't know," I said. "We haven't really talked about it. Things were just so good the way they were, I didn't want to think about changing them. . . ."

She looked at me over her shoulder, but said nothing. I looked down at the soapy water. I had spoken in the past tense. Teddy would not have missed that.

I knew then that things had changed, and I had not let myself see it. Not in the way we felt about each other; I was so sensitive to Luke's feelings that I would know almost before he did if there had been any lessening of the thing between us. It was I who had changed. Up to now, I had been content, as he was, to go on as we were, to live in the moment, let who and what and where we were fill me up, complete me. But sometime during the Christmas holidays that had changed. I found myself looking ahead now, wondering what would come next, wondering when he would tell me that he wanted to go to the war, or wherever the next siren call tugged him; wondering how he would tell me.

Wondering what he would say about coming back.

We had agreed that when either of us felt the need to change something we would say so, and he had not said. And I knew that the need had been born in him, and was growing, like a seed. But I also knew that a need had been born in me, too, a need for permanence, promises, reassurance—and I had not said. I had been, for some time, needy, anxious, clinging. He had been preoccupied, restless. I had put it down to the emptiness left by Tom and especially John Howard's leaving, and the worry over Matt. Maybe Luke had too.

But I could not think that anymore. I realized that for the past few weeks I had felt as if I were living in a dead place in the air, living on a flimsy bridge hung between two great tectonic plates, living in a white corridor with no doors at either end. I missed all of us and what we had been. I missed the old *Downtown* as a child might miss an absent mother. Most of all I missed Matt.

For the first time since we had been together, I rolled over on my side when Luke finished his shower and came to bed that night, and feigned sleep. But I did not sleep for a long time.

On January 30, the news came of the Tet Offensive. The nation, having been lulled by positive Pentagon reports that victory was within reach, took in the massive troop losses on both sides, and the grinding difficulty the combined allied force encountered trying to push back the North Vietnamese from Saigon and the heart of allied territory. Antiwar opinion flared like wildfire through the country.

Luke was wild to go to war.

"Go," I said over and over. "I want you to go. You should go. It's the only possible thing for you to do, careerwise. And you won't ever be satisfied until you do. You don't want to look back twenty years from now and regret that you didn't go shoot this war, and I don't want to look back and see that I'm the reason you didn't. I couldn't stand that. Let's start right now thinking who might send you."

He knew that I was upset, though.

"Christ, it would be absolute shit going off and knowing you were back here with all this stuff going on at

Downtown—or not going on—and me not here with you," he said once.

"There's no point in my telling you I wouldn't miss you and worry about you, but you have to believe that it's more important to me for you to go than to stay with me," I said, meaning it. "If you do go, you might get your stupid head shot off. If you don't, it would kill the part of you that's the photographer. And that's the part I love the most. I knew you'd go sooner or later. Do it and come on home."

"I do love you, Smokes," he said softly, and began to look around for someone to assign him to cover the war before it ended.

Life and *Look* both had men, as they said, in country, and did not need any more coverage, though they would be glad to have whatever he sent back if he went on his own.

"Cheap bastards," Luke said, and scouted the *Atlanta Journal* and the *Atlanta Constitution.* Both said they were using wire service material, but would keep him in mind.

"Cheaper bastards," Luke said, and went to try his hand with Matt.

But Matt was not even remotely interested. Luke took him out for a night on the town to soften him up, and put the idea to him, and Matt dismissed it with a grandiloquent wave of his hand.

"*Downtown* needs a war feature like a rooster needs socks," he said. "Order us another and let me tell you what I've got going."

It took him two more doubles, Luke said later, to spell out his grand plan of action regarding the Cup Wars. When he was done, Luke had to carry him home to bed like a child stricken suddenly with sleep.

*　　*　　*

All through February and into the tender, luminous early spring, the Cup Wars raged. The first strike of the new offensive started on a relatively small scale: one morning the statue of Henry Grady, which presided over the traffic island at the intersection of Broad and Marietta Streets, where our offices sat, was festooned with rattling strings of yellow cup holders. By noon Willie, the chamber's grave, decorous handyman, had retrieved them, and by twelve-oh-one Culver Carnes was in the office, his face a mask of restrained fury, asking for Matt. But Matt had not shown. He had called in around ten and said that he had a breakfast meeting with a former member of John Kennedy's cabinet and was hopeful of an interview. They were not to be disturbed.

"Tell him to call me the minute you hear from him," Culver Carnes said tightly to Cecelia Henley. But Matt did not call in. It was mid-afternoon before he appeared, looking as if he had slept in his clothing again, as if he might not have eaten for days. But his eyes, behind the round glasses, glittered with a kind of feverish glee, and his face was flushed. He smiled a lot. He would not say where he had been.

At five he blatted us into his office with the taxi horn and motioned to us to be quiet. He poured paper cups of Cutty Sark all around and took a great swallow from his, shuddered pleasurably, tossed the wing of chestnut hair off his forehead, and got Culver Carnes on the phone.

"Understand you were looking for me, boss," he said amiably.

A furious jumble of sound issued from the phone. Matt grinned ferally all around and held the phone out from his ear; it spit ducklike quackings for a full minute. It was impossible not to laugh. He shushed us gleefully.

At last he answered, "Yeah, well, it wasn't my folks. And I know you're not intimating it was me, are you, boss? Because I can prove where I was, if I have to. Of course you're going to look as paranoid as hell if you ask me to. But I'll be happy to. . . . No, that's okay. But while I've got you, let me tell you that I'm changing my routine for a while. This is just so you'll know. I'm going to be out of the office a lot during the day for a couple of weeks, maybe three. Yeah, I'm lining up a new section on the area arts, a much larger kind of guide thing, looking to bring in at least three times as much revenue. I'm going to have to see the arts leaders in the entire five-county metro area, though, and you know there's not anybody who can sell 'em like I can. Hank's going to hold things down here, and if you need me you can always get me through him. He'll know where I am. I'll be in and out, and I'll be working most nights, to catch up on office stuff. You can always find me down here at night if you want to hang around. I figure I'll have it nailed down in say, three weeks. Four at the outside. It's going to be worth it, Culver. It could double our circulation. Smoky will be doing it, with Luke Geary . . . "

There was more babble from the phone, but the heat had gone out of it. When Matt replaced the receiver in the cradle, he was grinning like a child who has succeeded in fooling his teacher. Glee fairly radiated off him. He all but clapped his hands.

We were all quiet for a moment. I don't think any of us knew quite what to say. We had never seen Matt in precisely this mode before.

Finally Hank said, "I assume you're serious about the new arts thing? And you really do want me to look out for things for a while? It's a long time to be without you in the office—"

"You're the managing editor," Matt said happily. "Manage. Teddy's the production manager. She can produce. I have great faith in you guys. You don't need me to hold your hands. And yeah, there's going to be a new arts section, eventually. I think, short range, you can look for some . . . startling works of art."

"Matt, if I take that on, it's not going to leave me any time for Focus," I said warily. "The county chamber review is taking up about half my time already."

"Oh, Focus is off, for the time being," Matt said airily. "Culver wants to downplay the quote, black angle, unquote, for a while. The Christmas thing spooked him worse than shit. Don't worry, we'll get back to it sooner or later, when I find somebody as good as John Howard to be liaison for me. You'll have time."

I said nothing. I felt hollow and diminished at the thought of losing Focus, but I knew that there was no sense arguing with Matt in this strange, bright, hard new mood. I knew that Luke would not be shooting the new arts section. There was nothing in it that would engage him.

Matt shooed us out of the office then.

"Out," he said. "Go home, all of you. I don't want anybody working late around here for a while. I've got stuff to do at night, and I don't have time to fiddle around with you guys. If you can't get it done during the day, take it home. Tell Hank if you need me. Begone."

He blatted the taxi horn and we filed out, looking back at him uneasily. He was lifting the Cutty Sark bottle to refill his glass as we closed the door on him, and he almost seemed to give off sparks of an interior hilarity.

"I think he's drunk," Sister said unhappily.

"I think he's nuts," Teddy said.

"There is absolutely no doubt in my mind that he's both," Hank said. "I wonder what the hell he's up to."

For the next few careening weeks, we saw very little of Matt Comfort except replications of that night: at five o'clock, the lifted Cutty Sark bottle, the brilliant smile, the closing office door. He was almost never in the office during the day. Hank almost never knew where he was. He did not call in at intervals and let Hank know where he could be reached, as he had said he would, and Hank could not raise him at his apartment. He thought Matt was there, he said, because he found his car in the underground garage. But there was no reply to his hammering on the door, and none to his repeated phone calls. Just when Hank was about to go to the resident manager, and demand the pass key, Matt would call in, or appear in the office. Maybe, I said once, he was with the Playboy PR person, but Hank said no, they had broken up over the holidays, and she had gone back to the mother hutch in Chicago. Matt was with a TWA stewardess now who had the Atlanta to New York to Rome flight three times a month, and was seldom at home. She slept in when she was, and did not answer her phone. All anyone knew about her was that her name was Maria and she had, as Matt said, an awesome fuselage. Matt Comfort had managed to vanish as thoroughly from the face of the earth as was possible without making an alarmed investigation of his whereabouts necessary. It was a masterful piece of legerdemain.

There was absolutely no doubt in any of our minds, after a few days, what he was up to.

The week after the Henry Grady incident, the Citizens and Southern Bank hung an exhibit, in its main lobby across the street from our building, of portraits of civic movers and shakers, painted by the incomparable local artist George Parrish. The morning after the private reception, early workers were startled to find that the portrait of Culver Carnes was festooned with strings of yellow cup holders.

Soon after that, Culver Carnes's car was brought down to him from the upper decks of our parking lot by a puzzled attendant who explained to the apoplectic Culver that he had tried to unfasten the slender metal cord that held the dangling train of yellow cup holders to the back bumper, but he could not. It would, he thought, take wire cutters, or maybe even a welder's torch. Nossir, he sure didn't have no idea who did it. Not one of them, nossir. She was like that when he found her. Culver Carnes went driving off, white faced, toward a downtown garage, the yellow cup holders clanging merrily behind his new Buick as if he were a newlywed.

That night he hired a Pinkerton guard for the chamber offices.

He was back in Matt's office at nine the next morning, but no one could reach Matt.

"I think he said something about Gwinnett County," Hank said earnestly, flushed with embarrassment and anger at having to lie for Matt, but hardly able to hold back his laughter all the same. Culver was practically dancing on the rug, like a child who could not wait to go to the bathroom.

About that time the Polaroid campaign began. Each morning for perhaps a week Culver Carnes would find, in his morning mail, a Polaroid photograph of a local scene with the yellow cup holders prominently featured: decorating Margaret Mitchell's grave in Oakland Cemetery; adorning the gates to Grant Field at Georgia Tech; hanging rakishly on the cage of Willie B., the famous and dyspeptic gorilla at the Grant Park Zoo; gracing the scrawny neck of the gospel shouter on the corner of Broad and Marietta, who could not remember how they got there and called down biblical curses upon Culver Carnes's envoy, sent to interrogate him.

At the same time Culver Carnes was opening his morning mail the local newspapers and radio stations were opening theirs, to find identical shots. In the muddy gray hiatus between news of winter weather and the Braves' spring training, the media fell upon the Cup Wars with alacrity. Culver Carnes would, at first, speak with no reporters, but of course, someone at the chamber ratted, and the Cup Wars went public with a vengeance. Most televised newscasts ended up with a shot of the day's Polaroid, and drive-time radio hosts kept the thing going by sponsoring call-in contests to name the culprit. Culver Carnes lost his head and gave one near-demented interview in which he called the whole thing insidious and insubordinate in the extreme, and promised to fire the culprit when apprehended. After a local deejay suggested that someone give him little steel balls to roll in his hands, like Captain Queeg in *The Caine Mutiny,* the chamber board called Culver Carnes in and told him to put a lid on it; he was making himself and the chamber look like asses.

"Be reasonable, Culver," Ben Cameron, who was board chairman, was said to have told him. "You can't fire whoever it is because he's hanging yellow cup holders all over town and taking Polaroids of them. You say yourself no cup holders are missing. And besides, there's no law that I know that says it's illegal to . . . oh, Christ. What is it with you and these goddamned cup holders? Can't you just grin and go along with it? He'll get tired of it in a minute then . . . whoever it is."

Ben is said to have grinned, albeit reluctantly, when he said it.

"It's Comfort, of course," Culver Carnes responded. "He's lost it, Ben. It's symptomatic—"

"It's actually funnier than hell, Culver, whether it's Comfort or not," Ben Cameron said. "Even if you catch him red-handed with a sack of yellow cup holders, you can't fire him. He has a contract. You'd look like the biggest fool since Boy Slattery. And besides, if it is Comfort, my money says you'll never catch him in a hundred years. Join him. He's beat you."

The next time the media contacted Culver Carnes he grinned a sick grin and said it was all a prank, and even if it was pretty silly and childish, he appreciated a good joke as much as anyone else.

The next day, an Academy Award–winning documentary crew, in town to shoot a film on "Atlanta, the City Too Busy to Hate," found the misty wooded park at Peachtree Battle Avenue, where they planned to shoot the film's opening sequence, literally cobwebbed with festoons of yellow cup holders strung on every available bush, tree, and crag. It took the crew a full morning to get them down, set shooting back a day, and cost many thousands of dollars. Culver Carnes announced to the reporters who jammed his office that the only decent thing for the chamber to do was pick up the tab for the delay. He gave the cameras a decent, good-guy smile and went back into his office. We learned later that he was on the phone to the chamber membership all afternoon, putting his plan to them. I think he must have known it would be approved. It would bring the chamber a significant cash windfall, and that, after all, was what made the corporate world go round. The business of Atlanta had always been business.

The Cup Wars ended that day, but we were all frightened. The film incident was over the line; it had all gone too far. The sense of that was strong. None of us had the least doubt that Culver Carnes was right and Matt was behind it, but no one was quite sure how he had accomplished it.

"Well, anybody can go to a restaurant supply house and buy yellow plastic cup holders," Luke said, grinning. He was the only one of us who did not seem unduly disturbed by the tenor of things. "And it would take Matt about three seconds to make a buddy for life of that Cro-Magnon Pinkerton Culver hired. For all we know he's got an absolute network of buddies among the nighttime security guys around town. Hell, maybe he even wears combat fatigues and crawls through vents in blackface. One thing's for sure, Carnes will never know and neither will we."

Days passed and Matt did not come back into the office. Hank, bone-weary from trying to carry on the work of the magazine and fend off Matt's callers, tried in vain to track him down.

"I can't keep this pace up," he said at lunch over his desk one day. "I'm not getting but three or four hours' sleep a night. Neither is Teddy. Neither are most of y'all. I've got all the advertisers on my back, and the sales department is acting like every day's a half-holiday. We're going to come out a week late this month, for the first time in a year, and it's going to look like my fault, and it goddamned well ain't. If he doesn't get his ass back in here, I don't know what's going to happen to the magazine."

"You ought to quit and leave him with it," Luke said, reaching for the uneaten half of Hank's sandwich. "He's not helping you. He's making you look bad. You know damned well he's somewhere drunk. The papers would hire you in a minute; any of the bureaus would."

Hank looked at him wearily, and shook his head silently.

"Smoky should, too," Luke said. "I've told her over and over, the national folks aren't going to keep asking her forever. She needs to get out of here if she's going to make her mark. It's obvious Comfort's not going to help her out anymore than he is any of the rest of you."

I looked at him and then at Hank, and all of a sudden I saw what Hank had meant by the silent shaking of his head. He meant that he could not leave the magazine. That it was, to him, a singularly good magazine, his own magazine—home—and more than that: it was a living thing, an entity in and of itself, apart from Matt Comfort, apart from Comfort's People, apart from any and all of us. *Downtown* simply was. Without Matt and us, it would not be.

"I just can't leave *Downtown,* Luke," I said. "Not until I know it's going to be okay. I sure don't know that now."

Luke smiled at me, but he shook his head.

Hank grinned, the first full grin I had seen on his tired face in a long time.

"I think you just became a journalist, Holy Smokes," he said.

Two days later, on March ninth, Luke got his assignment to go to war.

He came quietly into the apartment after a late meeting at the *Atlanta Constitution.* I had known he was going there, but not why. Somehow it did not occur to me that it could have been a war assignment, but I knew, the instant I saw his face, that it was.

My heart gave a great, fishlike flop and then seemed to close up shop deep inside me.

"You got it," I said. I was surprised that the words sounded normal.

"Yeah."

He came over to where I was reading on the sofa and took the book out of my hands and sat down beside me. He took my hands in his and pressed them to his mouth, first one and then the other, and bit the knuckles gently. I had a hard time trying to keep from jerking them away, from beginning to cry, from jumping up and running . . . anywhere. Far away. Very fast. Anywhere. *Nononononono* my mind wailed idiotically.

"Where? When?" my voice said calmly.

"They've changed their minds and now they want to do a thing on a First Cav company that left a week ago. The angle is that it might well be one of the last, if not the last, bunch deployed out of Benning, the way the war's going. They want to follow them through the first phase of whatever action they get. It shouldn't take long. They rotate those guys out of there fast. No longer than a couple of weeks, for me."

"So you'd be going with them. Wherever they go. Cavalry. That's foot stuff, isn't it?"

"It is, yeah. Don't worry, babe. The reason you get so many good photos coming out of that war is that photographers are notorious chickens. I'm not going to stick my neck out."

I simply could not think of anything to say to that. Images flew: virulent green, white mist, red. Splashes of red. Red . . .

"So when would you go?"

"Well, they're just about getting into 'Nam now. They want me to catch up with them before they go in country. I've got a ticket on Delta to San Francisco for day after tomorrow. A MATS flight will take me on from there. I'm not sure about the details yet. They'll let me know more tomorrow."

I got up and went into the kitchen to start dinner. A great, airless white calm had settled down on me, like a mason jar over a lightning bug. I could see, feel, hear, taste, but it seemed to be happening to someone else. I had the very clear notion that if I did everything exactly right, if I peeled the potatoes perfectly, if I brought the water to exactly the right boil, if I made just the right dinner conversation and got the kitchen and dishes spotless after we had eaten, I could make it through until bed-time, and then I could sleep, and it would all go away. All I had to do was be a very, very good girl. All I had to do was not to speak of it, not think of it.

He followed me into the kitchen and put his arms around me from behind, and pulled me back against him until his chin rested on the top of my head. I could feel that my body was as rigid as a piece of wood in his arms. I was very still.

"You're upset. I didn't want you to be. I thought you wanted this for me—"

"I did. I do. I'm not upset. But I can't talk about it now, Luke. Please don't make me."

"We have to talk about it, babe."

"No, we don't. No, we don't."

"You want to go out to dinner? We could call Hank and Teddy, see if they want to do a send-off thing—"

"Please don't."

We ate our dinner and watched television and read for a bit and finally we got into bed. We made love. He took a shower, and then I did, and we made love again. I did it all perfectly. The ticket to San Francisco, in its smart blue envelope, sat on his bureau like a poison toad. I woke several times during the night, and it seemed to me, when I did, that it pulsed and glowed there like a living thing.

He drove me to work the next morning and came upstairs with me, to tell Hank about the assignment, he said, and to see if he might want something from him while he was over there. When we got into the office, I still walking perfectly on my fragile bridge over nothing-ness, it was to find Hank and Teddy slumped in Matt's Eames chairs, coffee cooling unheeded beside them, staring at a crumpled piece of paper that lay on the floor between them. I could tell, even with the crumpling, that it was an interoffice memo. Hank looked at us mutely, his face a boiled white, and picked it up and uncrumpled it and handed it to me.

It was from Culver Carnes to the staff of *Downtown,* and it said, essentially, that he was, with the chamber's full approval, putting *Downtown* up for sale. It would be an open sale, strictly according to chamber of commerce policy, with the magazine going to the highest bidder. He had two extremely qualified prospects in negotiation at present, and hoped to have a firm buyer by the fifteenth of April. The staff would be kept on to help out the new corporate editor, whoever that turned out to be, but of course the new owners would want to bring in their own man for that post. Matt Comfort was being apprised of this action under separate cover. He knew that we would want to give the new owners our full cooperation, et cetera. I did not read the rest.

I passed the memo wordlessly to Luke. It seemed a very long time until he tossed it back down onto the floor. He did not speak, none of us did. There was nothing conceivable to say.

Another ball of paper hit the floor beside the memo, and I saw, at first uncomprehendingly, that it was the San Francisco ticket in the blue Delta envelope. I looked over at Luke.

He grinned the old shit-eating grin and shrugged.

"It ain't much of a fuckin' war, anyway," he said.

16

Y OU HAVE TO REALIZE THAT IT'S JUST FOR NOW," LUKE
said that night. "I'm going to stay until something is
settled one way or another. I want to do that, I have to.
But after that, I can't hang around, Smokes. I want to go
to that war. I'm going to find some way to do it."

"I know," I said, pressing closer into the curve of his
body. "I know that. I wouldn't ask you to stay. I didn't
this time."

"Just so you know," he said. "And just so you know
that I'll come back."

We were lying close together in the waterbed. It was
early, perhaps only ten o'clock. The night was soft and
fresh; we had opened the long French windows and a little green wind poured in, freighted with wet earth and
new leaves. I remembered the smell from this time last
year: Atlanta in the spring. Only last year, I had been all
over the city like a young terrier sniffing rapturously at a
new territory. This spring, I had spent too many of the
nights like this, huddled with Luke in the tidal refuge of
the waterbed. The thought made the tears that had

threatened all this terrible day surge up again. I swallowed them. I was, I thought, done with crying. This was past crying anyway.

"I can't believe how much has changed in one year," I said bleakly.

"Yeah," he said, tracing the line of my hip with his fingertip. "There's almost nothing that hasn't changed. But not everything has."

We lay in silence for a while. I felt leaden, enervated. I knew that we both were hungry, must be hungry. We had not eaten dinner, and I could not, for the moment, remember what we had done about lunch. But I did not feel hungry.

"It's time for you to move on now, Smokes," Luke said presently. "You don't want to stick around and work for some Culver Carnes lookalike. You don't want to watch what *Downtown*'s going to turn into without Matt. If you aren't ready to leave Atlanta, go talk to Seth Emerson at the *Newsweek* bureau. He'll hire you in a minute. He told me he would. It's the Southeastern bureau; you could stay here and still get into virtually everything that's going on all over the South. He's got some of his women reporting now."

I shook my head.

"I'm going to stay," I said dully. "I have to, for a while, anyway. Don't you see? It would be like walking off and leaving a friend to bleed to death."

He sat up swiftly and jerkily, and I knew he was angry, or as angry as Luke ever got. He never moved abruptly any other time.

"Jesus Christ, Smoky, what's the matter with you?" he snapped. "It's over. It's already bleeding to death. Neither you nor anybody else can stop it. Matt killed it himself. Why do you want to hang around trying to save his ass? He's fucked you just as royally as he did everybody else on staff. He knew damned well Culver would find some way to pull the plug, even if he couldn't fire him. You don't owe him a goddamned thing."

"It's not Matt. It's *Downtown*," I said. But even as I said it, I knew that it was Matt, too. It was too late for me. I loved Matt Comfort. I could not walk away from him.

I did not understand why Luke couldn't see that. I did not understand how he could walk away.

But something deep down and rock-hard within me understood: Luke was all eyes, all images. He could not exist in stasis.

"You don't owe anybody anything," Luke said. "You only owe yourself. Only you. Nobody owes anybody else."

"Do you really believe that?"

"I do. I always have."

"Then why are you here with me?"

"Because it's something I owe myself, to be with you."

"And when it isn't?"

"I'm not going to fight with you," he said. "You're strung out and I don't blame you. You aren't making sense. We'll talk more when you feel better."

He got up and went into the kitchen. I could hear him foraging in the refrigerator.

"And when will that be?" I said miserably into the pillow.

I did cry then, despite my resolve. But they were tired, thin tears, and did nothing to ease the solid block of misery that filled my chest, and so I stopped.

We ate the cheese omelettes he made, and drank some of the widow's flowery Rhine wine, and went to bed early, but I don't think either of us slept much. Instead, we tossed politely on our own sides of the waterbed, each trying not to disturb the other. When I got up, in the first cool gray wash of dawn, I looked back on my way into the bathroom and saw his eyes gleam whitely at me before he turned over and buried his head in his pillow. It was the first time I could remember that we had been unable to give each other solace.

We drank coffee and dressed and left for *Downtown* in near-silence. We moved like people who have lost a lot of blood, heavily and carefully. He kept his hand on my shoulder or back or arm, lightly, but he said little. So did I. Every time I started to speak, I stopped. There seemed, now, little point. It was as if our entire context had been shattered. That was worse by far than anything that had gone before.

We heard it the minute the elevator door slid open: the roar of music. It was not the saccharine whine of the Muzak, but the thumping heartbeat of the record Matt had played over and over for almost a year, until Tom Gordon and Hank stole it and threw it out of the eleventh-floor window: "Don't sleep in the subway darlin', don't stand in the pourin' rain . . . "

The music filled the hallway and bounced off the dingy acoustical tiles of the corridor ceiling. Luke and I looked at each other and followed it through the open doorway of *Downtown*.

There was no one in the outer office, but all the office doors were open, and the mingled smell of fresh coffee and flowers and furniture polish hit us like a great sound wave. Desktops gleamed with lemon oil. On each woman's desk was a green florists' vase of red roses. The music bellowed and roared. Over it, the Bahamian taxi horn gave three ear-splitting blats, and Sister's face appeared in Matt's office door. It shone like a child's on Christmas morning.

"Y'all get y'all's butts in here," she screeched.

I dropped my purse on my desk and ran, my heart threatening to leap from my chest with something that did not, yet, dare to be joy. Luke was right behind me.

Hank said later that Luke running had been a truly amazing sight, like watching a scarecrow sprint.

They were all there, on Matt's sofa and his chairs, on his rug. Sueanne was sitting on his desk crying and wiping her glasses on her petticoat, and Sister was frugging madly on the little Oriental rug to Petula Clark.

Matt sat with his tiny feet up on his desk, holding the taxi horn and grinning. It was his old grin, the one I had seen the first day I had walked into this office, white and wolfish and world-igniting. His chestnut hair gleamed fire and his pin-striped suit was obviously new, even though it looked as if it had spent years in an attic trunk, and the blue eyes behind the round wire glasses were so crinkled that they were lost in furrowed flesh. The little Gucci loafers gleamed, and there was a red rose behind one ear.

"Sit down, dear hearts, and listen how we're going to pull this fucker out of the fire," he said. His voice was the old Matt voice when he was fully engaged, rich and honeyed and just on the brink of sardonic hilarity. There was nothing in it, that I could hear, of the awful cracked, canted glee that had been there for so long. I sat down on Hank's lap simply because my knees went out from under me.

It was a short speech. Later I wondered, fleetingly, why we all bought it without reservation, but almost by the time it ended we all had, and there was no doubt in any of our minds that Matt's plan could and would work: he was going to buy the magazine himself. He knew it could be done and he knew how. It was simply a matter of finding a backer, the right one, the one with enough money and sense to know what he had in *Downtown* and leave us alone to run it. He would have a major share and the editorship; that was the deal and it was not negotiable.

"I can do it in a week if I have to," he said. "You all know I can do it. All I need is a telephone. But we have some time and I'm going to take it, to find just the right people, so we don't ever have to go through this shit again. Don't glare at me, Teddy, I know where most of the shit came from. I never apologize, so you'll have to make do with that. All you need to know is that Comfort's back and one month from now this will be a done deal. I absolutely guarantee that. Anybody who doubts it should leave by that door there."

For just a fraction of a moment we were all silent. The past weeks hung in the air like a rancid odor. We stared at him and I knew that we were all looking for signs of the mania that had spawned the Cup Wars. But it was not there. Only Matt Comfort was, Matt Comfort, cool and arrogant and real. Power came off him like smoke.

We broke into cheers and applause. They lasted a long time. When we stopped, he ran us out. "Go on," he said. "Get busy. Bust your butts. Don't talk about this to anybody. I want to be the one to tell Culver myself. You've got your assignments; Sister has the list. I did it last night. Let's make June the best fucking issue we ever put out. Let him eat his heart out. Smoky, stay for a minute."

When the others had left I sat in his Eames chair and looked at him. He looked back, studying me. His eyes were rimmed with red, I could see now, and there was an almost imperceptible trembling in his hands. But the rest of him shone as if he had just been cast in new gold.

"Two things," he said. "YMOG this time is Culver's son-in-law. You'll hate him. He's the worst dickhead I ever met. Do it right. Lick the dickhead's boots if you have to. I want Culver to think he's won the whole nine yards."

I nodded, hypnotized. I would lick many boots for this man, I knew.

"Second thing. Starting with June you're the new assistant managing editor with as much pay raise as we can get you. It probably won't be much. You'll be back on Focus full-time, and I want you to go on with that little black girl with the voice. Luella what's-her-name. Don't talk about that, either; by the time it runs it'll be way too late for Culver to yell about that or anything else. I'm going to call SCLC and get Dr. King to suggest a new liaison for Focus. You've done a good job, Smoky, and I'm proud of you. I probably won't tell you that again until nineteen seventy."

"I love you, Matt," I said, my lips wobbling like they do when you have just come from the dentist and the novocaine has not yet worn off. I could taste salt.

He looked at me for a long moment, and then shook his head slightly.

"Ol' Smoky," he said. "Be careful who you love. They'll be part of you always. Even after the love is long dead, the fuckers'll be part of you."

"I hope so," I said, and went out with the others to bust my butt for Matt Comfort.

Somehow we did not talk much about it among ourselves. Maybe it was because we were afraid to break the new bubble of elation that contained us all, but I don't think so. There was a powerful feeling around all of us in those first new days of Matt's return, a sense of deep, quiet power, a conspiratorial happiness. We knew that, upstairs, the chamber buzzed and thrummed like a hive of bees with the news of Matt's vanquishing, but few of them came into the camp of the vanquished, and we were not often required to act humble and sorrowful. With the cessation of the Cup Wars and the issuing of the fateful interoffice memo, Culver Carnes retreated into his thirteenth floor lair. We did not see him in our offices again. We worked, prodigiously, and we smiled at each other, and we smiled at the closed door of Matt's office. The red light that meant his telephone was occupied glowed steadily all day. It was still glowing when most of us left in the evening. Hank, who often stayed late riding herd on the day-to-day business of the magazine while Matt poured his honey over the wires from Atlanta to Texas and Oklahoma and New York, said that it glowed late into the nights. He said also that Matt drank a great deal of coffee and smoked incessantly, but that he was not drinking at all.

"There's no way I wouldn't know," he said.

Only once did we really speak of the transformation, and that was the day it happened. Luke and I and Hank rode down on the elevator together at the end of the day, and Luke said to Hank, "So what happened?"

"I still don't know," Hank said. "I took the memo over to his place after I couldn't raise him on the phone and pushed it under his door. It was after midnight. I knew he was in there. I could hear the stereo. And then I went home and went to bed. When I came in this morning, there he was. That's as much as I can tell you."

After that, the tide of the spring turned abruptly toward joy. It was as if the city and the world swung themselves into synchronization with the elation that bore us along like a great wave. On March 12, Eugene McCarthy captured an astounding 42 percent of the vote in the New Hampshire Democratic primary, running as a peace candidate. On March 16, Robert Kennedy announced his candidacy for the Democratic presidential nomination. Two days later he opened his campaign by announcing that if he was elected, he would actively seek a peace settlement. In our giddiness, we cheered McCarthy and Kennedy alike. It seemed to me, crazily, that both, like us, were invincible.

On March 17, when they were dyeing the river green and getting sodden drunk on green beer back in Corkie, Matt came out of his office grinning incandescently and said that he had a fucking great nibble out of Oklahoma and to stay tuned. Then he went back in and closed his door.

On March 21, Francis Brewton paid us a long and fragrant visit and sold us his entire stock of antique periodicals, and on March 22, Mr. Tommy T. Bliss came and stood on his head in the lobby to celebrate Henry Aaron's first home run, in a preseason exhibition game with Pittsburgh. We were delirious with joy. There could not, Matt said, be better auguries.

On March 30, Matt called Luke into his office and asked him if he could get in touch with John Howard in New York.

"Yeah," Luke said. "I probably can. You want to tell me why?"

"Not especially," Matt grinned. "But tell him if he'll come down here for an overnighter in a few days we'll pay his airfare and put him up. Tell him he can pick the hotel. Tell him all he has to do is eat a dynamite dinner and drink some dynamite champagne and wear a suit instead of a caftan or whatever those things are the Yankee liberals are all running around in now."

"Dashikis," Luke grinned. "I doubt if John's into dashikis yet. I'll tell him. Anything else?"

"No. Just tell him . . . I need him, and I'll be beholden to him," Matt said. "And that he won't be sorry. It's for an honorable cause. Tell him that."

Luke did tell John Howard that, on the telephone that night, but at first John was reluctant. In the end, though, he agreed.

"How'd you get him to change his mind?" I said, when Luke came back into the living room grinning triumphantly.

"Told him it mattered an awful lot to you and me," he said. "And that Culver Carnes would absolutely shit. You know he always did think Culver was an asshole."

I went to Luke and hugged him.

"I'm so glad he's coming," I said into his neck. "I

didn't realize how much I missed him till I knew he might come back."

"Me either," Luke said.

On March 31, Matt came capering out of his office, blatting the taxi horn, and herded us all over to the Top of Peachtree to tell us that deliverance was at hand and to brief us on it. We sat late, while blue dusk fell over the greening city and the downtown lights winked on, drinking champagne and eating hors d'oeuvres and listening to Tony, who played "Downtown" over and over in an excess of delight at having Matt back. Matt himself only drank coffee and smoked, but he crowed as loudly as the rest of us.

"He's a Texan, but he's based in Oklahoma City now," he told us of our savior-to-be. "I knew him when we both worked on an oil rig off Galveston, both of us about eighteen, I think. I doubt if we weighed a hundred and fifty pounds together. He calls himself Cody Remington, and sometimes—I swear to God—Bubba, but his name's Duane Heckler. Hell, I don't care if he calls himself Alexander the Great. It would fit him perfectly. I always knew the little fucker would own the world one day. He's got the goddamn chicken parts market in the entire Southwest cornered, and he's looking to get into the media game, as he calls it. He's got a better cash flow than God. I convinced him he ought to start with a magazine with social conscience as well as fancy national awards. He's looking to be socially relevant now, he tells me. Well, I guess you would, if you'd made your pile from chicken parts. He requires, and I quote, a strong black presence in any venture. I'm gonna bring him over on the third and set up a presentation right here, under the mural, with storyboards and flip charts and the whole nine yards, and then I'm gon' wine him and dine him and hit him with the Andre piece and John Howard to boot. We'll have a special display with all our awards, and I'm going to get Ben

Cameron, and maybe even Dr. King, on tape, talking about what assets to the universe we are. I thought I'd get that little Luella gal to come sing 'Downtown' for us when I walk him in; you all will all be here under the mural, see, and Tony will hit it when we get off the elevator, and when we come through those doors she'll start belting it out. I'm going to rent the bar for the night. Just us and Cody Bubba. What do you think?"

"I think ol' Cody Bubba is a gone goose," Hank exulted.

"It's absolutely perfect!" Teddy cried.

"He'll be begging us to let him buy us," I said, laughing with sheer joy. It was an inspired scenario. It could not fail to move the chicken parts king of the Southwest.

"Chicken parts?" Luke gasped, doubled over in his tilted-back chair. "Chicken parts? Holy shit!"

"How are you going to pay for all this?" Hank said finally, sobering up a little. He could never quite stop being a managing editor.

"Put it on Culver's tab, of course," Matt said matter-of-factly. "By the time the bill comes he'll have one less magazine to pay for."

We were still crowing and preening when a commotion around the television set at the far end of the bar broke through our euphoria. We looked over at it just in time to see the lugubrious, Dumbo-eared face of Lyndon Johnson fading from the screen. I had forgotten he had called a special news conference for that evening.

"What is it?" Matt yelled over to Doremus, the weeknight bartender.

"Says he's stopping the bombing of North Vietnam except in the DMZ," Doremus yelled back. "And he ain't going to run again."

We sat stunned for a moment, and then Teddy began to clap. After a moment we all joined her, clapping and cheering and laughing and whistling. All except Luke.

"Shit," he howled. "I'll never get to the goddamned war before it's over! Shit!"

Still laughing, we rose and poured our champagne over his head, one by one.

On the afternoon of April 3, I went with Luke to pick up John Howard at the airport. It was one of those spring days that lures photographers outside in droves: so clear that you could see every delicate vein in the lacquered new leaves; so soft that you felt the air on newly bared arms like velvet; so suffused with every shade of green that it seemed that your very blood ran green, in harmony. The sun was warm at mid-afternoon, and Luke put the top down on the Morgan for the first time since October. The drive out the expressway was like swimming in foaming light.

I was giddy with sun and the air and the prospect of seeing John. The coming evening loomed like a radiant iceberg over everything. It was possible not to think of it, but it was not possible not to know that the grand shape of it was there. Passing the stadium a sudden sweet gust of wisteria washed over us from some tiny lawn in the warren of old houses behind it, and I closed my eyes and took a deep breath and smiled. It was the very scent of childhood springs and home, and though I wanted neither of those two things now, still, it enchanted as only sudden scents can do.

"This minute, just right this second, is absolutely perfect," I said to Luke, stretching my arms over my head and arching my back. The driver of a passing big rig yelled something cheerfully and admiringly obscene, and I laughed aloud with joy and the power of my young body. I felt, for a moment, as I had last summer at the Cloister, when I realized for the first time what a formidable weapon sheer youth is.

"I simply can't imagine being old," I said.

"You're not going to live to be old if you don't stop sticking your tits out at truck drivers," Luke said mildly, but when I looked at him from behind my sunglasses, he was grinning. His freckled arms were bare, too, and the wind whipped his sun-struck red hair around his head. He had stuck a plastic daisy in the ear piece of his glasses, and he looked about thirteen.

"Tom and Huck, running away from Aunt Polly," I said, and squeezed his arm. "Oh, Luke, I can't wait to see John! I can't wait until tonight! I can't wait to get everything all settled and tell everybody!"

"My mama would say you're wishing your life away," Luke said.

"No, just the next few hours of it."

We parked the car in the short-term lot and went into the terminal and down the concourse to wait for Delta flight 459 from La Guardia. It was a turnaround flight, and the passenger lobby was full of people who looked exactly like passengers for New York. They were well-dressed and impassive, scanning newspapers and magazines, lining up for the telephone. Most of them were men. There was only one other woman near us, a square, blue-rinsed matron in a flowered silk Lilly, inspecting the crowd as if for vermin.

"Buckhead grandmama come to pick up the grand-kiddies from Manhattan," I whispered to Luke. "The chauffeur is circling outside."

The flight was late, and John was one of the last to deplane. I had been peering anxiously as passenger after passenger filed out of the arrival gate, all of them looking somehow stunned, like people coming out of a darkened movie theater, none of them John. And then he was there, tall in a gray suit with a vest that I had never seen and a blue oxford cloth shirt and a striped tie, his narrow head turning slightly from left to right, looking for us. I smiled involuntarily. His presence smote the air. Everyone in the crowd waiting to board stared at him. It was impossible not to. He looked so totally collected within his taut skin, and so gravely and imperturbably correct, that I wondered for a moment why I had ever thought he was, could be, my friend. And then he saw us, and the sharp-planed face broke into a small smile. I felt my own smile grow.

"Oh, Luke, he looks wonderful," I said, and started forward to meet him. Behind me, the square Buckhead grandmother said something indistinguishable and unmistakable, not bothering to lower her voice. I stopped and looked at her over my shoulder, gave her a brilliant smile, and rushed at John Howard shrieking in delight. When I reached him I threw my arms around him so hard that he stumbled backward, and then he swung me around in the air, laughing aloud. I hugged him, smelling new oxford cloth and warm skin and some bitter, green-y aftershave.

"Smoky," he said, laughing. "God, Smokes . . . I'm glad to see you. Luke. Hey, Luke . . . "

Luke hugged him, too, and we started back down the concourse, each of us squeezing one of his arms, talking and laughing. The Buckhead grandmother gave us a long, venomous look as we passed. She moved slightly aside, as if to remove herself from contamination.

"My husband," I said loudly to her. "Haven't seen him in months. I just can't wait to get him home."

And I gave her a showy leer.

"Jesus Christ, she's going straight to the phone and call the White Citizens' Council," John said in the rich, beautiful voice that I had already almost forgotten. He was grinning broadly.

"Screw her and the White Citizens' Council," I said. "Is this all the luggage you brought?"

"You got a bad mouth on you, girl. I'm going back first thing in the morning," John said. "Lordy, jetting down to Atlanta for dinner and going straight back is such a *white* thing to do. Usually us po' blacks stay three weeks once we get somewhere. I almost didn't know how to act on that airplane."

"The simple darky shit don't wash, bro," Luke grinned at him. "You look like you just made the House of Lords. You look good."

"Thanks," John Howard said, "but the simple darky shit is pretty close to the truth in this case. Do you know, that's the first time I've ever been on an airplane?"

"Well, don't feel bad. Chances are not one of those cats on that plane ever rode a mule," Luke said, and we went out into the crystal afternoon toward the parking lot. I walked decorously between them until we reached the far curb, but then I clutched both their arms and gave a great skip and swung myself between them, off the earth, like a child.

"Can't take her anywhere," Luke said.

On the way back into the city, crammed between them, I simply hung my head back and let the wind take my hair and the sun lie heavy on my closed lids, and listened to them talk, shouting a little over the rush of the sweet wind.

"How is it up there?" Luke said.

"It's . . . funny," John Howard replied. "Queer. I mean, there's nothing particularly difficult or foreign about it; I know my way around pretty well, I fit in okay, my job's not all that different from what it was at AU. I like it fine. I like the people I work with. I've met some congenial new folks. It's just that nothing seems real. I can't seem to plug into what's important to them up there, and the stuff that was important to me down here just three months ago seems like it happened in another lifetime. The . . . I don't know, the fire, the heat . . . it all seems so artificial now."

"You got some new fire going?"

"No. I can't seem to find anything up there worth it. It's all the war now, or social protest, or fifty different kinds of drugs, or pure politics. The movement seems almost quaint outside the South, outside Atlanta. I feel like a dinosaur. Or a mercenary, flogging something that somebody paid me to flog. Like my horse got shot out from under me."

I felt a small chill that had nothing to do with the slanting sun. It struck me suddenly: how many mercenaries were simply people who had had their horses shot out from under them and couldn't find another? It was a queer insight for a giddy spring day, and it made me uncomfortable.

"It feels a little realer back here," John said tentatively. "It really does sort of swing into focus now that I'm back here. I didn't think it would. Not all the way real, but like something that fit once, that mattered once—"

"Come back," I said, and he looked over at me and smiled. I could not see his eyes behind the dark glasses, but I could see the cruel gray slash of the scar clearly in the sunlight.

"Don't know if I can," he said. "Don't know if anybody can, really. Didn't Thomas Wolfe say you couldn't?"

"Because of your kid?" Luke said.

"No, not really. I could see him as easily from here as I can from New York, I guess. Probably for longer at a time, too. It's a matter of money, not distance. I'm not really sure what it is."

"Juanita?" Luke said casually, and John looked sharply at him. I did not think he was going to answer, but after a moment he did.

He shook his head, and shrugged. I could feel the movement against my shoulder.

"Nothing there," he said. "I was looking to get Lowndes back, I guess. But that's gone, too. . . ."

There was a longer silence, and then he said, "When you gon' tell me why Matt Comfort is flying me down here and feeding me champagne and putting me up at the Regency? Not that I care, long as his voucher's good."

But he smiled, and I knew that he did care.

"Let's go back to the apartment," Luke said over the wind. "We'll tell you all about it then."

We did, laughing and interrupting ourselves in our eagerness to savor it again, to watch John savor it. He smiled as we talked, grinned outright at the saga of the Cup Wars, and was laughing with us when we outlined the shape of the triumphant night ahead of us. We were sitting on Luke's tiny balcony, like a ship's deck again, its prow thrust out into the luminous green of the new leaves and the motionless snowfall of the dogwood. Across the street the little park shimmered in a surf of pink, red, and white azaleas. Stiff, formal tulips bobbed and bowed along the steep driveway of the widow's house and Luke's carriage house. John had taken off his coat and loosened his tie and we were all drinking wine.

"Long way from Pumphouse Hill," he had grinned at us when we first sat down.

Now he stretched and shook his head and said, "It's sure gonna be worth the trip down here to meet the chicken parts king of the entire Southwest and get Culver Carnes's goat at the same time. Y'all sure Matt can pull this off?"

"It's a done deal," I crowed. "Tonight's just the . . . the celebratory parade. The last hurrah. You, of course, are the clincher. The 'strong black presence' that ol' Cody Bubba requires. So see that you act strong and black."

"Shit. You mean I can't chat with him about my squash game and my mutual funds?"

"No, but you can tell him about choppin' your daddy's cotton."

"I'll tell him about my daddy's squash game and mutual funds. Daddy don't know from cotton except swabs. Come on, Smoky, if I'm going to be a token I at least ought to get some fun out of it."

"You could sing 'Old Man River,'" Luke said, and we all laughed.

"I've got to go get dressed," I said. "Is there anybody you want to call while you wait, John?"

He looked out over the pastel sea of trees and flowers and shook his head.

"I don't think so, not this trip, Smokes," he said. "Maybe next time. Thanks, anyway."

I stood looking at him, feeling the laughter seep out of the moment, and then turned and went into the bedroom. As I turned on the shower I heard him yell, "Hey, Smoky!"

"Yes?" I shouted back.

"Wear that red dress. You know, the one you wore the night we did the presentation at the Top of Peachtree before? The Andre dress? Wear that."

"I always heard y'all were fools for red," I yelled, and they laughed again, and I pulled out the red linen sheath I had worn three seasons ago, on another night of luminous triumph, and hung it in the tiny bathroom to unwrinkle in the steam while I showered.

And so we went, in our cheeky joy and finery, down Peachtree Road once more in the lucent twilight, the air so sweet that I thought I could never breathe enough of it, to sit with the city at our feet and wait for Matt to bring our deliverance to us.

They were all there when we came up on the elevator. Doug Maloof had partitioned the bar off from the restaurant with a folding leatherette partition, and Tony's piano was stationed against it, banked in spring flowers. Tony himself was at the piano, noodling soft rock and show tunes and grinning hugely, and the staff of *Downtown* sat together at a long table before the wall of windows that looked North over the heart of the city. They were dressed as for a party, in bright spring silks and crisp summer-weight suits, and all the women wore corsages of little blue daisy-like flowers. The men had single flowers in their buttonholes.

"Doug gave them to us," Teddy smiled. "They're as near as he and the florist could come to Texas bluebonnets. Isn't it a fabulous idea?"

"It is," I said, pinning mine on and waving my thanks at Doug Maloof. He beamed at me from behind the bar, where he and Doremus were putting fat green champagne bottles into silver ice buckets. Over their heads the mural gleamed, our own smiling faces seeming to shine out of it like small moons. I thought that Doug must have had them cleaned, or something, just our faces, so that they would dominate the long painting as if spotlights were trained on them. Bless Doug. He had been a wonderful friend to all of us; a surrogate father, really. I knew that the news of the magazine's sale would have cut him to the quick, and that this elaborate palace coup taking place in his bar must delight his heart. He would talk of it for years to come. He had been one of the first of Matt Comfort's People; he would be one of us until he died. He had swept and polished and decked and shined his bar until it was fit to receive any royalty, even the Chicken Parts King of the Entire Southwest. There was no surface that did not bear fresh flowers. Even the black-veiled easels that held the presentation boards and our awards were festooned with blossoms. Even the portable recorder that held the tape of endorsing civic voices had a single perfect long-stemmed red rose laid on it. At a small, white-skirted table beside Tony's piano, hors d'oeuvres waited under heated silver domes. Everyone at the table already had a long-stemmed glass of wine or a cocktail. Doug would, I knew, save the champagne for toasts, when Matt arrived with Cody Bubba Remington. It would, I knew also, be the best that money could buy.

John went around the table, shaking hands with everyone. I slid into a seat at the end of the table beside Luke. I looked down the long table, letting my eyes go slightly out of focus, trying to see the familiar faces just anew, as if I had not looked on them for a long time, had just returned to them from a far time and place. I felt a great turning in my breast, not quite tears, not quite joy, perhaps merely and purely love. Comfort's People. My people. For more than a year now my community. My eyes went to the gentle brown hawk's face beside Matt's simian one in the mural, the face that was missing from this table. Tom Gordon's face. Tears did sting, then. Be careful who you love, Matt had said. They'll be part of you always . . .

Beside me, Luke followed my gaze.

"I know," he said, and squeezed my hand.

"I wish he could be here," I said. "Wouldn't he love this, though?"

"He would. We'll call him in the morning and tell him all about it."

"Oh, yes! Oh, let's do."

Across the room Luella Hatfield sat on the piano stool beside Tony, her head close to his as they bent over a sheet of music. Hank and Teddy had fetched her from Spelman. I knew that she and Tony would be going over the words and music to "Downtown." She wore a pretty chemise of yellow silk and had a corsage of the little blue flowers pinned in her sleek chignon, and looked vivid and much older, far more assured than when I had last seen her at the concert in Sisters' Chapel. I wondered what she had made of that night, if she had been a part of the brief spurt of idiot violence or if it had somehow missed her. I hoped so. I loathed the thought of Boy Slattery's casual hate touching this ardent, golden child.

She looked up then and saw me looking at her, and smiled shyly, and I got up and went over and hugged her. John Howard came behind me, and kissed her on the cheek, and she beamed up at us both.

"Well, I hear you're on your way," John said to her, and her smile widened, displaying huge dimples. I looked at him curiously.

"She's been picked to sing with the Atlanta Symphony Chorus, and she's doing a solo at her debut in the summer season," he said. "And there's some heavy-duty talent scouting her from some of the record companies. I hear things about her all the way up there in New York."

"Who you been talking to?" she mumbled, ducking her head.

"I have my spies," he said. "We're gonna lose you sure as shootin'."

"Not until I finish at Spelman, nossir," she said. "And I'm not forgetting who made that scholarship possible. I'm not ever gon' forget that, Mr. Howard. When Mr. Comfort asked me to sing for y'all and told me you were gon' to be here, I told him I'd come sing for you till this time tomorrow, if you wanted me to. I really did tell him that."

"I'm grateful to you, Luella," John said, inclining his head gravely to her. "I wish someday you would sing for me until this time tomorrow."

"You say the word," she said. "We'll sing all the old songs."

"You got it," he said.

There was a small stirring at the bar then, and I turned to look at it, and then at the table. Everyone had fallen silent, and was looking toward the door. My heart gave a great leap, and my breath caught in my throat.

"They're coming," Doug Maloof called softly, and we heard the elevator bell chime, and I flew back to my seat, heart hammering, and slid in between Luke and

John. We all looked at each other and grinned, huge, incandescent grins. The room shimmered and swayed.

At the piano, Tony crashed into "Downtown":

When you're alone and life is making you lonely,
you can always go . . .
>*downtown!*
When you've got worries, all the noise and the hurry
seem to help, I know . . .
>*downtown!*

Two figures appeared in the door and stopped. We stood as if a common chord had jerked us upright. Luella Hatfield threw her sleek head back and picked the song up, and the notes rose rich and golden until they bobbed and swam at the very ceiling:

Listen to the music of the traffic in the city,
Linger on the sidewalk where the neon signs are pretty,
How can you lose? The lights are much brighter there,
You can forget all your troubles, forget all your cares . . .

The two figures stood arm in arm, very still, Matt in his new blue suit, grinning until his mouth seemed to split his pointed face, cheeks burning red, eyes glittering behind the swoop of red hair. The other man was only slightly taller but half a hundred pounds heavier, dressed in white, his face burnt dark with the sun, his head crowned with a great white Stetson. His mouth, too, was stretched in a smile. They smiled, and smiled, and they stood there, arms joined, looking at us and the room and the girl singing and the city spread out below, just blooming into light.

". . . and go downtown!" Luella Hatfield's voice soared. "Things'll be great when you're downtown . . . "

Matt inclined his head to us in a small, magisterial bow, and bent slowly from the waist.

"No finer place when you're downtown," Luella sang, and we all joined in, shouting our elation back at Matt and Cody Bubba Remington: "Everything's waiting for you!"

Tony finished on a great, crashing flourish, and we clapped and cheered, and Matt bowed lower and lower, and then, in the silence that still rang with the glorious voice of Luella Hatfield, he went over on his face, onto the rug, taking Cody Bubba Remington down with him, and lay still in a tangle of arms and legs and a crushed white Stetson and the glittering shards of a dream.

Later that night, or rather, early the next morning, we sat on the rock verge of the little pool in the park across from Luke's apartment, dangling our feet in the water. John Howard and Luke and I had gone there from the Top of Peachtree, not speaking of a destination, just going there as if it had been agreed upon from the start. Teddy and Hank had come later, carrying sacks of steak sandwiches from Harry's and a six-pack of beer. They had taken Luella Hatfield home to her dormitory at Spelman first. Then they had gone to Harry's, and then come straight to Luke's place. They had seen the Morgan parked on the shoulder of the park, and heard our voices down by the pool, and come scrambling and sliding down. We had drunk some of the beer, but no one had eaten the sandwiches. I did not know how long we had been there, only that it was long past midnight. Time had stopped for me when Matt had hit Doug Maloof's newly cleaned carpet. Ever since, it had been weirdly telescoped. It might have been days since we left the Top of Peachtree.

The Chicken Parts King of the Entire Southwest was gone as surely as if he had never appeared. He had excused himself and gone to the restroom to straighten up his white suit and mauled Stetson and never came back. Doug Maloof, white-faced with misery, said that he had ordered his car and driver and gone downstairs to wait in the elevator lobby. His Lear jet probably took off from Peachtree-DeKalb airport before we reached Tight Squeeze and midtown.

"You kids go on," Doug said, looking at our stricken faces and then at Matt, sprawled unconscious on the rug. "Doremus and I will take him home. We've done it before. We know where he lives."

And so we had gone on. We walked around Matt and got on the elevator, all of us, and went down and got our cars and left. When we walked past Tony, he said, "I'm real sorry." He was folding the top down over his piano when the elevator doors opened.

I knew that we must and would talk of it eventually, but we had not yet. There was, after all, nothing to say. I felt emptied out and endlessly tired, floating, unreal. I wanted desperately to climb the long driveway across from the park to the apartment and crawl into the waterbed, but I wanted more not to move. Not to speak. Not to think. Not to be. The night was fresh and only slightly chilly, and from the dense stand of newly unfurled ferns around the pool the peepers called their silvery call. I had not heard them this spring until tonight. Overhead the stars pricked the sky. In another month, I thought, we will not be able to see them again until fall. And then I thought, but where will I be in the fall, and felt a tear slide slowly down my cheek and into my mouth. I licked it with the tip of my tongue. I felt no grief. I truly and mightily did want to go to sleep, though.

Across from me Teddy gave a sobbing hiccup and scrubbed at her face. She had been crying silently since she and Hank arrived, trying hard not to, stopping, then beginning again. Hank sat with his arm around her, but he did not try to coax her into stopping. She had his sodden handkerchief clutched in her fist, but I thought that it was useless by now.

"I thought he would do it," she said finally, her voice rusty and frail, like an old woman's. "I thought it was just so . . . possible. Such a possible thing to happen. He always made everything seem possible."

"Well, where there's one chicken king there's probably another," Luke said, but he said it abstractly, as if his mind were somewhere else. I thought it probably was, but I did not know where. I could always tell when Luke had gone away from me in his head; I could not feel his mind touching mine at those times. I could not feel it now. Come back, I said to him in my head. Stay with me.

"No," Teddy said. "There's not going to be another one."

No one argued with her. We all knew that, for us and for *Downtown,* there would not be another chicken king.

After another long space, Hank said to John Howard, "So what will you do now? You going on back in the morning? This morning, rather?"

John shrugged. He had not spoken since Teddy and Hank arrived. He had sat with one hand lightly on my back, but had said nothing.

"I think I'm going over to Memphis a little later today," he said. "Martin's over there with the sanitation people. Some of the others are there, too; Rosser and Tony, I think. I need to see if I can mend some fences."

"Smokes?" Hank said. I started to speak, could not, cleared my throat.

"I'm not sure yet," I said judiciously, as if I were considering it carefully.

"Teddy-o?"

She shook her head mutely and turned it into his neck and he tightened his arm around her.

"Luke?"

I looked up at Luke. I had dreaded this moment, dimly and distantly, ever since we left the Top of Peachtree. I had thought, though, that it would not come until much later. Certainly not this blasted night. I was not ready for it. Don't leave me, I said to him with my eyes. Don't leave me.

"I think," he said, looking at Hank over my head, "that maybe I'll go on over to Memphis with John. Just for a day or two. It sounds like it could be interesting. *Life* could probably use something on it."

His arm was still around me. He looked down at me, and away. I said nothing. I knew that my voice had shut down along with everything else.

"You ought to stick around," Hank said after a while. "We can run this thing, you know. If you think about it, why couldn't we? The new guy's not going to know anything. Not that much has changed. What's so different, really? There's always the Monday morning meeting."

I began to laugh softly, surprising myself profoundly.

"And the Cup Wars," I said.

The rest of them joined in, one by one, until we were all choking on laughter, giddy with it.

"And there's always . . . " Hank gasped, pausing for breath, and we read the thought and shouted it together into the chilly spring predawn: "There's always YMOG!"

We were still laughing when we dispersed. And when Luke and I and John Howard got into the Morgan to drive John to the Regency, we were still laughing, and we laughed all the way back downtown.

Epilogue

"COME WITH ME," MY HUSBAND SAYS FROM THE BATHROOM, where he is shaving.

"You don't need me to do that," I say. I am doing stomach crunches on the rug in front of the fireplace. It is late May, but New York is having one of its long, cold springs, and I have lit the gas logs. They will not heat the big room, but the fire feels good just here.

"Yeah, I do," he says. "This time I really do need you."

And I stop the crunches and pad into the bathroom to look into his face, because we do not use "need" lightly, he and I. It is one of our rules.

I think again, as I walk, how much I love this place. We have lived here, in the top two floors of a small building on West Thirty-ninth Street just off Fifth Avenue, for almost fifteen years. Downstairs are a living room, a kitchen, a small bath and Toby's old bedroom, and our two vast work places. Up here is one great room that takes up the whole floor, and here we sleep, read, live.

In the summer and fall we branch out onto the wrap-around rooftop garden that initially sold us on the place. But this room has become home. When he published his first book, ten years ago, we added the huge skylight that runs the length of the ceiling. When I published mine, the following summer, we remodeled the bath and added the big Jacuzzi. It took me a year to collect the palms and ferns in it. Now it is not uncommon for us to lie in bed or in the Jacuzzi in the jungly dark and watch the moon on the face of the buildings uptown. Sometimes, in winter, we can watch the snow fall past the beautiful profile of the Chrysler Building. It is a magical thing. This room is the heart of us and our marriage. Wherever in the world our work takes us, either of us, this is where we fly to when the work is over, like children at the end of their day.

"Tell me why you need me to go with you," I say, looking into his face. He is wearing a white lather beard, and I reach up to pop a bubble or two.

"I don't really know. I just feel like you need to come this time. This will be the fourth or fifth time I've been back, and you never have. I guess I'm sort of proud of myself. But it feels like more than that. I just need you."

We have the rule about honoring need because both of us know the real and savage hunger under the word, and we cannot use it lightly. It is a consciously made rule; all the ones that form the fragile tissue of our marriage are consciously made. The tissue holds us firm; we trust it. We have woven it together. We have friends who still, I know, think this marriage will not last, but he and I both know that the web will hold. Under it is love. That has held through everything, and will.

"Then of course I'll come," I say. We can and often have walked away from each other's wants, but never the needs.

And so I come with him, on the last weekend in May, to Atlanta where he will receive an honorary doctoral degree at Emory University.

It is a sultry, thundery weekend. The city is hot. I have forgotten these early hot spells. The graduation ceremony is planned for outside, but chairs are set up in the great gymnasium just in case. We do not know until the morning of the ceremony where we will be, but the muttering showers retreat long enough, finally, so that it is outside, surrounded by flowers and vivid new green, that I watch him incline his head to receive the beautiful satin doctoral hood, and take from President Meade the degree of Doctor of Letters *honoris causa*. Tears of pride stand in my eyes, and I wish again that our son, Toby, was here to see this ceremony. But he is far away on the coast of Oregon, my tall child with eyes, as a young man of this city told me mine were, long ago, the color of rain. He is an architect and a self-professed tree-hugger, and in the midst of a project that will both use and spare the great Oregon pines and spruces.

"Take lots of pictures," he says when he calls before we leave. "You know he'll never put that hood on again."

Toby: where did we get him? We are both so inalterably urban. But from the start he was a creature of earth and sky and water. We spent long summers shivering in rented houses beside Northern waters so that Toby could keep his first loves.

It is, somewhat to my surprise, a nice weekend. The old Druid Hills section of Atlanta is not one I used to be familiar with; there is nothing in the wooded hills and the old dowager houses to pull cruelly at me. Even the city that we ride through on the freeway coming in does not pull at me. There is nothing of that great, beetling skyline that I know. It could be any of the cities I have worked in and out of these long years; I have racketed through a great many of them in taxicabs.

The Friday night reception and dinner is pleasant; the academic world is the same everywhere, and we are both at home in it. Both our names and work are known to the people who attend, and that is pleasant, too. I am feeling, on the whole, rather mellow as we stand on the steps of the Emory guest house on Saturday afternoon, waiting for the taxicab that will take us to the airport to go home. Only later will I realize that the feeling is one of relief, of well-being at having escaped something I had expected to hurt me, and which, after all, did not.

"I still don't have much sense that this is Atlanta, do you?" he says as we stand there.

I shake my head, no. I have no sense of that, either. No sense, during the whole twenty-four hours just past, that this is the city I loved so totally and passionately more than a quarter-century ago, that I left so easily four years after that. I have come into it and through it, and now I am going out of it again, and I still cannot feel Atlanta. For some reason this makes me uneasy, restless.

Something feels unfinished.

Luke did go to the war, of course.

He came back from Memphis the night after we all gathered in the little park, back with Martin Luther King Jr.'s body and the silent, anguished people who had been around him at the Lorraine Motel. I will never forget John Howard's face then. I thought that he looked like a dead man walking.

Luke's were the most vivid of the images to come out of that terrible time in Atlanta. You saw them everywhere; you see them still: black and white, young and old, civil rights heroes and Dr. King's cherished little people, celebrities and politicians and movie stars. Luke shot them all up close and in their faces, as we say today.

Every newspaper and magazine in the country carried those faces. They are in many books still in print. His name is under them all.

"You will shoot their faces," I had said to him that day on Pumphouse Hill, and he did that. It has always been what he does. Faces, faces. Lucas Geary's faces. All eye and image, that is Luke.

Two days after the funeral he left for San Francisco to catch up with the First Cav in the Mekong Delta.

"I'll be back," he said all through the night before he left, while he held me and I cried. I cried all night, until I thought I would never cry again; that there were no tears left in me, and never would be.

"I'll be back. I'll be back. Wait here for me. I'll be back."

But I knew, even as I dropped him off at Hartsfield airport and drove away in the Morgan, that he would not. Luke could love me endlessly, and laugh with me, and even be angry both at and with me, but he could not grieve with me. I went back to the apartment behind the widow's house and garaged the Morgan and took a shower and crawled into the waterbed and slept for the better part of three days. When I awoke at last I showered again and dressed and went to see Seth Emerson at *Newsweek.* He hired me that day. I did not cry again for Luke Geary.

I moved to a small apartment near downtown. I could walk to work from it. The *Newsweek* office was nearer uptown; I had little occasion to go near Five Points, and unless I had to, I did not. I do not know what Luke did about his clothes and books and records, or the Morgan. For all I know they are still there, in the pretty little carriage house of the widow, dreaming under dust through the long seasons in the park. I never saw anyone else driving the Morgan around town, but then I did not expect to, anymore that I would have expected to see someone wearing Luke's clothes.

I did see his credits, though, on the faces that came out of that sad, awful, never-ending war. I think he must have missed much that he would have loved to shoot at home: the riots in the streets after Dr. King died; the assassination of Robert Kennedy; the incredible convention in Chicago; the dreadful, musical-comedy election to the presidency of the United States of Richard Milhous Nixon; the long death by hemorrhage of the Civil Rights nonviolent movement. I never saw his name on the faces that came out of those, only the faces of his war.

I may have missed some of them, though. Seth Emerson was the best imaginable boss; my byline was coming more and more often, from cities all over the South. Under the names of many people, my name.

". . . and you will write their names," Luke had said to me on the same day that I had said to him, "You will shoot their faces." It had been the second half of my sentence.

We had done that, both of us. We had simply not done it together. After a while it no longer mattered to me. I was, if never again so deliriously happy as I had been in my first year at *Downtown,* infinitely content to do what I did. I loved my job with most of my heart. The little bit that was left I simply closed off, as you do an unused room.

I was in New Orleans when Teddy and Hank called to tell me that Matt Comfort was dying. I had had dinner with Tom Gordon and his lover and was planning to come home the next afternoon. Instead, I left at dawn the next morning, on the first flight out of New Orleans to Atlanta. Even as I was doing it I wondered why. Matt Comfort was almost nothing to me by then.

But of course, he had been everything, and that was the answer. I smiled a little as I thought of what he had said: "Be careful who you love. They'll be part of you always. Even after the love is dead, those fuckers will still be part of you. . . ."

"You always did have to have the last word," I whispered to him somewhere in the air over Alabama.

Teddy and Hank met me at the airport and we drove straight to Emory University Hospital. Teddy was heavily pregnant with her second child and had been crying. She looked worn and nearly old for the first time since I had known her. Well, we were both over thirty now, I reminded myself. We are the ones we ourselves said we'd never trust. No wonder she's upset. She and Hank, of us all, were the only ones to have kept in touch with Matt Comfort as he self-destructed spectacularly all over the South.

From them I knew that he had left Atlanta almost exactly when Luke and John Howard did, just after the funeral of Dr. King. He had gone then to Charlotte and started a city magazine there and lost it; to Baton Rouge and done the same thing; to Winston-Salem, to found and edit a magazine for people who wished to sell their houses themselves, and lost that; to St. Petersburg, Florida, where he worked for a time for the Triple A, planning automobile trips for retirees going North. When he had been fired from that job, he had gone to Greensboro, North Carolina, and there hit bottom with the liquor; been fired from the McDonald's that he managed; gone into AA and gotten sober; found a lady friend there; and been sober for all of five months before they discovered that the headaches and blackouts that had plagued his last year were a malignant tumor in his brain and not the alcohol.

"It just seems so damned unfair," Teddy wept. "To go through all that and finally get sober and find somebody he really loves, and then to die of a stupid goddamned brain tumor. They were going to get married this fall."

"Maybe they still can," I said, but she shook her head.

"His doctor says he won't last two more days," she said. "It's a miracle he's hung on this long. He refused to marry her anyway, when he found out about the tumor. Said he'd be goddamned if he'd add a widow to his list of victims. She's with him, though. You'll like her. She's tough and she loves him an awful lot. Even like this, she loves him."

"Well, women always did," I said, trying to cheer her up.

"You won't know him," she said. "I want to warn you now, so it won't be such a shock. There's almost literally nothing left of the Matt you knew."

"Why'd he come back here for treatment?" I said. "Emory must cost the earth. Surely he couldn't have any money left."

Hank chuckled.

"He came back because the doctor who's treating him is the best young oncologist in the South and he's treating Matt free. He was the first YMOG Matt ever did."

"Oh, shit, of course he was," I said, and began to laugh helplessly. We all laughed for a long time, even Teddy. I'm glad. It was a long time before we laughed again.

He was in a light coma by the time we walked into his sunny hospital room. He lay in the narrow white bed hooked up to an intravenous drip, tossing a little, breathing slowly and heavily through his mouth. Except for the pointed fox's chin and the sharp, slack mouth I would not have known him. His face was waxen yellow and vastly swollen, and his eyes swollen shut and blackened, and the glorious red shock of hair was gone, replaced by a great turban of white gauze that made the yellow face seem deep saffron by comparison. He was so thin that his little body scarcely made a rise in the taut coverlet. The young doctor sat in a chair on one side of him, simply sat there, holding his left hand. On the other side of him, a youngish woman with dark hair pulled straight back from a strong, blunt face sat holding the other one. She looked up and smiled a little at Hank and Teddy, but said nothing. Later I would meet her and find that she was Claire Fiedler, the woman Matt was to have married, but for the moment I only smiled at her and went to stand with Teddy and Hank against the far wall. We had a hard time finding space. The room was full of people.

Hank told me about it later, when we went down for coffee. On the first day after Matt's surgery, when the doctors knew for certain that he would not leave the hospital, a strange thing happened. It was, Hank said, a rather wonderful thing, really. Somehow, he did not know quite how, the word simply went out, as Matt's word had gone out in the beginning: Comfort is dying. Come.

And for two days there gathered silently in his hospital room a good fifty or sixty people from all over the country. His people, young and old; Comfort's People. They came, and they simply stood, or sat on the floor or in chairs, watching the rise and fall of his laboring chest, listening to his breath. A crowd of once-young, once-lustrous people who had made it or not, who were okay or not, brought to that room by the common cord of a man who was still stronger, even in his dying, than anyone they had ever known or would, again. There were photographers and journalists and novelists and secretaries and aging YMOGs and shoe-shine people and city leaders, along with a few others so stoned or strung out that they thought they were still in MacArthur Park or the Haight or wherever their reality lay, leaning dreamily against the walls, far away in a better time.

Francis Brewton came on the first day, Hank said, and Mr. Tommy T. Bliss on the second, though he did not stand on his head.

Some of the people wept, but even as they did, they told the old Comfort stories, and they laughed. They drank coffee and they watched him and they all seemed to feel somehow that there was not another place just then that they could possibly be. It was not a quiet crowd. More than once, nurses came to shush them. But Matt's young doctor would raise his head and stare at the nurses and they went away again, shaking their heads.

When we got back up to Matt's room from the coffee shop on the afternoon of the third day the man that I would marry was there, standing silently in the space along the wall that we had just vacated, his arms folded across his chest, watching Matt and listening to him breathe. When we came into the room he lifted his head and looked at me, and I put my hands up to my mouth and stood still in the doorway, and he held his arms out to me and I went into them. I stayed there for nearly half an hour before we spoke a word to each other.

At six o'clock that evening the ragged breathing faltered and stopped. The young doctor pulled off his stethoscope and put his head down on Matt's still chest and cried. I turned my face into the shoulder behind me and cried, too. Everyone cried a little, but very quietly. We all hugged the woman on the right-hand side of the bed, and then my future husband and I went back to the hotel where he was staying. It was a new one, one of a national chain, on the fringes of the Emory campus. I remember that the air was fresh and cool and the dogwoods were spectacular in the green twilight. It was almost four years to the day since I had seen him.

When he left the next morning I went with him. We both knew that I could not stay in Atlanta.

* * *

And now I have come back for the first time since that morning, and am going away again, and I might as well have come and gone to Dayton.

We get into the cab that the university has called for us. It is an old one, one of the university fleet, and the driver is a white man past middle age, an anachronism to us who live in New York City. He is happy about nothing: not the heat, the trip to the airport, us as passengers. He clashes the gears and jerks the cab around corners and keeps up a spleenish running commentary to himself, just under his breath. I know that he watches us in the rearview mirror; I see his eyes on us. He knows that we are VIPs of some sort, though not which one of us, and I think that perhaps, if he did not know this, he would simply dump us out on a street corner. I am furious with him and long to speak sharply to him, but my husband merely shakes his head. He is quite capable of doing battle with cab drivers and often does, but he is also quite capable of simply going off somewhere in his head and not noticing anything at all, and I think that that is where he is now. So I do not speak.

Presently he leans forward to the driver and says, "Take the Courtland Street exit and head for Five Points. I'll tell you where after that."

The cab driver and I both look at him.

"I thought you said Hartsfield," the driver mutters.

"I changed my mind," my husband says equably, and the driver jerks the cab across three lanes of traffic and screeches up the Courtland Street ramp.

My husband directs the driver through a maze of streets that I do not recognize and finally bids him stop. When he does, we get out, and all of a sudden I know where we are.

"Oh, no," I say. "No way. I'm not going up there. I don't need any damned sentimental journeys."

"Maybe I do," he says, and leans in the window of the cab.

"We won't be more than half an hour," he says. "If you want to wait for us I'll pay you for your time."

The driver scratches off without looking back.

"Be happy in your work," I mutter after him. "We'll never see that jerk again."

"It doesn't matter. We can get a cab anywhere down here. Come on, Smoky."

"I really, really do not want to do this," I say.

"You'll be glad you did," he says. "They're going to gut the whole building next week and put in some kind of county government offices. The guy who owns it told me at lunch; he's on the Emory board. He's given us a safe conduct for the guard. Come on. I'm not leaving until we see it."

And so we walk to the revolving glass doors of the building that houses the Top of Peachtree, locked and empty now, and tap on the glass until the young guard sees us and comes to let us in. I remembered the building as being tall, but it is dwarfed now by the monoliths around it.

"The old mural, huh?" the guard says. He has on bell-bottom jeans and a ponytail; we have come full circle. "Yeah, I see it almost every day. I've always wondered about it. Y'all artists or collectors or something?"

"The lady's in it," my husband says, grinning.

"No kidding," the young guard says, examining my face as if to assess its mural-worthiness. "You were some kind of celebrity, huh? You still live here?"

"No. New York," I say.

"Ah. Local girl makes good. Well, if the boss says you can go up, I guess you can. I'll open the express elevator for you. Watch your step up there, there's stuff piled all over the floors and the lights are off. There ought to be plenty of natural light, though. I'm afraid you'll find that your face is plenty dirty."

"I'll bet," I say, and he puts a key into a keyhole on the elevator panel in the lobby that I remember and yet, somehow, do not, and presently the elevator comes rumbling down for us.

We are silent as we rise. I remember the mirrored elevator walls, but they do not give me back the same people that they did, and it is off-putting. The same thing is true when we step out into the lobby of the old restaurant. I remember the green carpeting and the quilted peach walls, even the springy feel of the carpet underfoot, but it is as if I remember pictures from an old book. Still without speaking I follow him through the long space where once there were white-clothed tables overlooking the great sweep of the city and now there are piles of lumber and insulation and acoustical tiles and debris, and the window walls look out into the blind eyes of the taller buildings all around. Dust felts everything, thick and pearly gray. It is very hot and very quiet. There is no furniture of any kind in the long room except two or three tables pushed into a far corner and stacked one atop the other, and, covered with a dusty tarpaulin, the shape of a grand piano.

Tony's piano, almost certainly. I walk by it without looking.

We go around the corner into the bar area and there we all are. There is the mural, on the wall over the padded leather counter that once served as the bar, looking half the size it once did in the huge, empty space, so faded and grimed that it is almost impossible to make out the faces in it. But I know where we all are in the mural, know our positions in this small firmament, and so, once my eyes get accustomed to the dim light filtering through the dirty plate glass, I see us once again. I go to the window wall and sit down on the ledge and look at the mural, and he comes and sits beside me and looks, too.

I start at the left and work to the right. Hank first, looking very much like Hank still does, and Teddy, looking too like Teddy now. I don't think that they will change until they are very old, if then. Then Sueanne, looking matronly and nurturing in her dark shirtwaist, and Sister, the perennial University of Georgia cheerleader in her perky headband and ironed hair. She is now, I know, one of the top trial attorneys in the city. I am next, looking only small and round and very, very young, and rather idiotically happy. I was afraid of what I would see on that face when we first entered, but what I see is mainly nothing at all except the overweening youth, and so I am able to move my eyes past it. Alicia Crowley is next, looking as old-fashioned as a Gibson Girl in her boots and fishnet stockings and fall of honey hair and beauty. Then Matt, the vulpine face sharp and grinning ferally, the red hair burning like live lava on his head. Of all the faces his is nearly a caricature; Matt was always the darling of editorial cartoonists. Beside him, on his other side, Tom Gordon.

Tom, dead of AIDS now these past eight years.

I am still and the room is silent. I feel, see, hear nothing. And then, just for a split second, it is as if someone has jerked open the door of a soundproof room and life crashes in. I smell the mingled odors of fresh-cut flowers and fruit garnish on the bar and the hot hors d'oeuvres from the silver trays; I feel the chill of the air-conditioning and the press of people around me; I hear laughter and the chink of ice and the sound of Tony's piano as we walk in: "When you're alone and life is making you lonely, you can always go . . . downtown . . . "

The door slams shut and I am back in dust and silence and emptiness. The mural is only that: an old painted wall, faded, dirty, set now for destruction.

I lower my head so that he won't see me cry. He is often impatient with my easy tears, but now he only reaches over and wipes them away with his thumb.

"Was this a bad idea after all?" he says.

I shake my head and swallow the tears.

"Not really. In a way it was a good idea," I say. "From now on I'll see him like he is in this mural when I think about him, and not . . . that back there in that hospital room. That's what I've been seeing all these years. It's going to be good to substitute this for that. It's just that . . . oh, Lord, you know. There were always so few of us, and the best of us are dead. It hardly seems fair, does it?"

"I hardly think the best of you are dead. But no, it doesn't seem fair," he says. "On a lighter note, do you notice that Matt's face shines like new money on a bear's behind? All the rest in that mural are faded out, but his looks like somebody just cleaned it. What do you make of that?"

I do notice it then: Matt Comfort's fox face does indeed gleam out of the dirty mural like the sun. Around it, our faces seem like little moons scrimmed in clouds. It must, I think, be some trick of the light, some quality of the old paint when the artist laid it on.

"He's got his own holy miracle ray," I say, smiling.

"More likely the sonofabitch made some poor asshole promise to come up here and clean it off every day in exchange for being YMOG," he says, and we both laugh, looking at Matt in the mural.

"That was really the end of it, wasn't it?" I say. "At least, the start of the end. When he went down on the rug that night. After that everything changed—"

"Everything was already changing," he says. "I refuse to accept Matt Comfort as the definitive metaphor for the collapse of the sixties."

I smile at him, and look back at the mural.

"But still," I say, "he was the centerpiece. You have to admit that he was. Just look at him. It was always like that. Him in the middle, holding all the strings while we danced around him. He was the maypole for the whole dance."

"He was the maypole," John Howard says, pulling me into the curve of his arm. "But you all were the dance. I brought you down here to see that. He was the maypole, but you were the dance."

We sit there in the hot gloom for a while longer, and then he says, "Let's go home."

"Let's," I say, and we get back into the elevator and go down to the street lobby once more.

"Did you guys say good-bye to yourselves?" the young guard grins as he lets us out onto the street.

"I guess we did, at that," John says.

I am surprised and none too pleased to see that the university cab is waiting at the curb. The driver's mood has not improved noticeably.

"Now for Hartsfield," John says, and the driver clashes through the gears and snarls off toward the expressway. It is very hot, and the windows are down; humid air buffets us. On the freeway, well past the blue bowl of the old Braves' stadium, we hit the first of the afternoon traffic, and slow down almost to a stop. The car's engine labors and the whole car shudders. The heat is fierce.

"We'd like some air back here, please," John says, leaning forward over the back of the front seat.

The driver scowls at him in the rearview mirror. John looks back at him levelly, deadpan. The scar gives his face a fine, frozen menace. We call it the Look. It has gotten us excellent tables in restaurants in cities all over the world. The driver drops his eyes and thumbs a button and the windows crawl upward. Cold air roars into the cab. To punish us, the driver turns on the radio as loud as it will go and gospel rock moos around us.

I begin to giggle, trying not to laugh aloud.

"I wouldn't want that face looking at me in my rearview mirror, either," I say.

"I'm his worst nightmare," John grins. "A nigger with a doctoral hood."

I laugh aloud then, and lay my head back against the seat and close my eyes. When I open them again John is shaking my knee and we are careening far too fast around the last long curve toward the Delta terminal.

We are high in the thundery air over the Blue Ridge Mountains before I realize that after we left downtown Atlanta, I never once looked back.

$1,000.00

FOR YOUR THOUGHTS

Let us know what you think. Just answer these seven questions and you could win $1,000! For completing and returning this survey, you'll be entered into a drawing to win a $1,000 prize.

OFFICIAL RULES: *No additional purchase necessary.* Complete the HarperPaperbacks questionnaire—be sure to include your name and address—and mail it, with first-class postage, to HarperPaperbacks, Survey Sweeps, 10 E. 53rd Street, New York, NY 10022. Entries must be received no later than midnight, October 4, 1995. One winner will be chosen at random from the completed readership surveys received by HarperPaperbacks. A random drawing will take place in the offices of HarperPaperbacks on or about October 16, 1995. The odds of winning are determined by the number of entries received. If you are the winner, you will be notified by certified mail how to collect the $1,000 and will be required to sign an affidavit of eligibility within 21 days of notification. A $1,000 money order will be given to the *sole winner* only—to be sent by registered mail. Payment of any taxes imposed on the prize winner will be the sole responsibility of the winner. All federal, state, and local laws apply. Void where prohibited by law. The prize is not transferable. **No photocopied entries.**

Entrants are responsible for mailing the completed readership survey to HarperPaperbacks, Survey Sweeps, at 10 E. 53rd Street, New York, NY 10022. If you wish to send a survey without entering the sweepstakes drawing, simply leave the name/address section blank. Surveys without name and address will not be entered in the sweepstakes drawing. HarperPaperbacks is not responsible for lost or misdirected mail. Photocopied submissions will be disqualified. Entrants must be at least 18 years of age and U.S. citizens. All information supplied is subject to verification. Employees, and their immediate family, of HarperCollins*Publishers* are not eligible. For winner information, send a stamped, self-addressed №10 envelope by November 10, 1995 to HarperPaperbacks, Sweeps Winners, 10 E. 53rd Street, New York, NY 10022.